KAREN S

FLESH ON THE BONE

A NOVEL

LIED SCOTTSBLUFF PUBLIC LIBRARY
SCOTTSBLUFF, NEBRASKA 69361

About the cover photo:

Photographer, Dorothea Lange is remembered for her work documenting impoverished and displaced people, especially during the Great Depression and World War II. She won the prestigious Guggenheim fellowship for her work. I was enamored with Lange's amazing cover photo, as well as two others used in the text of my novel because they spoke volumes to me. The photo of men and boys riding on a freight train and the photo of men lined up in serpentine work lines during the Great Depression are also attributed to Dorothea Lange. Her numerous and remarkable photographs need no title as the images speak for themselves.

KAREN SCHUTTE

This novel is dedicated to my husband, Michael

FLESH ON THE BONE

No part of this book may be used or reproduced, stored in a retrieval system or transmitted, in any form or by any means, electronic, mechanical, photocopying, recording or otherwise, without the prior permission of the publisher.
For further information contact Green Spring Publishing, at www.karenschutte.com

Scripture quotations are taken from the *King James Version of the Holy Bible*.
Permission, all rights reserved.
The opinions expressed by the author are not necessarily those of Green Spring Publishing, Fort Collins, Colorado.

This novel is a work of fiction. Most names, dates, incidents, and descriptions in this novel are based on the lives of real people.

Copyright © 2014 by Karen Schutte. All rights reserved.

ISBN for printed material: 978-0-9904095-0-2

ISBN for e-book: 978-0-9904095-1-9

Author's photograph by Skillman Photography, Fort Collins, CO.

Historical cover photo by Dorothea Lange, used by permission of National Archives and Records Administration as original source.

Interior Book Design by Elizabeth Klenda at Frontier Printing, Fort Collins, Colorado, 2014.

© *Cover Design by Thayne Sturdevant Graphics.* All rights reserved.

Historical Fiction: The Family Saga Trilogy by Karen Schutte
The Ticket – First Edition 2010; 2nd Edition 2012; 3rd Edition 2013; 4th Edition 2014
Seed of the Volga – First Edition 2013; 2nd Edition 2014
Flesh on the Bone – First Edition 2014

Introduction:

The third novel in a trilogy, **Flesh on the Bone** picks up the story of the married children of the first two books. Jake and Raisa Kessel emigrated with their respective parents as seven and eight-year-old children in 1907. Their immigrant parents came to this country with only the 'flesh on their bones'. They struggled to make their own way even with all America had to offer. Karl and Katja Kessel (**The Ticket**) prospered, but their marital relationship withered on the vine. Raisa's parents, David and Sofie Steiner, (**Seed of the Volga**) barely made ends meet, moving from one rented farm to the next, but at the end of the day they loved each other. Jake and Raisa were products of these parents, these beginnings, these lives.

This story is written in an ethnic voice that reflects Jake and Raisa's sixth grade education, with an expected mingling of the German and English languages. As adults, Jake and Raisa hoped for a better life than what they knew growing up in America. They had many memories as young children of destitute immigrants. From the age of six, they were expected to go into the sugar beet fields with the others from sunup to sundown. The entire family signed on to work in the beet fields, thinning, hoeing, and then harvesting. For most, it was the only way they knew to make money, to put a roof over their heads and food in their bellies. If they were frugal and saved every nickel, maybe in a few years they could rent a farm. When that happened, it meant more years of scrimping, saving, and going without—until they had enough to buy their own farm.

The skeleton storyline of this novel is true, as are the main characters. Their life story is woven into a vibrant, breathing account, infused with illuminating historical research and the far reaches of this author's imagination. To protect key characters and those still living, names and dates have been altered.

This photo and several others used in this novel are the work of Lewis Hine, an American sociologist and photographer who used his camera for social reform during the Great Depression. His photographs were instrumental in changing many unfair and cruel child labor laws in the United States. As a teacher he urged his students to use photography as a medium for educational purposes. Permission to use his work in this novel is attributed to the archive of public domain. My deepest thanks and acknowledgement is extended to the Library of Congress and the National Archives.

KAREN SCHUTTE

PART ONE

1925

LOVELL, WYOMING

JAKE AND RAISA

CHAPTER ONE

NEW YEAR'S EVE, 1925: Just past 5:30 p.m., Jake Kessel flung open the front door of their rented four-room house on Miller Street. He shook the snow from his thin blue coat and tossed it onto a shabby over-stuffed chair. Already primed for a good time, Jake called out, "Hey Raisa, we're going over to Jack Watson's place for New Year's Eve; how about you wearing that pretty green dress—and get a wiggle on, will ya?" Jake paused in front of the cracked hall mirror and ran a comb through his thinning brown hair. His ice blue eyes sparkled as he said, "It's been a while since we celebrated anything and tonight, we are 'goin' out on the town'!"

Raisa Kessel's hazel eyes narrowed with anger as she walked quickly from the kitchen, the heels of her second-hand black shoes clicking with a staccato sound as they hit the bare wood floor. Irritated by her husband's tardiness and the demanding tone of his voice, she didn't care that she must have been a sight with her head of thick auburn hair coiled up in strips of rags.

Raisa wiped her hands on the skirt of her bib apron as her eyes flashed with annoyance. "For crying out loud Jake, I've been expecting you for the past two hours. Where have you been?" She laid her hand against her flushed cheek and cocked her head, then sarcastically answered her own question, "Ohhhh, let me guess--the pool hall!"

Jake's biceps flexed as he raised both calloused hands in defense. "Now, honey, you know I enjoy relaxing down there with the boys and playing a few hands of cards now and then, so just can it, will ya? I'm home now and I'm waiting for you to get all gussied up so we can go out and celebrate for once." He crossed the room in six long strides and wrapped his arms around his wife of five years, pulling her close. But Jake could feel the annoyed resistance in her body as they stood eye to eye. He instinctively knew he wasn't getting off that easy. It wasn't the first time he was in trouble for staying too long at one pool hall or another and they both knew it wouldn't be the last.

Raisa's hazel eyes continued to glint with irritation and disappointment as she pushed him away. "Jake—you stink! You smell like pool hall smoke and stale beer. Don't be thinking you are going to kiss me with that booze on your breath! This 'store' is closed!"

Jake stepped back and a throaty peal of laughter rolled from deep in his chest. He reached into his front pocket, pulled out a little red tin, and sliding it open, popped two of the tiny black mints into his mouth. "Okay, now sweetie---this Sen-Sen should take care of that little problem; so, how about the kiss?"

Before Jake could collect 'that kiss', he had two scrappy kids wrapped around his legs, pulling at his coat and filling the small house with their shouting. "We want some Sen-Sen too Daddy, pleeeeese!" Jake pulled the tin from his pocket again, doling out two of the tiny mints per child. "Now, Beth, you go change your clothes and comb those snarls out of your hair because we are going visiting tonight! If you're a good girl, you might even get to dance the polka with that little boy friend of yours." Beth tossed him one of her special looks as she marched indigently out of the room.

New Year's Eve was a traditional opportunity for celebration especially for those of German heritage. However, even during the Roaring Twenties, celebration in rural Lovell, Wyoming didn't include any fancy dress balls or shindigs. There were plenty of hall dances around, but the old gang was all married with kids and mighty thin wallets. They had a long history of making their own fun and they were pretty good at it.

As the last frigid day of the old year began to fade, Jake and Raisa bundled their freckled-faced, five-year old daughter, Beth and tow-headed, two-year old son, Arnold in the back seat of the harnessed horse and buggy. Raisa wrapped a heavy, hand-made wool quilt across her legs as Jake cracked the whip through the frosty air. The horses were eager to get moving and set off at a fast trot down the snow-covered dirt road and up the hill to the south of town.

Raisa snuggled closer to Jake and inhaled his masculine cologne, "I don't think I will ever get tired of hearing the clip-clop of the horses' hooves—there's something soothing about the sound and the motion." She smiled mischievously and planted a quick kiss on Jake's cheek. "You also smell better!" Raisa pulled her wool scarf up over her mouth. "Brrrr--it's colder out here than it looks. Oh, Jake look up there at the moon, see the ring around it? My dad always said that a ring around the moon meant there was a storm comin'!"

Jake put his arm around Raisa's shoulders and pulled her closer to him. "Don't want my best girl getting the chills, do I? It's to my advantage to keep you warm, isn't that right?" Jake winked at her as a smile of pure satisfaction broke across his face. He drove the matching team over the snow-covered dirt road for about a half a mile. They could see the golden glimmer of lamplight from the white clapboard farm house where they'd been invited to join a group of their friends. In those days, nobody considered hiring a babysitter. Everybody just bundled their kids up and took them along whether it was church or a dance. Everyone was pinching pennies and trying to have a good time along the way was just a way of life.

As they pulled up in the farm yard, visions of tables heaped with hearty German food rushed through Jake's head—he could almost smell it. He turned to Raisa and asked, "What did you put together for our carry-in dish tonight?"

Raisa smiled. "I made your favorite dish----Huhn und KloB, my mother's recipe for German-style chicken and dumplings. By the way, did you remember to get a little something to drink? You know everyone's supposed to bring their own *hooch*." No one cared where you got the illegal stuff, only that you brought your own. There was an unspoken rule that you didn't mooch off the others when it came to booze. Being good Germans, most of them knew how to brew their own beer. In fact, you could drive down any street and usually tell if a German lived in a particular house just by the tangle of hop vines growing up the porch or along the fence. Those who didn't brew their own hooch knew where to find it—in someone's barn, a gin mill, the backroom of the pool hall, even at pre-designated areas alongside the road. Sure, it was illegal, thanks to Prohibition, but for a price, it wasn't hard to find; the better the booze, the higher the price.

Jake took care of the horses while Raisa and the kids headed for the house, which was glowing with light and laughter. After several hours of eating, drinking, playing pinochle, and dancing, the adults were ready to put the little ones down for the night so they could get serious with their merrymaking. Jake helped Raisa make a bed of coats in a secluded corner for Beth and Arnold. It didn't take long for them to conk out.

Jake slid his hands around Raisa's slim waist. "You sure look pretty tonight, honey. You know that's my favorite dress." He winked and squeezed her tiny waist. "It always amazes me how that color makes your eyes look so green. You are a regular 'Sheba' tonight and don't you forget—you're all mine!"

Raisa liked the feel of Jake's hands on her waist and rewarded him with a knowing smile as she replied, "I'm glad you like the dress; I wore it just for you." She placed her hand on her hip in a coquettish pose. "It's made of that new material called rayon; it's supposed to be as soft as silk, but not as expensive." Raisa beamed as she looked down at the emerald green print; she was glad she had added the splash of lace at the deep plunging neckline. She wasn't comfortable showing even a little cleavage.

Before Raisa could object, Jake spotted the mistletoe and in one fluid motion, he moved her under it and laid a long, slow kiss on her luscious, full lips. "Jake! Now you behave yourself." Raisa giggled in spite of herself as she pushed away from her ardent husband. At five foot six inches, she was only two inches shorter than Jake, who had inherited his lean, wiry build from his father; he was the spitting image of his dad, Karl.

To make more room for dancing, an odd assortment of second-hand furniture had been pushed against the living room wall. Someone was playing a familiar German polka on an accordion as two couples circled out onto the floor and began dancing the 'Dutch Hop'. Jake grabbed Raisa's hand and twirled her across the room, "*Hochzeit*! Waaa-hoo, *hochzeit*." Jake threw his head back and hollered merrily as they hopped, stomped and whirled around the room in time to the festive music.

Raisa tipped her head of thick auburn hair back as her green eyes sparkled; she laughed as her dress flew up over her knees. "Oh Jake, not so fast or I'll be sick, I am telling you, slow down!" They danced the next four dances without a break before Raise complained, "Oh my, I am completely out of breath."

Jake smiled down at her as he kissed her rosy cheek, "Okay, okay—I'll give you a rest. I need a smoke anyway. Can I bring you a glass of elderberry wine, before I go outside?" A minute later, Jake brought the glass of rosy-colored wine to Raisa and then headed for the back yard where some of the guys were hanging out.

After checking on their two little ones who were sleeping soundly, Raisa threaded her way through the dancers to where she spotted an unoccupied straight-back chair next to her friend, Emmie. She wiggled out of her shoes and spread her toes. "Oh mercy, that feels so good."

Emmie leaned over and in a low whisper, said, "Raisa, did you notice that low-cut dress Frannie wore tonight? My Joe wouldn't let me out of the house in something like that—it just isn't proper for a married woman to look like that in public. She's advertising for trouble; that one is a real hussy if you ask me." The two friends sat for a few minutes scrutinizing the other women in the room and sharing tart bits of local gossip as they sipped their glasses of wine.

Raisa stood and looked at the clock on the wall, "Goodness, how the time goes by, it's almost midnight. 'Spect the boys will be itching to go do their thing soon." She peered out the frosted kitchen window. "I have to make a trip to the outhouse; I sure hate going out when it's so cold. Do you wanna come with me, Emmie?" The two women grabbed their coats and arm in arm, headed out the back door and across the yard to the unpainted outhouse. They hurried their pace when they heard the guys heckling them, "We know where you're goin'."

FLESH ON THE BONE

Jake stood shoulder to shoulder on the back porch with four other men, having a smoke and shootin' the bull. His friend, Hoot Westin slapped Jake on the back and declared, "Hope you don't mind my saying so Jake, but your woman has some nice-lookin' flesh on her bones! Yes sir-ree, she's a ritzy-lookin' dame!"

Jake laughed; the corners of his mouth curled up forcing his deep dimples to appear, "Nope, I don't mind you saying so, Hoot. Just you remember she's my woman!"

Hoot put his thin lips on the rim of a half-full pint canning jar of beer and took a long swallow. He shook his head feeling the liquid burn all the way down. "Whoo, that's some stout stuff. Hey, Jake, by the way I was wonderin' if you knew what happened out at Wilbur's farm the other day. I heard they had some sort of explosion."

A twinkle lit up Jakes ice blue eyes as he slapped his friend on the back and chuckled as he took another nip, "Yeah, I sure do. Now, that's a story. You know those two big Norwegians who work out at Wilbur's place? I guess it's no secret they like their booze? Well, the other day I happened to be out there hauling in some hay for Wilbur's horses; those two come up to me and asked if I knew where they could get the makings of a still, that they would make it worth my while. I told them I could probably round some stuff up for them and they was downright excited about that. So, I got the stuff for them and then a couple days went by so I stopped over at their house to see how they was doing." Jake's amused chuckle rippled through the night air as mental images filled his head.

"It was the damdest thing, Hoot. There they were out back in this here shed; they had this heavy corn syrup they were going to run through the still to make whiskey. I told 'em it was too thick, that it wouldn't go through the tubing. 'Oh, we'll make it work' they said. They told me to come on back that night cause they were going to run it through after they was done workin' for the day. So, that night after supper I went back over there. We sat around the still and waited and waited for that syrup to run through. One of 'em was even sittin' at the end of the pipe with a little glass to make sure he caught the first drop."

Jake burst out laughing, "I'm tellin' you Hoot, I took another look at that whole contraption. The boiler, she was belching, smoking, and grinding-- and I said, 'No sir-ree, I am going to beat it, cause that thing is going to blow up!' I got on my horse and I headed for home. Well, I was just reining my horse onto the main road when that still and the whole side of the shed, she blew sky high! I didn't even look back a second time; I high-tailed it back home laughing my fool head off all the way. I kept imagining what those fellows looked like after that thing blew. "

Hoot slapped his beefy thigh and began to laugh as images materialized in his own head. "Are you telling me the truth or are you stretching it as usual?"

Jake draped his well-muscled arm across his friend's broad back, "No sir-ree, that's the way it happened. I don't know if they tried it again, but that first batch didn't turn out so good! They weren't hurt none when that thing blew, except for their dignity!"

Jake stamped out his cigarette butt and went back into the house. He snuck up behind Raisa and grabbing her around the waist, bent forward and whispered into her soft, fragrant neck, "The boys and I are settin' to mount up, it won't take long. We should probably head on home right after us guys get back."

Raisa blushed profusely as she pushed Jake away in mock irritation. As usual, he just laughed, winked, and headed for the backdoor, throwing her an exaggerated kiss as he went. Raisa and the rest of the women moved to the frosty windows, each one wiping off an icy porthole so they could watch the men mount their horses. Impatient and skittish, short puffs of steam shot from the horses' nostrils as they pawed the frozen ground. Covered with hoarfrost, the cottonwood trees shimmered and the night sky literally glistened with sparkling pieces of floating ice and distant twinkling stars as the men began to mount up.

With nimble fingers, Jake untied his horse from the back of their buggy. The big roan stud tossed its head up and down as Jake slid his left foot into the stirrup and swung up into the saddle. Jake reached down and patted the sinewy neck of the horse as he shied to the left and snorted. "Whoa there--looks like you are ready to get going and have a little fun tonight, huh big boy?" Settling himself in the saddle, Jake wound the reins around the saddle horn then unbuttoned the bottom half of his coat so his holstered .45 was unencumbered. He glanced around and counted close to a dozen of his fellow German merry-makers. *There's a handful of fellows here who aren't really German, but for tonight they wanna be; that's just fine with me, the more the merrier!* "There was no question that most of the men had consumed their fair share of hooch for the night and were itching to bring in the New Year according to the old German tradition! Hank Zellner was the first to gallop down the lane and onto the road heading north towards Lovell's Main Street. Once they were down the hill and in the center of town, the merrymakers made a spectacle of themselves galloping up and down the main street hollering, "Happy New Year" and shooting their guns into the frigid air.

The fellows chose a few of the 'friendly' businesses that were open, like the pool hall and the Horseshoe Bar. They pulled their horses up in front and all together, wished the customers a prosperous and a healthy New Year as they fired off a few rounds. The local sheriff didn't raise a finger; he knew those boys weren't hurting a soul—just some wound-up Germans feeling their oats and having a time of it.

When they had enough of their New Year's tradition, Hoot gave a signal and the group wheeled their horses around and headed back up the snow-covered hill, to the house at the edge of town where their womenfolk waited. A couple of the guys were still shooting their guns as they raced up Shoshone Avenue. Jake and Hoot were bringing up the rear in a fast trot, chatting as they rode. Suddenly, Jack Wagner's horse slipped on the icy street just as he was about to pull a final shot off with his Colt revolver. The shot went wild and slammed into Bob Miller's leg. There was a second rogue shot as Bob tried to rein in his horse. The sudden scream of the horse split the night air as horse and rider fell to the rutted, frozen street. The frigid air was filled with frantic shouting and profanities as the rest of the fellows reined their horses in, jumped off and ran to where Bob was laid out cold on the icy street.

Jake noticed Bob's horse struggling to get up and trotted over to see about it. He jumped down from the saddle; he didn't like what he saw. Blood was pulsing from a gunshot wound near the horse's hip. It looked pretty bad. "Hey Mutt, it looks like Bob's horse has a shattered flank bone. That second bullet must have hit an artery from the looks of it. There's only one thing to do 'bout that'." Jake pulled his gun and put it to the temple of the struggling, wild-eyed bay. He squeezed the trigger and all was quiet. Jake looked down at his blood-splattered coat and tried to brush the blood off best he could. "Hell, those head shots always send blood and brains every wheres. Sure as hell messed up my coat; Raisa isn't going to like that one bit, no sir-ree!"

Jake looked at the dead horse lying in the street in a pool of blood. "We got to drag him off to the side so someone don't run into him in the dark. I suppose Bob can get some help to drag the horse out to the dump tomorrow or the day after that." Jake and Hoot bent to pick up the front legs, "Hey, will a couple of you guys get down from your nags and help us pull Bob's horse into the ditch here?"

Some of the other guys were tending to Bob. Jake walked over to where Bob lay, just as his friend was coming to. Jake knelt down beside Bob, "Hey there Bob, how are you feelin'? That was a nasty bit of luck." A piece of white cloth appeared and Jake helped as they wrapped the wound tightly and lifted Bob to his feet, he was pretty woozy. Lefty gave him a foot-up to sit behind the saddle on Helmut Fink's horse. That's when Bob noticed his own horse laying in the street. "Damn, did Jack shoot me and my horse?"

Trotting his horse up alongside Bob, Jake reached out and laid his hand on Bob's shoulder. "I wanted to tell you before, but we didn't have any choice, Bob. I hated like the dickens to have to do it, but that horse of yours took that second bullet. It looked to the rest of us like he had a shattered flank along with a ruptured artery, with blood spurting everywhere and all. It was obvious there weren't nothin' we could do for him but put the poor devil out of his misery. We pulled him off the road for now; tomorrow or the next day you can see about draggin' him out to the dump."

Jake looked down at the frozen street, "That was a hell of a way to end our New Year's Eve! Was just something that happened, I guess. How are you doing, Bob? Do you want us to take you over to doc's place now or wait and let the women take a look the wound back at the house? It looks to me like the bullet went through the fleshy part of your thigh."

Bob replied, "Thanks for taking care of my horse, Jake. I was just in the wrong place at the wrong time. It coulda' happened to any of us, I don't blame Jack for shootin' me or you for putting my horse down. Actually, I don't think I'm hurt that bad; I'll let Betty take a look at it when we get back up to the house."

~~~~~~

When Jake and Hoot rode into the front yard of the farmhouse, they noticed that a couple of the guys were already spilling the beans to a group of women folk who were waiting outside. Jake smiled to himself as he listened to their accounting of the events. Of course, the guys who were doing the talking enjoyed the female audience and described an even gorier version of what had actually happened.

Jake paused outside the back door and attempted to rub snow over his blood-splattered coat but it didn't do much good. As he walked into the house, Raisa took one look at him and nearly swooned! "Oh, dear Lord, Jake, are you hurt? Were you shot too?" Jake assured her he was fine that it was blood from the horse he had put down. "I think we've all had enough fun for one night. How about you, Raisa? Are you ready to head on home? Let's get the kids and put 'em in the wagon." As she and Jake attempted to bundle their sleeping children into their coats, Raisa couldn't help herself. "Jake, I keep telling you that this shooting guns and all, is dangerous. A bunch of grown men with families and you all acting like kids."

Jake laughed then cupped her sweet face in his cold hands, "Its tradition Raisa, German tradition, *mein Liebchen*!"

~~~~~~

Several couples were saying their goodbyes and heading out the front door with their children asleep in their arms, when out-of-the-blue, Ruby Miller slapped Frannie Waltner hard across the face. Ruby grabbed a handful of Frannie's brassy bottle-blond hair and yanked as hard as she could as the two women fell to the floor. All hell broke out as Raisa pushed Jake out the back door. "Let's get out of here. I'll tell you what happened on the way home. Those two have been at it all night; it was something else! Shameful hussies—just shameful that's what it is!"

Jake and Raisa said their goodbyes and headed for their rig. Raisa shivered as the frozen snow made crunching sounds with each step; she felt the freezing chill bite into her face and shimmy up her green dress. As Jake secured his roan horse to the back of the buggy, Raisa made sure their two sleeping children were nestled under a heavy down quilt in the rear seat. Jake took her by the arm and helped her up and onto the front seat; he cracked the bull whip through the frosty night air as the team lunged forward. The still of the frigid night was disrupted by the sharp clicking sound of horse hooves pounding against the frozen road; puffs of hot breath shot from their nostrils as they headed for the warmth of their lean-to barn.

Raisa cuddled closer to her husband. She turned momentarily to check on their two sleeping children and tucked the heavy blanket tighter around them. They passed a brightly lit house and heard the sound of singing, "Listen Jake, they are singing Auld Lang Syne. I wish our party hadn't ended like it did; it would have been nice to sing something like that before we all left." She laughed into her hand, "It might have been sorta hard to sing with those two hussies wrestling on the floor like they were."

Raisa twisted to the side in her seat so she was facing her husband. She cocked one eyebrow and said, "Well, Jake, you really missed something tonight. We probably had more excitement there at the house than you did out on those cold icy streets with your six-shooters. You could have watched a real honest-to-goodness cat fight if you'd stuck around. What you saw back there between Ruby and Frannie was actually the end of the fight or maybe then again, they never quit in the first place. It all began just after you fellas left. Ruby and Frannie were talking back there in the kitchen, the rest of us were in the living room playing another hand of pinochle when all of a sudden we heard the sound of breaking glass and yellin' coming from the kitchen. The rest of us women--well, we ran in just as Frannie knocked Ruby to the floor; she was sittin' on top of her screamin' and pullin' her hair. I've never in my life seen women act like that, Jake." She put her glove to her mouth and stifled a giggle. "Really, it woulda been pretty funny if it hadn't been so disgusting."

Jake glanced over at his wife with a sarcastic grin on his face. "Well, actually it doesn't surprise me much. Those two haven't liked each other from day one. That relationship is just like a fat pimple filled with pus; sooner or later it's gotta pop. Do you know what prompted the final showdown?"

Raisa raised her carefully plucked eyebrows as she faced her husband. "Well, it's no secret is it that Frannie's been carrying a torch for Ruby's man for quite a spell. Ruby just came right out with it and accused Frannie of flirting with her husband; we all knowed it wasn't just tonight. Frannie took offense to what Ruby was insinuating---well, you know the rest of the story."

Jake looked down at his wife. "Well, like you said, we have all seen the signs that Frannie has been, uhh—steppin' over the line for a while now. This is what happens when people start drinking--things get out of hand!"

Raisa hooked her arm through her husbands as he drove the horses down the hill to their house. "Are we almost there Jake, huh?" She smiled sleepily as she gazed up at the star-studded winter sky. "Just look up at the sky Jake. It's all lit up to the north. Is that what they call the 'Northern Lights'? It's a beautiful sight, isn't it? The sky all shot with blue, pink, yellow, and purple like that. I wonder, what makes it do that?" Raisa tipped her head back to get a better look at the studded canopy of night sky. "I swear it looks like a million diamonds just flashing and twinkling at us!"

Jake slid his extra arm around Raisa and pulled her close. "None of them shine as bright as you do though—not even close!" He shifted in his seat a bit, taking both reins with one hand then casually remarked, "You know Raisa, we have sorta' talked here and there about someday, trying our luck someplace else. I have been seriously thinking about packing up the kids and leaving Lovell. We've been married over five years and just aren't making any headway here; I'm getting frustrated. Most of our friends are doing pretty well for themselves and we seem to be stuck in a rut. Maybe it's time we look in a different direction and 'get out of Dodge', as they say. What do you think? Any place special you'd like to try our luck?"

Raisa sat up straight in the seat. Jake had her full attention. "Really, you want to leave here? I don't know, Jake. I have always thought I had my fill of moving from place to place as a kid. I suppose it wouldn't hurt if we pulled up stakes and tried to make it somewhere else. Our kids are still little enough; Beth won't start school for another year. Let me think about where we might go." She gazed off into the distance, her mind already flirting with a world of possibilities.

Jake dropped Raisa and the kids off at the front door as he headed for the small stable out back. He unhitched the two horses from the buggy and led them into their stalls. Then he hung the harnesses on the wall pegs and threw a bucket of oats into the feed trough. With his chores done, he headed for the house, where he slipped out of his winter coat and shook the snow from his boots before lining them against the wall.

Rubbing his cold hands together, he headed for the kids bedroom to kiss them goodnight. They were both huddled underneath the down coverlet that Raisa had made. Jake leaned down and laid a soft kiss on Beth's freckled cheek. She opened her eyes and howled, "Daddy, you are freezing, and you knew that, didn't you? Goodnight, Daddy, and don't play any more tricks on me!" Jake chuckled as he tousled Arnie's blond mop of hair and retreated for his own bedroom.

The door was shut and as he gently pushed it open, he hoped that Raisa wasn't already sleeping. The first thing Jake saw in the dim bedroom light was the green silky dress on the floor, puddled around two gorgeous long, bare legs.

The next morning as Jake and Raisa lay in their rumpled sheets, Raisa snuggled close to her husband and curled a small tuft of his chest hair around her little finger. "Here it is, the first day of the New Year. I wonder what this year will bring." She rolled over on her side, facing Jake as he stretched his cramped limbs and wiped the sleep from his eyes. "Jake, we need to talk some more. We need to get serious about what we are going to do this next year. I don't mind telling you, again, that I'm sick and tired of working in the fields, especially with two little kids to watch out for. Beth is getting old enough to go out with us and work in the sugar beets. I just don't want that for my kids, Jake, to have to work in the fields like we did growing up—it was so darn hard."

Raisa's gaze went to the window and out into the fields that lay frozen under a blanket of snow. "I can't get it out of my head how when I was thinning the sugar beets last summer; Beth just  followed me up and down them rows, holding her doll. I was so glad Mama took care of Arnie, so I didn't have to leave him at the end of the row in a box, like most folks usually do."

Raisa wiped the tears from her eyes. "You were right last night when you said that we don't seem to be getting any wheres financially!" She sat up straight in the bed, "You know, I just remembered that my uncle Wilhelm lives in Michigan, in Port Huron, right there on the lake. I know he's written my folks there's plenty of work and nice little places to rent." Raisa curled her legs underneath her as she sat in their rumpled bed and enthusiastically said, "Jake, I really would like to try it. I loved living in Michigan when I was a little girl. Everything is so green and you wouldn't believe the rain, it's so gentle and warm. It does get a little hot and muggy in the summer, but we could adjust. Hopefully, we could find a place to rent near Lake Huron; you would love the lakes there Jake, the way you like to fish and all!"

Jake chuckled as he rolled over onto his back, folding his hands under his head. "You really want to get out of here and try our luck don't you?" He gazed at his wife. "There's something else

I want to know. How can you look so beautiful in the morning without even combing your hair?"

Raisa got a tight grip on the bed pillow and bashed him over the head. "Jake, for cryin out loud; I am serious, so don't try to change the subject and fill my head with your talk!"

Jake pushed himself up on his own pillow, "Okay, okay Raisa Kessel, we will strike out for Michigan and give that a try if that's what you want. Get your uncle's address and we will start making plans. Probably can't travel until early spring, so I need to see if I can get on at the Great Western Sugar factory and earn some extra dough, until we are ready to go. I am thinking maybe we should put a lot of our stuff into storage out at my folks' farm and just take the train. I'm sort of leaning toward a bigger city—lot more opportunity for me as far as a new kind of job. I don't think I want to farm out there. I've had a craw-full of farming. Problem is--I'm a jack-of-all trades and master of none. But you know me, I'm willing to learn and try something new. I think a change of scenery might just be what we need. Who knows, maybe we'll find us a pot of gold out there."

Jake plumped his pillow and leaned back against the headboard. "So, you think Port Huron would be a good place to go, huh? Before we pack up and move all the way out there, maybe we should send your uncle a letter and make sure it's as good as your folks said."

Raisa leap-frogged across the bed and wrapped her arms around her husband, "Oh Jake, I am so excited to get out of Lovell and go back to Michigan. I think it is going to be good for us. A new beginning! We'll make new friends, have new experiences—our great adventure. I think the kids will love it too, especially the ride on the train!" She scooted to the edge of the bed as a million thoughts raced through her head, "And, Jake—in Michigan, our kids won't have to go into the beet fields, they'll be city kids." Raisa ran her fingers through her hair and licking her fore finger, she daintily smoothed her eyebrows. Tipping her head back, she said, "I've always thought I was better suited for the bright lights and glamour of city life." She giggled and jumped on top of Jake, tickling him until he rolled her over onto her back.

The very next day she went out to visit her folks at their farm. "Mama, can you find Uncle Willie's address for me? Jake and me are talking about moving out to Michigan to see if we can do any better there. I was also wondering if I might borrow the big traveling trunk that you and Dad used when we was movin' back and forth across the country all those years. It sure would help. We don't have but two suitcases and they are pretty small."

Sofie poured a cup of coffee for her oldest daughter and one for herself, and set a chipped blue plate of apple kuchen down on the oil-cloth covered wood table. She pulled a wooden chair out and sat, heavily. Sofie took her handkerchief from her apron pocket and dabbed at the sweat that had beaded up on her forehead. "Of course you can use that old trunk. Your Dad and me are here to stay—no more moving for us." Sofie pushed a forkful of the apple cake into her mouth, chewed, then said, "Raisa, are you sure you and Jake want to pull up stakes? Do you think it's going to be that much better out there? I thought you always hated moving?"

CHAPTER TWO

"We are leaving—to fling into the unknown—to transplant in alien soil; to see if it could grow differently, if it could drink of new and cool rains, bend in strange winds, respond to the warmth of other suns—and, perhaps, to bloom." **Richard Wright**

Jake stared at the feisty blades of tender, green grass that pushed their way up through the crusty brown snow. Little groups of brave April flowers clustered together in the protective shelter at the base of the unpainted wood station platform. Jake raised his head to gaze at the small corpse of trees that grew across the street, their branches pregnant with swelling buds. A soft fragrant breeze wafted over the little town, bringing with it the hope of spring. *This is the best time of year—ripe with promise. I pray that this decision has more than possibilities for Raisa and me; it's high time we had us a real break.*

Pensively, Jake looked off toward the blue Big Horn Mountains to the east. *I hope we're doing the right thing, leaving Lovell, our families, and moving clear out to Michigan. But, guess one's gotta take a chance once in a while and see what's on the other side of the hill. It might be good and then again, it might not.* His head snapped up when he heard the wailing call of the train whistle. "Okay, everybody get your stuff together, the train is coming!" Jake called to his young son, who was busy exploring the nooks and crannies of the wooden platform. "Arnie, come here boy. Do you want to ride on the train, huh? Look, your sister is already in line with Mama."

They all climbed onto the 'bare bones' train, and settled in. Raisa handed their two children some dried fruit to nibble on. "Now put some of that in your pockets for later when you get hungry." Filled with excitement, the children were glued to the window of the train as it snaked alongside the Shoshone River out of Lovell. Jake leaned back in his seat and took out the *Lovell*

Chronicle. He read for a few minutes and then began to chuckle. "Listen to this Raisa. '*Early last Friday morning, about 2 a.m., the Big Horn County sheriff and his deputies' raided two rooms at the Greybull Alamo Hotel. It seems the desk clerk tipped the sheriff off that some of his guests where having a very noisy party in a private room. The law officers hauled off five men and three women along with several quarts of liquid which seemed to be the source of the good time. Some force was required by the law officers to convince one of the men, to come along peacefully.*" Jake slapped his knee and laughed some more, "Guess them guys are cooling off in the clink! I wonder where they got that much booze."

    It took three long hours for the impatient Kessel family to ride the slow, north-bound train as it headed across the border to Billings, Montana. Jake complained during the long ride, "Son-of-a-gun, I could run faster than this train. But, I guess it has to stop at all the little Podunk towns along the way and pick up their mail, passengers, and whatever else they need to send north to Billings. Sure am glad our two kids decided to take a nice long nap so we can catch our breath!"

    It was late in the day when they arrived in the bustling Montana town. After they stored their luggage at the station, Jake found an inexpensive cabin for the night. The next morning they slept in, then ate a leisurely lunch and headed back to the spanking new railway station on Montana and 25th Avenue, to wait for the faster, modern east-bound train. Leaving Raisa in charge of their two squirming children, Jake rose from the varnished oak benches in the passenger waiting area and got in line to buy their tickets to Michigan.

    Protectively, Jake fingered the cash in his front pocket. He stood patiently in the line that had formed in front of the middle ticket window where a uniformed man sat. Finally, it was his turn. "Good morning sir, I want to buy two adult and two children's tickets, straight through to Port Huron, Michigan, on that there Pullman passenger train." Jake fidgeted with the money in his pocket as the railroad man behind the window studied the detailed price schedule.

The middle-age ticket agent lifted his head, his finger remaining on the schedule pointing to a particular line. "I need to know, sir, if you have considered upgrading from straight coach tickets to a combination of coach and sleeping accommodation tickets for two adults and two children. You can purchase an upper or lower berth in the tourist-class Pullman car or if you prefer, we also have individual private rooms in a first-class sleeper car, for an additional fee, of course. What Pullman arrangement would you prefer to make for the trip?" He spoke so fast, throwing out the prices and different accommodations that Jake felt overwhelmed.

Nervously shuffling his feet, Jake ran his right hand back through his thinning hair as he bought a little thinking time. He swallowed hard, looked the ticket agent straight in the eye and replied, "I definitely want to buy a sleeping berth for our two kids and honestly, I can't see me and the wife sitting up the entire trip, so I think I will need an upper and lower berth added to the price of the ticket. We don't need no private room, that ain't necessary." Jake looked over his shoulder at the line growing behind him and added quietly, "Ah—those—uhh t-those beds will be one over the other, right? And, if you don't mind my asking—are they wide enough for two adults in one?"

Without raising his head, the man behind the barred window glumly replied, "Yes, Mr. Kessel. In fact, I am going to assign you the berths at the end of the sleeping car, that way it will give you more privacy with your young ones and, they are wide enough for two adults. Would that be satisfactory?"

Jake opened his coat and tucked their train tickets safely into the inside pocket. Watching from across the room, Raisa gave a big sigh of relief as Jake turned and with a confident expression, headed back to where they were waiting. "Okay, that wasn't too bad. I used some of the extra cash Dad gave me to buy sleeping berths all the way to Michigan. I thought you'd all like that!"

Raisa jumped from her seat and threw her arms around Jake's neck. Suddenly realizing they weren't alone, she quickly withdrew her arms and hugged onto Jake's arm instead. "That's wonderful Jake, I am so excited and I know the kids are going to love sleeping on the train. This will be a first for you and me, too. I don't think either of us has ever slept in a bed on a train. This is going to be a great adventure for us all."

Jake settled down beside Raisa on the shiny oak bench to wait for their train. He reached inside his jacket and pulled out his pipe. Raisa glanced at her husband out of the corner of her eye. "Jake, I don't think you are supposed to smoke in here, are you?"

Jake looked around the enormous hall. "Well, I see others smoking; why would they have those big ash trays around if people weren't supposed to smoke."

Jake put a match to his pipe, inhaled and blew the smoke far out into the room. "That's just what I needed, something to relax me a bit" He turned to his wife, "The ticket agent told me that a porter will prepare our beds at night and make them up in the morning while we're eatin'. Pretty fancy, don' you think? Just don't you go getting used to this high livin' now!" Jake laughed as he tweaked Raisa's rosy cheek.

None of the adult conversation missed five-year-old Beth, who was all ears. "Daddy, do we really get to sleep and eat on the train while we ride? I am so excited! I've never been on a train like this in my whole life!" She paused and then added, "You aren't teasing me again, are you Daddy? Because I don't think that would be funny at all." She ran over to the station window, pressing her freckled pug nose against it as she gazed at the impressive silver train waiting on the tracks. As usual, Arnie tagged along, not wanting to miss a thing. Irritated by her little brother's constant presence, she roughly pushed him away. "Do you have to follow me everywhere I go, Arnie? Really, you are such a pest." She turned and ran back to where her parents were sitting and talking.

"Mama, will you please make Arnie behave and stop following me everywhere and doing what I do? He is getting on my nerves and I'm about to bust him in the chops!"

Jake picked Arnie up and gave him a good 'horsey ride' on his knee. "Now listen boy, you stop pestering your sister do you hear me?" Arnie sat with a pouting scowl on his face. As soon as his parents took their eyes off him, he stuck his tongue out at his older sister.

Raisa stared pensively off into the distance for a few moments then turned to Jake who sat next to her on the oak bench. "Jake, I can't forget the look on both of our parents faces when we told them we were leaving for Michigan. It must have brought back memories for them of when they left their parents and their homes back in the old country. But I think they understand that we need to try something else, just like they did. Besides, we aren't even moving to another country—it won't be forever, like it was for them."

Jake's expression was reflective as he nodded in agreement. The Kessel family waited patiently for the conductor to announce boarding. Soon, they heard the conductor's booming voice announce their train. Adrenaline rushed through them as they hastily gathered their belongings and headed for Gate Three. Jake noticed Beth had a death grip on his coat as they walked up to the impressive, silver train. She tugged at his coat tail to get his attention. "Daddy, who are those men standing beside the train? They're all dressed alike. They look different than us. Are they Indians, Daddy?" Jake smiled down at her and in a low voice explained the men were the train porters and they always dressed in uniforms. Beth pulled hard on her father's coat. Loudly and impatiently she asked again. "Daddy, I said—are they Indians?"

Jake bent down, scooped her up in his arms and firmly replied, "Beth, I will answer your question when we are settled on the train. Lower your voice, you are being rude. Do--you understand me?" Jake put her down and gripped her little hand tightly in his.

Beth was well-acquainted with that particular tone of voice and trembling, she hid her face in her father's coat. Jake stepped aside so Raisa and Arnie could board, then he climbed the steep steps with Beth in tow. They found their bank of four seats, facing each other. Raisa reached up to stroke the magnificent mahogany carving on the seat edges. "Jake, look at the beautiful wood on these seats, and velvet upholstery too—oh my goodness, I never dreamed it would be like this. Trains have changed a lot since we rode on them as children. Do you remember how hard those wood seats were back then?" Raisa smiled as she looked at her children with their noses pressed against the glass windows. She thought to herself, *this is going to be a wonderful journey--I pray.*

The massive silver train began to move as the state-of-the-art engine built up pressure. Steam hissed loudly from beneath the train as iron wheels groaned and straddled the iron rails. Frightened by all the unfamiliar noises, Beth and Arnie scrambled onto the laps of their parents. As the train began to pick up speed, Beth looked up with determination at her father. "Okay, is now the time Daddy that you are going to tell me about the Indians?"

Jake tried in vain to stifle a smile at his daughter's naïve persistence. "Sweetheart, the men are not Indians, they are Negros. They are just like us except their skin is a different color." He forewarned his daughter that she would more than likely see many more dark-skinned people during their trip, especially in the big cities. "You must not be disrespectful and stare or ask rude questions. I want you to be polite and remember to say excuse me sir, thank you sir, and please. Do you understand me Beth?"

The rhythmic sound and sway of the train had a hypnotic effect on the two children as their heads began to nod and soon they were both fast asleep. The sleek passenger train headed east out of Billings toward Glendive and the Montana border where they would cross into North Dakota. Later that day, Jake gazed out the large dining window as the sun began its descent behind the majestic Rocky Mountains to the west. After a pleasant meal in the dining car, they returned to their prepared sleeping berths. That first night they changed into their pajamas, all except for Jake.

Jake and Raisa tucked their excited children into the upper berth; drawing the curtain, they climbed into their own bed. Raisa wriggled under the soft blanket and settled back against the fluffy pillows as Jake pulled their itinerary from his pocket. Raisa turned over onto her side and pulled the bedcovers up to her chin as her eyelids began to flutter shut. Jake leaned over and whispered, "Raisa, I can't settle down, I think I'll go down to the smoking car and have me a smoke. You go ahead and get some sleep, I'll be back soon."

Jake leaned over the edge of their berth and slipped into his shoes; cautiously, he made his way down the narrow, swaying hallway to the smoking car which was located at the rear of the train. He found a window seat and lit up a cigarette. He drew in the smoke and exhaled, closing his eyes in relaxing gratification. Even though it was nighttime, light from a full moon reflected off the lingering mounds of melting snow. Jake could easily make out the countryside passing the window. As he had expected this far north, there hadn't been much to see except for snow and more snow. There were still areas of large, impressive ice jams on the Yellowstone River, but they were beginning to melt and break up as the encroaching warmth of the spring thaw woke the frozen water and sleeping land. *I wouldn't be a bit surprised if there was some flooding around these parts in a few more weeks; there's a lot of ice jammed up there.*

It took half an hour before Jake felt his mind and body giving in to the day. He took a final drag on his third cigarette, stubbed it out in the glass ashtray and headed back to where his family slept.

Crossing the border that first night, the train cut a diagonal line across the southwest corner of North Dakota. Staying a respectable distance from the ice-jammed current of the Missouri River, the track shadowed the river's southeast direction.

The next morning, the sun was just peeking over the wind-swept plains of South Dakota's flat horizon as the steam train eased into a small station outside of another 'Podunk' town. Jake had been awake for the past hour, unable to get comfortable in their unfamiliar, lower berth. He slipped from the bed and bent to kiss Raisa softly on the cheek. She opened her eyes ever so slightly as Jake whispered, "I'm going to step off and have me a smoke at this wide spot in the road. It's pretty early, you go back to sleep honey."

Jake made his way down the aisle as quietly as possible. He was still amazed by the luxury and comfort of the sleeping cars. He remembered last night and what the Negro porter had told him. 'The Pullman Palace Car Company began making these sleeper cars around 1870 to 1880 and now they had a fleet of about 9,800 heavyweight steel coaches from coast to coast.' The sleeper coaches looked pretty snazzy painted in two-tone Pullman grey and they were usually attached to the middle of the train where there was less sway.

The sharp spring wind stung Jake's face as he stepped down the narrow, steep train steps onto the wooden station platform. Pulling his coat collar up against the penetrating early morning cold, he dug down deep in his pocket, pulled out his smokes and cupping the flame, he lit one with a stick match. Inhaling deeply, he released the warm tobacco smoke to blend with the morning dew.

Looking back at the Pullman cars, Jake remembered how amazed he had been at the clever, functional design. They had created a substantial horizontal upper berth built above the facing seats below which folded out flat into a rather narrow double bed. The design engineers even thought to install a curtain that could be pulled for privacy. He smiled when he recalled how adamant both kids had been, insisting they were big enough to sleep in the upper berth. Raisa had agreed, only if Beth was on the outside. Jake smiled in spite of himself as he remembered how she always complained about Arnie kicking her in his sleep.

Jake walked up and down the station platform, stretching his legs and enjoying his morning smoke. *I might have time for another quick cigarette before I have to get back on that train.* Curious, he watched as the workers filled the sleek water reservoir behind the engine. He noticed an engineer nearby and struck up a conversation with him. "Excuse me sir, but I have a question that has been nagging at me. I read somewhere that the Ingersoll-Rand company was trying out a 300 horsepower locomotive that was fitted with an electrical generator and traction motors. Is this rail line using anything like that yet? I've also heard some talk about diesel engines."

The engineer rubbed his day-old growth of whiskers and replied, "Yeah, well they are working on lots of things but nobody seems in any big hurry to change everything over to a new system until they tweak it some more. Probably be another five, six years before you see a diesel engine replace these old steam babies! Change comes slow when there's a healthy price tag attached!"

Jake stood for a few minutes longer, taking it all in. He took a final drag on his cigarette and then stamped it out on the icy station platform. He bid good day to the engineer and pulled himself up the steps, back onto the train.

As the train pulled out of the station, Jake strolled to the dining car to get a cup of coffee before Raisa and the kids woke up. He ordered his coffee then chose a vacant seat near a window and watched as the snow-covered country side began to move past. *I don't think this country would be any better to farm than Wyoming. It looks pretty barren and downright windy to me. I hope we are making the right decision, picking up and taking off to Michigan. But I guess it's worth a try. There's still a lot I don't know, but I'm not afraid of learning and/or working hard, nosiree! I remember back when I left home and went to work at the new sugar factory in Lovell. I was still wet behind the ears and I found a job that very same day. That foreman asked me if I knew anything and I told him the truth. 'I'm sixteen and straight off the farm. I know how to do a lot of things, but the main thing I know is how to work hard.' He hired me on the spot, damn right. I started at the bottom and worked my way up. I learnt something different every day.*

After he finished his coffee, Jake walked the length of the dining car and paused to wash up in the men's washroom. After he washed up, he walked back down to the sleeping car.

Reaching their berth, Jake pulled back the privacy curtain and cautiously lay down on top of the blanket next to Raisa. Trying not to wake her, he unfolded the newspaper he had purchased and began to read the local news. Suddenly, he was aware of a bright-eyed little freckled face, hanging upside down from the top berth watching him. Jake raised his index finger to his lips in warning for Beth to be quiet. He eased out of the lower berth and reached up to plant a kiss on her silky, freckled cheek. In a low voice he whispered, "Good morning sunshine. How did you sleep last night? Was it fun sleeping way up there?" Jake tweaked her cute little nose as she flashed a big smile.

Beth cocked her head to the side, her short-cropped hair fanned out onto the blanket as she whispered disgustedly, "Oh Daddy—have you ever slept with Arnie? He kicks like a mule! How about trading me tonight? I'll sleep with Mama and you sleep up here with Arnie—deal?"

Jake winked at her and backed up, raising his hands in protection as he replied, "No deal—don't think your Mama would like that and besides, I know I don't want to sleep with a mule either!"

Beth's face darkened with a scowl as she laid back down next to her little brother. Rebuked, she thought to herself, *well then, tonight I am going to lay a coat or something between us so he can't kick me. That should fix him and if it doesn't, I guess I'll have to pinch him good and hard.*

After Raisa and the kids washed up, they made their way to the dining car for breakfast. Jake spotted an empty table as Beth and Arnie scuffled for the window seat. A uniformed waiter appeared to take their food order. As he walked toward the kitchen car with their breakfast order, Raisa commented, "Now this is what I call livin' high on the hog. I think I could get used to this service real fast!" Her green eyes sparkled as she smiled across the table at her husband.

All that day and night, the train headed southeast across the state of South Dakota. They crossed the border and pulled into Sioux City, Iowa the morning of the third day. As usual, Jake woke early and made his way quietly down to the dining car to watch the landscape unfold past the window as he peacefully sipped his coffee. He was impressed by the size and appearance of the obviously successful farms. Most had two or more brick silos with enormous white barns. *This Iowa country looks mighty good— looks like they raise a lot of corn—I see the wintered stalks poking through the melting snow. I've heard that these folks put up with pretty heavy winter snows, even this far south. I suspect Michigan gets a fair amount of snow, too. I know I'm not looking forward to the eastern humidity. I still remember that feeling from when I was just a kid and we landed at Ellis Island. I remember Dad complaining about the humidity when he lived in Cleveland, but it sure is pretty country---that, it is!* He noticed the train was slowing for yet another stop, at yet another wide place in the road.

It's funny that neither Raisa nor I have ever been away from our folks. I guess this little experiment of ours is going to be a test for both of us. We'll get a taste of what our own parents went through when they left their villages and families back in Europe.

Jake rubbed his unshaven face as he thought about farming and signaled the waiter for more coffee. After pouring half the pitcher of cream into the potent black brew, he looked back out the window of the moving train. *It's darn right interesting to me that the farther east we travel the more paved roads I see. Most all the bigger cities have real nice asphalt paving along with concrete sidewalks, curbs and gutters. I hear even the small towns have shaped, permanent roads covered with crushed rock. Earlier this morning I remember seeing a crew building a new road. It looked to me like they was using well-drained, compacted dirt as the road bed. They ditched out the gutter or barrow pit to handle the water flow from the road. Then there was other guys coming up behind laying down the top layer of a Macadam road—the combination of asphalt and rock. Wish they would put in more of those roads in Wyoming but guess we are at the end of the chain when it comes to improvements on roads or anything for that matter. The big eastern cities get the first cherry off the tree!*

By mid-afternoon, the sleek silver train pulled into Des Moines, Iowa. They had an hour layover in the large city so the Kessel family took the opportunity to stretch their legs, especially since the sun was shining and it looked so warm outside. They secured their berth and stepped down from the train. "Look, Mama, look Daddy, there is even green grass here!" Beth pulled them along toward a small manicured park that skirted the Des Moines River. She was amazed at the size of the river. "That's a lollapalooza! Daddy, this river looks like a lake--look how big it is? I bet it's the biggest river in the whole world—is it, huh?"

Jake laughed at his daughter's exuberant expression and replied, "Well, from what I hear, we are going to see an even bigger river, called the Mississippi. We should cross it before it gets dark today. Why don't you and Arnie run some of that energy off and play tag for a while? Your Mama and I are going to sit here under this tree and look at the pretty sights." The kids ran and played until they were pooped out. Jake hoisted Arnie onto his shoulders as they walked back to the train and Raisa held Beth's soft little hand. Settled back in their seats, it wasn't long before both kids were asleep and the train continued its trek across the state of Iowa, headed for Davenport. Raisa closed her eyes and leaned her head against the window as her own memories of the past five years filled her.

I remember the first time I laid eyes on Jake Kessel—was when we was both seventeen and working at the Great Western Sugar Beet Factory in Lovell. It had just opened a year before and we were lucky to get jobs. Mercy—I remember watching Jake pitch sugar beets from the pile into the vats—how his sweaty shirt stuck to his muscles. His shoulders were wide and straight, narrowing down to slim hips. His light brown hair was already receding and he always wore it slicked back. Jake wasn't what lots of girls would call a big man. He was about five foot eight inches and weighed 150 pounds soaking wet. But he was all man and I couldn't get him out of my mind. It wasn't long after that, he noticed me too.

There was that day I remember purposely taking the sanitary cap off my head after working all day in the factory and shaking my long thick auburn hair loose. My hair was so pretty, clear past my waist and that's what caught his eye, so he says!

Jake and I kept steady company, mostly went places with the gang. Gosh, I think there were usually about ten of us—went all sorts of places together, like camping, picnics, and dancing. We always had a good time and it wasn't long before Jake and I became a couple. It sure didn't take that man long to ask me to marry him, especially when he noticed a couple other guys taking an interest in me. He wanted me all to himself and I pretty much felt the same way about him. There was just something different and exciting about Jake Kessel—made me feel alive. It didn't hurt that he was Lutheran like me and came from a good Lovell family. I think it was those twinkling blue eyes of his and the way they sorta crinkled in the corners when he laughed. Jake loved to tease me and he wasn't anything like my Dad. Jake has a temper, like his father. I didn't realize that it would be a problem for us later on, but for the most part, he's a good man.

Raisa and Jake Kessel on their wedding

February 1st, 1920: our wedding day. It was such a beautiful warm winter day. We said our vows in the yellow and white clapboard Lutheran church on Shoshone Avenue. Mama made me the prettiest dress. She ordered the pale peach chiffon fabric, clear from Billings, Montana. I picked the lace out for the dress and veil myself. I felt so beautiful that day. I remember Jake's face lit up like a Christmas tree when Papa walked me down the aisle. The Lutheran church was filled with our families and friends. After the service, we had us a big celebration in Dad's barn. Even though it was illegal us Germans had to have our beer especially when we dance the polka. We were so young and innocent. I had no idea of what was going to happen from that moment on. I just remember when we was alone for the first time. Jake took the pins from my hair and let it fall down my back. He got this look in his eyes when he wrapped his fingers through my long thick hair and then kissed me hard and slow; I almost couldn't catch my breath.

FLESH ON THE BONE

We learnt things pretty fast during that first year. I think I must have got pregnant on my wedding night because Beth was born nine months later. We named our baby girl Elizabeth Katherina after our mothers, but some way or another her name got shortened to Beth. During those first three years, we moved from rented farm to rented farm —from one filthy shanty to the next. Good thing I have experience cleaning out dirty houses, what with my folks moving all the time when I was a kid.

Bare-bones renter's shack in the late 1920's

Being the oldest, I was the first one called on to take charge. We had it tough those first years, but like my Dad always said 'This is the only way we are going to eat and the only way we are going to get ourselves up and out of this hole. This country promises us freedom to work or not to work, and I can tell you this, we are going to work!'

I remember when us kids didn't want to go out to the beet fields, Mama would always say, 'Spend a few hours a day in the garden or the field and you will have something to eat; spend a few hours a day caring for an animal and soon you will have something to eat; share what you have with a friend and you will have a friend for life.' Those were good words and I have often thought of them and how hard my folks worked to feed us kids.

No matter how hard he tried, my Jake just hasn't made much of a go of it on the farm. I am sure part of it was because he felt like his dad was still watching and criticizing everything he did. I took in extra work, cleaning houses and working at the laundry when I could. Jake took on any and all jobs he could find in the winter months, from feeding cattle and hauling hay, to building brick silos. I lost count of the number of them brick silos he built. He got the bricks real cheap right there in Lovell.

I didn't want to get pregnant again for a while after Beth was born—tried everything I could and even things Mama suggested. But in spring, 1923, Arnold was born. He came early and we near to lost him. We gave him a strong name but he was pretty scrawny at first. I will never forget, after he was born, Mama wrapped him tight and put him in a shoe box. She sat the box on the oven door to keep him warm. That's how folks done it then. Shoot, I don't think he weighed but four or five pounds, but I took real good care of him and look at the little imp now—ornery and healthy as the day is long! I know one thing for sure--I don't want any more babies. I am not going to be like my mother or Jake's mother—having kids clear into my 40s, and having a tough time of it too. No siree, two is plenty for us and Jake agrees.

Arnie. Jake. and Beth with her doll.

I am lookin' forward to livin' in the city, not some wide place in the road. Beth will be startn' school next year and that means finding a good place to live once we get there. I can't believe it when I look at our kids. They are growing up so fast. I keep thinkin' of that picture I snapped before we left Wyoming, of Jake and the kids. Beth carries that baby doll with her everywhere, even sleeps with it. I remember when Arnie stole Beth's baby doll and drew red dots all over the doll's face with Mercurochrome!

～～～～～

Raisa felt Arnie stir as he woke from his nap. He sat up, rubbed his eyes and stretched his little arms out wide, then reached up for her, giving her a big hug as he laid his head of unruly blond curls on her shoulder and stuck his thumb back in his mouth. Beth was awake as well, sitting quietly and coloring in the little picture book Jake had bought at the last stop. She guarded her little nickel-box of crayons with a vengeance, refusing to let her brother touch them. "No, he can't hold even one. I know him and he will break them—he's too little and just plain ornery."

As they neared Davenport, Jake made sure the kids were looking out the windows so they could see the enormous Mississippi River. When Beth spotted the river, she exclaimed, "Oh Daddy, never in all my life have I seen a river that big—it's even bigger than that one we saw in 'Desss Moans'."

Jake winked and tweaked her cheek, "You are looking at the largest river in America. See how many big boats and barges there are on it? They are carrying things up and down the river just like big trucks carry things on the highway. It is a very important river, Beth."

After a lovely dinner in the dining car, the two kids began to yawn. Jake carried Arnie back to their berth. "Think this little tyke is plumb tuckered out. That's good, maybe he will sleep all night."

They put the kids to bed early; then slid into their own berths below to wind down a bit. Relaxed and sitting side by side, Raisa leaned into Jake; they were both mesmerized by the glittering lights of the flourishing industrial tri-cities of Davenport and Bettendorf, Iowa and Rock Island, Illinois. After leaving the three cities and crossing the Mississippi, they headed almost due east toward Chicago where they would change trains the next morning.

At the crack of dawn, the two kids were glued to the window as the train pulled into Union Station in the center of Chicago. Beth said, "Papa, look at all the trains here. There must be a hundred." Jake and Raisa were also captivated by the number of tracks and trains either waiting for passengers or freight—it was something neither of them remembered seeing when they were young. When it came time for them to disembark, Raisa carried Arnie and Beth held onto her father's coat as he carried their suitcases. They were directed to a large building where they were instructed to relax and wait for their next train. Once inside the recently completed, magnificent Great Hall of the Chicago train station, all of the passengers experienced a jaw-dropping moment. Jake and Raisa walked over to a commemorative plaque concerning the Great Hall. Jake read out loud—"This building was designed by Chicago architect Daniel Burnham whose inspiration was his favorite slogan, *'Make no small plans, they have no magic to stir men's blood.'*

Raisa looked around the room at the eighteen massive Corinthian columns. The glistening pink, Tennessee marble floor butted up to blush-colored terracotta stone walls. She tipped her head back to gaze up at the five-story, barrel-vaulted atrium ceiling. "Oh Jake, have you ever seen anything so grand?" As the family of four waited for their train, they continued to enjoy the vast beauty of the Great Hall, that is until Beth pulled on Raisa's arm. "Mama, I have to go potty. Do they have a potty in this place?"

No sooner had Beth and Raisa returned from the restroom when Beth remembered seeing an ice cream stand across the great room. "Daddy, can Arnie and I have a penny each to go over there and get an ice cream cone. Don't worry, Daddy, I'll take care of Arnie. Huh Daddy, can you give us each a penny? Come on, be a sport."

Jake and Raisa saw the ice cream stand a few hundred feet away and figured it would be all right. Jake dug into his pocket for two cents and giving the money to Beth, he instructed, "Okay now Beth, you hold on to his hand and don't let go, you hear me? Mama and I'll be sitting right here, go on now."

Beth and Arnie raced across the gleaming marble tile, to stand in line for an ice cream cone. Beth had a death grip on Arnie's hand and he began to squirm. "Sister, don't hold so tight, you hurt my hand." Beth relaxed her grip just a tad but she still hung on to him. She knew him and his escaping tricks.

Next in line, Beth ordered two vanilla ice cream cones; without letting go of Arnie's hand she paid for the cones and handed one to Arnie which he immediately dumped on the floor.

After a two-hour wait, they boarded their train and settled in as they began their trek eastward, across Michigan to Detroit where they were scheduled to change trains again. Looking at their tickets, they saw that from Detroit to Port Huron, they would travel on a basic local train. It took both Jake and Raisa a while to fall asleep that night because they were consumed with visions of what lay ahead as the future danced in their heads. Would it be all good?

CHAPTER THREE

Port Huron, Michigan: Uncle Wilheim, Aunt Gerta and a collection of curious cousins stood waiting on the platform as the train pulled into the small rural station. Jake, Raisa and their two kids climbed off the train and after everyone was properly kissed and hugged, they piled into two waiting farm wagons and headed out to Uncle Willie's farm.

On the way to the farm, Uncle Willie said, "Well, I have some good news and some bad news Jake. That job that I had for you went up in smoke, but I am sure you can land something else in Port Huron if you are serious about not wanting to rent a farm. You all are welcome to stay with us for a few days until you find some work. I have to warn you that we don't live in a castle and the kids will have to double up. Laying all that aside, welcome to Michigan"

~~~~

Jake and Raisa stayed only a few days at Uncle Willie's farm. The second day pounding the pavement, Jake found work as a Fuller Brush salesman in Port Huron. He was also fortunate in finding a small, partially furnished house to rent. The house wasn't much to look at and was situated in a back alley behind a small local movie theatre, but it served its purpose. Raisa scoured the flea markets and second hand stores to pick up a few necessary items and in no time she turned the little house into a home. Raisa beamed when Jake said, "Well, I've always heard that you can't turn a sow's ear into a silk purse, but you came darn right close with fixing up this place. I am going to keep looking for a regular, hourly job. I already know I don't much care for this kind of sales job, although I do get to meet some nice folks now and then. What I don't like are the cold calls and not feeling welcome when I knock on a door."

The sales job at Fuller Brush didn't last long, or perhaps it was that Jake didn't last long. He quit after finding an interesting and better paying job on the assembly line at Wills St. Clair auto factory. Jake was very interested in the new line of automobiles and the job was right up his alley.

Two weeks later, on Friday after work, Jake came waltzing confidently through the front door sporting a big smile and a nice fat paycheck. "Get your coats and hats, we are going out for supper and then see what we find to do after that." They walked several blocks to the south of their house and found a nice little café. After a savory home-cooked meal of meatloaf and fluffy potatoes swimming in brown gravy, they walked on down the street. Right there on the corner of Lake and Brighton Street sat an impressive theatre. Jake turned to his family, "How about we take in a moving picture show? It says up on that there sign that they also have a vaudeville show. Sounds like some good entertainment to me. Let me check to see how much the tickets are." Jake walked up to the ticket booth and liking what he heard, he bought two adult tickets. He turned and walked back to where Raisa and the kids were waiting patiently.

With a twinkle in his eyes, he said, "Well, them ticket prices cost a pretty penny-- so I just bought two, for Mom and me. You kids will have to stand out here and wait until the show is over. Can you do that?" Beth's eyes opened wide and her lower lip began its trembling downward pout as she looked to her mother for sympathy. Before Raisa could respond, Arnie began to bawl in earnest.

Raisa looked at Jake with annoyance, "That was not funny, Jake. Now see what you've done. What's the real story on the tickets?"

Jake scooped Arnie up in his right arm, holding him like a sack of potatoes. "Sorry kids, I was just having some fun with you. You two get in free, how about that? Come on, let's go inside."

The attendant found them four seats in the middle of the theatre and they settled in to watch their first vaudeville show and silent moving picture. The two children were busy sucking on lollipops Jake had bought for them at the candy counter. Unable to contain her curiosity any longer, Raisa leaned over and whispered in Jake's ear. "Jake, those girls... I was wondering—those women we saw standing on the street corners---were they, were they, those women who-?"

Jake couldn't help but chuckle. "Boy, nothing much misses your eyes, does it my sweet, innocent country girl? Yeah honey, those women were what are known as 'ladies of the night'. Some of them gals looked pretty rough. That's a heck of a way to make a living if you ask me. But, what with no education and probably a kid or two at home, they have to make money some way and for most of em', it's on their backs!"

Raisa put her left hand over her mouth as she looked down in shock. She felt pity for the women—sorry they felt they had no choice than to take something so beautiful between a man and a woman and make it so—so, so common.

In a matter of minutes, the theatre's gas lamps dimmed and the enormous, burgundy velvet curtain rose magically. The master of ceremonies walked onto center stage and announced in a very deep voice-- "La-dies and gentle-men—for your en-ter-tainment to-night, we have a world-class show di-rect from Paris, France. After the vaudeville performance, please keep you seats for a wonderful moving picture show starring Charlie Chaplin. Thank you for coming this evening and----enjoy the show!"

The theatre reverberated with enthusiastic dance music as twenty or more scantily clad, shapely young girls skipped onto the stage and began to dance. Beth and Arnie wiggled to the edge of their seats. When the girls all kicked their legs over their heads in unison, Beth literally gave out a squeal. Arnie soon tired of the show and laid his head on his mother's lap. Beth however, continued to sit on the edge of her seat during the entire vaudeville show, her eyes devouring every move of the high-stepping girls in the chorus line. In a loud whisper, she asked, "Daddy, where do those ladies learn to dance like that and kick their legs so high? Can I do that when I grow up?"

Jake said, "I don't know where they learn that but that's not something you are going to do when you grow up, if I have anything to say about it." Beth didn't like her father's answer. In response, a frown wrinkled her freckled face and she kicked the seat in front of her.

FLESH ON THE BONE

After six months on the job, conditions and opportunities at the Wills Sainte Claire Automobile[1] factory seemed to be slowing down, and they cut Jake to four days a week. To make ends meet, he found a new part-time job driving delivery truck for the nearby ice house.

Jake had the last Sunday of the month off. "I don't have to work tomorrow, so after church, how about we hop the trolley and have us a little adventure?" True to his word, after church, they walked two streets over and caught the trolley which took them down by the river to where the icehouse sat. The desk clerk smiled as he told them, "Yes sir-ree, during the winter theys about a dozen men who wait for the river to freeze real deep. That's when they go out on that there ice. They cut chunks out and haul them up to this here icehouse. When they built this here ice house, they built two walls about six inches apart then stuffed the area between them walls with wadded-up newspapers to keep the cold inside. The icehouse its self is all cut up into small rooms packed floor to ceiling with ice blocks. It's easier to keep a room cold if it isn't too big."

Beth looked with distaste at the unpainted wood that was permanently stained a mottled moldy color. Jake explained the shabby appearance of the exterior of the building. "It's never been painted and it's stained like that because of the mold that comes from all that continuous moisture inside and out. Paint just will not stick to the damp wood."

On the trolley ride home, Raisa turned to Jake and under her breath asked, "So, Jake—just how did you get the job driving a truck? I didn't know you knew how to drive."

Jake smiled as he continued to gaze out the window of the trolley then replied in a cocky tone, "It's simple Raisa—I didn't tell Mr. Rogers that I had never driven a motor car. I figured I would catch on by myself. I rode along with another driver the first day and hell, I just watched what he did. The next day, I climbed behind the wheel of my truck and--nothing to it. You step on the

---

[1]

clutch with your left foot and brake with the right. Then you grab onto the gear shift that sticks up from the floor on the right and shift it into low gear to start out. You let the clutch out real slow like, as you take your right foot off the brake and step ever so slightly on the gas and away you go. Nothin' to it, just keep it on the road!"

Jake was making pretty good money driving the ice truck. It was a little trickier to keep the ice frozen during the hot summer months. His truck was installed with copper coolers but they didn't help that much. He learned to make frequent and quick trips to the customers, dividing his route into tighter trips, which also meant he made more trips to the ice house during the summer months compared to when it cooled off. Jake liked the job because he got to meet different people along his route, but lifting the large chunks of ice day in and day out started wearing on his back and he knew he was going to have to look for another job.

Along his route that summer, Jake found a small pool hall close to home and several times a month he enjoyed stopping in after a long day. He usually had a cold beer and played a round of pool or a hand of cards. It was a way for him to unwind, light up his pipe and shoot the bull with some of the guys. One Friday night Jake stayed longer than he meant to and it was dark when he got home, smelling of pool hall, smoke, and stale beer.

Raisa looked up from the tin dishpan where she was washing the supper dishes. She wiped her hands on a dish towel when she heard him open the front door. She turned to face him. With her hand on one hip and her eyes blazing, she shot him a question, "For Pete's sake Jake---where have *you* been? I know you got off work hours ago and I held supper as long as I could, but the kids were hungry. I had to go ahead and feed them. There's nothing left for you, I threw it out."

Bravely, yet cautiously, Jake crossed the room and gave his wife a quick kiss on the cheek, obviously forgetting he reeked of smoke and stale beer. One sniff was all she needed as she pushed him away. "Pee-U, Ja-ke Kessel, I figured that's where you were---at some pool hall. A real family man, aren't you? No matter that the wife and two little kids are at home, waiting supper on you. You just had to get in one more hand of cards, am I right?"

Jake gave her a sheepish grin as he pleaded, "Aw, come on, Raisa, a man needs a little time to himself once in a while. Shoot, I haven't been to the pool hall or had a beer in months. I just had a hell of a week and needed to unwind before I came on home, and well you know how it goes--I lost track of time!" He shuffled around while Raisa continued to glare at him.

Raisa sat his supper plate on the table harder than necessary. "So, you lost track of time did you? I don't call that very considerate and I certainly don't have any sympathy for you."

Pushed just a bit farther than he could tolerate, Jake hit the surface of the kitchen table so hard with the palms of his hands that the plates jumped. "Okay, Raisa, here's the plain truth. I lost my job at the ice plant—I got sacked today and I needed some time to lick my wounds, are you satisfied?"

That next week, on every one of his days off from the automobile factory, Jake pounded the pavement looking for a second job. He'd already tried selling insurance and Fuller Brushes and knew he didn't like those kinds of jobs. He liked to sell but he knew he wasn't a door-to-door salesman. He hated the cold call. What's more, times were getting tougher and people weren't buying insurance. He finally found a job as a repairman at an electric appliance shop. When they were short-handed, Jake even sold a few washing machines to folks who walked through the door. He had always liked to fix things and he could sell an ice cube to an Eskimo!

Friday evening after supper, the Kessels were sitting around listening to their small Philco radio when Jake reached over and turned the volume down and said to Raisa, "I had a pretty good week, how about I take you and the kids' downtown tomorrow? We can ride the streetcar and catch some lunch."

Beth and Arnie heard the part about riding the streetcar and started jumping up and down with expectation. "Oh, Daddy, can we really, can we?"

Early Saturday morning, they walked a couple of blocks and caught a streetcar which took them to downtown Port Huron.

Jake and Raisa hung onto the coat tails as their two kids leaned out the windows of the street car. Arnie was thrilled with all of the different automobiles. "Daddy, look at those cars and trucks. The buildings are like giant houses!"

When they arrived in the downtown area, Jake made a quick decision to exit the street car as he stood up. "Come on, let's get off here and take a stroll up the street. Maybe we can find a nice place to have a bite to eat later. Kids, watch your step, the cobblestone and brick-paved street is tricky to walk on."

After an hour of strolling up one side of the street and down the other window shopping, the kids began to complain. Just down the street, Raisa spotted the sign of a small café advertising German food. "Look Jake, let's try that little restaurant down there.

The restaurant was small and clean and they chose a booth near the front. Jake picked up the menu and smiled, "Looks like you picked a good one Raisa—the daily special is bratwurst and sauerkraut—just up our alley!" After a leisurely lunch, they headed back toward the streetcar station. Jake hoisted Arnie onto his shoulders because the little fella was plumb tuckered out. As they neared the trolley station on the other side of the street, Raisa took Beth by the hand. They stood waiting on the corner for the cars to pass. Just as they stepped off the cement curb, Beth slipped her hand from her mother's grip and began to race across the street toward an ice cream vendor she'd spotted. Raisa screamed, "BETH, stop—BETH watch out for that car, it's backing up!"

But Beth didn't stop and she didn't see the Model T car as it backed out of the parking space. There was an audible thud as Beth and the car collided. Jake and Raisa were horrified as their child flew up in the air, landing hard on the cobblestone street. She didn't move, her eyes were closed and she was deathly pale.

Jake and Raisa were beside Beth in an instant as people came running from all directions to see what happened. The driver of the car had obviously felt the impact and had jammed his foot on the brake. He threw the door open and leaped from the car. His face went completely ashen as he saw the child lying on the street. He hurried to where the little girl laid on her side. "Is she okay? I didn't see her, she came out of nowhere. Oh my God, I am so sorry. Is she breathing?"

Beth lay at a twisted angle on the brick street[2] near the trolley tracks. Jake and Raisa were on their knees beside their daughter. "Oh dear Lord, please, please let her be okay." Raisa cradled her daughter's head in her hands and smoothed the hair from her freckled face. Blood was oozing from a cut on Beth's cheek. Someone in the crowd offered a glass of water which Raisa took and dipping her fingers into it, splashed Beth's face, hoping to revive her.

Jake's eyes frantically scanned the crowd. "Is anyone a doctor? We need a doctor here!" It was music to his ears when he heard Beth moan. Her eyelids fluttered and then opened. "Wha— what happened? Ohhh, Mama my head really hurts bad."

Raisa attempted to calm her daughter, "Beth, sweetheart, can you move? Can you sit up?" With her mother's help, Beth struggled to move to a sitting position then soon was able to stand on her own. When Beth attempted to talk a step, she wailed again in pain, "Oh Mama, my leg hurts, I can't walk so good; it hurts up here, above my knee. Oh, Mama—I hurt all over, but my head and leg hurt the 'worst-est'."

A well-dressed man pushed his way through the crowd that had gathered. "Let me through, I'm a doctor." He introduced himself to Jake and Raisa. "Excuse me folks, I understand a little girl has been hit by a car. I am Dr. Carl Boegher and I have an office down the street. May I take a look at you daughter? No charge of course." After checking to make sure there were no broken bones, the doctor turned to Jake and Raisa. "I think she is a very lucky little girl. All I can find are some deep bruises and she'll probably be gimpy for a week or more. I suggest once you get her home, put ice on the leg area several times a day for four days. That should take care of it. You might watch her for a concussion. If she begins to complain of a headache and vomits, do not let her fall asleep. Please call me immediately. Here is my card."

---

[2]

Jake dug into his pocket for some money. The doctor laid his hand on Jake's arm. "No charge, I was just glad to help."

As Jake anticipated, the job at Wills Sainte Claire Auto factory finally gave out. People simply weren't buying expensive cars—the market was flat as a pancake! After that, Jake worked at several different part-time jobs over the next year, never quitting one job before he had found another. Sometimes he worked two or three part-time jobs a day. "I tell you Raisa, it's not easy to find a good-paying job now days, but I might have an opportunity to work in the Ford garage on Broadway. They tell me they need another good mechanic and they know I learnt a lot working at the Wills Sainte Claire Automobile factory. I'm going down to talk to them again over the weekend. Keep your fingers crossed!" Sure enough, Jake came home two days later with a big smile on his face—he had a new job, and a used Ford Model T.

"Oh Jake, we can't afford a car, can we? Raisa was excited at the mere thought of actually owning a motor car, yet scared of debt at the same time. Jake assured her, "It was a repossessed car and the boss wanted a couple hundred for it. I couldn't pass it up honey. It'll make our lives a lot easier 'cause now I can get to work on my own instead of using the streetcars. And besides that, we can go where we want to go. Would you wanna take a little spin in it now?" Raisa and the kids didn't need a second invitation as they piled into the car.

That next weekend, Jake, Raisa and the kids headed out of town in the Model T with a picnic lunch packed into the trunk. Beth and Arnie squeezed into the small back seat and Raisa sat proudly in the passenger's seat up front, next to Jake. About two miles out of Port Huron they spotted a picnic ground. Jake signaled with his left arm and pulled off the dirt road into a nice shady spot. He braked and clutched as he shifted to neutral then cut the engine and pulled the emergency brake out.

Jake and the kids retrieved the picnic basket from the trunk while Raisa spread a blanket on a soft grassy place. Another family was picnicking nearby and Jake asked the man if he would mind snapping a photo of them. Later that afternoon, Jake and Raisa packed up their picnic, while the kids got in a final game of tag. Suddenly, Arnie let out a blood-curdling scream. Alarmed, Raisa turned in the direction of the scream and saw her little boy running toward her, holding his arm. "Mama, Mama, it hurts, that bee bite-ted me!"

On a family picnic in Michigan, Raisa, Beth (6), Arnie (3), and Jake Kessel.

Raisa bent down to take a look at Arnie's arm as Beth stood watching. "Yeah, Mama, a bee stung him right on the arm, I saw it all. Boy, look how it's swelling all up and it's so red. Is it gonna bleed, huh?" At the mention of blood, Arnie cried even harder.

Beth turned away—giggling into her hand. Raisa gave Beth one of her withering looks. "You, missy just behave yourself and go check in my pocketbook. Get a penny out of the coin purse and bring it here."

Beth rummaged through her mother's purse and, finding a penny, ran back to where her brother and mother were sitting. She handed Raisa the shiny penny. "What are you going to do with a penny, Momma, pay Arnie to quit bawling?"

Raisa smiled and replied calmly, "This is something I remember my mother always did. I don't know why, but it really works. Usually, we try to tape the copper penny over the sting, but we don't have any tape, so I'm just going to wrap it with this piece of rag I have with me." She gave Arnie a big kiss on the cheek. "You are going to be fine—that penny will take the 'bad bee juice' out of your arm. Now, let's get back in the car, I think your dad has it all packed up."

The Kessels piled back in the car. Jake released the brake and wheeled it back onto the road, heading west. Out of the blue Jake said, "I think next weekend when I have a day off, you--Raisa Kessel, you are going to learn how to drive. How about those apples? Now you watch everything I do Raisa, cause next week it's gonna be you behind this steering wheel."

Raisa glanced over at her husband in disbelief. In the back seat, Beth and Arnie looked at each other and immediately got the giggles at the thought of their mother driving a car. They could hardly wait!

The next weekend, they loaded the car with another picnic lunch and Jake climbed behind the wheel. They headed out of the city limits, into the country side. Spotting a nice stretch of road ahead, he pushed the clutch in as he stepped on the brake, pulling the Ford off the road. He turned to Raisa who was slightly pale and said, "OK, Raisa, it's now or never." Raisa felt like she was going to pass out from the excitement and fear. Her hands were sweating and she was shaking like a leaf as she dutifully climbed behind the wheel. "Now, before we take that ride—in case none of us survive your mother's driving, we need to have a picture of this. You sit there, behind the wheel Raisa; Beth, you and Arnie get out and sit on the running board.

Port Huron, Michigan---
Raisa Kessel at the wheel of their Model T. Beth and Arnie Kessel.

FLESH ON THE BONE

Jake snapped the photo with their new camera then put the kids back in the car as he walked around to the passenger side. He ran through all the preliminary instructions and suggestions. "Okay, Mrs. Kessel, you're on your own. Let's drive down this dirt road. Just take it easy and don't turn the steering wheel too fast. And another thing—it's not like driving a horse and buggy; you can't say, 'Gee' and expect it to turn left or 'Haw' and expect it to turn right. You have to turn the steering wheel to guide the car. Just take it slow now."

Self-consciously, Raisa bit her lower lip so hard she drew blood, as her sweaty hands gripped the oversized steering wheel. She pushed in the stiff clutch with one foot and slowly lifted the other foot from the brake to the gas pedal. She took her time and worked through each gear. Driving on the gravel road was tricky, just like Jake had told her it would be. After driving for ten minutes without incident, Raisa relaxed and pressed a little harder on the gas pedal. She was grinning ear to ear and her blue eyes sparkled with excitement as she said, "This is fun Jake, it's really fun. I am driving a car; you bet your boots I am. How do you like those bananas?"

Raisa didn't realize how fast she was actually going—they were all laughing and having a time of it when suddenly, there was a sharp corner dead ahead. The seriousness of the moment was upon them before she had a chance to react. Jake yelled, "Take your foot off the gas pedal, step easy on the brake. Gol damn it, Raisa, I said e-asy, e-asy!" Jake grabbed the wheel and pulled hard to the left as the car went around the corner on two wheels in a cloud of dust and gravel. Raisa and the kids were screaming as Jake yelled above the mayhem, "Stomp HARD on the damn brake, Raisa, NOW!" Suddenly there was a loud BANG and the car swerved and headed for the ditch. Jake grabbed the steering wheel for a second time, pulled the lurching car out of the shallow ditch and back onto the road. The kids continued to scream and bawl as they were thrown from one side of the car to the other.

When the careening car came to a stop and the cloud of dust cleared, Jake pulled the emergency brake and jumped from the passenger side of the car. He slammed the door as hard as he could. Anticipating what was coming, Beth and Arnie dove under a coat in the back seat. Raisa seemed frozen at the wheel as Jake jerked open the driver's door. He pried her fingers off the steering wheel and grabbing her by the shoulders none too gently, he physically pulled her out. "What in the bloody hell did you think you were doing? You coulda killed us all, woman! You cannot take those corners going that fast on these skinny tires and with a top-heavy car. And furthermore, driving on a gravel/dirt road is like driving on ice; you can't trust the surface. Now, on top of everything, I've got to change a gol damn tire."

The ride back to town was not much fun. Raisa retreated to the far side of the front seat, head down and shoulders shaking with silent humiliated sobs. Jake let her cry until they pulled up in front of the house. "Okay, Raisa, I'm sorry I got mad at you, but driving is serious business. We'll go back out next week and we'll try it again, and don't you dare tell me you don't want to learn to drive!"

The Kessels moved again when their lease was up. This time they found a nice little house on Jay Street not far from where Jake was working. Raisa loved the partially furnished house because it had an icebox in the kitchen and the previous tenants had left it relatively clean. "Oh Jake, look over there in the corner, a real icebox. Look at the nice oak cabinet it sits in, isn't that grand? I've never had an icebox, but I know how nice they are because your mother has one. Now, all I have to do is find an iceman to bring us chunks of ice to put inside and we can keep all sorts of things cool during the summer."

After getting settled, they searched the nearby neighborhoods to find an Evangelical or Missouri Synod Lutheran church. Going to church to worship God on Sunday was something they were used to doing and an important part of their lives. The first thing Monday morning, Raisa located the elementary school where Beth would begin second grade. It was just four blocks from where they lived.

When Raisa and Arnie walked down to pick Beth up after the first day of school, Beth was bubbling over with excitement.

"I've met this new girl, her name is Shirley Walker and we are going to be best friends! Anyway, that's what Shirley told me." Beth began to skip along the sidewalk as they strolled back home. "And, and—you know what else Mama? Shirley lives one block away from where we live. Isn't that swell?"

Every day after school, Beth and Shirley played outside until they were called home for supper. They especially liked to play out when the skies opened up rain poured down. Raisa stood by the window and watched them as they opened their mouths and stuck out their tongues to catch the rain drops. Sopping wet and shrieking with laughter, they ran up and down the cement sidewalk out in front of the house, making the most of the storm.

Raisa heard Beth remark "You know Shirley, I remember when I was little, back in Wyoming, the rain was sooooo cold and it came down so hard. It wasn't fun to play in like it is here. I'll tell you something else—we didn't have cement sidewalks to mark with chalk when we played hopscotch either! I'm glad we moved to Michigan." Beth put her arm around her friend's shoulder and squeezed. "And, the best thing is—you are my friend, forever and ever, let's promise, okay?"

Most of the time Beth and Shirley skipped rope, roller skated, played hide and seek, and a new game called Jacks. One evening after supper, Beth tried to explain the rules of Jacks to her mother. "The game is played with a little rubber ball and these metal things that look like two X's. Shirley and me, we sit on the ground, Indian-style; then we take the jacks, there are fifteen of them—and throw them across the ground." Beth became impatient with her mother as Raisa threw the Jacks out of the circle. "Oh Mama, you can't throw them too far; you have to be able to reach them. Now, watch me— you bounce the ball like this--- and before it hits the ground, you scoop up as many jacks as you can with the other hand." Beth paused to catch her breath. "That isn't too hard is it? Its soooo much fun Mama. My favorite game is 'Plainsie Double Bouncies". Raisa smiled to herself as she recalled her own best childhood friend, Ruby. *I'm so happy Beth has found herself a best friend; she is making lots of memories.*

All the new 'flapper' styles in the magazines and on the street had caught Raisa's eye. She liked to be stylish, even though their cash was on the low side. One afternoon, feeling frustrated and behind the times, she decided to do something about the situation. Raisa got the scissors out and gave herself a new modern, flapper haircut. Looking in the mirror at her image, she decided to add one more thing to update her appearance. Raisa went to the closet and pulled out the new chemise dress she had finished sewing two days ago.

Raisa Kessel with new haircut and dress

When Jake walked through the front door after work that afternoon, he stopped dead in his tracks. With one hand on her hip, Raisa posed fashionably in the doorway to the kitchen, dressed in her mauve chemise. She was smiling ear to ear, waiting for a compliment from Jake. Instead, his eyes opened wide as he took one more step toward her and stopped, "What in the hell did you do to yourself, Raisa? What happened to your beautiful hair? Who cut your hair like that? And, and that dress is new too. It doesn't show off your curves at all; it just hangs straight, like a sack!"

Shock, embarrassment, and disappointment filled Raisa's eyes. Her hand flew to cover the sobs that escaped from her mouth. Without saying a word, she turned and fled into the bedroom slamming the door behind her. Jake realized he had made a big, mistake. Knocking on their bedroom door, he pushed it open. Raisa was standing in front of the window, her face in her hands and shoulders shaking with sobs. Jake crossed the room in long strides and wrapped his arms around her.

Raisa and Jake Kessel in Michigan

"Awww, honey, I'm sorry, I didn't mean it like that. It was just such a shock to come home and find a 'different woman' in my house. Come on, turn around and let me look have a better look. It's just gonna take some getting used to--that's all. I know you like to be fashionable; just give me a bit to get used to it all, okay? You know, I think you look very modern—very, uh—very *citified*! That's it—you look like a city woman, not a country gal." Jake put his arm around her shoulders and said, "Come on outside so I can take a snapshot of you!"

That night after the two kids were tucked into bed, Jake and Raisa were sitting in the front room. Jake was reading the paper and Raisa was working on her fancy work. Suddenly, out of the blue, she said, "Uhhh, Jake—I have something else to tell you."

Jake looked over the top of his paper, he'd already had one good shock from his wife today. "What else have you been up to?"

Raisa laid her fancy work on the couch and stood, "I-I-I am going to register to v-vote in the next national election for president. It's s-something I've been thinking about ever since women were given the right to vote in 1920. I've been thinking about it and so, I'm going to do it. Is that okay with you?"

Jake put the newspaper down, "Sure, Raisa, that's fine with me. But you are starting to worry me a little bit. I think you might be getting pretty citified—new haircut, new dress style, now you are going to vote with all the other suffragettes." Jake laughed as he stuck his head back behind the newspaper. Raisa grabbed the paper and threw it onto the bare wood floor. "Jake, this is not funny. I am serious about staying up with the times and being a modern woman."

Jake stood and wrapped his arms around her. "Okay Raisa, just don't go getting so modern you don't need the likes of me!" Jake grabbed her around the waist and pulled her into his arms.

Later that week, Raisa took advantage of a special offer that Spearys Department store was having on children's photos. She took her two kids down and got their picture taken. She sent copies home to her folks and to Jake's parents as well. Raisa couldn't stop looking at the photo. *Our kids are both growing up and just blooming out here in Michigan.*

Beth and Arnie Kessel in Michigan

Jake was working the late shift down at the garage and so after a light supper that evening Raisa opened the screen door and went out to sit on the front porch to pass the time and watch as Beth and Shirley jumped with their ropes and chanted numerous little catchy rhymes to keep time with.

"Teddy Bear, Teddy Bear, turn around. Teddy Bear, Teddy Bear, touch the ground. Teddy Bear, Teddy Bear, show your shoe. Teddy Bear, Teddy Bear that will do." Both girls collapsed onto the lawn in a fit of laughter.

Things went along pretty well for the next six months until that spring. It was near the end of the school year in 1928 when Beth woke before dawn one morning with a high fever. Not knowing the cause, Raisa kept her home from school. "I don't know what is wrong with you sweetheart, but measles are going around and to be on the safe side, we'll just keep you in bed." Beth didn't seem to mind because frankly, she didn't feel like doing anything, especially going to school. All that day, Raisa kept sponging Beth down, trying to keep the fever as low as she could.

Around eleven o'clock that night, Beth's fever broke and she was soon covered with bright red spots-- the measles. It was common knowledge that they were going around school and they spread from one child to the next like quicksilver. Raisa didn't take having the measles lightly. She knew that some kids actually died while others just were plain miserable and sick with a frightful high fever and red spots. Raisa was homebound for a whole month because after Beth was well, Arnie came down with the disease. Beth had missed a couple weeks of school but managed to make her work up and pass to the third grade at the end of the year.

Everyone was happy the winter was over and now, summer was here to stay. During the warmer summer months, Jake and Raisa often enjoyed packing a picnic lunch on Sunday afternoon and heading for the shores of Lake Huron to try to beat the heat and humidity.

~~~~~

After church on a particular summer Sunday, they spread the picnic blanket out and Jake flopped down. He took his shoes and socks off and to Raisa's surprise, wiggled his toes in the warm sand then lit his pipe while he watched her take the picnic from the box. She was in a chatty, happy mood as she said, "You know Jake, this reminds me so of when I was a little girl and we lived here in Michigan, farther up the shore in Port Sanilac. We used to go to the shore all the time too. I loved running up and down the cool sandy beach at the water's edge, just like our kids are doing.

I've been sort of worried about something that happened the other day. I didn't think it was anything to be telling you about, but I found Beth crying. When I asked her what was wrong, she said, *I miss my Oma and Opa. I think I liked it better living in Lovell, even though there are lots of things to do here and I have a special best friend. I miss my cousins too."* Raisa looked off into the distance. "I hate to consider it or even say it Jake, but I am beginning to think the time away from our families and friends is beginning to take a toll on us and our two kids. We grew up without grandparents, so we didn't realize what an impact they can have. Our folks were so close to both our kids and I know they miss that love and support." She finished putting out the picnic, then said, "How about you, do you miss your folks?"

Jake pulled his newsboy cap lower to block the glare from the lake. "I have to admit, I agree with you in that I think sometimes we forget how important our folks are to the kids. As a little kid, I thought about my grandparents a lot and wished I could have seen them again. Sure, I miss my folks once in a while. We could start saving some money and make our plans to go back to Wyoming after the spring thaw next year."

Tears clouded Raisa's eyes as she looked over at her husband, "Yeah, Jake, we've had some good times and some interesting adventures out here, but we need to be closer to family."

Later, after they all ate their fill, Raisa started packing up their picnic. "I'll start watching what I buy and maybe start saving that way."

Jake nodded in agreement. "I am going to take on a second job—they need a bar tender at the pool hall four nights a week and that extra money could help."

Raisa put her hand on Jakes' shoulder. "Jake, I been thinking. When Arnie starts first grade this fall, I would like to look for a part-time job—you know, to help out a little."

The first day of September, Raisa walked her two children to school and then took the trolley downtown. She applied for a job at Speary's Department Store, the largest department store in Port Huron. When that job petered out, she worked at the Beanery Café. She even tried her luck as a door-to-door saleswoman for Watkins Products. Raisa never made a lot of money but, like she said, "What I make helps out and besides it makes me feel like I'm doing something positive."

Even with both Jake and Raisa working, they were just barely making enough to keep their heads above water. They couldn't seem to get ahead by much and save enough money to go back to Wyoming too. It was going to cost a lot more than what was presently in the savings can. It seemed like it was one thing or another that kept knocking them back down and they knew they were one step ahead of the bill collector.

Late on a Saturday night, Jake and Raisa sat at the kitchen table, going over the stack of bills they owed. Jake ran his fingers through his thinning hair, "Son-of-a-gun Raisa, where the hell does all our money go? I know things don't cost that much and we should be able to make ends meet with us both working, but we just don't make any headway. I'm gettin' darned frustrated with the whole damn thing---I work and work and work and we still don't have nothing!"

Raisa sat with her hands in her lap; her eyes were on the floor as Jake let off steam. She watched as he walked to the cupboard and reached to the third shelf and grabbed the bottle of whiskey. Raisa winced, she never liked to see Jake take a drink when he was already upset. Jake opened the bottle and poured himself a stiff one! "You want a little nip, Raisa?"

Raisa looked up at him, cocking her head to one side and said softly, "No thanks, Jake—not tonight. My stomach hasn't been feeling too good lately."

Jake tossed down the half-filled glass of whiskey and refilled his glass before he headed back to the table. He sat heavily, head down as he stared into the amber liquid. "Ya know what Raisa? Before we married I was consumed with fear that I couldn't live up to what my Dad expected of me. Then we got married and for a while I didn't have that fear, you helped me to feel like my own man, that I didn't have to live up to my old man's expectations. But for the longest time now, I've had a gut full of fear. I'm so tired of being afraid, so tired of always feeling fear--- fear that I won't be able to provide for you and the kids. Truth is, I'm just plain tired of fearing how long this job or that job is going to last, fear fills every waking thought that our kids are going to get some terrible illness, fear that something bad will happen to one of us. It's like I live on fear, like that's what keeps me going."

Raisa reached across the table and laid her hand on his. "Jake, no matter what, we have each other and we have our kids. We've always got our faith, Jake. God always finds a way where we think there is no way—we know that. I have to admit that I am scared too, what with the way the economy and the world is going and all. Maybe we need to pray harder, pray that God helps us find a way to get the money so we can get back to Wyoming where things will be safer and better for us. Something tells me that things here are going to get a lot worse before they get any better. "

    Raisa stood and went around to where Jake sat. She pulled him to his feet and they held each other. Finally she kissed him and stroked his ruddy cheek. "I'm going to bed, you can come with me or you can sit out here and drown that fear of yours in the rest of that whiskey bottle. But Jake, if that's what you do---don't wake me up when you come to bed!"

CHAPTER FOUR

IT was that next Tuesday when Raisa woke in the dark of the night. *A sound, I thought I heard something, someone.* She sat up in bed, fully awake now as she quietly swung her feet to the floor and sat on the edge of the bed. *Jake's working late again. Maybe that's why I'm so jumpy; I was probably imagining it all. Who would blame me with the assorted creeps moving in and out of the neighborhood?* Then, she heard the sound again--coming from down the hallway. It was Beth, crying and calling out for her. Raisa jumped to her feet, threw on her worn blue chenille robe and turning on the hall light, she hurried to the bedroom where her two children slept.

Raisa knelt down beside Beth's narrow bed as her daughter moaned. She put her hand on her daughter's forehead. *The child is burning up with fever and it looks like I'm on my own. Why is Jake never around when I need him? Beth has never had a fever this high before, even with the measles.* Raisa was scared and she knew she had to make a decision, quickly. She went into the front room and dialed the family doctor. She hated bothering him in the middle of the night, but it's what he told her to do if needed.

An hour later, after checking Beth over, Doctor Hadley motioned for Raisa to come out into the living room so he could talk to her. "I'm quite sure, Mrs. Kessel, that Beth has scarlet fever. I hate to see her get another childhood disease so soon after that bad case of the measles. Her immune system is weak because of that and she doesn't have much resistance. We have to watch her carefully because she doesn't have what it's going to take to fight this off easily.

"You may or may not have heard that we are going through a pretty bad epidemic of scarlet fever. I don't have to tell you that it is very contagious. She has all of the classic symptoms, sore throat, high fever, and a strawberry-red tongue with a white patch at the back." The doctor washed his hands and then closed his bag. "Try to keep that fever as low as you can. I suspect she will break out into a rash in the next day or two. Watch for it under her arms, behind the ears, and on her chest. I'm sorry but I'll have to quarantine you—you and both kids. You can't leave the house. Where is your husband?"

Raisa told the doctor that Jake was working. "He can't come back into the house until Beth's fever has broken. I'm sorry about the quarantine Mrs. Kessel, but we have to try our best to hold this disease down. It's pretty serious. I want you to watch your daughter closely for complications. We may have to put her in the hospital if she gets any worse." The doctor slipped into his coat and picked up his doctor's bag. "We've been using a new antitoxin medicine that has been successful in treating the bad cases. If Beth complains of ear ache or aching in her joints, I want you to call me at once. Here is a list of instructions—and like I said, try to keep that fever down as much as you can with cool cloths and sponge baths. I expect she's not going to like the cool baths. I'll stop by in a day or two if I don't hear from you."

When Jake came home from work that first night, he was stopped by a large white quarantine sign nailed to the front door. He knocked on the door and Raisa opened it a crack. Her eyes were large with fear. Tears streamed down her face as she explained what was happening and how she had to take care of their daughter without him. "Just go back to work Jake, we are going to need the money if she has to go to the hospital. Maybe you can stay over at the Carters' house while we are quarantined." Raisa spent that night and the next day bathing Beth's face with cool water. Arnie, who was usually in perpetual motion, seemed to realize he needed to be quiet and entertained himself playing on the floor of the bedroom where he could see his mother and sister.

For three days and nights, Raisa did her best to nurse her daughter. She made herself a pallet beside Beth's bed, catching a cat nap when she could. Raisa watched in alarm as Beth's frail chest moved up and down. Finally, the fever broke before sunrise on the fourth day and as predicted, the rash began to appear with a vengeance. At first, it looked like severe red-streaked sunburn with tiny, raised itchy bumps. Later in the morning, when the light in the room was better, Raisa pressed her fingers across Beth's arm.

The rash temporarily turned whitish just as the doctor said it would. On the fifth day, there wasn't much change. Raisa kept hoping that by now, Beth would be showing signs of healing. Instead, she seemed to be getting worse. She cried and whimpered constantly--mostly that her ear hurt. At her wits' end and exhausted, Raisa called the doctor again. After listening to Raisa describe Beth's symptoms, he arranged for Beth to be transported to the local hospital.

Later that morning, Raisa was trying to catch up on her housework when the phone rang. It was the doctor. "Beth not only has scarlet fever but a 'mastoid' ear infection; she's in a quarantine ward with other victims of the disease. The other doctors and I think she is a good candidate for a new treatment for scarlet fever, an intravenous anti-toxin." Raisa couldn't leave the house because of the quarantine so she called Jake at work. He hurried to the hospital to be with his daughter and to sign the permission papers for them to begin the new treatment. As weak as Beth was, they had to hold her down when the nurse put the needle into her tiny arm. By the tenth day the symptoms began to subside, and Beth's skin began to peel.

The following week, with the quarantine lifted, both Jake and Raisa visited the hospital. Jake parked the car while Raisa waited in the lobby. They had moved Beth from the quarantine ward to a children's ward. After they checked in at the desk, they walked quickly down the sterile white hallway to where Beth was still being treated. When Beth saw her parents walking toward her bed, she put her face into her hands and began to cry.

Raisa wrapped her arms around her daughter's frail shoulders until the sobs subsided. "Honey, for heaven's sake what is the matter, why are you crying?"

Beth wiped the tears from her red eyes and push up the sleeves of her hospital gown. "Look, look at my ugly skin. It's all peeling off and I look like a monster." The tears began again in earnest.

Jake stepped forward and took command of the situation, "Beth, now stop it. This peeling is a final part of the disease. It's like when you get a bad sunburn—the burned skin comes off after a few days. It's no big deal—your skin will look like new in a few days—in fact, it may even be prettier!"

That explanation seemed to satisfy Beth as she blew her nose and wiped her puffy red eyes. Jake and Raisa talked a little longer to their daughter then bid her goodbye, promising to return in two days to take her home. "Oh Daddy, I can't wait to sleep in my own bed and even to fight with my little brother. He hasn't been getting into my things or sleeping in my bed when I was gone, has he?"

Beth stayed in the hospital for a couple more days and then was released to return home. The doctor instructed, "I want her to take it easy, keep her home from school until Monday and make sure she takes in plenty of fluids."

Things were back to normal, at least for three days. On Thursday, October 24th, Jake unexpectedly walked through the front door of their rented house on Jay Street. Raisa was kneading a batch of whole wheat bread on the kitchen table. She looked up with surprise as Jake walked into the room. Raisa paused with her kneading as a sliver of fear ran down her back. Neither of them spoke. Jake tossed his jacket across the back of a sofa and then slowly crossed the room to the table where Raisa was working. He pulled out a mismatched wooden chair and dropped down onto it as he laid both hands on the table, palms down. He looked up at her, confusion filling his face.

After taking one look at Jake's clenched jaw and pale face, Raisa knew something was wrong. She covered the bread with a towel and laid the mixing spoon down on the countertop. She walked slowly around the table to where he sat; she reached out and put her hand on his shoulder. Raisa felt how tense he was and yet he was shaking. "JAKE, what is wrong, what's happened? You are scaring me, talk to me. Why are you home in the middle of the day? I can tell something is very wrong—did you lose your job again?"

Jake stared at the oilcloth-covered table and finally, he looked up at her, "I'm not sure what it all means Raisa, but everyone is hysterical. The stock market crashed in New York

City. They say men are jumping off skyscrapers and committing suicide. Banks are closing their doors all over and people are running in the streets in a panic." Jake rubbed his hands back through his thinning hair. "Honest to God, Raisa, people were lined up outside that big bank, the one down on the corner, trying to get in and get their money out. The doors were locked and shades down. There's a sign in the bank window that says, 'Bank Closed', 'Bank Insolvent'. Them people were pretty damn hot and then the cops came and tried to break the crowd up, bashing in heads and all."

Jake got up and walked to the window, looking out into the alley; he put his hands against the upper sash and leaned into the window, staring out through the permanent haze of grime. "I don't understand all that stock market stuff and just how that all works—I'm just an ignorant country boy. But I do know this—whatever is wrong, it's bad, real bad. I don't know how this 'crash' and all will affect the rest of us yet, but I'm sure it will, in one way or another. That's probably why everyone is so upset."

Jake turned and walked back across the room. He wrapped his arms around Raisa. "Sorry to scare you honey, but I don't know what's gonna happen, Raisa. I don't have a good feelin' in my belly. Them peoples was shoutin' that it was their money in them banks and the banks won't open their doors and let 'em have their own money. I heard they have lost it all in bad investments. Can you believe that—taking people's money and using it to make money for themselves? All I can say is I'm glad we didn't open a bank account, that we kept the money we made out of them banks. Those bankers are a bunch of damn thieves if you ask me, and theys been caught red-handed at it!"

Jake slumped back down in the wooden chair. He put his elbows on the kitchen table, wrapping his hands around the cup of coffee Raisa had fixed for him. "I didn't tell you 'cause I didn't want to worry you, but we've noticed a big change at the appliance store too. We are taking back darn near half of what we sell, 'cause the peoples can't make the payments. It's damn sad to see the look on their faces when they have to admit they can't afford the washing machine or ice box and we have to take it out of their house and back to the store. It makes me feel like shit to take their appliance or whatever it is. Seeing them stand there, stunned as I move it out of the house because they can't pay for it. Frankly Raisa, I don't know how long my part-time job at the store is going to last if the store ain't making any money."

After several months of cinching their belts in tighter and watching every penny, they realized the contents of their saving can wasn't getting' any bigger. One evening, Jake asked, "How much money is in the 'Wyoming' can, Raisa? Did you cash my last check, like I told you on Monday?"

Raisa went to her hiding place to retrieve their stash of money; he opened it up and counted the money. "This isn't going to get us to Wyoming." As he put the money back in the can, he continued, "The appliance store closed today Raisa, so I'm out of that job now as well. I think things are going to get real bad around here---real fast, and we may have to get out before we planned. I'll see if I can find extra work, maybe even at night and in the meantime, save every penny. Start using up the food we have and don't buy anything we can't use today. I'm glad I bought that used Model A sedan when I did. Now, all we need is a small trailer to haul a few things in, and then we can get the hell out of here and back to Wyoming. I'll ask around down at the garage and see if I can come up with a trailer. I've got a hunch the big city isn't where we are going to want to be, because this thing, whatever it is, is going to get ugly before we ever see 'happy days' again."

For the next few months, Jake stood waiting in long job lines that snaked up and down the streets of Port Huron. He stood on the corners and in other lines with other anxious men, waiting for a job, any job. Every day that Jake stood with the others, he noticed tempers growing shorter as desperation set in. Fear was his constant companion as he pounded the pavement, asking everyone he knew if they had a job for him, anything. He still had his job at the garage but they had cut his hours by half. He felt lucky when he was hired on as a baker for a couple of months then found a seasonal job with Muriel Best Co. down by the docks, loading iron onto barges. One thing Raisa knew about her husband, he was a hard worker and he wasn't particular or above doing anything as long as it paid. He wasn't afraid to try something new to support his family and put a few dollars in the 'Wyoming' can. The writing was on the wall, fear had put it there—they had to get out of Michigan.

Photo courtesy of Dorothea Lange/National Achieves - 1935 Job Line

When the time came that Jake and Raisa couldn't pay their rent on the house on Jay Street, they picked up and moved their meager belongings in the middle of the night to a small, second-story apartment on La Pere Avenue, close to downtown.

Raisa hated the apartment from day one when they climbed the creaking stairway to the second floor. Out of breath and overwhelmed, she thought, *OHHHH, this place stinks to high heaven! The accumulation of years of neglect and--hordes of dirty, unwashed people and the odor of cabbage and garlic is everywhere. Combine those smells with mold, vomit, and urine and this is what we get. It's so disgusting I don't even want to breathe. I can only imagine what the inside of the other apartments look like. I won't sleep nights worrying about things crawling on us because nothing I do will stop them, they are living in the walls and between the floors.*

Jake stuck the key in the lock and turned the doorknob. He gave a gentle push to the door and not getting a response, he pushed harder. Finally, with an audible groan, the door swung open to reveal their apartment. Raisa stepped through the door, took one look and instinctively gasped as her hand flew to cover her mouth.

She never uttered a word, but her eyes spoke volumes. Her jaw was clenched and her lips pressed together tightly. They stepped inside as Jake closed the door. Turning in a complete circle of inspection, Raisa was rooted to the spot with disbelief and revulsion. What was left of the numerous layers of faded tan paint was blistered and bubbled on the weathered window sills. The flowered wallpaper was peeling and covered with a multitude of unidentifiable stains. She looked at the wall where a picture had been—the paper had been pretty at one time, sort of faded lavender with a gray squiggly design. She looked down at the splintered, stained wood floors. They must have been beautiful too, when they were first laid. Now, they were covered with deep gouges and were gray with layers of greasy sticky grime.

Raisa swallowed twice before she spoke. "Oh Jake, t-t-this is---this is not what I expected. How am I going to get this place clean enough so we can live in it?" Not waiting for Jake to answer, she went to the window facing out to the street below. She stuck out her index finger and attempted to gently rub through the grime on the window pane. "This is absolutely disgusting. These windows look as if they haven't been washed in years—inside or out." She narrowed her eyes tightly, attempting to hold back the tears that threatened to spill down her cheeks. *I can't cry in front of Jake, I know he's doing the best he can.*

Jake walked over to a window and wrapped his arms around Raisa. His voice faltered as he said, "It's all we can afford right now, Raisa. It won't be for long, not for long, honey. I need you to help me. Together we'll get through this."

In the days that followed, Raisa attacked the apartment with a vengeance. Using white vinegar and baking soda, she scrubbed and scoured until her hands cracked and bled. She tried to kill the cockroaches, but they simply migrated through the thin walls from the other apartments. It was a losing battle and she knew it. *Why do I feel like this is all I've ever done and all I will ever do, clean up other people's disgusting slop? Scrape the years of grime from tacky floors so we can walk across them without our shoes sticking to them? Year after year I helped my mother clean one filthy shack after another and now, I'm married and still cleaning up after the pigs that lived here before we moved in. I am getting a gut full of it---I am so tired and so discouraged.*

As the days without a steady paycheck increased into weeks and weeks into months, it became painfully obvious that times weren't getting any better. All they had to keep the apartment warm was a small, wood-burning cook stove in the kitchen. It helped some that their place was sandwiched between the first and third floor and these tenement apartment buildings were so close together you could touch the other building by just leaning out the window.

But when winter hit that year, it hit with a vengeance. The glacial north winds blew off Lake Huron seeping through the cracked and warping windows frames, resulting in a light layer of frost on the north wall. Raisa tried hanging blankets over the drafty windows but there weren't that many blankets to spare for window coverings.

During the weekends or after school, Raisa and the kids made a game of walking the frigid streets of Port Huron seeking scraps of wood or anything that would burn. They walked until they all complained of stinging ears, cold hands, and running noses. Beth and Arnie weren't shy about asking store keepers and neighbors for old newspapers and magazines. They dragged the bags of paper home then spent evenings rolling them tightly, tying them and soaking them in the tin bath tub overnight. The next morning, Raisa laid the "paper logs" on the southwest window sill to dry; it took days for them to dry out and often they froze instead. If and when they were dry, they were used in place of the scarce and costly wood to burn in the ancient iron stove. While they worked together, Beth and Arnie pleaded with their mother to tell the story about the 'Old Country' and how they burned bricks of dried manure in the winter to stay warm. Raisa laughed as she recalled helping her mother stack the dried bricks of manure and straw, the '*mistholtz'*. "You two have heard that story a hundred times, no sense in me telling it again!"

During the frigid winter mornings Raisa would wake her children for school and let them lay in their warm beds for a few moments. She gathered their clothing, laying them near the stove to warm. When their breakfast was ready, she called from the kitchen, "You two better be gettin' up now; I've got the stove nice and warm in here. Your hot oatmeal will be ready in a minute." She could always tell when they finally abandoned the warmth of their beds and their little feet hit the icy-cold floor. Raisa smiled as she heard their squeals of protest as they made a bee-line for the warmth of the stove. There was always a race to see who could dress the fastest. Raisa noticed that Beth usually let Arnie win, just to keep him moving.

The bitter cold weather finally broke around the first of March and the ugly drifts of crusted brown snow began to melt into muddy streams. One Saturday morning, midway through the month, Raisa walked into the cramped kitchen and was startled to see Beth crawling across the counter top, opening every cupboard. "Beth, what in the world, are you doing?"

The skinny ten-year-old looked up with tears running over her freckled face. "I'm hung-ry Mama, I'm so hung-ry and I can't even find a cracker. Where is our food?" She doubled over and held her stomach. "I'm so hungry my stomach hurts."

Raisa went to the hidden money can and pulled out a dime. "I'm sorry money is so short. We are only buying a little food at a time. Daddy and I are trying to save everything we can to go back to Wyoming." Raisa hugged Beth and handed her the dime. "Here sweetheart, walk down to the corner market and buy a loaf of bread. When you get back I'll fix you and Arnie a butter and sugar sandwich. Bundle up now." As Beth scampered toward the front door, she heard her mother add, "And Beth, you should get a penny back after you pay for the bread—go ahead and buy yourself a penny candy."

Raisa watched from the window as her daughter skipped down the sidewalk toward the corner grocery store. She crossed her arms over her stomach and thought, *I never noticed those dark circles under Beth's eyes before, and she has gotten so thin. What are we doing to our kids? We can barely feed them.*

The Michigan sky was bird-egg blue with only a cloud here and there as Beth walked back home from the grocery store, the brown bag of bread clutched in her fist. She paused at the front door of the apartment building. She wiped the tears from her eyes and then began to climb the stairs to their second-floor apartment.

Raisa heard the front door open and close. Beth stood just inside the door, her head was down and she held tightly to the twisted-neck of a brown paper bag. "Beth—Beth, what is wrong? What's happened? Look at me."

Beth dropped the sack to the bare wood floor; she covered her face with both chapped hands as sobs wracked her thin little body. "I'm sorry, Mama. I'm so sorry, b-b-but I was just so hungry and, annnd I---I was just going to eat only one piece of bread. It s-s-smelled s-s-so good and then I ate two pieces---and n-n-now—now, the bread is half gone!"

Tears filled her own eyes as Raisa wrapped her arms around her daughter and hugged the frail child to her chest. "Oh, my baby girl, it's okay. I'm sorry you are so hungry and we don't have food in the house." Raisa pushed Beth back so she could see her face. "Sweetheart, can you keep a secret? We are going to leave soon—back to live in Wyoming. We are going back to see your grandparents in Lovell and we will have food to eat there. Just don't tell any of our friends or neighbors—can you do that?"

Beth asked, "Mama, would it be all right if me and Arnie collected old paper, rags, metal, and stuff like that to sell to the junk man at the end of the block? I know lots of kids do that and we could earn a few cents or maybe even more to put into the can. Can we try it, Mama, huh?"

In their spare time and weather permitting, Beth and Arnie scoured the garbage cans behind the neighborhood stores and factories. They learned pretty fast where the good stuff was, which houses threw out the most, and where the mean ladies lived who chased them off with a broom and ugly words. In those moments, Beth would grab her little brother's hand and they would run off down the sidewalk. "I'll bet she rides that broom just like a witch—I bet you a penny she does!"

One Saturday morning, Beth and Arnie got an early start on their search for rags to sell. While walking home from school yesterday, Beth had noticed a dress shop tossing a bunch of old dresses into the garbage bins in the alley. Beth grabbed Arnie by the sleeve and pulled him into the alley. Arnie put his heels down. "I don't wanna go down there in that dark alley, sister; it looks too scary."

Beth persisted because she was sure they could fill their bags and be on their way home before anything happened, though she was aware that there were gangs of kids, mean kids who were also on the watch for just this kind of opportunity. Beth inched her way along the wall, down the dark alley toward the huge garbage bins. Once she thought she heard something and roughly pushed Arnie into a dark doorway. Arnie began to sniffle when Beth gave him an elbow and hissed, "Shut up Arnie, do you want them to find us?"

When the coast was clear, Beth and Arnie crept out of their hiding place and made a beeline to the bin. Beth looked around just to be sure they were alone. She opened the heavy steel door and peered inside. "Shut the front door! Will you fill your peepers with that?" Beth pulled Arnie closer and instructed, "Here Arnie, you hold the bag and I'll put the clothes inside; hurry up, will ya? We gotta get the stuff and get out of here." Beth's hands were shaking as she hurried to get their share of the discarded clothing. Arnie had tears and snot running down his face. "Quit your sniffling, you big baby, and wipe your snotty nose for Pete's sake!"

When their two bags were stuffed full of the old dresses, Beth pulled on the drawstrings and she and Arnie started dragging the bags toward the light at the end of the alleyway. Arnie saw them first and stopped dead in his tracks. He pointed back behind them, back down the dark alley. "Sister, look—there's them Rafter Street boys and they are gonna beat us up, I knowed it for sure!"

Arnie dropped his bag and started running toward the illuminated end of the alley. Beth grabbed both bags and threw them behind a parked car that looked like it might have grown roots it had been there so long. Suddenly, out of nowhere, one of the boys grabbed Beth tightly from behind as another chased Arnie around a mismatched set of garbage cans. Beth felt his arms encircle her and squeeze. That's when her adrenaline fueled the anger that came from deep within. Shoving her elbow hard into his soft, unsuspecting belly, Beth let out a blood curdling scream and stamped on the instep of his foot. Gasping for his breath through the searing pain in his foot, the hoodlum made another move toward Beth, just as she connected a solid punch to his left eye. No waiting for his buddy and wanting no more of that little hellcat, the bully limped quickly but steadily out of the darkened alley. It had not been a good idea to turn down that alley and go after those kids, not good at all!

Beth could hear Arnie yelling; she saw the other boy on top of her brother and he was pounding on him. She ran as fast as she could and flying through the air, hit the boy with her body, knocking him off her brother. They both rolled onto the street; Beth had a softer landing as she was still on top of the tormenter. She grabbed his long greasy hair with both hands and began slamming his face into the dirt. "Have ya had enough yet you sorry piece of shit? If not, I've got more where this came from. Nobody hurts my brother, ya hear, nobody! And if you was a wondering, your friend ran home to his mama! So it's just you and me, got that?"

Beth let the boy up after he promised he was done trying to take what wasn't his. Beth stood beside Arnie as they watched the boy stumble toward the street. Arnie looked up with admiration at his sister. "Boy, sister, you are real tough. You sure made those boys cry, ha ha—wait till I tell Mama!"

Beth turned and, grabbing Arnie by the scruff of his collar, said, "You tell Mama any of what happened and you will get what's left over, got that? Now, let's go back and get our bags and get out of here."

On the way home, Beth looked down at her little brother. "Arnie, I feel bad that I hurt those boys, but a girl's gotta do what a girl's gotta do. We need the money that we are gonna get for these rags and I wasn't about to let those bullies take them or hurt us. I don't know what it is, but something comes over me when I see you in trouble or even when someone tries to hurt me. I just get mean right back." They walked a little further when Beth stopped and pulled Arnie around to look him in the eyes. "And, don't you ever---ever, ever tell Mama or Daddy that I said 'shit'; if you do, I will tell a story on you and you know I got a lot of things on you!"

As they climbed the stairs to their dingy apartment, Beth reminded her brother, "Now you remember, Arnie—when Mama asked where we got these rags, I'll do the talking. And, if she asks how we got so dirty, we'll just say we wanted to look like the other rag pickers—to blend in. I can't wait to take these bags to the Exchange; we are going to make a ton of money this week."

Raisa was at the dry sink when her two children came walking through the apartment door like nothing in the world was wrong. But Raisa knew something was up; she could tell they were trying to hide something and so she just gave them a little rope and waited. "So, did you two have a good day with your collections? How did you get so dirty? Arnie, you look like you rolled in the street; is that a bruise on your face?"

Beth pushed her brother to the back as she volunteered certain information. "Well, Mama, it's like this---we were real lucky today and found a garbage bin with a bunch of old dresses in it from this shop. We stuffed our bags full and then these boys came along and wanted to take them. I had a little trouble convincing them to leave us be."

Arnie escaped his sister's grasp and, eyes wide, gave his version. "Mama, you should have seen Beth---this here kid knocked me down and he was wrestling me on the ground and Beth flew out of nowhere and smashed him to the ground—hard! That kid was sure bawling when he got up and ran away. Sister saved my life today, she's a hero!"

Raisa looked from Beth to Arnie and burst out laughing. "Well, I don't know what really happened, but that is a pretty good story!" She turned back to the corner kitchen and continued preparing their dinner, smiling at the wild stories her children came up with.

Beth grabbed Arnie by the collar and pulled him into their room. "You little moron, you just had to start blabbing didn't you? Lucky you---Mama thinks it was just another one of your goofy stories."

When Beth and Arnie collected enough metal things like bottle tops, cans and the like, they took it to their dad who melted it down. At an exchange shop where they took their loot, they got a nickel for melted metal and two pennies for ten pounds of paper. Old rags brought in three cents, maybe four if they were clean. Everybody was looking for anything with copper in it because copper brought ten to fifteen cents depending on how big the piece was.

Arnie and Beth saved their money in a special canning jar their mother kept up high in the kitchen cupboard. Every Sunday they would ask to see their jar, and sat cross-legged on the wood floor, counting their pennies. Beth liked the money part of their collecting but hated going to people's houses and asking for their old stuff. They always had to watch out for the bigger kids, the mean kids who pushed them and called them 'rag pickers and beggars'. Beth usually got the last word in when those kids picked on them; when she was a safe distance, she'd yell back, "I'd rather be a rag picker than look like you!" Good thing she and her brother were both fast runners.

After she and Arnie screwed the lid back on the canning jar and it was safely hidden away, Beth wandered over to the grimy front window and looked out at the bleak street scene below. There weren't nicely dressed ladies strolling along the sidewalks showing off their beautiful dresses and hats. There weren't fancy motor cars driving up and down on their street. The houses all needed paint, but nobody had extra money for paint. Tears trickled down the hollows in her cheeks as she realized where and how she lived. Beth angrily wiped the tears away with the back of her hand, turned and walked into the kitchen where her mother was making soup out of odds and ends. "Mama, are we poor?"

Shocked, Raisa put down the wooden spoon and took her little girl by the hand, leading her over to the chair. She lifted Beth onto her lap and held her close. "Sweetheart, there are all kinds of people in the world, good, bad, rich, poor, ugly, and pretty. You will find out someday that everyone goes through some bad times in their lives but that doesn't mean they are ugly or bad or any less than those who have money and a nice house. I know it's hard, sweetheart, not to have the things you want, but it only makes them better when you finally get them. We just have to get through this bad time. Someday things will be easier. We have each other and God is watching over us—he will help us through. Just think about leaving here soon and going back to Wyoming where your grandparents and cousins live. Think about the good times we'll have."

A couple of weeks later, Raisa noticed that Arnie had been waking frequently during the night. He cried and complained that his arms and legs hurt. At first, she thought it was just growing pains, but as it continued, Raisa had a nagging feeling it was something more. Arnie didn't seem to hurt in his joints or muscles, but in his bones. After discussing it with Jake, they decided they didn't have a choice. They had to take Arnie in to the doctor, paying him with cash money from the 'Wyoming' can.

Dr. Riley did a thorough examination of the little boy, taking x-rays and testing his urine. He asked, "How long has it been since Arnie's front teeth fell out? Have you noticed if he is growing or staying about the same?" Raisa didn't understand the questions or what they had to do with her son's condition. After the examination, she dressed her squirming boy and they went into the doctor's office. Raisa sat across from him, holding Arnie as he snuggled in her lap. She silently prayed, *Please Dear Lord, let it be something little, please don't let Arnie be real sick. I ask this through Jesus' sake, Amen.*

"Mrs. Kessel, if it's what I think it is, it has to do with diet and a child's body trying to grow normally, without proper nutrients. I think Arnie has a case of what we call rickets."

Raisa felt perspiration bead up on her upper lip as a shiver of fear crawled up her back. She tried to remain calm, but growing panic and a hundred questions crowded her mind. "How serious is this, this rickets disease, doctor? Is there some medicine for it? Does he have to go in the hospital? What should I do?"

Dr. Riley smiled warmly as he wrote out several prescriptions. "Don't worry Mrs. Kessel, there are simple things we can do to take care of this disease. First of all, this lad has to have a better diet. He needs foods that are rich in calcium and phosphate, like calcium-fortified milk, fish, liver, and green leafy vegetables. I want you to buy some whole wheat, cook it until tender, then drizzle honey over it and feed this to him, warm or cold. Arnie needs to be out in the sunshine more. I know most folks are pretty short on money to spend on extra food and I also realize the cold, cloudy winter days haven't helped him. It wouldn't hurt to feed this diet to both of your kids while you are at it."

Over the next few months, Raisa tried her best to buy better food for Arnie, but their funds and food sources were so limited. It seemed like the stores didn't carrying the fresh produce they once did and if they did, they were asking an arm and a leg for them. Raisa bought what she could and tried to stretch the food out. Lately, she just picked at her food, finally dividing it between her two children. Raisa pushed back her chair and rose from the table, carrying her plate to the sink she ran the dish water.

Jake had noticed what Raisa had done and he didn't like it. "Raisa, what's wrong with you, you've been eating like a bird, are you sick?"

Raisa turned blushing and stammered, "N-n-no Jake, that's not it. I just haven't had much of an appetite lately. It's nothin' to worry yourself about; it's just one of those things." Raisa turned quickly before Jake could see her eyes well up with tears; she put the dirty supper dishes in the hot water and began to scrub them. Suddenly, a wave of dizziness washed over her and she grasped the edge of the sink. "Jake, Jake, can you put the kids to bed tonight while I wash these dishes? It would sure help me."

Jake pushed back from the kitchen table. "You heard your mother, come on, get your pajamas on and wash your faces!" He finished the newspaper article he'd been reading and then walked across the front room towards the kid's small bedroom. They were both jumping into bed as he walked through the door. "Okay, who wants to say their prayers first?" After hearing their prayers, Jake kissed them both good night. As Jake turned to go, he felt a little hand pulling on his shirt sleeve. Beth cocked her blond head to the side and begged, "Daddy, before you go, will you tell me and Arnie a story about when you was little, please, Daddy, please?"

Jake stopped in his tracks and sat down on the edge of the bed. "Well, now, let me see—what story haven't I told you yet? Hum...When I was little, like you, it was Uncle Christian and my job to gather the chicken eggs, every night. If we didn't gather them, then the skunks or the coyotes might get them. Our dad would be mighty mad and probably take his belt to us. So, this one night, it was really dark out and we had forgotten about gathering the eggs. We had to walk down to the chicken house in pitch blackness and it was awful scary. We had with us this here kerosene lantern to light our path and to see where the eggs were in the nests.

"We pulled open the old creaking door. Neither one of us wanted to go inside cause it was double pitch black inside. That there lantern we had gave us a little light, but we knew it didn't light up those dark corners where the monsters hide. Then we realized we had another problem---we had to get the chickens off their nests in order to gather the eggs. We learned firsthand that if you don't get a chicken off the nest and you reach your hand in there to get the eggs, that chicken will peck you. So Chris and me, we got this here board and hit the side of the wall where the nests were. Those chickens was so scared, they flew off their nests. Boy, we was glad about that. We hurried and grabbed the eggs, putting them carefully into the basket so they wouldn't crack. Chris started crying when he dropped one of the eggs and it broke all over the place. I just kicked a bunch of straw on it like it never happened, no need to fuss over that egg. I picked up the basket of eggs and Chris carried the lantern as we headed for the doorway. We couldn't wait to get out of that spooky chicken coop.

"It was about as dark and scary outside as it had been inside the chicken coop. We could see the lights of the house not far away, but it seemed far away to us 'cause we were just little. I remember hooking my arm through my brother's and we started walking, real fast like towards the house. Suddenly, out from behind a bush a big coyote jumped right in front of us. Its eyes glowed red and the fur on the back of its' neck was all bristling and stiff; there was drool coming from its mouth as it moved closer and closer to us. It smiled at us and I swear it said, "I want to eat those eggs AND you little boys!" With that, Jake leapt onto the bed and grabbed the tummies of his two children. He tickled them until they could hardly breathe.

Just then, Raisa walked into the bedroom and sternly admonished her husband. "The bedtime stories are supposed to calm them down, not scare the heck out of them. You've got them so worked up now, Jake—that it'll take another hour for them to go to sleep."

But Jake, undeterred, leaped from the bed and began to chase Raisa around the bedroom. She laughed in spite of herself as he caught her and laid a big kiss right on her lips. The two kids shrieked and laughed, "Do it again, Daddy, do it again!"

Trembling, Raisa pushed Jake aside and kissed each of her children good night. "Now, you two settle down or no more stories from Daddy. He's got to go to work and you two have school in the morning. Goodnight, sweet dreams, I love you."

Jake was still chuckling when he walked into their bedroom, where Raisa was turning down their bedcovers. "Jake, really—do you think you should tell the kids those kinds of stories before bed? They'll both probably have nightmares now."

"By the way Jake, I've been thinking about something and we need to talk. We are plumb out of options and choices; we have to get out of here and back to Wyoming and the farm, where we can get better food for Arnie. It's just so expensive here and we can't afford what he really needs. What do you think about that? Do you think we can go pretty soon?" Before Jake could answer, Raisa added, "I was also thinking that we might write and ask your folks to help us out, temporarily of course. I know that's probably the last thing you want to do, but truth is we are down that far."

Without speaking, Jake turned his back to her to pull down the window shade and began to dress for work. He needed some time to think about an answer. Before Jake turned around to face her, Raisa took the opportunity to slip her flannel night-gown over her head. She opened the dresser drawer and pulled out her hair brush as she began the nightly ritual of brushing her hair with long, slow strokes. Looking in the cracked and filmy mirror, she said, "I know you wanted to wait until spring when the snow has melted off the dirt roads, but our boy is sick and I am running out of hope." Tears welled up in her eyes. "If it isn't one thing, it's another lately. Just, when I think nothing else bad will happen, it does! I just don't know how to manage anymore; I'm at my wit's end with all this---all this hopelessness!" Raisa was horrified as the tears rolled down her cheeks.

Jake crossed the room and wrapped his arms around Raisa as she melted into him and cried on his shoulder. He tried to console her, "Please honey, come on, it's not all that bad, nothing is that bad. No more tears now. We have to try and hold on until the spring thaw is over and the roads back west are half way decent. I don't want to get stuck out on those dirt and gravel roads across South Dakota and Montana during a late snow storm or a two-day rain. The problem isn't back here in the east. These main roads are mostly paved. It's when we cross the Mississippi and start heading north and west that we are gonna run into those blasted dirt and gravel roads again. Just another month or two, Raisa, then I think we should be pretty good to go. We gotta hang on a little longer honey, just a little longer and hope we can keep the kids well and nobody needs a doctor."

Raisa looked at him with red, puffy eyes, her arms crossed over her stomach. "But Jake we owe everybody in town, the grocer, the doctor, and the landlady. What with this Depression it's getting harder. I'm trying to put any spare change I can find in the money can, to travel back to Wyoming on. As a result, there's not much left to pay the bills; I've been holding everybody off with the promise to pay more next month. I don't expect people are going to be able to let us charge what we need much longer. Everybody has bills to pay and no money to pay them with." Raisa looked down at the worn bedspread as despair and more tears clouded her eyes. *I can't tell him now, I just can't tell him.*

Jake hung his head, feeling responsible for not finding steady work or providing for his family. "I know--I know we have a bunch of damn bills, Raisa, but we gotta save our cash. I will write letters to the people we owe money to and promise to pay what we owe when we get back on our feet, back in Wyoming. I don't want to leave with them holdin' the bag, but we can't be paying those bills now. We have to save our money for the trip, do you understand me? Just try and keep those two kids well; it's the doctor bills that are killing us."

Jake leaned over and kissed her goodnight. "I'll try to be home before two a.m., I don't want you worrying about me. Get some sleep—I love you." With that, he put on his worn coat and newsboy hat then slipped out the door, closing it softly behind him.

Raisa went to the front room window and looked out. She saw Jake get into the car and drive away. Tears began to fall from her eyes again. "I've got to try harder to control my emotions but I've been so weepy lately? I've got to stop this crying over every little thing. I know getting all upset isn't good for me. I just don't know how I am going to tell Jake—how did we let this happen?" Raisa turned away from the window as the first pain hit her and she dropped to her knees.

CHAPTER FIVE

"A man's mind plans his way, but the Lord directs his steps and makes them sure." Proverbs 16:9 KJV

Jake worked at the Ford garage, when there was business. Raisa noticed he had also been keeping some late hours working another job or so he said. He never told her much about the night job or exactly what it was he was doing. He let her think he was working nights at the bakery. It was just best that way, her not knowing what he really did. Sometimes he picked up jobs down at the docks loading iron. For a while, he even sacked bags in a grocery store. It was a kid's job and he got paid less than fifty cents an hour; Jake wasn't proud and he told himself that every little bit helped. He knew lots of guys that had jobs just like this: sweeping up after hours, washing windows, taking care of old people. It didn't matter as long as it paid.

Jake had a way of stepping past a question with a few carefully selected and brief answers. But Raisa wasn't buying it— she knew he wasn't telling her everything, but there were things she wasn't telling him either, things she was still trying to deal with.

One dark night, several weeks later, Raisa was restless and couldn't get to sleep—just lying in their bed, waiting for Jake to come home. She threw back the thin blankets and grabbing her worn chenille bathrobe, she made her way to the kitchen where she put on the teakettle. After pouring the hot water into a cup of tea leaves, she walked barefoot into the front room and stood by the window, sipping her tea and looking out into the street as the darkness was swallowed by the first bits of daylight. She closed her eyes as the warmth of the tea radiated into her body, relaxing her. Only a handful of houses were lit. Everything was dark and silent. Raisa shivered, *I wonder just exactly where Jake is tonight and every night that he says he is working late. It is becoming a habit and I don't see any of this money he says he is making, working extra jobs, late at night. What is he really doing? Is he seeing another woman? No decent man stays out this late without getting into trouble!*

Try as she may, Raisa couldn't get the images of Jake with another woman out of her head. She was practically convinced that this is what was keeping him out until the wee hours of the morning, night after night.

It was close to the end of June when Raisa's curiosity and active imagination got the better of her. Suspicious thoughts kept nagging at her until she couldn't bear it any longer. "Jake, I need to ask you a question and I want a straight answer. Don't sugarcoat it or dance around the truth like you usually do. Just spit it out—I need to know." Raisa took a deep breath and then blurted out, "Are you in cahoots with another woman on these nights when you say you are working late? Sometimes you don't come in until three in the morning. So, tell me the plain truth. I deserve to know if I have some competition. Because if I do-- if there is someone else, then the kids and I need to make plans to go back to Wyoming alone. I won't stay around here a minute longer, and that's that!"

Startled, Jake felt the start of a smile touch the corners of his mouth, then decided this probably wasn't the time to smile. Trying to buy some time to come up with the right answer, he looked at the floor and ran his fingers back through his thinning hair, then taking a deep breath, he replied, "Okay Raisa, here it is. I can't tell you exactly what I'm doing, but it certainly isn't seeing another woman or anything along that line. I love you and only you. You are more than enough woman for me."

He recognized the no-nonsense look Raisa was giving him and switched gears. Jake paced the floor like he was thinking of the right thing to say, and then turned. "Before you ask me, NO, I haven't been going to the pool hall lately. I don't have the spare money to drop around a pool hall anymore. You knowed I never was much for gambling, just a few hands of cards, or shooting darts. I never have and never will get into the heavy bets. I know you've been worried about the night job. But Raisa honey, honestly, this job that I work at nights now--it's a delivery job.

Frankly, I don't know what it is I'm delivering. I don't know from nothing what's in them boxes, but I'm getting paid well for doing the job. I don't ask any questions—that's the way them guys want it. I get my delivery instructions and I get the job done. A few more deliveries and maybe we'll have enough to get on the road back to Wyoming. Just be patient honey, and don't ask me nothing more 'bout it, ya hear?"

Jake was stunned by the look on Raisa's face, as if he'd slapped her. He crossed the room to where she stood, arms folded across her stomach. "Is there something else besides my night job that's bothering you Raisa? Is something wrong—are you…keeping something from, me? You've been so weepy and emotional the last couple of months."

Raisa spun to face him; she couldn't keep her secret any longer. *Who does he think he is, coming down on me like that? I've tried to help, tried to do what I could, tried to save money—but how do you save money when there is so little coming in?* Raisa stood there, her face pale and tense. She couldn't hold it in any longer, she just couldn't.

"Yes Jake, yes there's something I haven't told you, something I been keeping to myself to try and protect you until the time was right. But it seemed like the time was never right, it's been one bad thing after another for longer than I can remember. There's just one doctor bill after the other. God knows we have had more problems than we can handle and I just didn't have the heart to dump one more thing on you." Raisa looked out the window, not seeing anything in particular. "I w-w-was, I—was pregnant!"

Jake reached out and took her by the shoulders. "What do you mean you, you *'was'* pregnant. What happened? So, you aren't pregnant now? Raisa what did you do? How did you lose the baby? I never thought you could do something like that?"

Raisa looked him in the eye and without thinking, she slapped him. She slapped him hard. Jake reached up to his face and tried to rub the slap away. Shock filled his eyes. "What in the hell is wrong with you, Raisa? Why did ya slap me like that?"

Raisa began to fight the tears that welled up in her eyes, "Because, Jake—because you assume I did something to cause the miscarriage, you actually think I would do something like that? You need to be horsewhipped, not slapped." She pulled out a wooden chair and sat heavily at the kitchen table. "I was maybe three or four months along and things weren't right from the start. It wasn't the same as the other two. I spotted all along and had sharp pains. I didn't have any good food to eat. I think that my body couldn't nourish the baby and so my body or God or whoever, stopped it all. I didn't tell you because there was no need---I took care of it and I'm fine now. I didn't even go to the doctor 'cause everything came out like it was supposed to." She put her hands over her face and cried. "He was so tiny, so scrawny—just a little bit of a thing."

Stunned, Jake stammered, "You was able to tell it was a boy? Oh, Raisa, Raisa---why didn't you tell me, honey? Why did you keep something like that to yourself?" Jake walked around the table to where Raisa sat and pulled her to her feet. I'm your husband and we're married—you are supposed to tell me things like that. I know there wasn't anything I coulda done so it didn't happen, but I coulda helped you get over it. We could of gotten over it together. Don't you ever do that again; I can take it. I can take it for the two of us! They stood together in each other's arms and cried for their infant son, for the bad times they were going through, for Wyoming.

Two weeks later, as Jake was getting ready to leave for the night, he turned to Raisa. "I've been thinking about this and I think it's time. I want you to start packing the trailer tonight. It's parked out in the shanty garage with a tarp over it. Don't tell anyone what you're doing and try not to bring any attention. If someone asks, just tell them we're going camping. Be careful, honey." She didn't know why, but Raisa felt a shiver of fear slide down her spine as Jake pulled his light brown tweed jacket on and turned the collar up. "By the way, how much do you have in the savings can?"

Raisa stammered, "Uh---I think there's about forty dollars, give or take a few cents. I had to use some to pay the doctor when

Arnie got sick again last week, but I been savin' everything I can and still feed the kids what they need."

Jake gave her a peck on the cheek as he turned for the door. "That's good honey, because I think the writing is on the wall, if you know what I mean. Start getting things ready cause we might be leaving sooner than later!"

Raisa trembled with raw fear at the implication of Jake's words. She knew him, she knew he was fearless, determined, and desperate---a dangerous combination for Jake Kessel. After he walked down the front steps, she thought about what he had said. *I know that man and he still isn't telling me everything. Oh please, dear Lord Jesus, keep Jake safe in whatever he is doing so we can get out of here. We gotta get back to Wyoming and our folks. Please hear my prayer.*

After she put the two kids to bed, Raisa packed up the remaining bags and quietly hauled them down the stairs and out to the shed. She lifted the tarp and stuffed them inside the trailer, then retied it nice and tight. She made another trip up to their apartment and grabbed two sleeping bags and pillows for the back seat. On her way down the stairs, she bumped into Mrs. MacTully.

"And, what are ye doing with those bed rolls and pillows this time of night. I seen ya taking some things out to your trailer there. Planning on skipping out on the rent, are ye?"

Raisa felt herself flush with anger as she narrowed her eyes and stared down the nosey neighbor. In the sweetest voice she could muster, she replied, "My my, isn't that sweet of you to care? For what it's worth, Jake and I are planning a camping trip with the kids come the weekend, you know, to get them out in the fresh air a little more. Do you have any plans for the weekend, other than peeking out your door to watch who goes and comes?"

Raisa had to stifle a giggle as Mrs. MacTully gasped in indignation and without another word, turned tail and marched up the stairs to her own apartment. Still carrying the bags and pillows, Raisa continued on down the flight of stairs and out the back door to the trailer. She laid the bags and pillows under the tarp. Once Jake came back with the car and was ready to leave, she planned on making the kids a nice bed in the back seat.

Raisa hadn't been back in the apartment more than five minutes when she heard a knock at the door. *Oh for heaven's sake, if that's Mrs. MacTully again, I don't know what I'm going to do! I've about had a belly full of her nosing around in our business.* Raisa opened the door a few inches and to her shock, came face to face with a middle-aged man in a long overcoat, a black fedora pulled low over his eyes. Fear, alarm, and surprise crawled up Raisa's back. She tried to maintain calm as she planted her foot on the other side of the door to stop it from opening any further. "Yes, what do you want and who are you?"

The man looked up and down the dimly lit hallway before he spoke in a muffled voice, "Mrs. Kessel? I work with your husband or rather he works for us when we need him. May I come in for just a minute? I know you don't know me and all, but I assure you, you don't need to be scared of me, I'm not here to hurt ya. I know Jake isn't here, but I have some information for you. Uhh, the name is, Frankie, Frankie Menellie."

Raisa noticed that Mrs. MacTully's door was ajar. Against her better judgment, Raisa opened the door and let the man into their apartment. He stayed right by the door and didn't try to come any further into the room, mainly because Raisa stood with her arms crossed blocking his way.

He looked around the dingy apartment and said, "I won't keep you long Mrs. Kessel, it's just that Jake has some extra dough coming and he's somewhere on the other side of town, delivering tonight and I thought he'd like to have this here cash." Menellie arrogantly cocked his head to the side as he handed Raisa the envelope and sneered, "If ya don't mind my saying so, you might want to skim a couple bills off the top and get yourself something nice to wear. A woman who looks like you should have nice things. Jake didn't tell us boys his wife was such a looker."

Raisa felt her face redden with embarrassment as Menellie reached up and ran his hand slowly down her arm. Anger and fear flushed her face as she quickly took the envelope and backed out of his reach. Suddenly, Beth was standing beside her.

Beth cocked her freckled face to the side and with an impertinent expression she stared a hole right through Mr.

Menellie. Taking a step closer to the man and giving him the 'eagle eye', Beth asked, "Who are 'you' and what are you doing in our apartment when my Daddy isn't here?"

A sneer curled the corners of Menellie's mouth as he replied, "I work with your dad little girl; shouldn't you be in bed? It's past your bed time, isn't it? Actually, your Mother and I are having a conversation here that doesn't concern you."

Beth took another step closer and lifted her chin in defiance as her ice blue eyes narrowed, "Well now, I don't know about that, but I do know that right below us lives a good friend of mine, who told me that any time we have any trouble up here, to just yell and stomp and he'll be right up. Yes sirree, Officer McDermot doesn't take kindly to people bothering us, no he doesn't. Got that mister?"

Menellie's eyes widened and he looked at Raisa, "You got yourself a pretty brassy little tart there Ms. Kessel. High time you taught her a lesson or two!" The smile disappeared from Raisa's face as she quickly reached around to open the door to the hall. Briskly, she responded, "Thank you for stopping over, Mr. Menellie, I am sure Jake will appreciate you bringing this by. Good night."

Raisa pulled Beth back into the apartment and swiftly locked the door. She turned with the intent of glaring at her daughter, but instead of a glare, a smile crossed her face and the two hung on each other as laughter bubbled out. Firmly grasping her daughter's shoulders, Raisa pushed her back and looked into her face, "Where, did you learn to talk like that? I have a feeling you've been watching too many movies. But, I have to admit, it did the trick and I don't think Mr. Menellie will be wantin' to come back here anytime soon!"

After Raisa got Beth back into bed, she retreated to her own bedroom but not before checking to make sure the door was securely locked. Climbing into her cold bed, she propped the pillows up, laid the envelope on the bed and reached for her Bible. She stared off into the dim light of the bedroom. *Who was that slime ball really? What is Jake doing with those kinds of men; and, they know where we live? They know where we live; that is not a good thing.* Raisa opened the envelope with shaking hands and peered inside. It was filled with twenty dollar bills. She didn't count them, but it had to be a couple hundred dollars. *Jake's right, we need to get out of here----tonight. This is it!* She took the envelope and stuffed it into the Wyoming can, then put the can into her valise. *I'll tell Jake about the extra money when he gets home.* Still shaken, she opened her Bible to her favorite book of Psalms and began to read.

It was just past midnight when Jake drove his trusty Model A down a deserted city street to the address of a rundown warehouse, down on the wharf at the south edge of Lake Huron. *Sure am glad I got rid of that Model T, it was a real hay-burner. This little baby is no jalopy, no sir-ree!* He killed the lights a half block from his destination and coasted down the street, parking on the opposite side. Jake sat inside for a few minutes, perfectly still just watching the dark side streets—watching for trouble or anything out of the ordinary.

When the coast looked clear, Jake pulled his cap brim down low to partially conceal his face. His ice blue eyes flashed in the dim night light and his face took on a menacing scowl. Tugging his tweed coat collar up, he shoved his hands deep in his pants pockets and then quickly crossed the street. A dog barked at a disheveled old drunk, who staggered down the other side of the street and then disappeared into an alley.

Jake paused on the street curb, leaned against a street lamp and lit a cigarette, taking the opportunity to again survey the street. Trying to ignore the baseball-sized knot in his belly, he moved quickly to the second doorway on the left and slipped into a shadowy archway. Jake knocked twice on the weathered wood door. Then, as instructed, knocked once more and turned the door handle. He pushed the door open just a hair and slipped inside, closing the door behind him. It was pitch black in the room and it smelled of rats, mold, and fear. A voice growled from the darkness, "Took your sweet time gettin' here. Where's your car?"

Jake's gut tightened as he took on a street persona, trying to appear as tough as the hoodlum he was dealing with. He cleared his throat and in a matter-of-fact voice said, "I parked it down the street. I didn't think pullin' right up in front of the address was such a good idea. Ya know, in case there's 'eyes in the night', *Capishe*? Just tell me where I make the pickup and I'll blow this joint. There's just something in the air tonight, can't put a finger on it, but it's got me on edge."

The voice replied, "Okay, Okay, quit beatin' your gums. Now listen real good, 'cause I'm only gonna tell you once. Go back out to the street; take a left at the third corner, pretty sure it's Ash Street. Then turn down the sixth alley on the left. There's an old garage at the end of the alley. You'll see an open bay, just drive in and the boys will shut it behind you. Once you get the merchandise, ya blow, got it? You head back to Decatur Street and swing around to the other side of the wharf on Market Street. Go two blocks down to warehouse number nine, pull up to the double doors and don't honk for hell sake. Just gun the motor once and if it's clear, the doors will open."

A hairy, well-manicured hand came out of the gloom and shoved a piece of paper at him. "Here's where you make the delivery; they will have an envelope ready for ya, as usual. This ain't a load of coffin varnish you're packin' around in that jalopy." The goon grabbed Jake by the lapels to get his point across. "Now, get this straight--you be on the look for plain-clothes dicks and don't be stoppin' along the way at some juice joint to get your courage up. We have reason to believe it's getting pretty hot out there. The coppers have eyes all over the place. Just keep doin like you're doin--be on the watch and if something happens and you get yourself pinched, well, ya know what we do to a snitch! If it comes to that you'll be lucky to end up a gimp, 'cause our boys take their business real serious, if ya know what I mean?"

Jake left the same way he came in. He waited in the shadow of the doorway, took a final drag on his cigarette and flipped the butt into the street. He walked quickly to his car; his hand shook as he pulled on the door handle and climbed inside. Jake stepped down on the clutch and shifted into neutral, letting the car roll slowly down the steep street before turning the key in the ignition. Sweat beaded up on his forehead as he clamped his teeth together in dogged determination. *Ya'd think that by now, I'd be used to this routine and these slime balls, but I ain't. I don't like breakin the law, but we all gotta do what we gotta do to make a buck and put a little food in our kid's bellies.*

A half hour later, the job was half done. He did what the goon had told him to do to and made the pickup. So far, everything was going like clock-work. Jake was about two miles from the drop when he noticed headlights in his rearview mirror. He slowed and purposely turned off the route, onto a side street— the car followed at a discreet distance.

Jake took another left turn at the next corner and sped up. His eyes shifted to look in the rearview mirror again. The car was still behind him, keeping up, but staying back just far enough so Jake couldn't see who it was. The hair on the back of Jake's neck stood up and a shiver skittered down his back. *That's all I need now, is for some plain-clothes cop or one of the other gang's goons to try and hijack me. I gotta keep cool and play the part---a regular guy out for a drive. Maybe I'll grab a cup of coffee and see what happens.*

Spotting an all-night café, Jake pulled up in front and cut the motor as the other car drove slowly past. He couldn't see who was in the car or how many there were. Nervously, Jake pulled the brown newsboy cap lower so it sat just above his eyes. Flipping his coat collar up again, Jake got out of the car, locked it and walked into the café.

He picked a side counter seat with his back to the wall, where he could watch the street and his car. If there were cops or thugs in that maroon car and they decided to come for him and his load, he planned on slipping out the back door. *You just gotta play it smart and don't get caught with the goods.* After drinking his coffee, he waited a bit longer. *No cars or customers--that's a good sign.*

Finally, Jake paid for the Joe and walked quickly out to where he parked his car. He climbed inside and sat in the dark for a moment, exhaling deeply. Then he turned the key in the ignition and backed into the street, shifting into first gear. The Model A lurched forward and Jake took the corner on two wheels, headed in the direction of his drop. It was all clear.

Caution ruled as Jake's eyes continued to glance in his rearview mirror and up the dark side streets as he headed to the drop. So far he hadn't seen anything else out of the ordinary. Finding the address easy enough, Jake drove around the block once, then twice--looking for anything suspicious. Then, he made his move. He pulled up in front of the dark building, gunned the Model A's motor and the double garage doors swung open like magic. He drove through and the doors slammed shut behind the car. Jake made a sharp U-turn inside the cavernous warehouse, so his car was pointed back at the doors he had just driven through. The interior of the warehouse was dimly lit as four men emerged from nowhere and descended onto his car. As instructed, they began to unload his trunk and the hiding place under the back seat.

Jake stood off to the side and watched as the men did their job. He had never looked inside the boxes he delivered, but he had a hell of a nose for booze and he knew what he was doing was as illegal as it could get. If he got caught, he could get twenty to thirty years up the river. That is, if he lived through it. Transporting, dealing, even drinking illegal hooch had been against federal law for the past ten years and he knew it. However, like a lot of other desperate men, he needed the money. *You bet-cha; desperate times make for desperate men and desperate deeds and I'm sitting right here in the middle of it all. Forgive me Lord and help me to do what I have to do. Just let me get this last run over with, without any hitches. You know we've got to get the he___--sorry Lord; we gotta get out of this town. I gotta get my family back home to Wyoming.*

Jake felt the beads of sweat slide down his back. His hands were damp and shaking as the goons finished unloading. Some swell took his time walking out of a back room; he was wearing an expensive suit and casually puffing on a fat Cuban cigar. He took his pudgy hand out of his inner coat pocket and shoved a fat envelope into Jake's hand. "Here ya go, Mac. There's some extra *moolah* in there for you. That was a special load you had tonight, real good stuff and worth a shit-load of dough. You've done a good job so far—been minding your potatoes. Smart, that's real smart."

He turned to leave, then walked over to one of the boxes, ripped the top off and pulled out a bottle of prime Canadian whisky. He looked over his shoulder at Jake and a slow grin spread across his face as he walked back. "Here's a bottle of the best hooch you've ever tasted. This is what it is before we cut it with some cheaper stuff and sell it at an, elevated price. Anyway, call it a little symbol of our gratitude. Oh yeah---just a word to the wise, keep your eyes and ears open when you leave here, ya might even take a different route back to where ever you came from. A little bird told us that the place is crawling with coppers!"

Jake thanked the guy and moved quickly toward his car. He pulled open the front door and stuffed the bottle under the seat. Turning back to face the boss man, Jake said, "Uhhh, do ya mind if I use the can before I take off, I won't take long. I'm anxious as hell to get out of here."

The big cheese took another drag on his fat cigar, sneered and pointed in the direction of the restroom at the far rear corner of the building. Jake trotted off around the corner and hurried into the filthy hole they called a restroom. He bolted the door and turned to take care of business.

He had just finished when a rapid pop-pop, followed by rat-tat-tat echoed through the rat-infested warehouse. *What the hell is that? For a minute, I thought it sounded like gun fire.* Then he heard it again. *Someone out there is shooting and it sounds like one of em' has a Tommy gun! Holy crap--it sounds like an all-out war! This is a hell of a place to be-- and me without a gun. What in the Sam Hill am I going to do now? I gotta get myself out of here, and fast!*

Jake listened at the door, trying to clear his head and think rationally about what he should do next. Turning out the restroom light, he opened the door just a crack; the explosions of gunfire and men swearing was even louder. Out in the hallway, with his back to the wall, he inched his way down the dimly lit hall and around to the side where boxes and crates were stacked to the ceiling. *I figure I can squeeze between those boxes and make my way back to the car without them seeing me. It sounds like they are all on the other side of the warehouse. Whoever it is must have come in the* back door. *There's no way to know if it's the cops or another gang. All I know is I want out of here and the faster the better.*

Smoke and the smell of gunfire filled the air, making it hard to breath. Jake crouched behind a stack of boxes and peered out. He could see his car, about thirty feet away with the front door hanging open, just like he had left it.

Crouching low, Jake cautiously inched forward using the stacks of cartons and barrels as cover. He took his time moving forward when suddenly a bullet whizzed by his head and slammed into one of the boxes. That was all Jake needed to hasten his departure. Seeing his chance, he made a run for his car. Once inside, he slouched down in the seat and gently closed the door until he heard it click. *Okay, here goes—nothing ventured, nothing gained—help me dear, God*!

Jake stuck the key in the ignition as he pressed down firmly on the clutch. *My best bet, if I'm gonna make it out of here alive, is to make a run for it. Just gotta keep my head down and aim the car for those flimsy double doors. Just hope to hell I hit the center of the opening!* Just before he turned the key in the ignition, he stuck his head up for a last look at the gun battle and the double doors that were closed, dead ahead.

Just as he had hoped, the sound of gunfire drowned out the sound of Jake's ignition as it turned over. Jake shivered, remembering seeing a couple of guys down on the floor—they weren't movin'. *Obviously no one has noticed me--they're too busy killing each other; this is my only chance to get out of here alive. Okay boys, here goes!*

In a matter of seconds, Jake shifted down hard into first gear—at the same time he stomped on the gas. He felt the Ford lurch forward as he gunned it and headed straight toward those closed double doors. The Model A shot through the flimsy doors like a bullet through a cardboard box. Split lumber and dust flew everywhere as the Model A hit the street and Jake cranked the wheel hard to the left, away from the warehouse. He was out and flying down the street as one of the goons ran out of the warehouse and managed to get a couple of shots off before Jake got out of range.

Jake didn't take the time to stop and have a look-see; he knew they were shooting at him 'cause he felt the thud of a couple of bullets as they hit the rear of the car. *Thank God, they didn't put a hole in one of my tires, the gas tank, or me!* Jake took a zig-zag route of escape as he roared around another corner and down the street, away from the warehouse and the gun battle.

When he was about a mile from the warehouse, Jake eased up higher in the seat and gripped the steering wheel. He made a hard left turn at the next street, stomped on the clutch again and shifted swiftly into second, then third gear. He went a couple of blocks before turning right onto a main thoroughfare. Relaxing a bit, Jake reduced his speed and drove as casually as possible down the street, heading west—west towards home. Taking a deep breath, he wiped the sweat from his forehead and ran his fingers through his thinning hair before he put his newsboy cap back on. *"Now that was a little too close for comfort. Thanks God, for helping me get out of that jam."*

As far as Jake was concerned, he couldn't get out of this place fast enough, but he knew he had to be smart and not bring any attention to himself. He smiled in the dim light of the gas-lit street. *I didn't even take the time to look inside the envelope to make sure they paid me the agreed amount. In the past, they've always paid me what they said they would, for the delivery. Frankly, at this particular moment, that is the least of my concerns--I need to spread out and do it as fast as possible.* Jake took one hand off the wheel and patted the bulky pocket of his light jacket where the cash envelope was stashed. Reassured, he was surprised to see that his hand was still shaking.

Jake's eyes moved to the right and left at every intersection, watching the side streets and his rear view mirror, all at the same time. *Judas Priest, what in the hell happened back there? Was it another gang that moved in on them guys or maybe it was the cops? Whatever, whoever it was, I'm thankful as hell to have made it out of there alive. That was about as close a call as I could have had! I don't know who got killed, but there were about four guys that I saw lying on that cement floor. I just have to hope that none of them come lookin for me now. I gotta put some distance between them and me!*

He shook his head to clear it. *Okay, I guess that was a sign—I'm not stupid, it's getting too damn hot out there for me to be involved in this any longer. That was my last delivery! I didn't realize that, until this minute—getting too damn dangerous—can't take any more chances. Now, all I have to do is make it back home, pick up my family and blow this town. I'm probably real lucky to get out of that operation with my skin intact, period. Whew! That was a relief to get rid of that load of hooch! If I do get stopped there's no evidence. That's all the flat foots would need---to get the goods on me.*

Jake's eyes opened wide as he slammed his right hand onto the rim of the steering wheel. Damn*! I do have a bottle of that booze in my car—the one that goon gave me. I would hate like hell to have to give that a sail out the window. I'll just have to hope-- hope it's worth it—hope I don't get stopped by some curious flatfoot. Just have to relax and drive the speed limit. I need to try and not bring any attention to myself—look and act like a regular 'joe'.*

About a mile or two from the drop, Jake tensed when he heard police sirens coming from every direction. Two squad cars passed him, going like a bat out of hell. As he crossed the next main intersection, he saw two more cop cars barreling toward him. Jake took a deep breath, signaled and turned the car down a side street, taking a round-a-bout way back to the apartment. He kept one eye on the road ahead and one on the road behind him. After a few minutes, he shook his head hard and drew in a deep breath, trying to relax a bit. Nobody was following him—the street was dark. The cops were all going in the direction of the wharf. They'd probably gotten a call about the gun battle at the warehouse. *Even if someone remembered my car, there are thousands of Model A's in the city. I just have to hope and pray no one took down my license plate number.* Jake said another prayer of thanksgiving to his maker as he headed home!

It was just after two in the morning when Jake killed the lights and turned the Model A into the alley behind the apartment house. He coasted up to the garage. Backing up to the trailer, he hopped out of the sedan and quietly hitched the two-wheel trailer to the car. The moon hung low as slivers of dark clouds slid across the dark night sky like skaters on a pond. Jake paused, looked around and not seeing another living soul he crossed the dark backyard, tripping on a tin can. He jumped a vertical foot as some mangy alley cat knocked over a trash can lid.

Finally, Jake turned the door knob to the building slowly and slipped inside. *I will never get used to the stench that hits me in the face every time I walk into this dump.* He took the apartment stairs two at a time. Reaching the second floor, he paused at his door and tried to clear his head. He quickly reached and wiped the sweat from his brow. His chest heaved and his shirt was damp with sweat as he unlocked the door and moved silently inside their apartment. Jake eased the door shut behind him and flipped the lock. The room was dark and hushed with the sound of sleep as he crossed the front room to their bedroom door.

When Raisa heard Jake's key turn in the lock to their apartment, her eyes flew open. Recognizing his gait, she breathed a sigh of relief. Lying motionless, she watched through half closed eyes as their bedroom door opened. Jake moved silently into the room and to the side of the bed where she slept. He sat heavily on the edge of the bed; the ancient bedsprings creaked and groaned under his weight.

Alarmed, Raisa sat up in bed. Even in the dimly-lit room, she knew instantly that something was very wrong. Her slim hand rose to touch Jake's shoulder, she felt him trembling. "Jake, what happened? Are you okay?" Raisa tossed the bedcovers back and sat up on the edge of the bed, next to her husband. The light from the street lamp was enough for her to see his face and her hand flew to cover her mouth.

Jake's face was ashen, sweat beaded across his forehead, and he was shaking like a leaf. In a low voice he spoke urgently, "Get the kids up—no need to dress them, just wrap blankets around them. We can make them some beds in the back seat. I'll take the suitcases out to the trailer. Do you have everything else ready to go, Raisa?"

Her hair still coiled in rags, Raisa grabbed his arm and pulled him back, "Jake, Jake, answer me, what is wrong? Why are we leaving in the middle of the night and since when do you wear your hat all low like that?"

Jake grabbed the newsboy cap off his head and stuffed it into his front pocket. He shook her hand off his sleeve as he turned and looked her full in the eye, "B-be-cause Raisa, we have to blow this town tonight, now! I'll tell you everything when we are on the way out of Port Huron. Now get a move on, we don't have a lot of time. Just pipe down—our dance ticket is full if ya know what I mean." Jake turned and said, "And, don't forget the Wyoming cash can—we are gonna need that!"

The hardest part was getting the kids out of their warm beds and down the stairs without making a sound. Raisa woke Beth up first and put her finger to her lips, signaling her to be quiet. Whispering into her daughter's ear, Raisa said, "Daddy just got off work and we are going to leave tonight for Wyoming, I'll explain later. You are going to have to walk to the car, we can't carry you. Daddy made you a nice bed in the back seat and you two kids can snuggle down and just sleep while we drive. Hush now and tippy-toe out the door, real quiet like!"

Scared and bewildered, Beth began to whimper. Jake stopped dead in his tracks and glared at her, "If you don't shut up, we are gonna leave you here. Now, lets' see how quiet you can be missy!"

Jake carried Arnie down without waking him and as soon as both kids were settled in, Jake turned the key in the ignition.

Within an hour, they were on the asphalt highway, heading out of Port Huron. The night was pitch-black except for a sliver of moon. Jake decided to head straight west to Flint, then angle southward to Lansing and on through Kalamazoo. The roads were always better around the big cities and he wanted to make some good time while he could. He pressed on the gas and watched the speedometer climb up to fifty. *I think that's all the faster I'm going push this rig, specially pullin' that trailer. That's all we need, to have a wreck or something—better safe than sorry.*

FLESH ON THE BONE

After three hours on the road, the sky to the east blushed with the imminent arrival of the new day. Jake took his foot off the gas and braked gently as he pulled off the dirt road into a secluded clump of trees. He killed the engine and rested his head against the steering wheel. Raisa reached over and touched his shoulder. Jake jumped and whirled to face her, "Damn it to hell Raisa, don't do that. I'm just trying to take a breath here, get some control of myself. I'm still shaking like a damn leaf."

Tears welled up in Raisa's eyes as she stammered, "But Jake, I just wanted to comfort you. You need to t-tell me what is going on. Why are you so jumpy and why did we have to leave Port Huron in the m-middle of the night like that? Are you in trouble—is someone after you?"

Jake reached under the driver's seat and pulled out the amber bottle of Canadian whisky. Raisa took one look at it and everything became all too clear. "Jake Kessel, where on earth did you get that? Is that what you've been doing Jake, running hooch? Isn't that illegal? For God's sake Jake, you could have been caught, then what was I supposed to do--me and the kids, alone there in Port Huron."

Jake twisted the cap from the bottle and took a good long swig of the premium whisky, gasping and shaking his head as the booze burned its way down to his stomach. "Ya, well, that is all history. We're out of it and on our way back home. I just had to take a few chances, honey; it's just how it was. There weren't any way else for me to make enough money in a short time to get us out of there. It's over and done with now." He shook his head again and smiled wickedly. "Whew—now that's some good hooch."

He turned to his wife and saw she was white as a sheet and visibly shaking. Jake reached across the seat and wrapped his right arm around her shoulders, "With everything we've gone through tonight, honey, I think you need to take a little nip too. Come on, take a swig, it'll help you settle down." Handing the bottle across the seat, he said, "Here, let's see what you can do with that!"

She looked across the front seat at him. "I don't know if I should do that Jake, with the kids in the back seat. But, they are asleep and maybe you are right, I need something to settle me down a bit. But---Jake, I've never had a drink of whisky, what's it like? Does it taste like it smells?"

Jake chuckled as he pushed the bottle closer to her, "Go on Raisa, I wouldn't tell you to do something that would hurt you. Just take one swallow. Go on now it will help you, honey."

Raisa reached for the bottle, put her full lips to its mouth, tipped it up and swallowed once. "Yeeeee-ow!" Immediately she coughed and patted her chest as her eyes filled with tears. "That's some mean brew, Jake Kessel! I can't believe people really like that stuff. One swallow is all I want. Here, take it back." She handed the bottle back to her husband, who was quietly laughing, in spite of himself.

Jake took another short pull, then screwed the cap back on and stashed the bottle under the seat. He turned to face Raisa. "I think we should drive on down the road for another hour or two. When I get tired, I'll pull off and we can grab a couple hours of shut-eye while the kids are still sleeping. You go ahead and sleep, honey—I'll be okay. I'm not tired at all—pretty keyed up if you know what I mean." He put his right hand on the shift stick but before he could clutch and shift, he felt Raisa's hand on his.

"Jake, before we start up again, I want you to tell me why we left Port Huron so fast. Are you in trouble?"

Jake paused and thought before he spoke. "No Raisa, I'm not in trouble—not that I know of. I got out of the job before that happened. At least I think I did. There's no reason to think the law has any goods on me. Listen, it's a long story, let's get going and I will tell you everything, once we get back on the road heading home." Pausing, he added, "I will tell you this: I kept thinking of that passage in the Bible—I think it's in Ecclesiastes 3:1, *'To everything there is a season, and a time for every matter or purpose under heaven'*. I couldn't get those words out of my mind and I think the Lord was trying to tell me it was time to leave Port Huron."

At that moment, Beth's face appeared out of the darkness from the depths of the backseat. "Why are we leaving at night? I don't know where we are? I don't like sleeping in the backseat either."

Raisa reached around and cupped her daughter's face in her hands. "We are going home, to Wyoming! I told you it would be a surprise when we left, didn't I? Sur-prise! Now, get back under your blanket and close your eyes, we can talk some more in the morning."

Beth's eyes filled with tears and she began to sob, "B-but, but I didn't get to tell Shirley goodbye. She's my best-est friend ever!"

Raisa reached around and stroked her daughter's short-cropped brown hair as she tucked her back into her makeshift bed. "Sweetheart, don't cry. What if, when we stop for breakfast, we can buy a post card and you can write her a little note? Maybe it'll be fun to write letters back and forth. That way you will always and forever be best friends--okay?"[3]

Jake turned the car back onto the main highway and decided with the kids asleep, now was as good a time as any to tell Raisa about his former job. "At first I didn't know what it was I was picking up and delivering, but it didn't take long to figure it out. Sure, it was dangerous and I knew that, but the money was too good, too easy, and we needed the cash." Jake reached into the inside pocket of his coat and handed the fat envelope over to Raisa.

Hesitantly, she opened it and gasped. "Jake, there's fifty dollars in here. Is this for just one job?" Before Jake could reply, she said, "With the forty I have in the cash can that makes---ninety dollars. Can we get to Wyoming on that?"

Jake smiled as he casually remarked, "That ain't all the money I made over the past couple months. I got the rest of it hidden in the car. Yeah, I wasn't taking the chance we could get to Wyoming on seventy or eighty bucks—I've been saving most of my payoff. We'll be fine Raisa, just fine. We might even have a little bit left over to get us started, once we're back home."

Raisa smiled as she looked across the front seat of the car. "Well, I have a little extra in the Wyoming can as well! A Mr.

---

[3]

Menellie stopped by tonight and left off an envelope for you. I just happened to look inside before I stashed it in the can. So, my dear, I would say we are gonna be fine, just fine."

Jake smiled as he looked across the seat at her. "Menellie huh, he's a smooth one, thinks he's a real ladies' man. I hope you slammed the door on him after he gave you the envelope. Anyway, you get some shut-eye, honey, I'll drive until I get tired, then I'll pull over." Instinctively, he knew what she was about to say. "No, Raisa, you can't drive this car and trailer. You are a pretty good driver now, but pulling a trailer on these highways takes a lot of strength. [4]Sooner or later we're gonna run out of this here paved surface and onto a rut-filled, dirt road, and that's another story. You just aren't strong enough to handle this rig, so close your eyes—we are on our way back home! Let's hope these asphalt roads last for a while longer."

Jake stared at the road ahead, lost in his own thoughts. He assumed Raisa was asleep, but then her voice came softly and sleepily out of the darkness. "Jake, how far is it to, Wyoming? How long do you think it'll take us?"

Keeping his eyes on the road, Jake replied, "I think it's a little over 1700 miles as the crow flies. Course we aren't going in a straight line so, it's probably closer to 1800 or even 1900 miles. If the weather cooperates and this tin lizzie holds together, I figure it'll take us around a week or more---probably more if we have to stop a lot." Jake looked across the front seat and added, "Oh, uh, Raisa, there is one more thing I should tell you before you see it and get all upset. There's probably a bullet hole or two in the rear fender!"

Raisa's mouth fell open and her eyes went wide. "W-what did you say? There's a bullet hole in the rear fender? Oh, Jake, oh my heavens, Jake! Someone was shooting at *you*? I don't think I want to hear any more about your job. At least they missed and you are okay."

She gazed out the car window for a mile or two, working to get her nerve up to ask the next question. "Jake, I was wondering.

---
[4]

Do you think we can swing up to Mitchell, South Dakota and stop to see my sister Lizzie, George and their two kids? It's been over five years since I have seen her. It's not too much out of our way is it? You don't have to answer me now, I was just wondering. You think on it." She reached across the seat and traced the back of his right hand with her index finger. "Oh, and Jake---I love you! I'm so happy to be going back home." She kissed the tip of her finger and reached through the darkness to touch his cheek.

After a few minutes, Jake looked over at Raisa, who was sleeping with her head propped against the window. He smiled and said a prayer. *Thanks dear Lord, for getting us out of Michigan in one piece. Watch over us and help us find our way back to Wyoming without too much trouble. I ask this in your name. Amen.*

Hours passed. Eventually, Jake slowed up as they came to a small town. *Not a soul on the streets—pretty deserted if you ask me. Guess this is one of those towns where they roll the streets up after nine. It's just as well; I don't mind it a bit.*

Up ahead he spotted two cars parked along the side of the road, under a street light. As he got closer he saw that they were cops. Instinctively, his hands tightened on the steering wheel. As he drove slowly past the officers, he glanced over at them. They turned at the same time, giving him the once over. Jake touched the brim of his cap with his right index finger, nodded and kept driving.

Finally reaching the edge of town, Jake sped up and exhaled loudly. *Whew, that was a bit unsettling. Glad they didn't decide to pull me over. We're just a family here—on our way back home.* But something caught Jake's eye as he looked into his rear view mirror again. The flashing lights of a squad car were approaching fast. Jake swallowed and decelerated. "Well, shit—I thought it was going to be okay, but I guess I 'thought' wrong." He slowed and pulled off onto the shoulder of the road as the squad car pulled up behind him.

Raisa sat up in the seat, rubbing her eyes, then noticed the flashing of the police lights. Suddenly, she was wide awake. "Oh dear Lord, Jake—what did you do? Why are those police walking up to our car?"

Jake rolled down the window and swallowed hard as he said, "Good evening officer, I am not sure what I did to warrant you stopping me. I know I was doing the speed limit. What is the problem?"

The cop leaned down and washed the beam of his flashlight over Raisa and the sleeping kids in the back seat. "Well, you are right about the speed limit—no problem there. There is a problem having only one tail light. I don't know if you realize it, but your right tail light is out. I am not going to ticket you but do want you to get it fixed first chance you have. I, aaah---also noticed a couple of bullet holes in your rear fender. Has someone been shooting at you recently?"

Jake responded with shocked seriousness, "What? Oh, no sir—shooting at me? Not that I knew of. I have to park down by the wharf in Port Huron for my job and it's a pretty rough neighborhood as you probably know. Maybe that's where it happened. I sure didn't realize one of them tail lights was out; they were both fine last time I checked. You can bet the farm I'll get that fixed, first service station we come to. We might look for a place to pull over for the night pretty soon, we are headed back to Wyoming where our family is. We got a pretty long trip ahead of us and I was trying to make some time while the kids slept."

The officer turned off his flashlight. "Drive safe, and you would be wise to get that tail light fixed as soon as possible. You don't want someone clipping the side of the car because they didn't see you. Have a safe trip and watch out for those Hoovervilles; best to find some other place to spend the night if you can. We get nothing but trouble from those places and the people who camp there—rotten apples, if you know what I mean!"

Jake sat in the car for a moment after the police drove down the road. "Wheweeee, that plum scared the poop out of me. I'll bet that one of those bullets hit the tail light as I was racing away from that garage down by the wharf. It was damn lucky that's all they hit. I can get the fixed easy enough, first chance we get."

CHAPTER SIX

"He who is outside the door already has the hard part of the journey behind him."
Dutch proverb

The sun was just making its daily debut behind them as Jake drove the Model A along the southern-most tip of Lake Michigan. He decided to take the road that paralleled the extensive railroad system on the outskirts of Gary, Indiana. Raisa began to stir, rubbing the sleep from her eyes as she looked out the window at the large number of freight trains waiting on the tracks--waiting to get the go-ahead out of Gary.

Giggling, she said, "Oh my word, I really slept hard. I hate to admit it but that swig of whisky really conked me out." She smiled as she reached across the front seat and gently rubbed the back of her hand along Jake's whiskery jawline. Speaking in a low whisper so as to not wake their two sleeping kids, she asked, "Have you stopped at all? Have you caught any sleep yourself, Jake? I see you haven't shaved, so I assume we haven't stopped."

"Good morning, honey. Glad you slept so good. I hate to be the one to tell you, but you even snored a little bit!" He winked. "It wasn't near as good as me though! Hey, I was thinking that we'll just drive until the kids wake and then stop at a gas station where we can clean up and find a place to catch some breakfast after that. How does that sound?"

Raisa was busy looking out the car's passenger window at the freight trains. "Yeah, sure Jake, that sounds good. Hey—hey, did you see that? Pull over Jake, please. That cop is cha-cha-chasing that little kid along the tracks; the one that just hopped out of a b-boxcar. SEE—see him over there? Oh Jake, Oh dear Lord—he's beating him with that c-club! Jake do something, he's just a little kid!"

Jake jammed on the brakes, pulling the car and trailer off the road. Jumping from the car, he trotted towards the tracks and called out to the cop. "Hey, excuse me, officer, can you help us? We are trying to find the road to Joliet. Do I take the first or second turn?"

The bull momentarily took his eyes off his target as he looked over at the man calling to him across the fence. That brief interruption was all the time the young boy needed to make his escape. Seeing the lad was free, Jake made a beeline back to the car. He jumped in behind the wheel and clutched hard as he jammed the gear shift into first. The car and trailer leapt forward back onto the road. Realizing he had lost his prey, the bull hit the side of the boxcar with his baton in disgust and irritation. His eyes narrowed to slits as he glared at the car and trailer high-tailing it down the road.

Raisa turned and looked back to see if they were being pursued. "Oh Jake, thank you—thank you for saving that boy." Her breath caught in her throat as the image of the cop hitting the little boy with a club came back to her. "Why in the world was that cop beating a little kid like that?"

Photo, courtesy of Dorothea Lange/National Achieves.
'Great Depression transportation.'

Jake shook his head. "Raisa, Raisa—you haven't heard of how the rail yards and boxcars are full of men and kids trying to get to someplace, anyplace that might have work? Lots of the boys are anywheres from nine to eighteen. Most of them kids have left home, either on their own or their folks kicked them out because they had too many mouths to feed? That cop you saw back there probably works for the railroad and he's called a bull. It's his job to keep the hobos and bums, if you will, off the trains. I hear tell some of them get pretty ruthless and in fact not only maim but sometimes even kill the ones they catch." Jake made a left at the next stop sign and headed west on another main highway out of town. They passed a nice residential area with big white houses and Jake caught Raisa looking wistfully at the big homes and he winced.

Raisa turned, her expression was grave. "Jake, what is this world coming to? Did you see how many men and boys were on some of those freight trains? I've never seen anything like that in my life; I didn't realize just how bad it is for everyone. We aren't the only folks who is having a tough time. They are just trying to find honest work, it's hard times everywheres. I'm sure they have no money to pay for the train ride—who does these days? It's the only way they can find to get from one place to another, right? Oh, Jake, I can't wait to get back to our simple, country way of living in Wyoming."

Jake kept his eyes on the pothole-filled road as he wheeled the Model A and loaded trailer west. After a few minutes, he said, "I been thinking Raisa, that maybe we'll cut right across Illinois, to Davenport, Iowa where we crossed the Mississippi River when we was on the train coming out to Michigan. Then we'll cut straight across Iowa to Des Moines. From there, we'll maybe head north to Sioux Falls, South Dakota right on the border. I want to stay as far south for as long as we can to avoid those northern states. We don't want to run into any spring snow storms if we can help it."

About that time, two little sleepy faces appeared over the front seat from where they'd spent the night, in the backseat of the car. Beth had bedded down on the seat and Raisa had made Arnie a cozy little bed on the floor. "Good morning Mama and Daddy.

This is soooo much fun, but I have to go potty. I'm telling you, I have to go bad. Can you stop the car Daddy?"

Jake smiled as he pulled off the road into a wooded area. He opened the back car door for his daughter. "There you go sweetheart, find yourself a nice big bush."

Beth flashed her father a look as she blushed, "Oh, Daddy, that's really not funny."

Jake stretched his arms, attempting to work the kinks out. He smiled when he heard the morning call of a meadow lark, reminding him of Wyoming. About that time, he felt Arnie grab his coat tail and declare that he had to 'take a walk'. Jake reached down and, taking his son's hand, they headed for the nearest large tree. After everyone had attended to what they had to do, the family climbed back into the car and Jake turned the car and trailer back toward the highway.

Beth looked out the window of the car at the passing farms for a few minutes before asking, "When are we going to eat Mama? I sure am hungry! Are there any cafes along this road, huh?"

Arnie started jumping up and down in the back seat. "Me too-- me too, I wanna eat some breakfast; my tummy is saying, grrrrrrowl—feed me."

A couple miles down the road, Jake pulled into a gas station and while the attendant was filling the Model A with gas and washing the windshield, they went into the restrooms and washed up. Jake even managed to shave, much to Raisa's delight. After they climbed back in the car, Beth leaned forward and rubbed her little hand over her dad's cheek. "Oh that feels soooo much better Daddy, and you even smell good! Did you use some of that 'Burma Shave' stuff that's advertised along the road? You know Daddy, I think the saying I like the best so far, is the--- *'Eeny-meeny, miny-mo. Save your skin, your time, your dough— buy Burma Shave'* I'm going to keep track of all of those 'Burma Shave' signs we see along the road. I'm going to write them down in my book."

It wasn't long before they came to a little family-run café called 'Gerts'. "That must be the place the station attendant told us about," said Jake. "Looks okay to me, how about the rest of you?" Without waiting for an answer, Jake pulled off the road and killed the engine. Nobody needed further invitation as they piled out of the car and into the little café, ready for a good home-cooked breakfast.

An hour later, full of black coffee and buttermilk pancakes, they were back on the road; it was slow going from paved to intermediate areas of unpaved muddy roads still thawing from the winter freeze. Jake's knuckles were bone-white from his death-grip on the wheel. It was a constant struggle to keep the car on the road and the trailer from fishtailing.

Later that morning, they passed some camps along the road. Beth tapped her mother on the shoulder as she looked out the window. "Mama, look over there—I see a whole bunch of people camping in tents and stuff. Maybe we can stop and talk to them."

Jake turned, his eyes flashed with warning. "No, Beth we can't. Those camps are not safe places for families like ours. We aren't going to stop or camp in those places."

Beth began to whine, "But Daddy, I saw three little kittys that I could play with—see they are over there, beside that blue truck."

Raisa looked over and saw the skittish black and tan cats. She knew in an instant what they were, by their matted, dirty fur and the way they were slinking around looking for food. "Oh, my word, Beth—what are you thinking? No, you couldn't play with those cats, they are feral cats. They would sooner scratch you and run away than allow you to pick them up and cuddle them. Those are wild cats, sweetie, and they live in these camps. Maybe when we get to Lovell, your grandma might have a cat with some kittens. I bet she would give you a tame little kitten, how would you like that?"

Beth continued to watch the kittens until they disappeared from sight. Pouting, she spoke under her breath, "I bet-cha I could make one of those kittys tame. Momma doesn't know everything."

Fascinated by the collection of people, Raisa continued to look out the car window as they passed by several camps then turned to her husband. "Jake, were those camps those places I've heard folks call 'Hoovervilles'?"[5]

Jake clenched his jaw and, keeping his eyes on the road, responded, "Yep, that's what they are and I've heard nothing but bad about them. Places are full of thieves and all sorts—not someplace we want to be."

That afternoon when the kids took naps, Jake pulled over on the outskirts of Joilet, Illinois. "I gotta take me a catnap Raisa. I am plumb tuckered out."

Raisa sat in the car, keeping watch over her sleeping husband and children. She briefly closed her eyes as she prayed, *"Dear Lord, thank you for helping us get out of Port Huron safely. Please watch over us as we travel back to our people in Wyoming. Thank you, Lord for this day and for everything."*

After only two hours, Jake woke from his catnap. He climbed out, turned and walked to the rear of the trailer. Taking a look at the loose canvas tarp, he grabbed a rope and pulled it tighter, then moved on to the next one. His mind wasn't especially on what he was doing; he kept thinking about what they had left behind in Port Huron—about *how* they had left. *I hate like hell to leave in the middle of the night and run out on our rent like that. Makes me feel like a bum—not the kinda man I am at all. It's like we really had no choice—I had to get Raisa and the kids out of there—it was time. When we get to Lovell, I'll scrape up the money and send it to our landlord. They're all just folks like us with bills to pay and trying to stay afloat.*

Jake walked around the entire car, kicking each tire as he went. *The tires look good so far, just hope we have good roads the rest of the way. I do know the better roads are around the big cities and we are headed 'back to the sticks', so—suppose we'll run into more and more dirt and gravel roads the farther north we get. Well, time to get this rig back on the road. That reminds me, I have to get that tail light fixed at the next gas station.*

Jake backed the car and trailer up to where he could swing back onto the highway. He glanced over at Raisa as she nodded off

---

[5]

FLESH ON THE BONE

to sleep; both kids continued to nap in the back seat. *That's a good thing. I need a little time to myself, to think a few things through. We've been through the wringer the last day or so. I'm glad we went out to Michigan but I'm just as glad to be heading back to Wyoming. I learned a lot of different things, working in Port Huron, but nothing really clicked for me. I mean, I haven't found anything I know I want to do for the rest of my life to make a living for my family and that worries me some. I don't have a real good feeling about the future. But with God and our families in our lives, I know we'll make it somehow.*

Jake had driven for about a half hour when he suddenly heard a loud bang and the car and trailer veered to the left. He struggled to hold the rig on the road as he slowly applied the brake and brought it to a stop. That bang and Jake's cussing woke Raisa and the kids; both kids were scared and screaming in the back seat, not understanding what had happened and why their father was so upset.

Jake jerked back on the emergency brake and slapped his open palm against the steering wheel. "Well, hell's bells--as luck would have it, we have blown a tire. Raisa, why don't you take the kids over to that clump of trees and let them do their business while I change this darn tire. Glad I brought a pump and patches— I won't need them with this tire. I'll just put the spare on for now and stop at the first gas station to get this thing fixed. We just gotta keep our fingers crossed when we're out in the sticks rollin' over these sharp rocks and gravel. For sure, that's when we'll have a tire or two blow out at the same time and I don't intend on getting caught with my pants down!"

Beth cocked her head and looked at her father in confusion and slight irritation. "Daddy, your pants aren't down. I have no idea what you are talking about. Are you just trying to be funny again? Sometimes you say the silliest things!"

~~~~~~

They ran into an early summer rainstorm about fifty miles down a packed-dirt road. By then it was getting dark as the rain pelted their car and the roads were as slippery and sticky as black molasses. Jake was having a heck of a time holding the car and trailer on the road. He finally decided to pull off into a side-road. "I'll just drive this rig in here a ways and get off the main road. I think this is as far as I want to try and travel tonight Raisa. Guess you and me can try to lean back and get some shut-eye while we can. We'll take off again in the morning. I sure hope the rain lets up by then." Jake turned around in the seat, "Okay, now knock it off, you two. Beth, you sleep up on the seat and Arnie, get down in your bed on the floor. I don't want to hear another peep out of either of you kids—got that? If I do, I am comin' back there and you know what that means!" The two kids heard the warning tone of their father's voice and decided not to press their luck.

Raisa reached around to make sure the doors were all locked and the kids were covered up before she leaned her own head against a rumpled pillow. By the time she got settled in, Jake was already snoring. She sat there for a while, listening to her husband and the sounds of the night. She smiled as the low mournful sound of a distant train whistle drifted through the darkness and thought about when she was a little girl. *I've always loved the sound of a train whistle in the night—somehow it still comforts me.*

It was around three in the morning when Jake was wakened by something tapping on the driver's window. Startled, he stiffly straightened up in his seat and peered out through the rain-covered window. What he saw snapped him out of his drowsy state—it was a state cop.

Jake rolled down the window. "Yes officer, what can I do for you?"

The cop looked inside the car at the sleeping family, "I have to ask you to move on out of here. This ain't no campground, there's a Hooverville up the road about three miles—you can pull in there and sleep if you want, but you have to get this contraption off the public road, understand?"

With the sheriff waiting beside the road, Jake turned the motor over, clutched and shifted the gear stick pulling their rig back onto the highway. The road was snot-slick as it continued to rain. Tired as he was, Jake struggled to keep the car steady and the trailer from fish-tailing. It didn't take long for Raisa and the kids to go back to sleep and for that he was thankful. Around four or five in the morning, the rain stopped, but the roads were still slick and rut-filled.

It took two more days to get to the Mississippi River at Davenport, Iowa. They had another blowout, this time on the trailer and the weight of the trailer almost turned them over. Jake patched the tire as good as he could and as luck would have it right before lunch, they found a filling station that would fix his tail light and the blown tires. "Tell you what partner, the wife and kids and I are going to go over to that diner and have us a bite to eat while you are fixing that light and the tires. That should give you enough time, right?"

When Jake went back to check on his tire, he discovered that it wouldn't be ready until the next morning. Back in the car, he said, "Well, if that doesn't beat all! The guy can't have the tire fixed until tomorrow so I guess we might as well find us a cabin to spend the night in. Late the next morning they were back on the road. When they passed through Des Moines they turned and headed to the northwest corner of the state. Jake liked the good roads through the big cities but driving in heavy traffic put him on edge and besides that, the kids were showing signs of getting antsy and darn right tired of being cooped up in that back seat.

The peace and quiet was shattered by Beth screaming. "Mommmmmma---will you make Arnie quit picking his nose. It's reallllly disgusting!"

Then came another deafening scream, this one was even shriller than the one before. "Yeeeeeow---Momma—he wiped his booger on my sleeve." Beth immediately began to cry and pound on her brother, who was backed into the corner of the seat, laughing his fool head off!

Beth obviously made a good connection because the next thing—Arnie was bawling his head off and leaning on the seat directly between Raisa and Jake. Not saying a word, Jake reached around and grabbed his seven-year old son's belt, hauling him unceremoniously up and over the seat, dumping him directly into Raisa's lap.

Jake shouted, "Now you stay put, Arnie and don't be wiping your stuff on anybody. We've had this conversation before and if you don't straighten up, I will--stop this car and we, will--go behind the bushes, and I, will---teach you a lesson you won't forget. Got that? Now behave yourself or you'll be walking to Wyoming!"

Jake had to turn his face toward the window to hide his smile. *That kid just looks pure ornery with that tousled blond hair and that face all drawn up in a determined pout. He's a handful, that's for sure.* After what she determined was a safe length of time, Beth leaned over the seat and as sweet as pie asked, "Daddy, how much further to Aunt Lizzie's house in South Dakota?"

Jake rubbed his head in thought. "Well Beth, if we don't have any more blowouts and it doesn't rain or snow, we should be in Pierre by late afternoon tomorrow. Now, you be a good girl and color me one of your pretty pictures while I drive."

It wasn't ten minutes later before Beth's shrill squeal erupted from the back seat. "Oh lookie, there's another Burma Shave sign! Slow down, Daddy, so I can read it. *'Don't stick your elbow out so far. It might go home in another car.'* That's really funny, isn't it Daddy? I've gotta write that one down in my book."

It was near four o'clock in the afternoon of the fifth day on the road when they pulled into the farmyard of Raisa's sister, Lizzie, her husband, George, and their two skinny kids—eight-year-old Annette and seven-year-old Danny. It didn't take Jake and Raisa's own kids two seconds to hop out of the car and run off with their cousins, much to the relief of the parents.

After lots of hugs and kisses, arm in arm, Raisa and Lizzie headed straight for the kitchen and a cup of coffee, while George took Jake down to the barn to see his horses---and have a smoke. Once inside the barn, Jake pulled the whisky bottle out of his coat and offered a short nip to his brother-in-law. George's face lit up like a Christmas tree as he reached for the bottle. "Don't mind if I do—don't, mind if I, do. Did I mention you was always my favorite brother-in-law?" George slapped Jake on the back as he eagerly reached for the bottle of whisky. But Jake knew the instant he pulled the bottle out and George grabbed it, that he had made a bad mistake.

Back inside the run-down farmhouse, it didn't take Raisa long to find out that George hadn't stopped his old ways of pounding on Lizzie every chance he got. Hunched over, Lizzie sat across from Raisa at the shabby oilcloth-covered kitchen table, her tear-filled brown eyes downcast in shame as she poured her heart out to her older sister. "It's just that times are tough here and George gets so frustrated with trying to make a go of it and us not getting any wheres! He says it's my fault that he hits me. Honestly, Raisa, I really try to be a good wife and keep the kids quiet and stuff, but it's never enough, he always finds some excuse to land into me!" She reached up with her thread-bare hanky and dabbed at the tears in her eyes, "It seems the worse things get, the more he drinks and the meaner he gets. I just don't know what I'm going to do. I wish I had gone on to school like Emilie. Now she's able to support herself. I swear if I could, I would take my kids and leave him. I'm pure tired out being his boxing bag."

Raisa went over to where her sister sat, dejected and sobbing. She pulled Lizzie to her feet and folded her arms around her. "There might come a day when you have to leave him Lizzie. Why don't you come back to Lovell with us? It would be better for you to be around your own folks. Theres always things women can do to earn their own way. Any thing would be better than this."

Just then, they heard Beth scream hysterically as she raced across the farmyard and clambered up the broken-down wooden steps of the back porch. Once inside the house she made a frantic beeline for her mother.

"Mommmmma---get them off me, get them off me!" Raisa grabbed her daughter and saw what Beth was screaming about—grasshoppers! There was one big one crawling up her arm and another one clinging to her threadbare dress. The two wriggling 'hoppers' that were caught in her hair were the ones that were sending her into hysterics. Raisa plucked the grasshoppers from her daughters brown stockings and dress and then went after the spitting, clinging creatures in Beth's hair.

Raisa called out to the porch where Arnie and his cousin were happily pulling the legs off the grasshoppers they caught. "Arnie, come in here and take care of these hoppers that I pull off of Beth, and hurry up will you?"

Arnie flung open the pathetic-looking screen door and ran into the kitchen, where he began to gather the discarded grasshoppers. With blue eyes twinkling and the biggest grin of pure pleasure covering his angelic face, he declared, "Mama, this is the most fun I've had the whole week. There are so many grasshoppers—wow, I don't think I ever seen so many! Danny and I are helping Uncle George get rid of these damn hoppers!" Before Raisa could comment on his language, he smiled his most charming smile. "Oops, sorry Mama--that bad word just sorta slipped out all by itself, again!"

Lizzie apologized, "I am so sorry, I guess in my excitement to see you all, I forgot to mention that we have a terrible problem with grasshoppers again this year. We had a few last year, but with this drought, they are back and eating everything in their sight. I bet they ate my puny garden down to nothin' in two hours. They are only part of our problem, trying to make it here!"

Beth stood in the doorway, trying to decide whether to take a chance and go back outside or just stay put inside where the grasshoppers wouldn't crawl all over her. She turned to her mother as she said, "Oh boy, here comes trouble. Uncle George doesn't look very happy; in fact he looks darn right mad.

Raisa rose to look out the kitchen window. "Oh my, the fellows must have heard all the screaming and they are heading for the house. You are right Beth; your Uncle George does not look happy or too stable on his feet."

Lizzie joined her sister at the kitchen window. "Oh, sweet Lord, he looks like he's been drinking, Raisa. How could that be?"

It didn't take two seconds for Raisa to realize that Jake must have shared the last of that whiskey with George out in the barn.

George threw open the kitchen screen door and, with Jake following close behind, he crossed the kitchen floor to where Lizzie sat at the table. Raisa was startled to see her sister cower as

George grabbed her viciously by the arm. "What in the hell was all that fuss about? Why were the kids screaming like that, huh? Look at ya there; sittin on your fat behind like nothing was wrong. Why in the hell can't we have some peace and quiet in this place?"

With her eyes on the floor, Lizzie winched in pain as she pleaded. "George it weren't nothin' but the kids fussing with the grasshoppers. Some of them landed on Beth and she screamed like most little girls would. No harm, George."

George's face was red and his mouth sagged at one corner as he yelled, "And you didn't bother to tell em about the hoppers, right? You stupid, bitch!" With that, George hauled off and backhanded Lizzie across the face.

Jake was across the room in a second. He grabbed George's arms, pinning them to his sides as he pulled him roughly away from Lizzie. "Come on George. What the hell's wrong with you? That was nothing to slap your wife over, it weren't her fault."

George pulled loose, whirled on his brother-in-law and with a closed fist took a wild swing at him. That was all Jake needed. He landed a vicious punch to George's jaw that sent him sprawling against the wall. Jake paid no attention to the two women crying and carrying on. He was focused purely on George. Jake bent over and hauled the man to his feet then slammed him against the wall for good measure, oblivious to the huddled group of scared children watching their every move with wide eyes.

"Tell you what, George. That better be the last time you lay your hands on Lizzie or take a swing at me. Real men don't beat their womenfolk, got that? When we leave here, I'm going to stop at the sheriff's office in town and file a report on you, have him come out here and check on Lizzie every once in a while. I mean it, George. You leave her the hell alone."

George staggered over to one of the shabby kitchen chairs. Slumping down in it, he snarled, "And you, Jake Kessel, get the hell out of my house, and don't think you're invited back real soon. Still think you can take care of the world don't you? Why the hell don't you just mind your own got damn business? Now git the hell off my place, and don't be comin' back!"

Jake turned to Raisa, who was as pale as a ghost. "Round up the kids, we need to get back on the road." Jake drew Lizzie into his arms and kissed her goodbye. "If you have any trouble from him, Lizzie, you let the sheriff know. Just a thought, but you might think about moving back to Lovell and leaving this piece of no-good horse shit out here by his self. We love you. Take care of yourself and we'll say goodbye for now."

Not a word was uttered for the four miles into the next small town, where Jake found the sheriff's office and pulled up in front. "Raisa, you and the kids stay put, it's not going to take me long to file a complaint against that no-good bum. If you all are good, we will stop at the ice cream stand on the way out of town."

Jake stomped up the front steps and went into the building. True to his word, he was back in the car in minutes and on the road again. Lost in his thoughts about his no-good brother-in-law, he headed for the highway.

"Daddddy, stop; you promised, Daddy, you promised to buy us an ice cream cone and now you just drove past the place. That's not fair, not one bit!"

Jake slammed on the brakes and, looking both ways, made a fast U-turn in the middle of the street, throwing both kids into the corner of the back seat. Arnie untangled himself and stood up. "That was fun, Daddy, go back and do that again!" Raisa merely gave Jake one of her looks, telling him he better not even think about doing that again!

Ten minutes later, everyone was happily licking an ice cream cone as they settled in for the next long stretch of road. They only had three hours of daylight left when they got back to the main highway. Jake rubbed his two-day growth of whiskers and said, "I was hoping we could make Devil's Tower camp ground across the Wyoming border, but I don't think we can get there now. We'll look for a city park to camp in tonight, maybe in Rapid City."

Before they were five miles down the road, the two kids were asleep in the back seat. Raisa turned to gaze thankfully at her husband. "Jake, thanks for knocking George on his butt. He really deserved what you gave him. I'm sure Lizzie appreciated it too.

She's got to leave him before he puts her in the hospital. He's just not going to change. I pray she thinks about what we told her and comes back to Lovell."

~~~~~

They got an early start on the second day, heading west to the Wyoming – South Dakota state line on Route 90. It was mid-morning when they crossed the border. Jake let out a holler. "Wahoo, we are back in Wyoming! Just put your head out the window and smell that fresh air, kids." He pointed to a sign on the right side of the road. "How about turning off here and taking a look at that Devil's Tower I was talking about yesterday. I've heard that it's quite the sight and we need to stretch our legs. There's not much to see or do between here and the Big Horn Mountains, just a lot of wide open prairie, where nobody wanted to squat or homestead."

Raisa looked out over the vast dry land. "I can see why; there's hardly a tree in sight and no water either. The soil must not be good for farming or some homesteader would have given dry land farming a try. Just imagine all the big prairie schooners and people that crossed this land, loaded down with hopes and dreams of owning their own land"

Jake pulled to a stop in the parking lot at Devil's Tower. They all piled out of the car and headed for the information board. Jake read, "They say here that it's made of an uncommon igneous rock that pushed up through some sort of opening in the earth a long time ago. Teddy Roosevelt declared it as the first national monument in 1906—just about the time we came over to this country! The Indians thought it was big medicine, and that it is--- it's really something."

Raisa stared up at the towering, pleated-rock mountain. "I've never seen anything like that in my life. I wonder if anyone has tried to climb it and what's on the top?" She looked across the barren prairie to the south and then back at Devil's Tower. "There isn't anything around here that even resembles this thing—it's like it just grew out of the earth!"

Jake turned back towards the car, "Well, we better get back on the road; we have a ways to go before sunset!" Inspired, he put the pedal to the metal and they made good time traveling west over the flat, uninspiring prairie, through Gillette and then up to Sheridan. As the day was nearing its end, Jake pulled a ways off the main highway and they camped for the night near a crystal-clear stream at the foot of the majestic Big Horn Mountains.

Raisa smiled to herself as she watched her husband. She knew Jake was just itching to get ahold of his fly rod, but first he had to unload their camping equipment from the trailer. It was then that he and his son headed for the stream. Arnie didn't fish, he wasn't that patient, but he did manage to fall into the shallow creek three times.

In the matter of an hour, Jake had four fine rainbow trout for their supper. After he gutted and fileted the fish alongside the creek, the two of them headed back to their campsite. He could smell the distinctive odor of the camp fire as he walked into camp with a wet, soggy little boy in tow. While Beth helped her protesting brother change into dry clothes, Jake got busy pitching their tent.

Raisa searched around in the trailer and finally found the old black cast-iron frying pan. The campfire she had built with the sticks of dry wood Beth had fetched from the woods, was settling down now and there were some perfect glowing coals to fry the fish over. Raisa couldn't help but hum a little as she prepared their supper over the open camp fire. *This is what I call living. I love this simple life away from all the town folks. Sure, it was exciting, living in the big city and we had some great experiences, but that's not Jake and me—it just isn't.*

Raisa flipped the frying trout over and settled back into her thoughts. *I know one thing for sure, we won't starve and we won't be shivering in our beds back in Wyoming. It's nothing like the big city livin'.*

Later that evening, Jake and Raisa tucked the kids into bed inside the cramped tent and returned to sit by the smoldering fire. Jake reached down, retrieved a small burning twig and put a light to a cigarette. The full moon hung low and lazy in the night sky as he put his feet up on a nearby rock; Jake put his arm around Raisa and pulled her into him.

Raisa gazed into the flames and snuggled closer to her husband. She could feel the tears of emotion building in her eyes. "Oh, Jake, this is what we missed—this feels like home and smells like home. We are almost there, Jake. Think about it--just over the Big Horns is Lovell. If only we could fly like a bird, we'd be there. How far do you think we can get tomorrow?"

Jake took a long drag on his cigarette and tilted his head in thought. "Oh, if nothing goes wrong with the car or the trailer, I think we might make Billings or even Laurel. Then it's a hundred miles to Lovell from there. We have a little extra money, I was thinking we could find us a little cabin for tomorrow night and all take some baths, wash a few clothes and stuff. I am beginning to smell myself!" Jake flipped the butt of his cigarette into the fire and pulled out his harmonica.

Inside the tent, Beth woke from a bad dream, but before she could cry out, she heard her father playing his harmonica. *Daddy can sure play that har-monica—I love to listen to it. It always makes me feel happy to hear that music.* She turned over and snuggled back down in her sleeping bag and went back to sleep.

The next morning, Jake woke early and slipped out of the tent. He foraged in the woods and found enough dry wood to build a breakfast campfire. As the fire built, Jake lit a cigarette and sat down on a large rock. He looked to the east and laid his eyes on first light as it painted a soft pink and apricot blush across the clear morning sky. *Looks to me like it's gonna be a good day for traveling, the mourning doves are singing already. I always loved to hear their call—somethin' soothing about it.* Jake took a final drag on the cigarette and flipped it into the campfire, then fished around in the canvas bag for the coffee pot and frying pan.

Inside the tent, Raisa turned over in their cozy bed to discover a cold spot where Jake had slept. She rolled onto her back and let her mind drift over the experiences they had on this journey back to Wyoming. She dozed until she smelled the coffee and bacon. *Oh my word, Jake got up and beat me to fixing breakfast.* She started to get up but had second thoughts. *I'll just let him fix breakfast today since he's probably already got it half cooked. A smart woman lets her man wait on her once in a while.*

After a leisurely breakfast of scrambled eggs, bacon and hot coffee, Jake declared, "I've got a feelin' that this weather is going to turn, even with a beautiful dawn. There's a new moon rising and we've got a slight breeze out of the north, but its building and the temperature is dropping like a rock. At first light, it looked like a clear day ahead, but I wasn't looking north, that was my mistake. See that bank of gray, dense cauliflower clouds? That spells trouble for us."

In no time, the Kessel family broke camp and piled into the Ford Model A, eager to get on the road. It was close to noon when they crossed from Wyoming into Montana, heading due north to Billings. By the time they rolled into Billings, it was late afternoon; the sky was filled with gray, boiling clouds and icy drops of rain began to fall. Jake stopped at a filling station and while the attendant was filling the Model A's tank, Jake went inside and got directions to some inexpensive road-side cabin where they would be warm and dry, as well as a small café just down the street.

After a quick supper they hurried back to the cabin through intermittent rain drops. Jake looked at the dark, threatening sky and said, "Well blast it! That's what I was afraid of and exactly what I didn't want—more rain on these dirt roads. We are going to have a hell of a time getting to Lovell if those clouds really let loose."

It rained off and on all night. The next morning they ate a cold breakfast in their room. Jake balanced the *Billings Gazette* in one hand while eating with the other. "Raisa, listen to this from former President, Calvin Coolidge: *'In other periods of depression, it has always been possible to see some things which were solid and upon which you could base hope, but as I look ahead, I now see nothing to give ground to hope.'* That sure as hell makes a guy feel confident about the future. If our president doesn't have much hope, then what the heck are we supposed to think?"

Jake shook his head and rubbed his hand back through his thinning hair. "I tell you Raisa, we got out of Michigan just in time. This here Depression is going to get worse, much worse, before it gets better, and 'home' seems like the best place to be. At least we know we won't starve, living on the farm."

The Montana sky was socked in and hung heavy with dark billowing spring rain clouds. An occasional flash of lightening sliced through the gray clouds, followed by rolling thunder. Jake rubbed his aching knuckles that were stiff and sore from gripping the steering wheel for the past week. He pulled the limp curtain back from the cabin window and looked out onto the street. To his disgust, a steady rain beat hard against the window pane. He turned back to face Raisa and the kids. "It's one hell of a mess out there, a real gully-washer. I'll put my slicker on and take the suitcases out and pack them under the tarp. I need to take a quick look-see to make sure that trailer tarp and straps didn't get worked loose."

Jake was back inside in a matter of minutes. "Okay, I guess it's now or never. Wyoming here we come!" He carried Arnie as Raisa and Beth made a run for the car. The roads weren't too bad from Billings to Laurel—they were blessed with a fairly decent upgraded road bed. Beth and Arnie stood up behind the front seat, eager to watch the storm and the road up ahead. Jake was a bag of nerves and didn't appreciate the kids breathing down his neck. "Will you two sit the hell down back there and play a game or something? You don't need to be standing up, especially if we should go off the road!"

They crossed the narrow, Yellowstone River Bridge just outside Laurel and headed due south toward the Wyoming/Montana border. Jake said, "I'm glad we had a bridge to cross the river, did you see how that thing was rolling full to the banks? The snow must be melting up in them mountains already and what with this rain, that river might just flood yet." The rain seemed to be slowing, but the blustery spring wind continued to bend the treetops and the road was soaked beyond slippery.

Right before they came to Bridger, Montana, things began to get real dicey. Jake swore under his breath as sweat beaded up on his forehead, "Gol damn rain! Gol damn roads! How in the hell am I supposed to hold this rig on this strip of gumbo and slime? Well, we just have to take our time, have a little patience and hopefully we'll make the next seventy miles in good shape."

Several times the car and trailer were headed for the ditch or sliding sideways on the slick, treacherous road as the rain continued to pour down. Beth spent most of the morning with her hands over her ears and the blanket over her head. Arnie was all eyes and ears; he loved the excitement. Every time the car lurched sideways or skidded in the muddy slop, he cheered loudly. After slipping and sliding their way southbound, they finally crossed the Montana/Wyoming border. They all let out a big 'Wa-hoo'! Just this side of Frannie, the rain let up and things seemed to get better the closer they got to Lovell.

Nobody in that car said a word as they drove slowly into their hometown, savoring every sight, every minute. The kids and Raisa were glued to the windows, looking at the familiar and unfamiliar parks, houses, the brick sugar beet factory buildings. Jake took Main Street straight through town without stopping. At the 'Y' junction, he headed east out of Lovell toward the Big Horn Mountains. In five minutes, Jake signaled for a right-hand turn and they pulled into the yard of his parent's farm. Jake and Raisa were speechless when they laid eyes on the new brick house Karl had built for Katja. Raisa said, "Oh Jake, look—it's the house your mother has always wanted. It's just like she described in her letters. It is just beautiful—I can't wait to see the inside." Jake pulled the car and trailer around and parked by the garage, then laid on the car's horn. Karl ran from the barn with a pitchfork in tow and Katja burst out of the back door of the house, wiping her hands on her white apron. Before Jake could set the emergency brake, the kids were out of the car, running into the waiting arms of their grandparents. They were home!

Katja wrapped her arms around her grandchildren. "Mercy, you kids don't have anything but a bit of flesh on those bones. Come on in here to Grandma's kitchen. We got to start fattening you two up! And, I need to catch up on some hugs and kisses."

Raisa and Jake Kessel, standing in front of the Model A and trailer they pulled back from Michigan.

KAREN SCHUTTE

PART TWO

1936

BACK HOME IN WYOMING

CHAPTER SEVEN

Life's blows cannot break a person whose spirit is warmed by the fire of enthusiasm.
Norman Vincent Peale

Lovell, Wyoming, 1936: Raisa looked up at the large clock on the wall of the Lovell laundry. She swept back the tendrils of damp hair hanging down from her top knot and thought. *Only thirty more minutes in this steam and heat and I can go home. I don't know how much longer I can take this kind of work, I can barely breathe. I never did do good with heat and the steam from them hot irons makes it even worse.* A wave of dizziness swept over her as she swayed and grabbed for the edge of the table. Silently and swiftly, blackness rolled in from both sides until that was all there was.

Raisa woke up in her bed with Jake and Dr. Welsey standing over her. She felt light-headed and undeniable nausea consumed her as she tried to sit up. Jake gently pushed her back onto the pillow. "My, gosh woman; you scared the heck out of me, fainting like that. You got a pretty bad cut on your arm from falling; you are lucky you didn't hit your head. It's a good thing you picked a pile of laundry to fall into. The doc sewed you up and you should be good as new, but Raisa, I'm telling you right now, you ain't going back to that laundry work. No way! There has to be something else you can do to make some extra money. When you are back on your feet, we can look around. For now, you just rest." Jake bent down and kissed her forehead. Closing the door behind him, he escorted the doctor to the front door. Self-consciously, he shoved his hands deep into his pants pockets, knowing far too well he couldn't pay the doctor today.

Jake pushed open the screen door and waited for Doctor Welsey to walk out onto the front porch. Dabbing the sweat from his flushed face, the good doctor walked down the steps, then paused and turned. "Jake, I agree with you about not wanting Raisa to go back to work at the laundry."

With a look of concern on his face, Jake reached into his back pocket and pulled out his thin wallet, but the doctor laid his hand on Jake's forearm. "Don't worry about paying me; I can get along without it. I think Raisa needs complete rest and time to rethink what she can do without compromising her health. You realize she isn't a very strong woman." He turned to walk down the steps. "Ask her mother to make a batch of her famous chicken and dumplings. That woman's cooking will cure anything. You call me Jake, if she takes a turn for the worse!"

Raisa was depressed and discouraged to learn she wasn't supposed to go back to work for a week, and when she did, it wouldn't be at the laundry. "Jake, what am I supposed to do? I hate lying around, not getting anything accomplished, it f-feels almost sinful."

Jake winked at her and said, "Well then, you'd better practice on being a bit sinful if you want to get better. I am sure you will find something to keep you busy: making curtains, crocheting, remaking a dress for Beth. You always seem to find things to do; the main thing is you need is to build your strength back up. Do you want me to move that little radio in here so you can listen to your favorite day-time programs?"

For his part, Jake had a steady job as head mechanic at the Ford garage in Lovell and was making decent money. Later that week over lunch with his boss, he happened to mention how his wife had fainted at the laundry and was looking for another job. Mr. Tomlinson's face lit up with interest. "I just had a great idea. Is or will Raisa be able to clean and do general house work, once she's well? Is that something she would be interested in?"

Jake slapped the desk and smiled, "You bet! Everything she cleans just shines and squeaks it's so clean—she is really particular. You know those German women and how they keep a clean house!"

Jack Tomlinson pushed back in his desk chair. "Well, tell you what Jake, let me mention it to the Mrs.—I know she's been wanting some help around the house."

Raisa spent the next two weeks recuperating and taking in mending for the Lovell Laundry. As she sat under the shade of the front porch one sultry afternoon, working robotically on the mending, her mind strayed to the past few years since they had returned to Lovell from Port Huron. *I still remember the day we drove into Karl and Katja's yard after our long trip. The kids were so happy to see their grandparents.*

Raisa smiled at the memory. *After smothering them with kisses, Katja took Arnie and Beth by the hand, leading them through the house to her bedroom. She made them sit on the rag rug at the foot of her bed while she unlocked her pierced tin storage chest. Smiling, she reached deep inside and pulled out two tins, one filled with dried peach slices and the other with dried plums. She told the kids to take three of each.* A warm feeling filled Raisa as she remembered her children's faces.

We unloaded the trailer that day and moved into the basement at the Kessel house. It wasn't supposed to be for long, only until we found a farm to rent. But as it turned out, we lived there for about six months.

We moved out when Jake got a job with my brother-in-law. Robert and left for Montana. Since the men were going to be gone for months and my sister, Maria didn't want to be by herself out on their farm, so the kids and I moved in with her and her two little girls. That was a lucky break for us. Robert needed help with a large contract he had up in Big Timber, Montana, and he asked Jake to come with him. He had a good dragline business going, digging canals and ditches for farmers in the surrounding

Jake running the dragline in Montana, building canals

states who were eager to put in irrigation systems. Maria and I had a swell time, catching up on our sister talk and taking care of our children, the chickens, and the garden. Arnie was happy because he had three girls to terrorize. The little imp! Before this, when our families were all together, the only time my sisters and I could talk privately at family gatherings was when we congregated in the outhouse. There are just some things we don't want our husbands and kids to know. Us sisters, we have our own little secrets. Raisa smiled wickedly to herself, *Oh, and if only they had an idea of our secrets!*

I always loved the Sunday afternoons after church when Jake and the kids and I would pile in the car and go visiting, either to my folks' farm, Jake's parents' farm, or one of my sisters. I was so happy when Lizzie moved back to Lovell with her family over two years ago. She finally divorced that good-for-nothing George after he darn near put her in the hospital. He left town, but not before Jake kicked his butt around the block a couple of times.

A couple businessmen from the Lutheran church helped Lizzie buy a rooming house close to the hospital and the telephone office. They said it was an investment; we all knowed they wanted to help Lizzie out. She rented out the entire top floor and most of the first floor to telephone operators and people who only needed one or two rooms. Lizzie and the kids lived at the back of the first floor in three rooms. It was perfect for her. She and her kids were finally safe and happy and she was making it on their own.

After three months working in Montana, Jake came back with some money in

Arnie (10) & Beth (13) in Lovell, WY.

his pocket. It felt good to be able to buy a few things we needed, like clothes for the kids. We got Arnie a tie and vest—he looked like a little man. I cut down one of Emilie's coats for Beth; it was blue-gray and had curly gray lamb on the collar and cuffs. We splurged on having Beth and Arnie's photo taken by a traveling photographer. It was so sweet—can't believe how fast they are growing.

I couldn't believe it when Jake told me he was going to get back into farming. I remember crying myself to sleep that night. I guess I knew deep down that he would try it again, sooner or later. I had to support him, even though I hated going back on the farm and into the fields. But, I knew Jake was itching to get back into farming and when he rented the Mueller farm out in Kane, we packed up and moved. The house wasn't too bad and his dad lent Jake a couple of horses and any equipment we needed. Those were hard years, trying to get started farming again and during the depression too. We sent Beth to live with Jake's folks for the school year so she could attend Lutheran catechism classes in Lovell and be confirmed in the spring.

After the kids were in bed one Saturday night, I remember sitting down at the kitchen table with Jake to go over our budget. He wanted to plant an entire field of oats because he could get $3.48 a bushel. We sat there and made a grocery/supply list of things we would need to get started: new horse harness $12.50, Kerosene 75 cents, 8 bags of grain $2.25, 6 boxes of matches 20 cents, a box of bullets 75 cents, 4 lbs. sausage 85 cents, 4 lbs. bacon 88 cents, 9 lbs. salt 75 cents, bag of rice $1.10, 5 skeins of yarn 75 cents, fabric 50 cents, kids winter coats $8, winter boots for Beth and me $2; long underwear $1.30, nails $1, coffee $1.15. There was more on the list but I can't remember it all. All I member is that we couldn't afford to get everything on that list—and everything on it was stuff we needed, not just wanted.

Raisa's eyes lit up with memories—*but somehow or another when we was done buying what was on 'the list', we always had a few pennies left over for a bag of peppermints, lemon drops, butterscotch candies, black balls or licorice. The kids looked forward to that bag of candy. Also they knew if they were good, the store owner would give them a treat.* Raisa smiled as she remembered, *they would stand so patiently beside the counter, watching his every move. With a twinkle in his eye, he knew what they were waiting for; he got a kick out of making them stand there and wait for it. They were practically drooling before he handed over a black ball or peppermint stick.*

I remember cutting down Jake's and my old clothes to fit the kids. After the kids were done with them I used all the scraps to make rag rugs, patches for other clothes, and just plain rags. Jake cut up the old leather shoes to use as patches for the horse's harnesses and saddles. We tried to make use of everything God gave us.

Raisa scooped up the mending that was left and headed to the back yard, where she settled herself on a chair in the shade of a cottonwood tree. She began to daydream again as she worked on a torn shirt, shuddering as she recalled the back-breaking work they all put in over the past few years, working the sugar beet fields. *After a year on the farm, Jake was bound and determined to have himself a cash crop of sugar beets, no matter what. He had his own*

**Thinning Sugar Beets from 6a.m. to 6 p.m.
The entire family went into the fields.**

system of farming; it was some of what his dad had taught him and part of what he had picked up from watching other farmers. First thing, he figured out was which twenty acres had the best soil. After plowing the ground he spread it with any kind of manure he could get and then he worked the manure into the ground with a disc and harrow. The final chore was to level it and then the field was ready to be cut into rows. Pert near the rest of raising sugar beets was done by hand—our hands! Sometimes other families came in to help folks like us, who only had two little kids.

Jake drove into Lovell, to the seed elevator and bought the sugar beet seed, which looked similar to peppercorns. Each one of them seeds sprouted a beet sprout. When the beets came up, the families went to the fields. It was the same for all of us. If we had a baby, it was left in a box at the end of the row in a shady spot, hopefully with a babysitter, while the rest of the crew started thinning the beets. We always packed us a cold, sack lunch wrapped in dish towels or old newspaper. Course, we took them chipped Mason jars filled with water or lemonade if we had any lemons, to the field with us. We'd find us some cold damp ground and dig a hole for the jar. Kept it nice and cool that way.

If you were six years old, you went into the field and thinned sugar beets, crawling on your knees.

Jake and I didn't have a whole bunch of kids to help work in our fields. Most Germans, especially the Russian/Germans like my folks, had as many kids as they could. They bred their own field help. Jake and I had two kids, one of each, and we stopped that business right there.

Raisa tried to erase the painful mental images of the grueling field work from her mind as she looked down and shook her head. *I can't forget how, before we went out into the field we all coated ourselves with a mixture of kerosene and mud from the ditch. Beth gagged and complained every time I put the mixture on her. But, I tell you this, it kept those mosquitoes and pesky blackflies off us.*

Jake and I would each take a long handled hoe and side by side we blocked a row of beet sprouts. We would chop out about a twelve-inch space between beet clumps. Arnie and Beth came crawling behind, thinning the clumps down to one plant with their little fingers. I remember how I sewed double patches onto their knees, hoping to cushion their tender flesh and make the pants wear longer too. Lots of times they cried because they didn't want to go to the beet field. They weren't the only ones that cried—there were plenty of nights I cried myself to sleep, with lard smeared over my sun-burned neck and face.

Raisa smiled as she thought of Arnie and how he disappeared one time when they were hoeing beets. *That little imp! We had just stopped for lunch under a bunch of cottonwoods at the end of the row. We'd been working all morning in the hot sun, not a cloud in that blue sky. Arnie ate his sandwich and drank his weight in lemon water. I remember him crying when Jake said it was time to go back out in the fields. Well, Jake grabbed him by the belt, lifting him off the ground and hauled him back into the sugar beet field. I remember him saying, 'If you want to eat and want to sleep inside the house tonight, you are going to have to work. Nothin' in this world is free. Get your lazy butt out there and work now'.*

Arnie worked alongside of us three, bawlin' with snot running down his upper lip mixing with the dirt. I tried to talk to him; he was just a little guy. I remember that after an hour or so,

Jake asked where Arnie was and Beth said that he had to go pee. Well, he didn't come back and didn't come back, so we laid down our hoes and went to lookin' for him. After about twenty minutes, we found him asleep in the shade of the bushes at the other end of the field. That's when Jake lit into him with his belt.

**Second Hoeing—of the sugar beets.
To make time go faster, they sang and told jokes.**

I never went against Jake when it came to disciplinin' our kids, except, for that one time. I grabbed Jake's arm and yelled at him to stop. 'You are turnin' into your dad, Jake. Arnie isn't strong and this heat is too much for all of us, we should wait and come out after supper.' I guess that wasn't the way to handle the situation 'cause it made Jake madder. But he didn't say or do anything else—just stomped off into the field and started hoeing the beets. Arnie came back and he worked a little while longer, then I sent him up to the house to gather the eggs and feed the chickens. I felt sorry for the little bugger.

We tried to wear long sleeve shirts, but one can only cover up so much skin. I remember how our hands throbbed with bloody blisters. There was just no gettin' round not gettin' blisters from all the field handwork. When the beets was finally thinned, the insides of our hands were often callused over, yet the back sides were chapped to the point they split and bled. Oh, mercy me, they hurt so bad and looked even worse—not like the fine, town lady's hands. Those of us who didn't have gloves, well—our hands got all chapped and as dark as coffee.

For us women---first thing in the morning, before the sun was even up, we had to fix breakfast and a bag lunch. Then we all headed for the fields before it got too hot; we worked all day with a half hour off for lunch. Sometimes if it was terribly hot in the afternoon, we took a drink break in the shade for fifteen minutes or so. When we finished the field work we headed back to the house there was supper to fix, cows to milk, chickens to tend to, and course we all had our own gardens to hoe and weed. I don't even remember fallin' into bed most nights I was so tired out.

We didn't bathe except on Saturday night, that's when we changed our underwear and the rest of our clothes too. No sense changing clothes 'cause we just went back out and got just as dirty and sweaty the next day. It was a bugger getting that dirt out of the clothes. We boiled them and then scrubbed them on the board. It's what we all had to do—just the way things was back then.

**Harvest time: they pulled the sugar beets up
and then top them with a hooked sharp knife.**

Those folks who could afford to hire, signed on Mexican families that came up every year from old Mexico to work the beets. We was never that rich that we could afford to hire someone else to do our work. After the thinning, came weeding and spraying for web worms. We all seen what happens when you don't spray for those worms. Jake mostly used a stuff called 'Paris Green' and it seemed to work pretty good. Course we had to irrigate them beets on a regular basis—let em get almost dry and then water them. Jake said that made the roots go down searching for water. Towards harvest when them beets started filling out, we had to irrigate a lot. It was best to have hot days and cool nights to bring the sugar count up in them. Nobody planned anything during the month of October. It was all work and everybody prayed for good weather. Nobody liked to go out in them fields in the mud or snow. Course, one good thing--when it got colder we didn't have to fight them gnats and mosquitos—just the wet and cold. Jake would drive this lifter machine down the row—it loosened the dirt around the beets and made it easier for the kids and me to pull them out. Then, we'd grab a beet in each hand and smack them together. Arnie loved this part of it—anything he could smash, he liked. It was the best way to knock off a lot of the dirt, providing it wasn't muddy, then that was another story.

We made one row of them beets between three field-rows, so actually six rows of beets in the ground ended up piled into one row of beets out of the ground. It was usually my job to come along with a hooked twelve-inch long beet knife—hook the beet with the curved end, grab the root and whack the top off and then throw those beets into another 'master' row. I remember every night we'd take those knives in and wash them, then sharpen them and put some oil or lard on the blade. When Beth got a little older, she got the job of toppin' them beets. She took a hunk out of herself every now and then with that wicked, long knife. Jake drove the truck along the master row of topped beets and with a pitchfork, threw them onto the open bed of the truck. That was such a great feeling to see that truck piled high with them big sugar beets. It told us we done something right.

Jake loved driving the loaded beet truck to the dump to be weighed. He never trusted me to drive the truck 'cause, like he always said, I was just a woman! Personally, I think he kept remembering when he first taught me to drive back in Michigan and I took that corner too fast. Raisa broke into a wide smile. I really scared the heck out of that man and he never forgot it either. We usually made between thirteen and seventeen tons per acre—just depending on the weather and a whole passel of other influences. Most farmers pulled their kids out of school during harvest time. Beth and Arnie didn't mind that much, but I'm pretty sure they hated working the fields as much as I did.

Jake Kessel beside a full load of sugar beets.

Jake and I've lived in some pretty shabby places when we rented farms, usually crawling with bed bugs, lice, and mice. I got my system down with ridding those places of the vermin and making them livable. They was always small houses, maybe three or four rooms if that. I remember this one place we lived in, it used to be a chicken coop. That one took the cake! But, I was pretty proud of how I done fixed that place up. Arnie liked it there because there was a passel of kids around including some little kids that belonged to the Mexican workers. We all lived in a group of shacks and worked the fields. Nobody was any better than anyone else, we was all in the same leaky boat!

Beth and Arnie shared a bed until she got older and insisted sleeping alone. We usually fixed Arnie a cot out on the back porch—summer and winter. I 'member that one winter when he caught a terrible cold, it 'bout went to neu-monia. I fixed so many mustard plasters for his little chest I lost count. Even put garlic under his pillow, trying to break the sickness. What finally broke the cold was putting a tent out of a sheet over him and setting a pan of boiling water with garlic and fever root in it. That steam got right to his chest and he got better.

Sharecroppers kids in front of the house that was once a chicken coop.

Raisa looked off into the distance, remembering that first winter back from Michigan. *Jake found us this farm to rent, out in Kane. We'd only been in that house a couple of months and winter was comin' on. It had snowed soft and steady all that night and when the sun came up from behind the Big Horns the next morning, it was still coming down. The kids were pestering me so much that I finally got them bundled up and sent them out the door. I remember how Beth showed Arnie how to lie down in the snow and stick his arms and legs out, moving them in and out, back and forth, to make snow angels. Mercy me, they must have made twenty snow angels all over the yard.*

We've had us some good memories, along with the bad times, I guess. When I look back now, I don't know how we got this far, and the Depression isn't over yet. I remember in 32' when President Franklin Roosevelt was voted in as president, he started giving those Fireside Chats. He told us that we were supposed to smile and keep smiling. That 'the only thing we have to fear is fear itself!' I think we have a good president, but he isn't in our shoes. He's come up with some good things for the country, trying to get us out of this here Depression. Them government agencies, like the Civil Conservation Corp (CCC), and (CWA) Civil Works Administration were successful in giving jobs to men, getting them off the streets. I heard that them agencies put over four thousand guys to work building roads and dams all over the country.

When we first moved back here from Michigan, wheat was going at thirty-six cents a bushel, eggs were four cents a dozen, and butter cost fifteen cents a pound. Why, you could even buy a 365-pound hog for around two dollars---if you had the money. Like all the other women, I've had to use my head to come up with ways to cook with purtin' near to nothing. We were always lucky to have a garden and when Jake's folks butchered a cow, they always shared it with us. I learnt how to can that meat and it was pretty darn good too. Whenever we was able get our hands on extra food, I would can it and keep it cold in the cellar or if we were lucky, a spring-well pit.

Off and on we had us a cow of our own, to milk and get cream from. When there was extra cream, I'd take it into town to trade for groceries. We kept us a few chickens around too—just fed 'em from the slop bucket and they wandered the yard during the day, pickin' up what they could find. At night we always locked them up in the hen house 'cause of coyotes and the like. Those chickens gave us a lot of good eggs. When a chicken was getting old, we'd wring his neck and he'd be in the pot along with some taters and carrots for a good supper. I had to cook the old birds long and slow to tender them up.

I know we aren't better or worse off than most folks. We all want to look our best, not let the others know how far down we are. If we're going to church, I'm particular that what we wear is clean, starched, and ironed. We have our pride left and that's about it. I guess you could say we are 'bout down to the flesh on *our bones. I've taught the kids how to take care of their clothes, saving the decent things for school and church.*

I remember one time placing an order with the Montgomery Ward catalog for a bundle of fabric pieces for two dollars. Shoot, I made all sorts of things for us from that bundle. The scraps are made into dish towels and rag rugs. My sister told me about the Spiegel catalog too. It lets peoples order and charge the amount owed. Then we'd pay a small monthly fee for a few months to pay for the goods.

We are in debt to every grocer and dry goods store in Lovell--us and everyone one else in town, we're all in the same boat. It's a rare day when we have any money for movies or new clothes. We live hand to mouth and are thankful for that. We put cardboard in our shoes like all the rest of the folks. Don't know where or when this is going to end. I'll tell you this much, we thank God for our folks. They have helped us out when they could, with meat and chickens and the like.

My little sister Emilie sends her last year's clothes for Beth. I learned all the tricks to adjusting and refitting those clothes for Beth and even me sometimes. I tore out more seams than I care to remember. But we were always mighty thankful for the extra clothes. Emilie made all the right decisions for herself—didn't have a lot of luck with men, but she has two sweet boys and a good job out there in San Francisco. I would hate for her to see my hands—bet hers look all soft and manicured. She was always so stylish and beautiful—a real stunner. She's got more gumption than me.

The mending lay in Raisa's lap as feelings of despair and defeat suddenly overcame her. A torrent of hot tears poured from her green eyes and washed down her porcelain face. She covered her face with both chapped hands and let the sobs come, and come they did. *Why doesn't our life get better, why can't we buy nice things, have nice things—live in a decent house like some folks in town do? I walk by the store windows in Lovell and all I can do is look and dream of what it would feel like to wear that pretty dress, or go to church with that nice hat on. I hate this life, our life. I wanted something better for Jake and me and our kids. But it* doesn't get better, it just gets worse. I know everybody is pretty much in the same boat as us, but we are so bad off we're almost on the street.

When am I going to have my own house, my own kitchen—things I can fix up and make nice for us? I've gone to my Dad and asked for his guidance, especially with Jake's staying until all hours at the pool hall. I know my husband doesn't mess around with other women, but he doesn't come home either. We've been having some real bad arguments over him playing cards and forgetting about the kids and me. I remember the advice my dad gave me. He said. 'You married Jake for some good reasons. In his heart he's a good man and that's what you have to hang onto. He has to let off steam one way or another, that's a man's way. I never cared much for going into town to the pool hall, but I did go in and stand on the street corner and talked to people passing by.' It was always the Good Book that I turned to and it never failed me.'

I try to explain to Jake that there's nothing here at home for me and the kids to do on the evenings he's at the pool hall. Oh yeah, sometimes he takes us along and parks the car on Main Street. He still goes to the pool hall, while me and the kids go to a picture show if we can afford it. Mostly we just walk up and down the street window shopping and day-dreamin' about the stuff we see in them store windows. Then, when the kids get tired, we sit in the car in front of the pool hall, waiting for Jake to finish up and drive us home. I do enjoy the times he drops us off at Lizzie's boarding house, so me and the kids can visit her and her two kids.

There are times I resent Jake having fun or time to his self, when all I do is work. I wish I had more good times in my life too. He goes to the pool hall to escape and socialize and I've got nothing like that except them picture shows. I guess that's my escape from our grim reality. I just imagine myself living like those folks in the movies live. I pretend it's me wearing those beautiful dresses, living in those grand houses with not a worry in the world. But then, it never takes long before I snap back to reality. Since Prohibition was repealed back in 1933, Jake's been drinking at the pool hall too and sometimes he drinks too much.

I don't know why I always remember this one time when we was pretty down, Jake had worked all week building silos. Come Friday night, I kept his supper warm thinking he was working late. Finally, it must have been around one in the morning. I heard him staggering in the back door and so I got out of bed, wrapped my thin flannel robe around me and met him in the kitchen. He was all stinkin' from the pool hall. He sat down at the kitchen table and commenced to eat the cold supper. I pulled out the other chair and sat across from him. Neither of us said anything for a bit, then he dug down in his pants pocket and slammed what was left of his paycheck on the table.

I remember just sitting there staring at that little heap of money. I said to him, "Jake, where is the rest of the money? I thought you was going to get paid today, paid forty dollars? That's not forty—Oh, Jake, what did you do? Did you gamble your pay in the pool hall? Jake—I was countin' on that money to pay some bills, and buy food for us and our kids. We can't expect our growing kids to live on rice and beans. You promised me that you wouldn't gamble a lot of money at a time. Jake you promised me!'

I can't forget how I felt that night. I was so disappointed in him--again. I felt the fear take ahold of me--felt my throat getting tight and the tears well up in my eyes, but I'd be damned if I was going to cry in front of him. I felt like I was going to burst but I didn't cry, no I didn't—not that night anyway.

All the memories finally got ahold of Raisa, and after she cried herself dry she dabbed at her puffy eyes with her apron, suddenly ashamed of letting herself go on like that. *I love Jake. I always have and I always will. We're blessed to have our kids. We just have to hang on a little longer. Things aren't always going to be this bad—I got to have faith—believe and have faith that it'll all get better. I've got to stop remembering all the bad times—like Dad always says –its water under the bridge. I think I heard on the radio that, 'things, good or bad, never last forever.'*

Raisa finished up the mending, packed the thread and needles away in the cardboard box and rose from the rocking chair. She looked out across the bare dirt front yard to the street. *I'm so thankful we finally moved into Lovell, even if it's into a rented* house. *I guess it was a blessing we lost the lease on that farm and Jake found work here in town. I hate everything about being out on a farm. I like living in town, at least I don't feel like a hick. I can't believe Beth is going to be a sophomore at Lovell High School this next fall and Arnie will be in the seventh grade. We want our kids to stay in school and get a better education than we got. Jake and I only got to the sixth grade, we don't know how to do nothin' but farm and do what other people tell us to do. It's kind of like that old Black Sea proverb; "For the first generation there is death; for the second there is want; only, for the third is there bread."*

Raisa recalled fondly the Confirmation photo they had taken of Beth along with Arnie. *She looked so sweet, so grown up—all dressed up like she was. Those two fight like cats dogs but are really inseparable—they look out after each other. Just last week, Arnie got in a fight with some guy who teased Beth about her freckles. Arnie still had a bit of a black eye in the photo, but I hid it with a little of my makeup.*

Beth (15) and Arnie Kessel (12)

Raisa got up early that Monday morning, before anyone else in the house. It was her first day of work at Tomlinson's. She stood in the doorway of the kitchen and listened to the soft sound of slumber wafting through the stillness of the house. She pulled the rag coils from her hair and ran a brush through the mass of curls. In her worn chenille robe and mismatched slippers, she padded to the east-facing front room window. The sky was clear and she could see a blush of red and mauve bursting from the gleaming silver crest of the Big Horn Mountains. As she stepped out on the front step to gather the milk bottles, Raisa smiled ever so slightly as she heard the early morning song of a meadow lark. Rubbing the back of her stiff neck, she headed for the kitchen to put the coffee on to boil.

Sipping a hot cup of coffee, Raisa thought about how last week, she had pushed open the white picket gate and walked up to the painted front steps of the white clapboard Tomlinson house to interview for the house-cleaning job. She and Shirley Tomlinson hit it off immediately and Raisa had the job by the time she left. Mrs. Tomlinson said, "I would like you to work five days a week, from nine to three, that way you can be home when your kids get out of school. Here's a daily agenda of what I would like you to do: laundry on Monday, ironing on Tuesday, baking on Wednesday, change the linens and clean the house on Thursday and grocery shopping on Friday.

"Also, Raisa, there will be days when I might ask you to prepare a light evening meal for us before you leave for the day. We can see how that works; Raisa, another thing, each day when you leave I want you to take the leftovers from yesterday's dinner as well as other things I will lay out. We are trying to get rid of excess things now that our kids are grown and gone from home. Harold and I just don't need all of this stuff. If there is anything you see, that you want or need, just tell me. I know times are tough and we need to help each other—agreed?"

I was pretty sure Mrs. Tomlinson would like how hard I worked. I always remembered what Dad taught us: 'Always give people more than they expect to get and you will keep your job!'

The Kessel family was all settled in and everything seemed to be going along fine for a change. Beth was involved with the Lutheran church youth group, The Walther League, which kept her busy with box socials or picnics up on the Big Horns. Sometimes they invited youth groups from other Lutheran churches in the Big Horn Basin, over to Lovell for a social evening. They had lots of fun, mostly just being around kids their own age and religion. Beth saved the programs, dance cards, notes from special boys, and the extra money she earned babysitting in a secret box, hidden under her bed.

It was around the beginning of Beth's sophomore year at Lovell High. Jake had gone to the pool hall, Arnie was at the picture show and Beth was at church where she and the Walther League group were entertaining the youth from the Lutheran church in Emblem. Arnie got home around nine and had gone to bed. Raisa sat in her rocking chair, listening to the radio and waiting for Beth to arrive. It was just after eleven when Beth burst through the front door.

"Mom, oh Mom—I had the very best time at 'league' tonight. I met these two boys from Emblem and I can't decide which one I like. They both acted like they liked me. They kept pushing each other away to sit next to me." Beth giggled with glee. "Isn't that just the best thing—I've never had two guys fuss over me before. Really Mom—one is tall, dark and handsome—his name is Arnold, but they call him Jimmy and his friend's name is Albert. He is shorter but has the curliest dark hair and sweetest dimples. I finally had to sit between them to keep peace! It was the best night ever, Mom!"

Later that fall, Beth decided she liked Jimmy the best. They dated off and on that year, going to dances, picnics in the mountains, and Sunday drives. She was still dating other guys, some that Jake and Raisa weren't that fond of. Beth was turning into a real looker and growing up so fast. Jake decided it was time that he set his daughter straight on how things were going to be with her dating and all. He waited for the right time, knowing he had to be careful in how he approached the subject.

One night after supper, Jake pushed back his chair from the kitchen table and said, "Beth, how about you helping me hoe the garden first thing in the morning. We need to get out there before it gets too hot—say, at sunup?"

Beth rolled her eyes as she walked from the room. "Sure Dad, rob me of my 'beauty sleep'---then you will have a heck of a time getting me married off!"

Just after the sun was up the next morning, Jake and Beth grabbed a couple of sharp hoes from behind the outhouse and walked to the huge garden. Jake pointed to the potatoes. "Why don't you start with them spuds? Hoe the dirt up around them in a mound so the spuds grow closer to the surface. I'll be a row over hoeing weeds out of the cucumbers." They worked for a few minutes before Jake stopped and leaned on his hoe, catching his breath. "Say, Beth, I been meaning to have a little talk with you since you have been dating quite a bit. It's like this—your mom and me, we got our rules: you can date whoever you want to, but when it comes time to getting hitched, it would be best to choose someone from our own religion. Just to keep the peace in the family and all if you know what I mean. If you decide to marry someone else, your mom and me won't be at the wedding and you won't be welcome in this here house anymore. That's the way it's been all along and I am damn serious about that. Things just turn out better that way for everyone involved, the families and all. Do you understand me?"

Beth stopped hoeing, wiped the sweat from her forehead and looked straight at her father. "Yeah Daddy, I get the picture. I know you don't like me dating Roger Hill, because he isn't Lutheran. But it's not like we are getting serious or nothing—he's just a really good dancer. I've got my eye on a good Lutheran—that fellow from Emblem. I just have to wait until he wakes up and gets serious--asking me out on a regular basis." Jake just smiled, gave a big sigh of relief and went on hoeing, happy that the little talk had gone so well.

Beth finished her part of the hoeing by 9:30. "I'm done with my side Dad. If you don't need me anymore or have anything else to talk to me about, I think I will go in and take a bath. Uncle Joe is picking me and Evie up to take us to that dance over in Cowley tonight."

Jake watched her walk to the house as he thought, "Where have the years gone? Our little girl is almost grown up. It's a darn good thing I had that talk with her so she don't go bringin' home someone who ain't gonna fit in with us. That would mean trouble, yes sir-ree—big trouble in my house!"

Beth thought this was as good a time as any to tell her mother of something she had done for a friend, impulsively. "Mom, Monday when Amy and I were walking to school, she admired the new scarf you knitted for me. She went on to say that she didn't get any presents for her birthday, not a one. Maybe I shouldn't have done it Mom, but I gave her the green scarf that Grandma crocheted for me. Mom, you should have seen her face. It made everything okay and she was so happy."

Raisa took her daughter into her arms and hugging her tightly. "You did the right thing. You make me proud, Beth. You always think of others and that is never a bad thing."

That next morning, Jake was eating and reading the *Lovell Chronicle* when suddenly he whistled and moved his chair back a ways. "Listen to this Raisa. 'Great dust storms spread across the Dust Bowl the normally dry areas of the Midwest, Texas, Oklahoma, southern Colorado, New Mexico and areas in Arizona are affected the most. The drought is the worst the United States has ever seen and the government predicts it covers over seventy-five percent of the country and parts of twenty-seven states.'

Jake stopped reading, shaking his head as he took another bite of his breakfast. He skipped over some of the article and then said, "Remember back in January when I told you about them cattlemen down to the east, who couldn't sell their cattle for more than they were worth? Lots of them just turn their herds loose to fend for themselves. Well, it seems that the federal government has gone in those areas and are buying them cattle from the ranchers for anywhere from $14 to $21 a head. Then, they go in there and herd them cattle into a hole and shoot all of of—just out right shoot them dead. The article said that they are saving some of the dead cattle to feed the poor, but most of them cows are nothing but a sickly bag of bones." Jake took a sip of coffee and turned the page of the newspaper.

"Over here it tells about how them farmers down on those prairie lands plowed up all the dry grassland, hoping to dry-land farm themselves some wheat. Well, with the drought, the wheat never came up and all that soil just blowed away. That prairie wind picks up that loose dirt and makes one hell of a cloud of dust. People can't even breathe and they are dying too. There's a picture of one of them dust clouds and it's downright spooky. Here, look at this."

FLESH ON THE BONE

Jake handed the newspaper over to Raisa so she could see the terrifying image of a monster dust cloud, as big as a thunderhead, rolling across the prairie and swallowing everything in its way. Raisa looked at another photo that showed fences buried half way up the posts, in dunes of wind-swept dirt. Farms were abandoned and left to die a lonesome death in the drought, wind and dust.

Raisa looked down at the table, thinking about all of those poor people. "You know Jake, we don't have it real good up here either, but it's not that bad. I guess that's why so many people are leaving those places and heading to California and other places up north to find a better way of life."

Jake pushed his chair back from the table. "That reminds me, the bank is having one of those foreclosure sales out at Heinrich Laubin's place today. I think I might run out there and take a look—see if I can pick up something at a low price. You know, Raisa, in a way I hate to go to them sales 'cause it's downright sad and depressing. Here's a guy that put his life's blood into a place, asked the bank to help out and then when the going gets tough, the banks come in and foreclose."

Jake was back at the house in a couple of hours. "Raisa, Raisa, where are you?"

Raisa came walking from the direction of the kitchen, wiping her hands on her apron. "Yeah Jake, here I am--what is it? Why are you back home so early? I didn't expect you back from the sale for another hour at least."

"Well, I tell you, that sale started off like most of them do, selling off a few of the livestock at rock bottom prices. There were farmers and ranchers there from all over the Big Horn Basin, hoping to get something for nothing. Then, the dam-est thing, I noticed, oh, about five fellows I didn't know, pulling the auctioneer aside and having a pretty in depth discussion with him. When the auctioneer got back up on the stage, he started right out, auctioning off the land. One of them fellows put up his hand and bid—six bits for forty acres. Then another of them gents bid eight bits. There was this one man, a stranger near the front, raised his hand to bid and suddenly the crowd pushed him out of sight. Then Heinrich Laubin bid five dollars for his forty acres and the auctioneer pounded the gavel down--- SOLD!"

Jake's steel blue eyes twinkled as he smiled widely and said, "I learned today that there sale is what is referred to as a 'penny auction'. It's what fellows do now-a-days—they get together to stop the banks from foreclosing on some guys' land—it'll work for a while anyways."

Raisa just shook her head and, looking at her husband, asked, "Jake, where is this Depression thing going to end up? So many folks is getting hurt, hurt bad. It almost makes me glad that we don't own a farm right now, 'cause we'd probably lose it.'

The next morning, bright and early, Raisa was up, cooked breakfast for her family, then gathered her things and was off to work. Raisa's house cleaning job with Mrs. Tomlinson had lasted just over a year. She liked working for Sally Tomlinson; they actually became friends and it was probably one of the easiest jobs she ever had. With the extra money Raisa made, she and Jake were able to put better food on the table and clothes on their backs.

Beth finished her sophomore year at Lovell High School and that spring; she was looking ahead to spending her junior year in Lovell with all her friends. Then, without warning, their world caved in.

Raisa was pulling weeds out front when she saw Jake's car coming down the dirt road in a cloud of dust. She straightened, stretching out her back as she looked up at the billowing white clouds that covered the sky with an impending storm. *I swear those clouds look like a whole crop of cauliflower just growing out of that blue sky.*

Raisa hurried up the front steps and into the house to tidy her hair and blot the sweat from her face. She watched through the screen door as Jake pulled up to the front of the house. He sat in the car for a bit before getting out. Keenly, Raisa noticed a particular slowness to Jake's normally quick pace as he walked up the dirt path to their rented house. A trickle of alarm slid down her back as he opened the screen door, hat in hand. Without speaking, Jake walked into the front room and sat heavily in the worn, over-stuffed chair. He just sat there, looking down at the floor. Instinct urged Raisa not to say a word. Sitting across from him, she waited for whatever it was he had to tell her.

"I just got let go at the garage. We are back at square one again, Raisa. I already checked around in town, nobody's hiring. So, I guess all we got is to try farming again. I heard of this place just outside of Cowley that's for rent."

That evening, Raisa and the kids cried and protested to no avail. Jake was adamant, "Damn it to hell—there are no jobs! What can't you understand about that? There is nothing I can do, I don't have me no education. All I know how to do is fix cars and farm. That doesn't mean I'm a no-account bum." He picked up the newspaper and threw it on the kitchen table. "Read it for yourself, what this federal man Harry Hopkins said just yesterday. *'Three or four million heads of households don't turn into tramps and cheats overnight, nor do they lose the habits and standards of a lifetime. They don't drink any more than the rest of us, they don't lie any more, and they're no lazier than the rest of us either. The earning population does not change its character which has been generations in the molding."* Jake was so angry his cheeks flushed red and his eyes bugged out. "I have to put some food on the goldamn table some way, any way I can--and that is all there is to it. So start packing, now!"

Later that week, Jake drove the car and loaded trailer into the farm yard of the old Jensen place. Raisa stared, unable to digest what her eyes were seeing. "Jake for heaven sake, are you telling me we have to live in t-t-this---this, shack? It looks like s-s-some falling-down outbuilding, not a house."

They got out of the car and walked toward the house. Jake took the broken-down steps to the front porch in one leap. Raisa stumbled as she climbed the steps onto the sagging porch. Hot tears rolled down her cheeks in spite of a weak attempt to hold back. She glanced back at the car where Beth sat unmoving in the back seat. Arnie stood at the foot of the front steps, hands shoved deep in his faded pants pockets.

Raisa turned to her husband. "Jake, please, can't we find something else? Anything would be better than this place. It's horrible—look at the floor; it's been used as a barn. The floor is full of manure and stained with urine. Jake, please!"

Jake stood, arms hanging limply at his sides. He glanced from his wife's face to stare out the grimy front windows, his eyes radiating the shame—shame he felt deeply because this was all he could give them. He wondered if he would ever be able to provide for his family—if he would ever feel like a man again?

`````

**September, 1938**

Jake and Raisa and their kids lived outside of Cowley and actually farmed the Jensen place for two years. Beth and Arnie were miserable at first, going to high school in Cowley where they had to make new friends all over again. They missed Lovell and the friends they had made there. Beth tried to make new friends, but she was never in the popular group because she didn't have the pretty clothes and the town ways, like some of the girls.

She started her senior year in high school that fall. One day after school, she burst through the front door. "Mom, Mom—where are you?" She found Raisa standing at the sink, up to her arms, canning tomatoes. "Mom, guess what? I've been elected president of the pep club. Isn't that just swell, Mom?"

Raisa dried her hands and gave her daughter a big hug. "I am so proud of you sweetheart, the kids must really like you." Beth beamed as she twirled around the kitchen, "And, that isn't all, I've been asked to the harvest dance in two weeks. Harold Regan asked me to go with him." She looked out the window, "That's not who I was hoping would ask me, but he's a nice guy and all. At least I'll get to go. Do you think you could finish that blue dress for me by then Mom?" Raisa knew her daughter was hoping Jimmy would ask her to the dance, but they were harvesting grain on their farm in Emblem and he didn't have time for dances.

Arnie didn't have the same issues with school and friends. He was always hanging around with a bunch of guys from school. They would find an old bushel basket, knock the bottom out of it and nail it to the garage or some building. One or another of the boys had a basketball. Raisa stood at the kitchen window watching Arnie and his buddies play a round of ball. *I love the sound of*
`````

those boys playing ball and the clunk of the ball as it hits the garage or ground. Arnie is getting pretty good at the game and growing like a weed! I think he is going to be tall and skinny like my dad. He's still got an ornery streak a mile wide.

On a lazy Sunday afternoon, about a week later, they were all sitting around listening to the radio when out of the blue Beth asked her mother a question. "Mom, I've been working on a paper for history class; it's a paper on family history, you know-- genealogy stuff. I don't even remember you telling us what happened to your grandparents and uncles, aunts, cousins, who didn't immigrate to the United States when your parents and you came over. Do you know what happened to them?"

Raisa stopped crocheting and looked up with a serious expression on her face. "We think we know; nobody knows for sure, but there were letters, letters that told of terrible persecution and famine. I remember one letter that my parents shared with us older kids. We all knew it was bad and getting worse around the time of the World War I; we'd had a few letters with only bad news. After the war, we didn't hear from many of our relatives again. We know that my grandparents all died from the harshness at that time, leaving their children and grandchildren. Those who still lived were persecuted by the Bolsheviks and the Russian people who hated and were jealous of the prosperity of the Germans. They took away all promises, land, and wealth, everything from the German residents. There were bad years of famine made worse by the greed of the Russians who took more and more of the grain as taxes. Josef Stalin escalated the persecution to a new level by taking control of everything and imposing collective farming, like sharecropping, on the German people. They executed village leaders, pastors, priests, anyone who talked against them.

"Over there, German people roamed the streets homeless and starved. Little children lay bloating and starving to death on the floors of their homes; they cried day and night until they cried no more. There was nothing the German people could do to help themselves. Stalin kept this news from the world for a very long time. If German peoples didn't have grain to give to the government, the soldiers ransacked their homes and dug up personal treasures they had buried to buy food with. The government took everything, everything. In the end, it is said that more than seven hundred thousand Germans perished at the hands of the Russians—executed by hunger, robbery, and pure brutality.

"Finally, the soldiers rounded up the Germans who were still barely alive and loaded them into boxcars or force-marched them to Siberia. Those who lived through the ordeal were forced to work in the mines and many more died. There were very few who survived. We know of no one in our family who survived."

When Raisa finished talking, Beth's cheeks were wet with tears. "Oh, Mom, that is horrible. What a terrible thing to go through and for those of us who are here, not being able to help them. Why didn't relatives here send them food?"

Raisa looked soulfully out the kitchen window. "We tried honey, but it only ended up in the hands of the Russians. There was nothing we could do to help them and they couldn't get out of the country."

Beth and Arnie found odd jobs on the weekends to make a little money. At least they were resilient and trying to make the best of the circumstances most kids during that time found themselves in. Arnie made the basketball team at Cowley High and that became his world. He didn't take much to girls those first couple of years in high school, but that too was about to change.

Beth saw how the other girls dressed and she tried hard to imitate them. She was determined to make a few dollars of her own to buy little extras with. Beth hired on to babysit and help women with their house chores. She knew there was little money for new clothes but her mother was really good at altering and restyling the skirts and dresses her sister Emilie or Mrs. Tomlinson gave her. Meanwhile, the Depression seemed to hang on and everybody wondered if and when it was going to end. They were all in the same boat—the one with the hole in the bottom!

One day, Raisa was at her ancient Singer sewing machine, working on a red skirt when Beth skipped into the front room with her hair all rolled up in rags. "Mom, is that skirt going to be ready by tonight? Uncle Joe and Uncle Adam said they would pick me up around seven. There's a big dance at Cowley and I would love to wear that red circle skirt. They are so good to me Mom, always watching out for any guy that might try to get fresh with me! And, I never have to sit out a dance, not when those two are around."

Raisa smiled to herself as she finished the red skirt later that afternoon. It was real pretty. She thought about her younger brothers and how they took Beth under their wing. Just then, the bedroom door burst open and Beth emerged. She had taken the rags out of her hair and brushed it until it gleamed. It laid smooth and soft in a perfect pageboy.

"I sure am glad I used a vinegar rinse on my hair when I washed it. Look how it shines. I think I finally got the idea of how to wrap the rags in my hair to set it. Does it look good, Mom?"

Raisa smiled as she handed Beth the red skirt. "It's real pretty honey. You'll be the bell-of-the-ball tonight. Go put the skirt on; the guys will be here soon."

That night, Beth danced every dance. She kept looking for Jimmy to show up and surprise her; she didn't really expect him because they were combining beans on his farm--but that didn't stop a girl from hoping. This one fella in particular came back several times, asking for a dance. Beth didn't like how Ned held her so close and put his face in her neck during the slow dances. But he was a great dancer and she was having fun.

At the end of a jitterbug, Ned suggested they go outside to cool off. He led her over to the corner of the porch where he spun her around. Holding her arms against her side, he pushed her back against the wall. Before Beth could respond, his lips came down on hers. Liking the kiss, he wanted more. But Beth's eyes opened wide as she shoved hard against his chest. "Stop it Ned. I said stop, please. Come on, Ned, this bank's closed! I don't do those sorts of things with you or anybody! Got that?"

Ned grabbed her arm and replied, "I don't get you. First you act like a live wire then you give me the icy mitt. You're nothing but a little teasing vamp." That was as far as he got as a large hand grabbed him by the shoulder and spun him around. The next thing Ned knew, he was literally sailing through the air—compliments of 'uncle' Joe Steiner!

Joe rubbed his knuckles as he took hold of Beth's arm and led her back inside the dance hall. "I've been watching that guy. He thinks he's a swank, a piker and you're his ripe tomato. I've noticed him laying his applesauce on you all night! Nothin' much gets by me, doll. You just gotta get more smarts when it comes to guys, and spot those drugstore cowboys before you get into a tight situation!"

Beth squeezed her uncle around the waist. "Oh, Joe, you slay me! Thanks for riding shotgun for me!" Beth stood on her tip toes and planted a quick kiss on Joe's cheek before as he twirled her out onto the dance floor.

Joe drove Beth home that night. He wasn't taking a chance that Ned might try to horn in again. Beth was all smiles as she watched her uncle drive off. She turned and walked up the front steps to the door. Her folks always left it unlocked when she was out and so she turned the knob and went in. She fell into bed and began to dream of being 'the belle of the ball'.

CHAPTER EIGHT

APRIL 1939: Jake rolled the Lovell Chronicle up in a big ball and threw it across the kitchen. "The news is nothing but bad, all over the world. It's a waste of time reading the papers or listening to the radio. The economy is still weak and that German lunatic Hitler is beefing up his armies and starting to push people around over there in Europe. He's going to mess around yet and start another world war if someone doesn't stop the greedy damn fool."

Raisa looked up from her crocheting and gently laid it in her lap. "Jake, I've been thinking we should drive over to Basin, to the courthouse and see about getting our citizenship papers. We weren't born in this country so we aren't natural citizens like our kids. It's something I've wanted to do—we should both do it. I've heard that a lot of peoples have been getting their papers, what with the way the world is going and all. If we do have another big war, we want to be legalized. What do you say; shall we drive over tomorrow, on your day off?"

Jake cocked his head to the side as he un-wrapped a stick of his favorite Black Jack gum and put it into his mouth. He chewed for a few moments, swallowed and then said, "Yeah Raisa, tomorrow afternoon is good for me---say we leave after the noon meal, around 1:30 or so?"

Two weeks to the day after they applied for citizenship, their official documents came in the mail. Raisa carried the mail to the kitchen table. Her breath caught as she carefully opened the official looking envelope. Slowly, she removed the document from the envelope and held it up in front of her face. *Oh my word, this is wonderful! It's really true--I'm a citizen of the United States of America. Now, we can really call ourselves Americans.* Raisa bought frames for their letters of citizenship and hung them on the wall in the front room.

~~~~~~

Beth had been waiting thirty minutes for her date to pull up in the front yard in his father's shiny black, Terraplane,[6] car. She hid behind the limp net curtain, spying out the window as he pulled into the yard. Jimmy cut the motor, opened the door and climbed out. Beth put her hand over her mouth to stifle a giggle. *He has a hairnet on his head. Why in the world is he wearing a woman's hairnet? Does he even realize he has it on?*

Jimmy paused a moment at the front door before knocking, he reached up with his right hand to smooth his dark wavy hair. Much to his horror, he felt the hairnet he used to hold down his thick, unruly damp hair as it dried. Blushing, he quickly pulled it off and stuffed it into his pocket, just seconds before Beth opened the door. "Hi, Jimmy, come on in, my folks want to say hi to you before we go to the dance. By the way, your hair sure looks nice. Did you just get it cut?"

Beth thought she noticed a slight blush as he quickly changed the subject and picked up a book lying on the table. "Oh thanks. Are you reading this book, *Grapes of Wrath,* by John Steinbeck? It just came out not too long ago, didn't it? I've heard it's pretty good."

Beth smiled sweetly, her eyes soft and glowing with love as she replied, "Well not really, my mother is reading it. She said it's all about the Great Depression. She sure does like it—says it tells it like it is. I'm not into reading about depressing stuff. Have you read it, Jimmy?"

Jimmy shoved his hands in the pockets of his dress pants, "No, not really; I've been too busy in the fields. I'm not much of a reader other than farm manuals and magazines—stuff like that. Well, are you ready to go? The dance doesn't get out until midnight and it'll take us at least an hour for me to get you back home. Is that okay with your folks?"

Raisa walked into the room just as Jimmy asked his last question. "Of course that's all right Jimmy. We don't worry when our Beth is with you. Have a good time and drive safely."

---

[6]

The front page of the local paper was full of the news that Germany had invaded Poland. On page two was a story about the graduating class of Cowley High School. Beth was both proud and relieved that she was finally graduating. Even though Jake and Raisa were very proud of their daughter, there were no big celebrations—nobody had extra money for something like that.

After graduation ceremonies, Jake and Raisa were waiting for her. They gave her a big hug and Jake said, "We are really proud of you, honey. With all the moving we did over the years and us pulling you out of school to work in the beets, we know it wasn't easy for you to keep up with your school work. But, you did it and so schooling is behind you! What are your plans tonight?"

Beth was all aglow with happiness as she kissed her folks. "Thanks Mom and Dad. You are right, it wasn't easy, but it's just like our speaker said tonight, *'Perseverance is not a long race; it is many short races one after the other'*. Oh, and—just don't wait up for me. Me and a bunch of the gang are going to a big dance at the ballroom in town." Beth smoothed her dress and gave her parents another hug. "I am so happy, now I can look for a real job and make some steady money to help out with all of our bills."

The next morning, Beth put her high school diploma in a drawer and went in search of a full time job. She found something, but it wasn't exactly what she'd been hoping for. She was hired to sweep up and stock shelves at the Lovell Rexall Drugstore. Beth really wanted to be a counter girl, but knew she had to wait in line for that job. Since her folks were still out on the Cowley farm, she was staying at the rooming house with her Aunt Lizzie. Out of every weekly paycheck Beth received that summer, she gave her aunt a dollar for room and board, held out a couple dollars for her own pocket, and the rest she handed over to her parents. All the kids she knew who were lucky enough to have a job turned their paychecks over to their parents to help pay off the family depression debts.

The spring thaw was in full force and Jake had been out in the yard all morning, working on the broken-down harrow. Beth and Arnie were both gone, working in Lovell. Jake's stomach told him it was dinner time so he headed for the house for the noon meal. After they finished off last night's leftovers, Raisa carried the dishes to the dry sink to soak in the dishpan. Jake was still at the table. She stood at the sink, slowly massaging her temples, trying to get rid of the migraine she'd woke up with that morning. Jake leaned back in the second-hand wood chair and out-of-the-blue, announced, "I have decided to farm this place another year!"

Raisa froze, and then turned slowly to face him. Her eyes flashed with anger; her head throbbed with a vengeance and her lower lip quivered. Raisa felt her grip tighten on the chipped white dinner plate she had in her hand. "Wha—what, did you just say Jake?" She took two steps toward him; her face was pale as death and her eyes narrowed in spite of the tears. "Did I hear you right? You are actually telling me that you expect the kids and me to live in this shack, on this god-forsaken pile of dust, for another year; live here another *year*, Jake? Our son sleeps on the back porch year round. The barn is even warmer than that place! The snow seeps through the cracks in the winter and in the hot summer months, the bugs invite themselves in!"

Raisa angrily wiped away the persistent tears. "I simply can't believe you expect us to live like this for another year. Another year of slaving like, like hired help in the fields we rent? You expect us to continue this humiliating nightmare? Well, it will be without me and the kids, do you hear me? I am not staying on this farm or any farm for another year or even another month!"

Without a second thought she raised the plate over her head and threw it against the far wall. There was not another sound in the room—no one moved, no one said a word. Raisa's whole body visibly trembled as she looked blankly at the floor, at the broken plate. Jake was frozen to the spot, shock flooding his face. He looked with dismay first at the plate and then at his wife.

Then simply reacting, Jake violently pushed back from the kitchen table. The chair he had been sitting in flipped backward, crashing to the worn wood floor. His lips were pinched tightly in anger as he slapped his hand hard, on the worn oilcloth-covered table. "Damn it, to hell, woman! Who do you think you are to question my decision of how I support this family? You know as well as I do there isn't much of anything out there for someone like me, but farming. You knew it when you married me. Face it, Raisa, you married a loser. I can't get a job because I had me no fancy education and I can't even make a living at farming. I'm good for nothing! That's what I am—end of story!" Jake gave the fallen chair a good kick, just because he felt like it.

Stunned and angry, Raisa remained rooted to the spot; her face was flushed and tendrils of damp hair clung to her forehead as she stuttered, "I, I have h-h-heard this story time and t-t-t-ime again Jake. I am tired of working like h-h-hired help. I work in the house and out in the fields until my hands crack and bleed. I know you've tried Jake, I know that. Even Michigan didn't w-w-work out for us. I know you've always felt your dad looking over your shoulder and it's even harder for you that some of your brothers are doing okay, but we continue to struggle. I know all this Jake and still I'm sorry, I just can't do this anymore. I can't stay here on the f-farm. It never ends, it never ever gets b-better and I am telling you---I am done with it. This life is killing me. I can feel it. It has devoured my spirit and all that's left of me is the flesh that's on my bones!" Raisa walked quickly past Jake toward their bedroom before pausing and turning back to face her husband. "I am moving to Lovell, with or without you!"

Jake's cheeks were red with anger and frustration as he shook his head in disbelief. "And how, Raisa, do you think you are going to support yourself and the kids? Have you even thought of that?"

Raisa inhaled deeply, squared her shoulders and took another step toward him. Tipping her head ever so slightly to the left, she said, "Yes, Jake I have thought of that and nothing but that for months, maybe even years. I can take care of me and the kids, just like my sister does. I will rent a room from her at the rooming house. God knows we aren't used to living high on the hog! I have already asked Ms. Tomlinson about getting my old job back. She said I can start as soon as I can manage. I'll work two jobs if I have to, to take care of me and the kids. Besides, they both have part time jobs and we will make it work."

She moved to leave the room, but had second thoughts. "Jake, have you ever thought of what it is like for me, living this kind of life? I've come to the end of the line of moving from one filthy rented house to the next. All my sisters and my friends have their own houses and I, I don't have nothin'. That's the pure truth. They might not live in fancy houses, but they have something to call their own—someplace to fix up and keep. I'm thirty-eight years old Jake, and I don't have nothin' nice, nothin' pretty, nothin' that I'm proud of except for my kids! You know, Jake, sometimes I don't even have hope. I feel like an empty shell, dried up and washed out. These sharecropper farms are sucking the life from me. I look and feel years older than I am, so I am just plain done with it all! I am sick and tired of having to smear mud and kerosene on myself and the kids to stave off the mosquitos and horseflies when we work in the fields. I'm just sick of it all and I'm not going to take it another minute! I've told you time and time again that I hate living on the farm. Of having people call us 'dirt farmers' and looking down their noses at us. You just aren't a farmer, Jake. God knows you have tried and I've hung in there with you, but now I'm done!"

Jake did the only thing he could think to do—he lit a cigarette, took a deep drag and blew the smoke out into the kitchen. He couldn't think of a thing to say to Raisa because he knew she was right and he knew he had some decisions to make.

Raisa kicked the shards of cheap glass to the side of the kitchen floor as she turned to walk out of the room. "I am going to pack up and if you won't take me into town, I'll call one of my brothers to c-come get me." She made it to the doorway this time before she turned around. "You know, Jake, you have to make your mind up now or we are through. I still love you Jake, but you ask too much of me---I c-can't live like this anymore. You have until tomorrow and then I'll be gone. And Jake, once I'm gone, I ain't comin' back."

Raisa crossed the floor to the bedroom. With all the anger and resentment in her, she slammed the thin wooden door as decades of dust exploded from around the warped door frame. She sat heavily on the side of the bed to collect herself, then rose and bent down to pull her second-hand suitcase out from under the bed. At that moment, she heard the car start up out in the front yard. Raisa pulled the limp window curtain back in time to see Jake behind the wheel of their old car. She watched as he angrily flipped his cigarette out the window, wheeled the Ford around and roared out of the yard, spinning gravel. He headed toward the highway in a cloud of dust.

Mortified by the reality of the situation, she stood, frozen to the spot. "Oh dear Lord, what have I done—what, have, I done? I just gave my husband an ultimatum and he walked out, he left!" Defeat, rage, hopelessness, and guilt filled her as her knees buckled and she slid to the floor. Raisa put her hands to her face as great gulping sobs came from deep within. After she cried herself out, her determination surfaced once again.

Raisa looked down at her hands---hands that shook with rage, fear, and being fed up. She stood up, turned and saw her image in the mirror on the wall. She said, "I can't believe Jake walked out. I've really fixed myself. Now, what am I going to do?" Raisa paused a moment and then, taking a deep breath, she looked straight ahead and with stubborn determination she declared, "I am going to do what I said I would, and I'm getting started right now!"

She stood for a minute longer, taking in the contents of the house. A wood table that had to be thirty years old, accompanied by five mismatched chairs, two long benches against one wall, a couple of kerosene lamps, an old wood cook stove, limp burlap curtains at the windows, two ancient, creaking iron-spring beds, orange crates nailed against the wall, acting as kitchen cupboards, and a rusty iron hand pump on the edge of the tin sink. She thought to herself, *I'm not leaving much, it has to get better than this, it just has to! I'll take the table and chairs, my sewing machine, rocking chair, the bed linens and a few dishes and pans.*

When Raisa got around to packing up the small kitchen, she was out of boxes, so she yanked the orange crates off the wall. *These orange crates will work better as my moving boxes.* It didn't take long to fill two of the crates up because there wasn't much worth packing. *I just feel dead on my feet with all this.*

She retreated to the bedroom. Plumb worn out, she lay down on the squeaky spring bed. Her eyes closed with exhaustion and she slept. When Raisa awoke, the room was dark and a deafening silence filled the house. It took a few moments for her to realize where and why she was in bed and alone in the house. A dark fear washed over her as tears clouded her eyes and rolled down her cheeks. *I guess I am going to have me a good cry whether I want it or not. I know I'll feel better to get it all out.*

Just as the sun broke free from behind the Big Horn Mountains, Raisa woke a second time. She lay in her bed for only a moment or so and then rolled over and sat up. Taking a deep calming breath, she prepared to face whatever awaited her. She swung her legs over the edge of the sagging bed then rubbed her red and puffy eyes; they stung from crying half the night.

She stumbled into the far corner of the front room they called a kitchen and lit the kerosene lamp. Raisa turned to the dry sink and poured some water into the bowl; she cupped both hands to splash the water onto her face. *Oh my goodness, that feels so good—just what I needed.* She gazed out the tiny kitchen window at the back yard. *It's a good thing both of the kids stayed in Lovell working this week. Jake still hasn't come back and only God knows where he spent the night. Where is he? What is going to happen to us now? I guess if he isn't home by the time I finish up in here, then I'm going to have to call Jack or Joe to come pick me up. They'll tell me I've made my bed and now I have to lay in it and, that's a fact. It's what I had to do—it's all I have left. I know one thing, Jake better not think that I've changed my mind, not this time!*

Raisa turned toward the yard when she heard a car pull up out front. It was Jake. Raisa put the last box beside the door and mentally braced herself for another battle.

She watched as Jake pulled to a stop, got out of the car and headed for the house, she noticed how stooped his shoulders were, his head was down and his steps were resolute. Jake climbed the broken-down steps to the porch and walked in. Without saying a word, he removed his faded wool jacket and his all too familiar

FLESH ON THE BONE

newsboy hat. He didn't hang them on the hook by the door like he usually did; he just held them in his hands.

Jake turned to face his wife. "Raisa, I want you to sit down. I have something to say to you before I drive you into Lovell, if that's what you still want."

Raisa took a deep breath and sat at the table, ready for another outburst of nasty temper from her husband. She crossed her legs and her arms in front of her body in a subconscious protection mode. Jake looked down and slid a kitchen chair out, sitting across the table from her. He fumbled around in his coat pocket and pulled a folded paper out, then spread it on the table. "This paper, Raisa, is the deed to a house! I went and bought us a house in Lovell—if you'll stay and give me another chance, we can leave this farm together."

Raisa reached across the table and picked up the paper, holding it up she read it. Slowly she lifted her face as her eyes met Jake's. "How did you buy a house? Where did you get the money, to buy a house?"

Jake stood, shoved his hands deep into his pants pockets. "Raisa, I'm sorry that I didn't see what this life is doing to you and the kids. I'm a stubborn, crazy damn fool and thought only of what I wanted or thought I wanted. I got the money for a down payment on the house by selling Babe and Bart along with a few pieces of farm equipment. Those things weren't worth much. Farmers aren't using horses to farm with anymore but Hugh Black at the horse ranch gave me a good price for both horses. Anyway, Raisa, that gave me enough to put a down payment on a small house on Shoshone Avenue, just down from the school and our church. The asking price was $375 and I got them to knock it down to $350. Our payments are less than what we were paying to rent. I think the monthly payment will be around eleven dollars."

Jake moved to stare out the one window on the east side of the house. "Raisa, I'll be the first to admit that I don't have much learnin', in a school house that is. I have learnt all my lessons by the seat of my pants, just like I'm learnin' this one." He turned to face her, his blue eyes filled to the brim with tears. "Raisa, if you leave me---if you take our kids, then I have nothing. I don't have no reason to breathe, I don't have no reason to work or keep on trying. What's the use of lookin at the sunrise or sunset? Why keep on tryin to find a new way to make us some money, if there ain't no us? If there's no us, Raisa, then there is no me, pure and simple. Raisa, honey—you and our kids are the reason I keep slammin' my head against the wall. Please, Raisa, please know how much I love you and our two kids—you are all I have that's worth a tinker's damn!"

Jake sat down at the table in front of her, hands lying flat on the table. "Honey, this house in Lovell ain't much. They moved it in from Frannie and sat it onto a concrete foundation. It's only four rooms. It has a garage and an outhouse. And, uhhh, Raisa—the outside of the house is covered in tar paper. There's no siding on it. B-but, but we can stucco it easy, when we get the money. It's got no yard to speak of, but there's lots of room for a big garden out back. For now, we have us a house of our own, in Lovell, some place we can fix up together."

Jake reached across the table, not knowing if she would let him touch her. He took her hand in his. "Will you stay with me? Will you move into Lovell with me—you and the kids? I know I'm not much, but without you and our kids—Raisa, I'm nothing, I have nothing. You're the only good thing I've done in my life."

Raisa started to say something as Jake put his hand out and a finger in front of his mouth.

"Raisa, I know I'm bad-tempered and I don't treat you and the kids like you deserve to be treated sometimes---but you've always been my rock, my safe harbor from everything that life has thrown at us. I love you, woman---I've loved you for too many years to throw it away just like that. I have no reason to go on, if I don't have you. Please Raisa, give me, give us another chance, 'cause I love you, I love you and our kids."

Jake walked to the front window and stared out before turning to face her. "You know, I remember all those years that my dad told me that I wasn't a farmer and I never would be one. It was something I think I kept trying to prove to him or to me—to prove him wrong. Who in the hell knows, but when it comes down to it, that isn't what matters, is it?" Jake pulled Raisa to her feet and took her into his arms. "I promise honey, I'll stop going to the pool hall so much, and I'll work two or three jobs to make the payment on that house and keep us going. Hopefully, something good will come along and you can quit working altogether. Is it a deal, huh? Please, Raisa, *please* say you will give me another chance."

With tears glistening on her cheeks, Raisa buried her face in his neck as her arms embraced his lean body. Gently, she pushed him back so she could look into his face. "Jake, I heard something the other day about not accepting someone else's definition of your life. That you should define yourself. I like that Jake, I think maybe you need to remember that—to be your own man, not who your father thinks you should be, and you need to stop trying to prove something, anything, to him. Now, let's go see this house you just bought! We'll stop and pick up the kids on the way."

Jake grabbed her and wrapped his arms around her tightly then laid a sweet kiss on her lips, one that she wouldn't soon forget. Raisa began to struggle in his arms, "Jake, Jake—you are hurting me—stop, squeezing me so hard!"

Jake relaxed his grip and Raisa wriggled free. She laid a quick kiss on his lips and grabbed her purse. "Well, let's get going."

Arnie and Beth sat in the backseat as they drove down the street toward what was to be their new home. Without looking or asking, Raisa knew what they were wondering—*is this place was going to be any better?*

When they pulled up in front of the house on Shoshone Avenue, Raisa was struck dumb. Somewhere from the backseat, she heard Arnie snicker. Then, Beth began to cry, "What is that? Noooo, we can't live in that house, it's ugly! It gives me the heebie jeebies, it's worse than the last place! Look at it, with that tar paper nailed to the outside, no siding? How can we live in that thing in the winter? The snow will come right through the walls! It's completely embarrassing, Dad."

The house was a literal cube, with the front door placed between two double-hung windows. There were two windows on each side of the house except the back where there was a lean-to porch and one rectangular window. The roof looked like a cone with a brick stove chimney poking out to the left of the peak. Somehow Raisa found the inner strength to open the car door. "Jake, can we go inside?"

Arnie jumped out of the car and ran around to the back of the house. He circled the entire house before his folks were even on the front porch. "Hey, it's got a little shed or garage where I can nail up my hoop and an outhouse clear to the back."

Beth shrieked, "An outhouse? You mean it doesn't have a bathroom inside? This is all too embarrassing, it's horrible. What are my friends going to think, for Pete's sake?"

Arnie looked with amazement at his older sister. "Beth, just quit being a wet blanket, will ya? It's got four walls and even a roof. Besides that, it's real close to school—it'll be perfect for me going back to Lovell High School in the fall." Grinning from ear to ear, he jabbed his sister in the ribs and added, "Ya just can't go out to the outhouse when it's recess at the school, 'cause they'll see ya!" Arnie slapped his newsboy cap on his thigh and crossed his arms over his stomach as he doubled over in laughter.

Jake opened the front door for Raisa and she walked slowly into the house. He flipped on the light switch. Hanging by a long cord from the middle of the room, a single blub glowed faintly through years of dust and fly droppings. "See Raisa, it even has electricity and a sink in the kitchen with running water! No more of those dry sinks or hand pump next to the sink. The next thing we will have to put in is an indoor bathroom; we already have running water in the house."

Raisa flung her arms around Jake, "I love that there is running water in the kitchen. I'd rather have that than siding over the tar paper, for now anyway. Are you serious about having a bathroom put in the house? That would be heavenly." She started to walk away and then with a sly grin said, "But Jake, where would my sisters and I go to talk secretly if we don't have an outhouse?"

Twenty minutes later, Jake and Raisa walked out the front door. Raisa had a pad and pencil in her hands and was busy writing things down as they headed for the car. Jake finally got up the nerve to speak, "Well, Raisa, I told you it wasn't much, but now that it's ours, we can fix it up a little at a time, when we have the extra money. We can fix it up, just the way you want it."

Raisa smiled as she tucked the pad into her purse. "I know Jake, I know. At least, it's *our* house and we don't ever have to move ever again. That makes it all worthwhile!"

They moved into their less than modest house in Lovell that early summer just as the earth was waking and new beginnings were in the air. They moved in with an odd assortment of furniture; some they already owned and some was donated by their family and friends. Raisa went back to work for Mrs. Tomlinson at thirty-five cents an hour. At the end of the month she cashed her first check and went to Winterholler's Grocery on the corner of Shoshone Avenue to stock up on a few things. Raisa bought a pound of coffee for twenty-five cents, two dozen eggs for twenty cents, and a loaf of bread for nine cents and two pounds of hamburger for twenty-six cents. After she paid the grocery bill, she went to the Lovell Rexall Drug and splurged on a jar of her favorite cold cream and a beautiful green-tinted glass sandwich tray. She thought to herself, *I love the sandwich tray. Now I have something nice to serve food to guests on. It feels wonderful to pay cash for things again and even have spare money to buy a few extras.*

Now when I walk down the street, I can hold my head up high and feel like I'm just as good as the rest of them. Things are gettin' better and I like it that way.

Jake Kessel building silage silos in Lovell, WY.

Jake found erratic work building solid brick silos for farmers in the area. At the end of July, he was hired on at the County Weed & Pest Control. He traveled the county spraying mostly Morning Glories and Russian thistle along the roads and ditch banks; it was a seasonal job he held for the next two summers. After the first freeze that fall, Jake's job ended with the county and he decided to pay a visit to the Ford dealership in Lovell. As luck would have, he got back on as part-time mechanic at the Ford garage. At the end of two months he was full time and that helped to ease the pressure of debt. Jake had been thinking about something special he could do for Raisa and now he had some extra money.

The next morning Jake was up before dawn. He dressed quickly and tiptoed through the house, then quietly let himself out the back door. He was smiling as he walked out back to the shack they called a garage and slipped inside.

When Raisa woke, she lay in bed for a while, and not hearing any sound, she crawled out of bed and slipped on her new pink chenille robe. Opening her bedroom door, she walked quickly to the kitchen. *The house is too quiet, I don't understand what is going on I didn't even hear Jake get up—where is he*? Raisa turned and hurried into the front room—still no Jake. Back in the kitchen she looked out the window, thinking he might have gotten up early to work in the garden. There he was in the back yard with a shovel, digging two holes in the grass about twenty feet from the house.

Raisa ran down the back steps and flew out the screen door. "Jake, what in the world are you doing?" That's when she saw the willow tree saplings laying on the grass, waiting to be planted. "What, w-w-hat, w-where did you get those willow trees? You are planting willow trees in our back yard? Oh Jake—Oh Jake, you remembered how much I love willow trees." Raisa threw her arms around Jake's sweaty neck and planted a big kiss on him. "Just imagine how nice it is going to be to sit under the shade of these trees. They will shade the house and help with the heat of the afternoon sun. Oh, honey—this is the sweetest thing I think you have ever done."

Pleased with himself, Jake replied, "Well, they grow pretty fast, but don't hold your breath. It's gonna be a while before they're big enough to shade the west side of the house. In the meantime, Mrs. Kessel, do you realize you are out here in your pink bathrobe for all the neighbors to see?"

During the summer, Beth moved up to counter girl at the Rexall Drug in Lovell and that fall, Arnie tried out for a spot on the Lovell High School basketball team. He made the team and was busting his buttons he was so proud to be a Lovell Bulldog. If he wasn't at home eating everything in sight, he was somewhere shooting baskets.

Beth was seeing a lot of that special guy from Emblem. Raisa thought, *I'm not blind: it looks like things might be getting serious. Jimmy is a few years older but owns his own farm along with his brother Ed. He's the youngest in a German Lutheran family of eight and lives in a large white-frame farm house with his widowed mother, Mazie. I'm not crazy about the fact that Beth is getting serious over a farmer, but he does have a house and he is Lutheran. He's pretty darn handsome to—reminds me of the movie actor, Robert Taylor!*

A year later, the Kessel house on Shoshone Avenue was still covered in tar paper but the family was making small improvements when they could. Things were beginning to work out just fine.

The first week in December, Beth picked up her check from the drugstore and when she went to hand it over to her parents, she held back a bit. "Mom, Dad—I need a little more out of my paycheck this month. Jimmy invited me to Emblem for Christmas to meet his mother and family. He said he'd pay for my bus ticket to Greybull and that he'd drive me home after Christmas. I need to get him a present and maybe something nice for his mother as well."

Jake and Raisa looked at each other, and smiling, gave their permission because they liked this young man and Beth was so happy.

That evening, Raisa knocked on Beth's bedroom door. "Beth, I would like to talk to you, do you have a minute?"

Beth opened the door, "Sure, Mom, what's up? I'm just rolling up my hair before I go to bed."

Raisa sat on the bed and patted a place next to her. "I want to have a little talk with you, about Jimmy." Raisa noticed that Beth's head cocked to one side and she seemed edgy.

"What do you want to ask me about Jimmy? I told you all about Christmas."

Raisa smiled and patted Beth's leg. "Oh honey, relax-- I was just wondering – well, how serious are you and Jimmy getting? Being invited to spend a holiday at his house, now that tells me this has gone beyond the boyfriend stage."

Beth pulled her feet up on the bed and wrapped her arms around her knees. A dreamy expression appeared on her face at the mere mention of his name. "Oh Mom, I am real serious about him, and I think he feels the same way. I think I knew he was the one when we were dancing at the Lovell Harvest Ball last fall. I just felt, well—I felt all warm and tingly inside when he wrapped his arms around me and spun me around on the floor. I wondered then if my feet even touched the floor. I never really knew what love felt like, but I think I know now. I'm in love with him, Mom—when he looks at me, I feel---I feel, well, real special. And, he treats me so good. He tells me over and over how much he loves me too, Mom."

Raisa wrapped her arms around her daughter and, swallowing a large lump, said, "We just want you to know that we think he is a wonderful young man; it helps too that he's a Lutheran. I guess I wish he didn't farm. I never wanted you to have to live on a farm because it is such hard work. But, Jimmy owns his own farm and you'd be starting off living in a big white house. It wouldn't be like it was for your Dad and me. Just take it slow, Beth, and make sure he's the one because once you are married, you are married for a very long time!"

"Aw, Mom, thank you. I'm glad you and Dad like Jimmy. I gotta get to bed—get my beauty sleep. I have to be at the drugstore by eight in the morning. 'Night Mom—I love you! By the way, there's a special present under the tree for you and Dad from Arnie and me---sure hope you like it."

BETH:

On December 24th, Jake put Beth on the Greyhound bus to Greybull. "Have fun, honey, and say hello to the family from us too." In a lower voice, he mentioned, "Just you make sure about the sleeping arrangements, you hear!"

Beth was mortified, "Daaaad, don't even say that. Jimmy already told me I would be sleeping upstairs with his sister. I'm so excited and sorta nervous too. I hope his mother likes me. You know, he has five sisters, but most of them are married! Oh golly, I've simply got butterflies I'm so excited! I always wanted a sister."

Beth (20) and Arnie Kessel (17)

Jake managed a crooked little smile as he waved goodbye to his first-born, his only daughter. Beth pressed her pert, freckled nose against the cold window of the bus and waved back, until she couldn't see her father standing at the curb.

Jimmy drove Beth back to Lovell the day after Christmas. She was absolutely bubbling over with excitement. "Oh, and Mom, Mrs. Wamhoff is so sweet and his sisters and their husbands and kids were nice too. The house is big. It has an upstairs and even an indoor bathroom with a huge pink tub and toilet! Will you look at what Jimmy gave me—Evening in Paris perfume. Isn't it divine?"

Raisa wrapped her arms around her daughter and teased her a bit, "Sounds like you've been bitten by that ole' love bug, huh? By the way, Dad and I love the picture, a last picture of you and Arnie before you go and get yourself all married!"

On Good Friday, Jimmy popped the question and put a ring on Beth's finger, after first asking her parent's permission to marry their daughter, that is. That next weekend, Raisa drove Beth to Billings to Hart Albin department store, where they bought her wedding dress.

On the way home, Beth turned to her mother and asked, "Mom, what makes a good marriage? What does a good wife do?"

Raisa thought for a moment then replied, "The best advice I can give you honey is, if you and Jimmy have a disagreement and you forgive him—don't reheat his sins for breakfast." They both laughed as Raisa added, "Marriage isn't easy Beth, there's a lot of give and take and lots of the time you are probably going to feel like you are doing all the giving. But nothing ever stays the same, just try to be a good wife and take care of the house and the children like I did." Raisa smiled as she thought of something, "There's an old Scottish proverb that my Dad shared with me before I was married—*'It is a sad house where the hen crows louder than the rooster'!* It's a good thing to keep in mind if you know what I mean."

Beth laughed nervously as she looked out the window then blurted out her next question, "Mom, uuuhh...I've been wondering, about t-t-the--what about the wedding night?" Raisa reached across the front seat and stroked her daughter's cheek, "Don't worry about that honey. Jimmy is older than you; it will all take the natural course." Beth continued to look out the window as she thought to herself, *well, that didn't answer anything! I still don't know exactly what is going to happen. I think Mom's a little embarrassed talking about that stuff. Guess I will just have to do what I have to do!*

The next few months flew by as Raisa and Beth were consumed with wedding plans and making bridesmaid's dresses. Beth asked her cousin, Lillian to be her maid-of-honor and Jimmy's cousin, Betty June to be a bridesmaid. Jimmy's best friend, Albert agreed to stand up for him as best man and Beth's brother, Arnold as a groomsman. Albert laughed and slapped his friend on the back, "Well, hells bells, I guess if I can't have that little doll, I am happy that my best friend is going to marry her."

Jimmy and Beth Wamhoff
on their wedding day

Beth and Jimmy were married on September 28, 1941, a beautiful crisp fall day, at the small, yellow clapboard Lutheran church in Lovell. Raisa looked adoringly at how beautiful her daughter appeared in her gown of soft white tulle with a wide satin sash. Her veil was edged with delicate Alcon lace and fell from a crown of seed pearls. Beth chose a lovely pale shade of peach roses for her bouquet. She was a beautiful, traditional blushing bride! Jimmy's white shirt was crisply starched and set off by a new double-breasted navy blue pinstripe suit. He was so tall and handsome, just like Robert Taylor the movie actor. Beth and Jimmy made a beautiful couple. Raisa and Jake couldn't have been happier.

After the ceremony, as they were standing to the side, Jake commented quietly, "Well, I can rest easy now; she married a Lutheran!" He laughed wickedly and then paused as he looked away, suddenly choked with emotion. "Ya know, Raisa, I have to admit I got pretty worked up, standing there with our daughter, waiting to walk her down the aisle. I asked myself, 'when did she get all grown up?' I had all these crazy thoughts about here I was, giving her away to another man. It dawned on me that she wasn't all mine anymore."

After the newlyweds left on their honeymoon trip, Jake stood up and addressed all of the wedding guests. "Raisa and I would like to invite everyone here to the *Hochzeit* dance this coming Saturday night at the community hall in Lovell. As most of you know, Raisa comes from a Volga German family and they have only one way to celebrate a wedding and that's with a *Hochzeit* polka band! Jake hired the best polka band in the Big Horn Basin and bought several kegs of good beer in preparation.

Beth and her new husband spent two days in Billings and then drove back down to Lovell in time for the *Hochzeit* celebration. People carried in heaping platters of traditional food which they put on a long covered table. The German band began to play as people flooded the dance floor. The band took only one break around 11 p.m. Most everyone stayed until the end, not wanting to miss a dance. They had themselves a good old fashioned Dutch Hop—dancing the polka all night with a few slow ones thrown in. According to tradition, the men who danced with the bride tucked money in the little purse attached to her belt.

After the dance broke up, Jimmy and Beth drove back to their home in Emblem in the wee hours of the morning, exhausted but happy. Jimmy had to get back to the farm to help his brother Ed finish threshing the bean crop. The new day was just breaking over the Big Horns to the east, when the newlyweds drove down the lane of cottonwood trees to the big white farm house. Beth had fallen asleep, leaning against her husband's shoulder. When she felt the car slow and turn off the highway, she opened her eyes and was immediately surprised to see the old farm house had a fresh coat of sparkling white paint. "Oh Jimmy, you didn't tell me you painted the house. It looks just wonderful. I can't believe we live in such a beautiful house. I'm a lucky girl to have you and a big white house too."

On December 7, 1941, Beth was preparing their Sunday morning breakfast and listening to the radio. Jimmy was out in the barn milking their three cows. She looked out the window and saw him close the barn door and begin walking toward the house, carrying two full buckets of fresh milk. She turned to the stove and began to spoon out their hot oatmeal.

Beth wiped her hands on her apron, turning slowly towards the countertop radio. Internal alarm gave her goose flesh; she moved closer to hear exactly what the broadcaster was saying. Her face lost all color as her blue-green eyes opened wide with understanding. She ran for the back door, flung it open and was halfway down the wood walkway as Jimmy came through the picket-gate with the milk. "Jimmy, come quick—the announcer on the radio said something about Japanese planes bombing some island called Pearl Harbor--someplace in Hawaii! There are thousands of Americans dead, Jimmy. It sounds real bad. I didn't hear it all." Beth moved in front of her husband. "Here, let me hold the door for you while you go inside. Just sit those buckets down by the separator and come on in here by the radio."

They sat at the kitchen table listening to the President of the United States address the country. Jimmy turned to Beth. "You know what this means don't you? We are at war with Japan." He rose and walked to the window, gripping the windowsill with his thick calloused hands. "I know a lot of guys will be signing up, but you don't have to worry, they won't take me 'cause I'm a cripple!"

Beth pushed back from the table and hurried to her husband's side, wrapping her arms around his shoulders. "Don't ever talk like that. You are not a cripple. You just have one leg shorter than the other from the accident. You do most things just fine and I love you just the way you are. I know you don't like it that you can't serve, but I am thankful you won't be going away from me to fight in a war. There are lots of things we can do here at home to help with the war effort." Beth turned her husband around and cupped his face in her hands, "Jimmy, they won't take you or your brother either because you are both farmers and the government needs food for the soldiers."

They spent Christmas in Lovell at her parents' house, which made Beth happy, in spite of having a 'touch of something'. As she and her mother stood at the kitchen sink washing and drying the dishes, Raisa remarked, "You didn't eat much honey, are you feeling okay? You look a little pale. Do you want to go in and lay down?

Beth forced a smile in spite of a persistent nausea. "Oh, it's nothing Mom. I just have a touch of something. I probably ate something that didn't agree with me or I picked up a bug that's going around."

That Christmas, most folks weren't in a celebrating mood; everyone was too worried about the war. Later, as the family sat around the dining room table playing a few hands of pinochle, the conversation again turned to the war. Arnie piped in nonchalantly, "Lots of guys who are graduating in May are talking about signing up." He shoved his chair back from the table and declared, "I guess I'm glad I'm only a junior. All I'm interested in for now is playing basketball and going to dances."

Jake, Raisa, and Arnie were invited to the farm in Emblem for Easter dinner. Beth prepared the entire dinner by herself. Raisa noticed her daughter had put on a little bit of weight. She thought to herself, *it's probably eating all this good food here on the farm and being happily married.* After dinner they were sitting around the table, finishing off the Easter Cake and coffee, when Jimmy rose and went to stand behind Beth. Proudly, he put his hands on her shoulders, "We have an announcement. You are going to be grandparents in August! Beth is in the 'family way.'"

Beth blushed profusely and her eyes filled with tears. Jake and Raisa were thrilled with the news as was Jimmy's mother, Mazie. Mazie put a protective arm across Beth's shoulders, "Don't you worry about a thing honey, I'm right here in the house in my apartment any time you need a hand. Oh my, a new baby in this house. It's been twenty-seven years since that happened. I am so excited to be a grandmother again." Mazie looked at Jake and Raisa, "This will be your first grandchild, am I correct?"

Jake and Raisa were beaming as Raisa replied, "That's right, this baby will be our first grandchild and in fact, it will be the first great-grandchild for both of our parents." Raisa turned to Beth, "I thought you had a special glow and I was right. You know, I think Grandma Kessel has a beautiful, hand-made cradle stored in the barn attic. We'll have to see about that, next time we are over there."

CHAPTER NINE

The end of May, 1942 proved to be a typical Wyoming spring, snowing one day and sun shining the next as the resilient green grass poked through the remaining spots of crusty brown snow. Jake had been working at the Ford garage all day and Raisa expected him home for dinner around six. It must have been close to 3:30 when she heard hurried footsteps on the back porch as the back door burst open. She turned from the sink just as Jake strode into the kitchen.

"Jake, what is wrong? You are home way early; I don't know if I can handle bad news."

Jake picked his wife up and whirled around the room with her in his arms as she squealed, "Jake, J-J-Jake, put me down. Have you been drinking? What is the matter with you?"

Jake pointed to the kitchen chairs, "Come and sit a spell with me, Raisa. I have some great news to tell you—it just might be the break we've been waiting for and I think you need to be sittin' down." He opened the cupboard and pulled out two small crystal glasses as well as the bottle of Mogan David wine. "We need to celebrate. I know I need something to calm me down and I expect you're probably gonna need a little calming down too, after you hear what I've got to say." He poured the wine into the two glasses and pushed one across the table toward Raisa.

Jake took a sip of the wine, wishing it was something stronger, "Honey, like I said, I got a feelin' that this is the break we've been waitin' for. I just signed Arnold and me up to help build what they call a relocation camp for the Japs they are rounding up from inside the States. Have you heard about that? The government is afraid the Japs might have strong alliances with their home country and they may sabotage important areas while we're at war with Japan. So they are roundin' them up, loadin' them on trains and putting them in locked-up camps all over the country."

Raisa's eyes opened wide and Jake couldn't tell if it was from the sip of the wine she just took or what he said. "Jake, you mean they are bringin' Japanese peoples here to Lovell? When, and how many are there gonna be? Are we gonna be safe with them living here right next to us?"

Raisa stood to gaze pensively out the kitchen window. She turned back to Jake as she said, "That scares me Jake. It really scares me that we'll have so many of those people living so close to our town. What if they break out?"

Jake smiled, "Aw, come on, Raisa. These people are not as big a threat as our politicians would have us think. Most of them are humble farmers and a few shop owners; they are scared and shocked that the government would do something like that to them. Our government went in and sold everything these people owned, out from under them and loaded them on trains. Does that sound wrong to you? It's like a witch hunt if you ask me.

Anyway, this is our big chance to get somewhere. The feds hired about two thousand of us guys and we're gonna build the relocation camp over between Cody and Powell—I hear they are callin' it the Heart Mountain Relocation Camp[7], but us guys call it Little Tokyo. They want us to start on it the first of June and it's gotta be finished by August. Guess we aren't gonna be putting a lot of finishing touches on those barracks." Jake stood and looked out the window. "You know Raisa that makes me wonder if we go to war with Germany, they could be building some of those relocation camps for those of us with German heritage."

Excited, Jake began pacing the kitchen floor. "Raisa, Raisa—hey, I am telling you, they're payin' us real good. So good that by the time Arnie and I help get the place built, we should have enough money to stucco this house and remodel the inside with an extra bedroom and a new kitchen/laundry room and that bathroom I've been promising. Think I'll have them dig a small basement area, big enough for a central air furnace and cool cellar to store your canned goods over the winter. And, we can get rid of

---

that gas stove in the front room. How does that sound to you, Mrs. Kessel?"

Raisa couldn't help herself as tears flowed from her eyes. She blew her nose and wiped her eyes as she stood and wrapped her arms around her husband. "Oh, Jake, oh, Jake—I can't believe this is happening." She pushed him back and looked him in the eye, "A new kitchen for me *and* an indoor bathroom--with a real tub and toilet? You aren't pulling my leg are you?"

Jake and Raisa danced around the kitchen, or what was actually a corner of the fourth room where they ate and did the laundry. Her head was filled with ideas for fixing up the house, *maybe even some big windows in the front room and dining room. And a nice wide cement porch out front where we can sit on hot summer nights. We could even get rid of that ugly cramped, screened-in porch in the back where Arnie sleeps with the dog year around. He could have his own bedroom inside the house.* They both went to sleep that night with visions of money and a decent-looking house dancing in their heads. "Happy Days" were here again, and they both hoped it was for good!

It was close to the middle of July when Jake and Raisa were finally ready to go ahead and hire a contractor to remodel their house on Shoshone Avenue. The Heart Mountain crew hadn't quite finished building the relocation center, but Jake had enough money in the bank to pay off their final Depression debts and get started fixing up their home. Raisa went down to the hardware store and picked out their new bathtub, toilet, and sink. That was the day she meet Sadie Ritter, book keeper, sales girl and general 'go-fer' at the store. She introduced herself and said, "I think I have seen you at church. Do you and your husband attend St. John's Lutheran church?"

Startled, Raisa thought for a few moments and then replied, "Well, yes we do and I think I have seen you there as well." Sadie showed Raisa everything they had in the store and in the catalog. Raisa kept going back to the cream-colored bathtub and allowed her fingers to slide over the smooth cool surface, daydreaming of what it would feel like to fill it full of hot water and bubble bath, then sink down in it up to her neck. A light bulb went on in Raisa's head, "Sadie, do you suppose you could come over to our house and take a look at our bathroom, maybe measure and see just what will fit in there?"

Sadie wrote down the appointment for the next day. Over the next few weeks, she was either at the Kessel's home or Raisa was down at the hardware store settling on the exact fixtures for her bathroom and kitchen. "Sadie, you have been a dear to go out of your way to help me wade through this all. There are just so many options that I have a hard time deciding. Let me take you to lunch on Thursday at the Lovell Drug's lunch counter. Can you make it?"

Sadie blushed and smiled, "Oh Ms. Kessel, you don't have to do that. It's all a part of my job and I have to say that I have enjoyed working with you. I don't have any folks around here and well, I just feel pretty close to you. You are such a sweet lady and all. I, ah well-- sure, I would love to meet you for lunch, say about 12:30, that's my lunch break!"

Arnold and Jake put in twelve-hour days working on the Heart Mountain Relocation Center. There was a big push to get it done by the first part of August and Jake was frustrated with the lack of materials. "Judas Priest, Raisa, if the government would just get the darn lumber to us and the other stuff we need, we could have had that thing built in a month. Now, they are jumping all over us because they have over six thousand Japanese internees they are holding, ready to put them on a train to Wyoming and we don't have the camp ready.

The fifth of August was Jake and Arnold's last day on the job at the relocation camp. By then Jake had his last pay check in the bank and was looking at other potential jobs. The government kept a skeleton crew on board to finish up the camp and they expected it would be ready for occupancy on August 13, 1942.

Raisa was looking at the calendar one morning after breakfast, "Oh Jake, they are going to finish up with our remodeling just in time. Beth is due to have her baby in about a week. It's so hot and she is so uncomfortable. She said she is going to stay out on the farm in Emblem for a few more days then Jimmy wants her to come on over here to Lovell and wait for the baby." Raisa smiled as she recalled her conversation with her daughter. "Beth says he's getting real nervous about driving her across those hills if she goes into labor over there. It's so hot here in Lovell, but I guess we can just turn the fans on her and try to keep her cool as possible. It's so exciting isn't it? A new baby—I think it's going to be a girl. I know Jimmy would like a boy, what man doesn't? I just hope my daughter doesn't have a hard time of it, that's all I hope."

Around nine in the morning on August 9th, Raisa pushed open the bedroom door and cheerfully said, "Are you going to sleep all day, sleepyhead?" Beth was curled up in a ball as Raisa opened the roller shade letting the bright morning light stream into the room.

"Ohhhh, Mom—I don't feel too good. I'm having some cramps and when I got up to go to the bathroom, there was some blood. I'm scared Mom, I don't know if I can do this or not."

Raisa sat down on the bed and stroked her daughter's flushed face. "You are going to do just fine sweetheart. This is something women do every day—have babies. Let's get you up and see what's going on, shall we?" Raisa pulled back the sheets and that's all she needed to see. "Okay Beth, we need to clean you up a little then I'm calling Dr. Welsey and we will get you over to the hospital."

Raisa timed the contractions; they were far apart, so she stalled. "I think you'll be more comfortable if we just stay here at the house for a couple more hours. If things pick up we can be at the hospital in five minutes. Is that okay with you honey?"

Around three o'clock, the pains were getting closer and lasting longer. Raisa wiped Beth's forehead with a cool cloth. Large salty tears rolled down Beth's cheeks as her stomach mounded up with a hard contraction. "Ahhhhhh, Mom—it hurts, that one really hurt. I think I want to go to the hospital. Can we go now Mom? I just don't know if I can walk to the car."

Raisa called the farm like she had promised her son-in-law and told Jimmy they were taking Beth in—that she was in labor. It was close to four o'clock on the 9th of August, when Jake backed the car out of the garage and waited beside the house. Raisa took Beth by the elbow as she waddled slowly and painfully down the front steps and out to the car. Raisa climbed into the backseat with their daughter. Jake backed the car out into the street and drove the four blocks to Lovell Hospital. Dr. Welsey was there to greet them and the nurses whisked Beth away to get her ready for her first birth.

After a quick examination, Dr. Welsey came out to the waiting room, "You might as well go back home, this baby is going to take a while. I'll have the desk call you when things get to moving a little faster." They were walking out the front door of the hospital when they ran into Jimmy as he hurried up the sidewalk to the hospital. He was pale and full of questions.

Around ten that night, they still had no baby and Jake and Raisa went back home to try and get some sleep. Jimmy bedded down at the hospital—no way was he leaving his wife there alone. The nurses let him go back to see Beth every once in a while, but it was hard for him to see his wife in pain like that. The last time he turned completely white and had to put his head between his knees, so he was banished to the waiting room. That's where he was at six in the morning when Jake and Raisa came rushing into the waiting room. Raisa was almost frantic. "Have they taken her to the delivery room yet?"

Jimmy was pacing the floor. He hugged Raisa and shook Jake's hand. "Boy am I glad you're here, she's been in there so long. The doc just said it won't be much longer though. I guess she's having a time of it. I had no idea it was this tough to have a baby!"

Their lusty baby girl was born just after seven in the morning on August 10. Beth was exhausted after more than eighteen hours of labor. Jimmy was waiting as they wheeled Beth out of the delivery room still groggy from the ether!

Later that morning Jimmy and Beth walked down to the nursery to look at their new daughter. "Jimmy, I want to ask you about a name. I wanted to name her Carole after Carole Lombard the actress, but I've been thinking more about it and would like to name her after my grandfather Karl. So, I was thinking about the name, Karlie Louise. Do you like it?"

~~~~~

Jake and Raisa didn't think things could get any better, but they were in for a big surprise. Around the first of August, Jake filled out an application at Marathon Oil Company for a job as 'well monitor'. Most of the younger guys had left for the war and the oil company needed workers to keep the flow of fuel going out to the military and the private sector. Almost two weeks had gone by without a call, and then out of the blue they called him in for an interview.

Jake drove over to Byron to the main office that morning and met with Bob Wentley, field supervisor. As expected, the interview didn't take long. Jake walked out of the Marathon front office, his hat in his hand; he climbed back in his car and headed back to Lovell. Parking the car at the curb in front of their house, Jake was deep in thought as he climbed the front steps. Opening the door, he began to call, "Raisa, Raisa, where are you?"

Raisa called out from the kitchen, "I'm in here Jake, up to my elbows in peaches." She inhaled deeply as she wiped her hands on the dish towel. She'd been so nervous about the interview and had worried about what they would do if he didn't get the job. She put on a happy face for him, just in case.

Jake practically ran to the kitchen, "Raisa, honey—oh honey—I got the job! I got the pump monitor job at Marathon and it comes with benefits and a great retirement. All I have to do is drive around to all the wells on my route for that day and check em'. If something is wrong then I report it to the front desk." Jake picked his wife up and swung her around.

"Jake, put me down. I've got a bushel of peaches to can yet today." She laughed as she gave him a big kiss. "I'm so proud of you, honey. Marathon got a good man when they hired you."

Jake took Raisa by the shoulders and said, "This is the second part---I want you to quit working. You take care of this house and garden. I want you to make a standing appointment to get your hair done every Friday. You've earned this better life too--do you hear me?"

Raisa smiled ear to ear. "I've got no problem with that. It will feel good to just take care of my own house and to do the things I want to do around here, like wallpaper the bedrooms. Yes sir—you've got a deal!"

It wasn't two weeks later when Jake pulled up into the driveway in a new black Ford sedan. He climbed out of the car, took the front steps two at a time and burst through the front door. "Raisa, R-Raisa—come look what I bought!" Jake searched all through the house then looked out the kitchen window. She was down on her knees in the back yard, planting three boxes of little purple and yellow pansies with their painted faces. Jake smiled as he watched her work. *I know those are her favorite spring flowers, other than our roses.* Jake trotted down the back porch steps and pushed open the back screen door, letting it slam behind him.

Raisa turned at the sound of the slamming door, startled to see Jake home already. Past experience told her when Jake showed up at an unusual time, it wasn't good—although recently, it had been the start of a good thing. "Jake, w-w-why are you home this time of day? What's the matter now? Is it serious?"

Jake motioned for her to continue with her planting, "I didn't tell you but today is my day off and I've been doing some shopping." Suddenly, he grabbed her by the hand and led her around to the front of the house where he'd parked the car. Raisa took her garden gloves off as they walked and wiped her hands on her apron. That's when she saw the new car. She was so relieved she burst into tears. "Oh Jake, oh Jake – a new car too?"

Jake led her over to the passenger side of the two-tone Mercury and opened the door. "Go on get in and we'll take it for a spin. Honey, I couldn't pass this up. Mr. Tomlinson made me a deal on this year-old car and I just couldn't turn it down. Some widow lady owned it and hardly drove it—it's like new! All I have to do is assume the payment. Come on, get in and we'll take it for a spin." Raisa slid into the passenger seat and Jake slammed the car door. He went around and got in behind the wheel. "You know honey, I really feel like a man, a successful man; earning my own way feels damn good!"

The first thing Raisa noticed when she got in the car was a funny looking knob on the steering wheel. "What in the world is that thing for? It looks like a door knob."

Jake laughed and took hold of the knob as he turned the steering wheel with it. It's actually a steering knob—an easier way to turn the wheel. I heard Arnie call it a 'Necker's Nob', and I won't go into that. I am sure you can figure it out!"

A week later, eighteen-year old Arnie approached his father with something on his mind. "Aww Dad, I was, uhhh, I was wondering if---if you would let me borrow the new car to take my date to the, ahhh, the senior prom next Saturday night?" Arnie took a deep breath and wiped the sweat from his forehead as he waited for his father's reply.

Jake cocked his head to the side as he thought about loaning out his new Mercury to his teenage son. He purposely made him wait for his answer. Jake walked away, appearing deep in thought and looked out the front window. Finally he turned and said, "Well, against my better judgment, I will let you take the new car, but not until we've had a chance to go over the features." Jake opened the front door and motioned for Arnie to follow. As they walked toward the garage, Jake began in earnest, "Don't be pushing too hard on that foot feed, and remember to let the clutch out slow when you shift. The dimmer switch is down there on the floor next to the clutch. You got to remember to dim the lights when you meet another car. In town, it's best to just leave them on dim." Of course, he went over everything at least two times, just in case the kid wasn't listening.

Arnie patiently listened to everything his Dad told him because he was itching to get his hands on that car. When the big night came, Jake watched as his son dressed up in a new suit. His hair was slicked back and the cologne he reeked of smelled slightly familiar. Before handing over the keys, Jake made Arnie listen to another ten minutes of instructions. Jake stood on the porch and watched reluctantly as Arnie backed out into the street. The boy waved and honked the horn as he drove off down the street, with the windows open.

It was midnight and Arnie still wasn't home. To make matters worse the weather had turned and a hard spring rain pelted the house as Raisa stood at the front window, looking up and down the street. Arnie was over an hour late when Raisa finally decided to wake Jake.

"Jake, wake up. Arnie isn't home yet. He's late and it's raining cats and dogs outside. I'm getting worried. Where could he be?"

Jake rolled over, pulling the bedclothes up to his chin. "Oh, for Pete's sake, Raisa, he'll be home when he walks through the door. If something happens I'm sure we'll hear about it. Now let me get some sleep; I have to work in the morning." She walked over to look out the window again, and that's when she heard the police siren.

Ten minutes later Arnie pulled into the driveway, turned off the headlights and cut the engine. A police car pulled up out front. Standing at the front door, Raisa's breathe caught as the circumstances became all too clear to her. She ran across the hardwood floor to wake Jake. They stood together out on the covered front porch, both in their robes. Arnie took his sweet time getting out of the car; he froze when he spotted his folks standing on the porch.

Locking eyes with his son, Jake walked down the steps toward him, "So, why in the hell are you so late and why, are the cops sitting at my front curb? What's going on here, Arnie, huh? Something tells me you got a hell of a lot of explaining to do."

Arnie's face was ashen and he was shaking like a leaf as the city policeman walked up the sidewalk. He looked at Arnie. "You wanna tell your folks about the wreck or do you want me to?"

After the papers were filled out, the policeman bid them a good night as he walked out the front door to his waiting squad car. Back inside the house, Jake's face was flushed and his fists were clenched tight as he struggled to process everything the police had told him. Maybe it wasn't the kid's fault, but his new car was still banged up and he was more than irritated. Jake crossed the living room in three strides. Grabbing Arnie by the suit lapels--he lifted him off the floor and slammed him against the wall. A picture fell to the floor with a crash.

"You irresponsible punk; I shoulda known you were still wet behind the ears! I let you take my new car to the dance anyway--- and you wreck it? What the hell were you doing? I told you and told you, that you have to watch out what the other cars are doing too. Maybe it wasn't all your fault, but that doesn't fix my car, now does it? It seems that there is only one way you learn anything--I'm gonna beat the ornery outta you!"

Raisa grabbed Jake's arm before he could strike her son and hung onto it with all the strength she could muster. "Jake, Jake, stop it. It's only the fender and a head light. It can be fixed."

Jake shook loose and his fist connected with Arnie's jaw, knocking him to the floor. The boy staggered to his feet, rubbing his face, "I ain't gonna fight you Dad. I just ain't gonna do it. I deserved it and so go ahead and get it over with. I said I'm sorry Dad. I'll pay to get it fixed with the money I made at Little Tokyo. I never meant for it to happen, it was an accident. The other car turned in front of me and I had nowhere to go."

Two weeks later, Jake retrieved his car from the collision shop. He was relieved to see it looked good as new. Besides his restored car, Jake felt pretty darn happy about the big paycheck in his wallet and the weekend ahead. He drove back home and parking the car in the driveway he spotted Raisa out in the backyard working in her rose bed. He strolled over to where she was kneeling in the dirt, pruning the roses. "How about we drive up to Billings tomorrow? We could do some shopping and go out to eat. We could even stay in a hotel if you'd like to: we can make a long weekend of it."

Raisa stood and wiped her hands on her apron, "Well, only if you will take me to Woolworths and later maybe even Hart Albin's."

Late the next day, Raisa and Jake walked down the streets of Billings, Montana, their arms loaded with packages. They were laughing and joking as they hurried back to their hotel. Raisa couldn't keep her hands off her new mink-tail coat. "Never in my life Jake, did I dream I would own a fur coat. I feel like I am in the movies" She turned to her husband, with a devilish smile on her face. "I might wear it all night!"

~~~~~

Arnie was in his senior year at Lovell High School and was scheduled to graduate in the spring of 1943. Raisa was disturbed when she overheard her only son and his buddies talk about signing up for the service. Arnie didn't like her fussing over him. "Awww, applesauce, Mom—come on now. We're at war and signing up is what all my friends and guys my age are doing. You have two brothers and a brother-in-law already serving—what's one more from the family?"

Raisa took her son by the shoulders and looked him in the face. "It's because y-y-you, are my only son and I fought s-s-so hard to keep you alive and help you grow when you were young. You are about to graduate from high school---you are just a boy. You really expect m-me to smile, let go and cheer as you go off to war—to shoot at other German boys and to have them shoot back at you? Men die in war, Arnold, don't you realize that? They get shot and lose arms and le-----." Tears rolled down Raisa's cheeks as she dabbed at them with her hanky. "No son, I can't even think about what that would be like."

Jake had a few things to say to his son as well. A couple of nights later, he sat alone on the front porch, waiting for Arnie to come home from a date. When the boy pulled up in front of the house, Jake took a good look at him as he walked toward the house. *When did he get so tall? He's a darn good-looking, strapping young man. He looks like the perfect 'German Aryan' with his blond hair and blue eyes.*

Jake pointed to the vacant metal spring chair next to him and Arnie plopped down, stretching his long legs out in front. "What are you doing out here on the porch Dad, having a smoke, are you?"

Jake smiled, "Yeah, it's nice and quiet out here. Your mom is at the pictures with Lizzie again. I wanted to talk to you about what you and your buddies did yesterday—signing up with the Army. What in the hell were you boys thinking? None of you realize what a big step that was—it's your life we are talking about here, Arnold, not some basketball game. But, you've never been one to listen much to us, so I guess what's done is done. At least the army is waiting until you all graduate from high school."

Arnold squirmed in his chair as he looked at the porch floor. "Aw Dad, us guys all have the 'war fever', we don't want to miss out on fightin' for our country and all that. Besides I didn't have any plans for what I'm going to do after I graduate, so it seemed like the thing to do. I'm nineteen and can pretty much figure my own life out. It's done now and there's no turnin' back, we leave for Cheyenne and Fort Warren for the official stuff in a couple of months."

Jake took a long slow drag on his pipe, thinking of what his next words would be. "Well son, I guess you've cast your lot and there's no turning back. Just some fatherly advice: I know you don't know exactly what to expect but I will tell you this, they aren't going to go easy on you boys when you get to boot camp. The sergeants and other officers have a job, and that's to get you ready to go into battle. I want you to listen real close to what they tell you and do your best to learn everything they are teaching. What they tell you is serious stuff and that's what is going to keep you alive or at least give you a chance at staying in one piece when them bullets start flying." Jake paused to take another pull from his pipe. "I don't like to see you going off to war any more than your mother does, but we aren't the only family in America who is going through this. Been thinking about what I heard the other day. 'It's the old men who make the wars and the young boys who fight them'. Maybe if the government sent the old men first, we wouldn't have any wars."

Arnold William Kessel graduated with the Lovell High School class of 1943. After graduation, he handed his diploma to his mother and packed his military duffle bag.

Two weeks later, the town of Lovell turned out to send their enthusiastic young men off to boot camp. After that they knew some were going to be sent to the West, to the Pacific and some were going to the East, to Europe. Jake and Raisa, Beth and Jimmy, as well as Arnie's grandparents and the rest of the family were all there—standing on the train depot platform as the troop train pulled out of the Lovell station, heading east.

When the train started to roll out, the Lovell boys were cuttin' up, hanging out of the windows, all eager for the last goodbye and the big adventure that awaited them. Jake spotted Arnie waving from the window as the seventh car rolled past. Tears welled up in Jake's eyes as he simply touched the brim of his hat in a farewell salute. Jake put his hand over Raisa's as she gripped his elbow. When the train rounded the bend and was out of sight, Jake felt Raisa go limp. He caught her in his arms as her knees buckled.

CHAPTER TEN

Be merciful to me, O LORD, for I am in distress; my eyes grow weak with sorrow, my soul and my body with grief.
Psalm 31:9 KJV

Late Summer 1943: Beth was married with a home and baby to care for and Arnie had left for boot camp. Raisa spent many evenings alone or at the movie theatre on Main Street. Jake still worked shifts for Marathon and was either working, sleeping, fishing or down at the pool hall. Raisa told her daughter she would babysit any time they wanted some time alone or wanted to head to Billings to do some shopping and take in a movie.

One weekend during a lull in the farming schedule, Beth and Jimmy dropped Karlie off and they drove to Billings. The first night Karlie woke around 2 a.m. and Raisa couldn't get her back to sleep. She bundled the baby and carried her into the front room. Raisa pulled her old rocking chair out from the wall and sat down. She began to rock back and forth, back and forth. A smile crossed her face as she remembered when Jake had surprised her with the beautiful wood and upholstered rocking chair right before Beth was born. She had rocked both of her own babies in it and now was rocking her first grand-daughter in the same chair.

Raisa looked up through the dimly lit room at the clock on the wall, which was making a rhythmic 'tick tock –tick tock'. *That clock is about to put me to sleep, I wonder why it isn't working on this little rascal.* Raisa rose from the rocking chair and held her wide-eyed grandbaby up to look out the window. She bent to kiss her silky curls as she murmured, "You are a little night owl aren't you? We better get you to sleep before Grandpa Jake comes home from work. How about a warm bottle of milk that should do the trick? Let's go in the kitchen and fix that."

With a warmed bottle of milk, Raisa carried Karlie back to the front room and settled back into the rocking chair. Raisa loved holding the chubby toddler close in her arms as she fed her the half bottle of warm milk. Then she began singing, "Bye, bye, bye, bye-yee", repeating the mindless tune over and over until sleep claimed the child. Raisa sat for a moment just gazing at the face of her granddaughter. She smiled as Karlie's little rosebud lips puckered and her jaws moved as she began to suck on a phantom baby bottle. Raisa leaned down and kissed the silky pink skin of Karlie's little cheek.

Reluctantly, Raisa rose from the rocking chair and carried her granddaughter back to her crib. She looked down into the peaceful face again. *What a blessing you are for all of us during this war and especially me having my son over there. We don't know what is happening until much later, sometimes we never know. It's such a welcome, positive distraction to have you in our lives.* As Raisa climbed back into bed, she heard their car pull up in the driveway. Jake opened the back door and tiptoed quietly in to the other bedroom. Raisa turned over in bed.

A week later at breakfast, Raisa said, "Jake do you think you can hitch a ride with one of the other guys tomorrow night so I can go to the movie? I'd like to call one of my sisters to go with me, there's a special one playing that I would love to see." Going to the movie was her escape from Jake's absence and the worry which constantly haunted her. That next evening as Raisa and her sister, Lizzie sat in the darkened theatre, waiting for the main feature to begin. Raisa said, "I hate the news reels they always show at the beginning of the movie. It seems they take pictures of the most horrible things happening in the war. I don't need to see that. It just puts more images in my mind and keeps me up at night. Maybe we should wait to come until after the news reels." She thought for a moment before changing the subject and asked, "Lizzie, who are your favorite movie stars?"

Lizzie shrugged her shoulders and between bites of popcorn giggled, "Well, frankly Raisa, there really isn't one or even two movie stars that keep me awake at night or that I dream about. I guess I just like 'em all."

Raisa took a deep breath then smiled sweetly and said, "I think my favorite couple of all time was Clark Gable and Carole Lombard. It was so tragic, the way she died, and so young too. Of course I love anything with Bing Crosby, Katherine Hepburn, Gary Cooper, Robert Taylor, and Jimmy Stewart. Let's face it; I pretty much like them all. I often imagine myself in those glamorous dresses and fur coats, living in mansions like they show in the movies. Wouldn't that be grand, Lizzie? By the way, have you seen the movie 'Casablanca' with Humphrey Bogart and Ingrid Bergman? It's just wonderful. I read a magazine article that said it was the best picture of 1943."

Lizzie smiled, "Aw, Raisa, those people really aren't any happier than we are. They have cheatin' husbands and wives, troubles with their in-laws, booze, and even with all the money they make, they have money problems too. It's just all on a grander scale!"

The last of July, Jake and Raisa finally got a letter from Arnie. He was stationed at Fort Carson where he and a few thousand other 'wet-behind-the-ears' young bucks were receiving their basic training.

Private Arnold Kessel – 1943

Dear Mom and Dad,
Well, I finally got around to writing. They keep us pretty busy here. The Army changes from day to day, most of the time I like it swell and at other times, it's the shits. They have so many men and are poorly organized in a lot of things. I am beginning to think this war caught them with their pants down, if you know what I mean.

We've been in training for the .22 and .30-caliber M2 machine gun; this last one is a honey of a gun. It holds eight rounds in one clip and it's gas operated and air cooled. What I like best about it is that it throws the shells out by itself and throws another one back in the chamber---auto—matic! You can really shoot straight just by adjusting the sight a bit. We've already had eight hours of instructions on the thirty caliber machine gun. There are a-hell-of a lot of parts on that gun and we have to learn them all, plus how to take it apart and fix it ourselves.

I hear that it's a part of our basic training, but our captain took us all in a room the other day and showed us some films on what kind of diseases we can get it we mess around with women. After seeing that film, I don't think I will be taking out any strange girls; it made me sick for a week. I had no idea about something like those diseases, it was really pretty bad.

This is real pretty country down here in Colorado Springs. The town sits right at the foot of Cheyenne Mountain; it's a huge granite mountain. The base and all is about fifty miles south of Denver. Me and the boys are itching to get a little time off to head to the big city.

Yes Mom, I'm reading the Bible you gave me so don't worry about that. And Dad—I am paying attention to what they are teaching us. Every bit I learn will help me once I get over there. Write when you can and if you have time, I'd sure like to receive a "goodie box" or two. Tell the family hello, for me. I should get a furlough to come back home for a visit when basic training is over. I am looking forward to that. Hope we can all get together before my company ships out.

Your son,
Arnold

PS: We got our picture taken and I thought you might like to have one. I enclosed one for Beth too-- so you don't forget my sweet mug!

Raisa's hands shook as she read Arnie's letter through twice, then laid it on the dining room table where Jake would see it when he got off work. She squeezed her eyes shut as she felt another migraine coming on and headed for the bathroom medicine cabinet. Raisa swallowed a couple of aspirin, pulled down the window shades and lay down on the bed with a cool cloth over her eyes. She thought about the Bible passage she had read last night when she was so upset about Arnie going overseas to fight in the war. *Be anxious for nothing, but in everything by prayer and supplication with thanksgiving let your requests be made known to God. And the God of peace will guard your hearts and your minds."* Philippians 4: 6 – 7

As Raisa tossed and turned in bed that night, her head continued to throb with blinding pain and her mind would not sleep. Finally, for the second time that night, Raisa put her hands together and prayed: *Dear Lord, please grant me peace and faith that our son will come back home to us. Watch over him as he goes to war. And Lord, please make these terrible stomach aches and headaches stop—pleasssse have mercy. Amen*

The next morning at breakfast, Raisa picked at her poached egg and toast. Jake noticed she wasn't eating again and decided it was time to say something. "Raisa, honey, listen to me. I am worried about you; you are dropping weight like crazy with not eating and worrying all the time. Arnie is still in basic training and you are making yourself sick with this worry. I want you to call Doctor Welsey and make an appointment to see him. Maybe he can give you something to settle you down."

Raisa looked up at her husband with tears in her pale blue eyes, "Oh Jake, I can't get all the worries and questions about Arnie out of my mind. I think going to the movies so much probably makes it worse. You know, before the main feature they always run those news reels; they are full of terrible things that are happening over in Germany and the Philippines. I just can't put it out of my mind and sometimes I feel like I am going to go crazy with worry." Raisa stood up and ran her fingers through her hair. "You know, Jake, I don't even know where the Philippine Islands are. We've each got a brother who is a prisoner of war in those Jap concentration camps, and I don't even know exactly where they are."

Jake pushed back his chair and reached out to pull Raisa to her feet. He wrapped his arms around her as she rested her cheek against the scratchy wool of his shirt. "Honey, you've got to get ahold of yourself. All this worry and stuff is making you sick. I need you and I know Arnie is going to need you to send him letters and boxes of your tasty baked goods. We all need you, Raisa, so you have to come to terms with this. Maybe you should go talk to Pastor Siebert too."

Jake released Raisa and reached for his aluminum lunch box that she had packed. He gave her one last peck on the cheek as he headed for the back door. "I've got to get to work. I want you to call the doctor and get an appointment—understand? I love you Raisa—I love you a lot! You just have to have more faith. None of this is in our hands."

Raisa stood at the kitchen window and watched as Jake backed his field truck down the driveway, into the street. She turned and looked at the black phone sitting on the little hall table. Walking across the kitchen, she picked up the phone and dialed Dr. Welsey's phone number. After making an appointment to see him on Thursday, Raisa hung up the phone and walked back into the kitchen and poured herself a cup of coffee. Wrapping her hands around the warmth of the cup, she moved over to the kitchen window again. She stood still as her eyes soaked up the beauty of their back yard. *It's so peaceful out there with the weeping willow trees, the green lawn, and our rose gardens. This place was worth everything we've gone through. Okay, I've got to quit daydreaming and get my laundry started. The morning's half over and I've done nothing!*

As Raisa ran the last load of clothes through her wringer washing machine, she noticed it was almost lunch time. She went into her small kitchen and fixed herself a cucumber, tomato, and basil sandwich. Sitting at the kitchen table she ate her sandwich and listened to the steady cadence of the washing machine's agitator. *What a wonderful invention the wringer washing machine is. I wish in those early days, that Mama and the women of her generation had been able to wash their clothes this way, instead of hauling water to tin tubs and scrubbing pile after pile of dirty clothes on a scrub board. Now, after their kids are grown, they both have wringer machines. Better late than never! After I run this last load through the rinse and get them hung on the clothes line, I can work a bit in the garden while the clothes dry.*

Raisa carried the heavy basket of wet clothes down the back steps and out to the clothes line. She reached into the bag of wooden clothes pins and pulled two out. One she put between her teeth and the other she squeezed open and pinched it over the tail of Jake's shirt. Bending down, she chose another shirt. Taking the clothes pin from her mouth, she pinched it over the first and second shirt tails.

I remember getting a lesson on hanging clothes from Mama when I was about ten. 'You always wash clothes on Monday and iron on Tuesday. We hang socks by the toes, pants by the waistband, and a shirt by the tails. Hang whites with whites, shirt and towels on the outside line and hide the 'unmentionables' in the middle of the drying clothes. That way the neighbors can't see our business. Try to line the clothes by same items and use one clothes pin to pin down two pieces. Never leave the clothes pins on the line after you take the dry clothes down—that tells everyone you are lazy. Take the last of the dry clothes off the line before supper, sprinkle and fold them, laying them in a basket to iron the next day. That's what she taught all us girls: her 'Ten Commandments' for washing clothes!

Raisa closed her eyes, remembering all the times she had to go outside in freezing temperatures and take the frozen-stiff clothes off the line. *It's always been a wrestling match just trying to bend them enough so they fit back into the basket. In a way being frozen is good because when I get the clothes back in the warm house they relaxed and I just rolled them up, ready for ironing the next day. But, oh my—my hands get so cold, no wonder I have arthritis in my hands now. Mama taught me a lot about running a house, just like I taught my daughter. There's a right and a wrong way to do things and that's all there is to it!*

After picking a basket of green beans from her garden and hoeing two rows in the afternoon sun, Raisa wiped the sweat from her forehead with the back of her hand. She felt light-headed and decided to head for the cool shade of the willow trees. *I hate how it feels when the sweat trickles down my back and across my temples.* Suddenly tired, she flopped down into a lawn chair in the shade and began to snap the green beans into a bowl that sat between her knees. *I think I'll fix the beans for supper with a couple strips of bacon thrown in for flavoring, just like Jake likes them. It's so hot. Perhaps I'll just put out some cold cuts instead of frying chicken and getting the kitchen all hot. Oh yes—and a bowl of sliced cucumbers with onion, dill, and tomatoes swimming in sour cream. Now that sounds good!*

After supper that evening, Raisa returned to the garden to hoe in the cool of the evening. *I don't know what I was thinking trying to work out here in the hot sun. I'm lucky I didn't faint again.* She thought about all the gardens she had hoed in her life. *There is just something I love about the smell of the damp earth when it's disturbed. And some of the plants give off a fragrance when they are brushed against, like the tomatoes plants.* When she finished the hoeing, she leaned the hoe against the garage and made a beeline for the dry clothes still hanging on the line. Swiftly, she removed the wooden clothes pins and systematically dropped them into the canvas bag hanging on the line. Piling the last of the dry clothes in a laundry basket, Raisa bent over and picked it up then carried it to the house. She sat the basket of clean, dry clothes near the kitchen table as she went in search of her husband. She found Jake on the front porch having a smoke.

"Boy, it's nice and cool out here. Wish this is all I had to do—sit on the front porch smoking my pipe." Raisa laughed as she scurried back inside, just missing the newspaper Jake threw at her. Jake called after her, "Sure is honey! Why don't you come on out and join me—relax a bit after you get your work done."

Jake grinned as Raisa replied, "Oh Jake, I can't, I still have all those clothes to sprinkle and roll up so I can iron them tomorrow. Maybe I'll come out when I'm done if you are still out here."

She walked back to the kitchen sink and filled the empty Royal Crown Cola bottle with water from the tap, screwed the pierced cap back on the bottle and began to sprinkle the clothes with water. When she finished sprinkling a piece, she rolled it up and laid it back into the clothes basket. Tomorrow morning, when she took them out to iron, they would be equally damp and ready to press. *Ironing is one of my favorite household tasks—there's something about taking a piece of wrinkled cloth and making it look all smooth and pretty.*

Raisa reached into the basket, and pulling out a cotton bed sheet, she held it to her nose. *I'll never stop loving the way the clothes smell after hanging out in the fresh air and sun all day. I know a lot of women don't iron their sheets and pillowcases any more but I like to sleep on smooth, ironed sheets.* Pushing her curly hair back under the mesh hair net, she smiled as she finished sprinkling and rolling the last shirt in the basket of clothes. Raisa covered the basket with a terrycloth towel and carried it into the laundry room. She took a deep breath and headed for the front porch to join her husband, kicking her shoes off as she went.

Out on the front porch, Raisa opened the small aluminum lined-milk box and left the milk man a written order for a bottle of milk and a pint of whipping cream. Sinking down into the metal spring-chair, she laid her head back against the cushion and listened to the doves, as their last 'coo, coo-coo' echoed through the fading evening light. She closed her eyes as the cool of the evening breeze brushed over her skin like a feather.

It was close to the middle of September, 1943, when Jake and Raisa drove back to the train depot to pick up their son. He had written to say he had a couple of weeks leave after completing boot camp, before shipping out to Europe. As they sat on the metal bench waiting for the train, Jake picked up a copy of yesterday's *Lovell Chronicle* as Raisa sat quietly, consumed with her thoughts. *I wish Arnie had longer than two weeks leave before they send him to Fort Knox tank school. After that training, he and the other boys there will be shipped out. This all seems like a bad dream and I just don't know how I am going to get through every day, knowing he is in a war. Raisa thought about the Bible verse she read last night. "Cast all your anxiety on him because he cares for you." 1 Peter: 5:7 KJV*

As she waited at the train station, Raisa's thoughts occupied her as she aimlessly looked at the other parents and families who obviously were waiting for a son or husband, just like they were. She smiled as she watched two little kids play tag, running up and down the wooden platform.

All of a sudden, they all heard the train whistle at the same time. Everyone stopped what they had been doing and crowded forward, eager for the reunion. Jake and Raisa rose from the bench and stood to the side, waiting for the train to stop—waiting for their only son to get off the train so they could take him home.

Raisa pointed toward a soldier hanging out of the window in the third car. "There he is--there's Arnold!" In a matter of minutes he bounded down the steps of the train, proudly carrying a duffle bag slung casually over one shoulder. Arnold was all smiles as he shook hands with his Dad and picked Raisa up and swung her around. As he put his mother down, she reached up, feeling his hard biceps. "Well, they put some more muscle on you didn't they? You look mighty fine in that uniform, yes you do!"

Jake slapped his son on the back, "You look good son, real good. Grab your bag and come on, the car is over here."

On the eve of his third day of leave, the three of them were having supper when Jake asked, "I was thinking of taking the day off tomorrow. Maybe you and me could head up to the Big Horns with our fishing poles? You got any plans?"

Raisa looked up from her plate and commented, "I think that sounds like a great idea. I'll have dinner waiting for you two when you get back. Anything special you'd like me to fix for dinner, Arnie?"

Arnie smiled as he reached across the table and patted his mother's shoulder. "Not really Mom, I like everything you make. On second thought, how about some chicken and dumplings with extra cream? That would sure taste good. I never get enough of that dish."

FLESH ON THE BONE

The next morning, just as the sun peaked over the mountains to the east, Jake and Arnie packed up the old pickup and headed for the Big Horns. They both looked forward to a day of fishing in a secluded mountain stream. On the ride up through the farming communities of Sunlight and Kane that nestled in the foothills of the majestic Big Horn Mountains, Jake took the opportunity to ask his son some questions. "So, they are sending you off to learn all there is to know about the Sherman tank in Fort Knox? Will it scare you at all being inside those things? Sounds like pretty close quarters if you ask me."

Arnie continued to look out the window at the mountains. "Naw, Dad, it doesn't scare me being inside of them, although some guys call them 'rolling coffins'. For Pete's sake don't tell Mom that!" He laughed and scratched the back of his neck. "Actually, I think it'll be a pretty good place to be when the bullets start flying. In war, Dad, there isn't any safe place if you know what I mean. If your number is up, it's up. I've learned pretty much everything thing there is to learn about the guns we carry on those tanks. The big cheese tells us they are working on a new model of the Sherman—one with more armor like the German Tigers and Panzers."

Arnie reached for the silver thermos, unscrewed the cap and tipped it to his mouth. "Is this all you brought, water? If so, we need to make a beer stop in Kane and pick up some cold ones. That's what we need on a hot day of fishing!"

When they reached the small Wyoming town of Kane, Jake turned into the parking lot of the general store and pulled the truck to a stop. "Okay then, lets you and me get us some cold beer—that's a good idea!"

When they were back on the road, winding up through the switchbacks, Arnie said, "I did real good in my basic training, Dad. I think all those hunting trips you took me on paid off. The sarge was pretty impressed by my marksmanship. At Knox, I hear that they want to start me out as a tank gunner. My goal is to be a tank commander; that would sure be swell. I hope I end up with a good bunch of guys. Would hate like hell to be in the situation where I had to be cozy in one of those tanks with some guy that was a bad egg. But then again, I get along with almost everyone except a loud-mouth bully type. You just watch. That's probably what will happen." He laughed as he opened his beer with a church key. "By the way, are you purposely hitting every pot hole you can?"

Jake looked across the seat at his son and thought to himself, *He's gotten so tall and the army training sure brought out the muscles in him. He might not be a boy anymore, but he's still wet behind the ears. If he isn't a man now, he will be when he comes back and by damn I pray he comes back in one piece. I don't even like to think about it, but I gotta be strong for Raisa and for my son. Dear Lord, please hear my prayer and bring our boy back to us—watch over him when he's over there dodging bullets. Just bring him back alive—Amen.*

Jake said, "How about opening one of those for me? We should be at the creek in about ten minutes. Did you bring some 'wooly eyes' or do you want to use my bait box?"

Arnie replied, "Yeah, I'll probably need to use your custom hooks. I've never seen anybody make better hooks than you Dad."

Jake pulled the truck off the road and parked under a grove of aspen trees. "This looks like a good spot. Let's grab our poles and get on down to that stream." Carrying their gear, father and son walked down a steep embankment to Whistle Creek, where Jake pointed to a large pine tree. "We can leave our gear here while we are out in the stream unless you want to fish from the bank? By the way---you better get used to some rough roads, cause I don't think it will be a smooth ride where you are going! You'll probably wish you were back in my fishing truck with me driving!"

Arnie laughed and held his hands up in mock surrender. He put his gear down and commenced to bait his fishing rod as his father did the same. Busy for a few moments, Arnie asked, "Say Dad, why don't you hand me that fuzzy red one in the top tray? I got a feeling these fish here, are gonna like a red hook today cause the water's a little muddy. Hey, not to change the subject, just something that crossed my mind. Have you ever shot a man or had one shoot at you on purpose?"

Jake shook his head. "Naw son, one hunter came close to hitting me one time but it weren't on purpose. How are you feeling about that; about some German shooting at you, trying to kill you? Does that bother you; do you think you could kill another man, looking him in the eyes?"

Arnie never hesitated. "You're damn right I could, without a moment's hesitation. That was all a part of our basic training. Dad, the enemy is the enemy and if you don't shoot him first, you are going to get nailed. There are very few second chances! They teach us to think of them as not men, not fathers, sons, brothers, but as the bad guy who will kill you if you don't have the guts to kill him first. Naw, I ain't got a problem with that in the least. In fact, I can't wait to actually fire those big guns on our Sherman and blow some German machine gun nest to pieces. Wish it was capable of blowing the crap out of a German tank, but they got us out ranked there. Our tanks are faster and more agile so we just have to be smarter and aim for their weak spots if we can."

Arnie was quiet for a couple of minutes, and then he said, "We just have to remember Dad, that we are going over there to stop a war and stop those who are making war. None of us really want to kill anybody, but if we have to, we will!"

It was a successful day of fishing and with both of their creels filled with squirming, glistening Rocky Mountain Trout they trudged back up the rocky trail to the truck. After Jake and Arnie stashed their fishing gear in the back, Jake turned to face his son. Clamping his weathered hand on Arnie's shoulder, he said, "Arnold, tell me something, truthfully, are you afraid at all to go to war? Have you thought about what it is going to be like over there?"

Arnie looked down for a moment then his eyes rose and rested on a high mountain peak in the distance. "Honestly, Dad? Sure, I've thought about it but I'm not going to make myself crazy wondering about things I really haven't experienced or can't control. I just plan on taking it a day at a time. They told us it isn't going to be a picnic or like anything we've ever seen or done. Fact is we just don't really know what we will face or how we'll react when it comes down to it. I remember in this one class I took, the

Major was talking about this very thing one day and he said, 'You men are going into something you have never experienced. You might have some doubts and fears, that's normal. But past experience has taught me that once men are caught up in the emotion of something, they stop being afraid and simply react. Frankly, it's the unknown that scares most of us because we make up things in our heads to scare ourselves with."

Then, Jake did something that he rarely did. He put his arms around his son and hugged him tight. Jake slapped Arnie on the back before he let go, they both stepped back and just looked at each other with tears in their eyes.

Then Jake said, "Well, we better get a wiggle on. Your Mom has probably been cooking all day." They climbed into the truck, Jake stepped on the clutch, started the motor, and, letting the clutch out, he shifted into first gear as the truck began the climb up the rocky dirt road to the highway. Looking straight ahead, Jake said, "Just one more thing and then we'll get off the subject. Never forget, Arnold, how much you are loved by the whole family. You make me proud, son, you turned out to be a hell of a man and I love you! Just promise me you'll keep your head down and don't try to be a hero when you get over there."

Jake felt himself getting emotional as a lump filled his throat. He waited a moment to regain his composure and said. "When you get over there, just do what you have to do to stay alive. There will be days when you might have to turn and run. Running away from a bad situation doesn't make you a coward, son. It means, you are picking your day and place to fight. It means, staying alive to fight another day. Just think about what the Germans are doing to other peoples and countries. They have to be stopped. I know you'll do what you have to do, you're just that kind of man."

Jake looked across the seat at his son and felt his eyes tearing up. Arnold sat with his head down, his jaws clenched in steely resolve. "Thanks Dad, I'll remember what you said. I'll do my best." Neither of them spoke for a few minutes as they headed back on the road to Lovell.

About five miles out of Lovell, Arnie turned and said, "Say, Dad, I've been meaning to tell you. You know the other night when a bunch of us guys went to that dance? Well, I met a real swell dame and I can't quit thinking about her. I think I might be carrying a torch for her if you know what I mean." Arnold grinned ear to ear and fidgeted around in the seat, "Well, that is, I think I might be stuck on her. Her name is Noreen Trask and she's a fine looking dame, not some dumb Dora. She's got these great looking gams and boy is she a hoofer. I think I danced about every dance with her. I got a date with her tomorrow night. Yes sir, she is one hotsy-totsy dame. The only trouble is I'm about to ship out and then I meet a dish like her. Maybe she'll write to me."

Jake looked across the seat at his son, amused by the expression of pure puppy love on his son's face, and thought to himself, *Yah—I think our boy's been bitten by the love bug!*

Private Arnold Kessel and his niece Karlie

Raisa outdid herself with the meal she prepared that night. At precisely six o'clock she walked into the front room where Jake and Arnie were sitting, listening to the radio. "Supper is ready, come on in the dining room. I wanted to eat in here because it's a special occasion." As Jake and Arnie were sitting down, she went back into the kitchen and beamed as she carried in a large steaming bowl of chicken and dumplings, setting the dish down in front of her son. She went back for a bowl of crisp snap peas and new potatoes from the garden that barely kept their heads above the thick, rich cream sauce. Arnie closed his eyes and shaking his head from side to side, inhaled the incredibly delicious aroma that rose from the table. Jake bowed his head and said, 'Let's pray."

Raisa and Arnie bowed their heads as Jake began, "Dear Heavenly Father, bless this food which we are about to partake of, that it nourishes our bodies. Help us to partake of your word to strengthen our spirits. And Lord, thank you for bringing our son home for a visit. Please watch over him when he leaves and bring him back to us. Thy will be done. Amen"

Raisa sat for a moment, just watching as her son dove into his plate of food. "Awww, Mom, this is what I'm talking about. I know I'm not going to get this kind of cooking where I'm going."

A dark cloud washed over Raisa's face, but only for a moment. *I can't think about where he's going or what he's going to be eating. We have to enjoy this moment, we have to enjoy this time together.* Raisa smiled proudly as Arnie and Jake heaped their plates high with the fruits of her labors. "That's right, dig in, there's more where that came from. And you just save some room for dessert too. I made a special Yagada Berry Cake for you because I know how much you like that, with a little vanilla ice cream on the side."

That night after supper, Jake lay in bed for almost an hour, thinking about the day and the conversation he and Arnold had on the mountain. *I hope there'll be more days like that when he gets back, that's what I pray for, that's all I ask for—more days with my son.*

The next few days were spent saying goodbye to his family and friends. *I hate leaving my little goddaughter, Karlie. I've never been much for kids what with their sticky hands and smelly diapers, but this kid is a sweetie-pie and I'm her godfather! I wonder how old she'll be when I get back home. Pretty sure she won't remember me—if I see her again.*

The last morning at home, Arnie woke early, at the crack of dawn. He heard the milkman climb the wooden front steps and deposit his order, then walk back to his truck and move on down the street. Arnie thought, *I guess I won't be hearing those kinds of sounds where I am going. I'm going to wake up every morning to the sound of a bugle and then probably even some gun fire!*

CHAPTER ELEVEN

Today the bus was right on schedule in spite of the rain and overcast skies. Mother Nature wasn't making this any easier, casting her gloom over it all. Gathered on Main Street at the Lovell Bus Terminal was a solemn group of parents and relatives. Some came to say goodbye and others came to, well—be a part of the occasion. Arnie was glad to see three other soldiers from Lovell who were obviously traveling back to their base on the special troop bus. There was one thing they had in common--they all agreed that their leave had been too short, especially when they knew they were being shipped overseas in a month or two. This was one bit of information that Arnie neglected to share with his mother.

Private Arnold Kessel –1943

Arnie walked to the edge of the crowd where he spotted Noreen standing. He stood shyly in front of her holding both of her hands, trying his best to act casual. However, when he looked into her eyes, all he really wanted to do was kiss her long and slow. "I hope you write to me Noreen; that would sure be swell." She looked deep into his eyes as she purposely moved closer. Arnie added, "I'll write first and let you know where I am. Just let me know what you are doing, how the old crowd is and well, you know—things like that. I, ahhh, I—don't know when I'll see you again, so do you think I could have a kiss goodbye?" Not needing a second invitation, Noreen threw her arms around Arnie's neck and kissed him long and hard, something she had been thinking about for a while. Arnie was smiling when they pulled apart. "Wow, guess that will have to last me for a while. You can bet I'll try my darndest to be back for more!" Reluctantly, they said goodbye as Arnold turned and walked back to where his parents stood.

Arnold felt his mother tug at his sleeve. "Come here, I want to get a photo of you and your dad in front of the bus. Ignoring the nagging knot in his gut and spiraling emotions, Arnold sucked it up and was all smiles as he stood beside his father as his mother snapped another picture.

Private Kessel and his proud father, Jake

With that, he quickly hugged his parent's goodbye and climbed onto the bus. Jake and Raisa had agreed the night before to try and keep a cheerful attitude along with, a smile on their faces, but Raisa was having a difficult time living up to her end of the agreement. Her hands were shaking; her face was ashen and somber. She knew she was plumb out of smiles. Later, Raisa would describe it like an out-of-body experience, standing there watching herself wave goodbye to her son. It was all surreal, like it was happening to somebody else—like watching one of her movies of a mother waving goodbye, sending her son off to war. They all knew this would be Arnie's last leave before he shipped out. She held tight to Jake's elbow as they watched the bus door close and listened to the driver shift down. The bus began its slow crawl down the street with Arnie and a few other guys hanging out the windows waving their last goodbye.

Jake and Raisa stood together, rooted to the ground and watched until the bus pulled away and their son disappeared around the corner at the east end of town. For a moment, both Jake and Raisa wondered if that moment would be the last time they would see their son alive. They wondered it, but neither of them said those terrible words aloud.

The rest of that day evaporated in a blur as Raisa retreated to her bedroom, shades drawn and a cool cloth over her eyes as another migraine descended upon her with a vengeance. Jake worked in the rose garden for a while, then fixed himself a sandwich and took it out to the front porch to eat. He sat alone in his green spring chair with only his thoughts for company, until darkness ended that dreaded day. Slowly, Jake rose and went inside, locking the door behind him.

Arnold was good for his word and wrote a letter to his folks a week after he arrived at Camp Fort Knox.

Dear Mom and Dad,

Well, my first impression of the South is that it's too hot, too humid, and they have too many bugs! Other than that, it's just swell. Fort Knox is a huge place—guess it's been around for a long time, training soldiers how to fight etc.

One of the squad leaders just told me that I am going to make a Lance Jack if I keep on the ball like I have been doing, not too bad, huh? It doesn't hurt that I speak some German too. I've heard rumors that those of us who can speak some German are pretty sure to get orders to go to Europe. We'll just have to wait and see which boat I catch.

I really like the Sherman tanks. I get teased because I grew up on the farm and knew how to drive a tractor—something these city boys don't know. So anyway, that put me a spot ahead of them guys when it comes to catching on how to drive one of these things. They have some pretty nifty features of which I can't tell you because it's secret war stuff and all.

Some of us guys went into Louisville the other night. I have to say I don't like it at all. There wasn't a shortage of good-looking girls there and they seemed pretty eager to get acquainted; most of 'em dance like we do back in the west. I kept remembering that film we saw back in boot camp and so that was it for me.

Well I better hit the sack; we are up at dawn for maneuvers!

All my love----Arnold

The next few months were a blur as Jake kept himself busy with work, an occasional fishing trip, and a couple hands of cards at least once a week. Lately, he'd tried to spend more time at home with Raisa. *I'm worried about her. She can't seem to quit worrying about our son, even when she's babysitting our grand-daughter. She's making herself sick with things she has no control over.*

Raisa went through the motions of taking care of their small house, the monotonous weekly grocery shopping, pruning the rose bushes, and endless weeding of the garden during the muggy hot summer months. She rarely ventured out to see a movie because the news reels upset her something fierce. This past year was the first time she could remember that she didn't can over two hundred jars of vegetables and fruits. Her heart wasn't in it. *What's the use in going to all that work, when there's just Jake and me? I just don't see the point in it and besides I'd rather spent time with our granddaughter.*

Raisa had a standing weekly appointment with the family doctor who was treating her for depression. Dr. Welsey advised, "I want you to see your chiropractor as often as you need if you feel you get some relief from his adjustments. It certainly won't hurt you Raisa. But, bottom line, you need to keep busy and get your mind off what is happening with your son. You aren't the only mother who is worried and concerned. Call me if you begin to feel worse or feel like you have had a setback."

Arnold shipped out to England late fall, 1943. He wrote interesting letters about their ship, telling what the censors wouldn't mark out. The opulent Queen Mary had been converted from a luxury passenger ship to a bare bones troop ship, carrying soldiers and supplies overseas. He wrote:

> *You wouldn't believe this ship. Wow, I've never seen anything like this except in the movies. Me and the rest of the fellas are living it up on this here tub. There's a card game in every room and most guys lose their pay check before they get it. Me, I'm holding on to mine. I only need a couple of bucks each month for a little fun here and there. I'd like to come back home to a nice bank account. By the way, word has it we are going into special training somewhere in England. Of course the brass doesn't tell us what exactly we're training for but I am sure looking forward to seeing England. I get a real kick out of listening to those guys speak English; it sounds so formal the way they talk. Well, better sign off for now. I'll write more when we land and I know where we are stationed.*
> *Love you both, your son,*
> *Arnold*

Jake was on the graveyard shift. He'd go to work at midnight and usually got off around eight in the morning. This morning, things were slower than usual. Jake's boss slapped him on the back and suggested, "Say, Jake, go ahead and head on home. You've checked all the wells and nothing is happening. I think it's safe for you to leave. I know you are concerned about your wife and all. We'll see you tomorrow."

Jake was plum tuckered out and looking forward to a few hours in the sack. It was close to six a.m. when he pulled into the driveway that ran parallel to their house and cut the engine of the truck. Just in case Raisa was still sleeping, he didn't slam the car door but pushed it shut. Once inside the house, he hung up his silver hard hat and shimmed out of his coveralls, hanging them on a hook in the laundry room. Jake turned and was about to walk into the kitchen when he spotted Raisa sitting in the dim light at the kitchen table. Jake stopped and watched her for a minute. She just sat, staring out the window. Finally, spotting him standing in the doorway she turned. Forlornly, Jake said, "Oh Raisa, what are you doing, sitting in here without the light on? Are you sick again?" Jake moved to the left to turn on the kitchen light.

Raisa held up her hand, "Don't Jake, don't turn the light on. I have a blinding headache and I haven't combed my hair or put makeup on. I'm sure I look a fright, but I don't care. I just don't care about anything at all." She laid a cool washcloth back over her eyes. "I wish I could describe to you what these headaches are like. Most of them feel like my head is in a vise grip, squeezing and squeezing until my head feels like it is going to pop like a melon. And t-t- that medicine the doctor gave me, j-j-just takes the edge off, it doesn't m-m-make them go away."

Jake poured himself a cup of coffee and pulled out a chair at the table. "Raisa, what am I going to do with you? You've gotten yourself all in a state again, haven't you? Honey, this has got to stop or you are going to end up in the hospital. What can I do, just tell me. I love you and hate like everything to see you getting all worked up and getting another one of those blasted headaches."

Raisa turned her head and looked blankly at Jake. Suddenly, it was like someone flipped a switch, as a terrible anguished expression crossed her face and she began to scream, "What can you do? What can anyone do? Just drive me out in the hills and leave me there. I don't want to go on like this. I don't want to think about what day it is, what time you're going to get home, what to cook for dinner. I don't want to think about where my son is today. Is he alive? Is he dead? Is he hurt and bleeding over there? I can't bear to think about any of it anymore."

Jake lifted her to her feet and walked her to their bedroom. When he tried to help her into bed, she verbally attacked him again. "Get away from me. I don't need your help. If you want to help me, bring my son home. Do you hear me, Jake? Make this all stop, please."

Jake put his hands firmly on her shoulder and shook gently, "Raisa, stop this. Stop this right now, do you hear me? Arnold isn't even in combat or danger yet—he's in England, training. Here, take this pill. Maybe it will help you rest." Calmly, he tried talking sense to her like he had a million other times. They had all tried to help Raisa, her sisters, brothers, Beth and Jimmy, their pastor, and of course her doctors. Yet, she continued to bury herself under a million possibilities of the imminent future and the daily peril facing their son. News from Arnold was purposely upbeat and last they heard he was still in England.

After making sure Raisa was sleeping, Jake walked back into the kitchen to fix himself a poached egg and toast. That's when he saw Arnold's letter laying open on the dining room table. Jake reached for it. He picked it up and walked into the kitchen where he turned the light over the table on. The letter was postmarked, *June 10, 1944.*

> *Dear Mom and Dad;*
> *By the time you get this letter you will probably know more about what I'm doing and where we are than I do right now. All I can say is that we are gearing up for something big. General George Patton addressed the entire battalion last week. He really didn't tell us too much except to 'make ready'. So we've been shining our guns and packing up, ready to ship out on a moment's notice.*
>
> *He was pretty damn disappointed that we didn't get the nod to participate in the big invasion of Normandy on the 6th of June. They don't call him 'old blood and guts' for nothing. But he's a damn good soldier and like he told us-- we don't have to like him but we damn better listen to what he tells us because it'll keep us alive. We're all itching to get across the Channel to France, and start killing us some Germans. My 81st Tank Battalion is gearing up. We've had enough of all this here readiness training. We want to start shooting, for real. I'll let you know as soon as I can where we're going. All I know is we are on the move.*
> *All my love,*
> *Your son, Arnold*

Jake's hands shook as he laid the letter back onto the table. *Well, it sounds like they are heading for France. We've heard how Eisenhower has been letting Patton cool his heels in England, not letting him back in the action. But it sounds now, like those boys are getting what they want—getting in the thick of things. Please dear Lord, watch over our boy.*

Jake walked to the back of the house and peeked into the bedroom where Raisa slept. *It looks like that pill I gave her is working. I need to call Doc and let him know about the way she's talking. He's gotta up her medication or I don't think I can leave her alone.*

~~~~~

The war news that August came over the radio in the evenings and in the movie theatre's news reels. The past week was focused on General George Patton's Third and Fifth armies landing on the south end of Normandy Beach in France, on Utah Beach. They met little resistance as they came ashore and onto French soil, but the carnage of the invasion was everywhere and it was emotionally jolting to the green soldiers. The movie reels showed U.S. Sherman tanks rolling down quaint French country roads, across or through the dense hedgerows, and finally--in a victory parade through the streets of Paris, with throngs of cheering Frenchmen and women throwing flowers at the American troops.

Another couple of weeks passed before there was another letter, in which Arnie told about the limited skirmishes with pockets of German resistance. It seemed to be a hide-and-chase sort of combat with no major battles to report, although he had experienced firing the big guns on his tank. Then another letter from Arnold was delivered, some time in late November. He didn't tell them much—just that they were heading northeast toward Belgium and the Ardennes Forest. He purposely neglected to tell them his tank had been hit by a Panzer shell and he had been blown out of the hatch. He'd been unconscious for most of a day and laid up in the field hospital for a few days after that before being released back to the front. He wasn't told right away that his entire tank crew had been killed. His captain waited until Arnold was stabilized before giving him the news. Arnold didn't pass that particular information on to his parents either. He did tell them he was promoted to Staff Sergeant and was commander of his own

Sherman tank. He didn't tell his folks that he didn't wear his stripes because he didn't want to be a walking target. Instead, he tried to make light of the escalating, harrowing battles they were experiencing, concentrating on a flowing description of the French countryside and the good-looking French women.

Nevertheless, Jake and Raisa realized that Arnold wasn't and couldn't tell them everything he was doing. After all, they listened to the news on the radio and read the papers every day. Of course, there was a gag order on combat information going out but Jake had a pretty good idea of what was happening. Raisa simply read the letters from her son and concentrated on the information he sent, she didn't want to know the details.

When Arnie's letters told of a foot of snow covering the French fields, what he didn't tell his folks was that two to three feet of snow actually covered the ground, their tanks, the roads, the quaint and burned out villages as well as the frozen bodies of the dead. For sure he didn't mention the gruesome sight of the red ground where mangled remains of bodies lay frozen in pools of blood after a battle. When he mentioned that winters there were about the same as back in Wyoming, he left out the part about the miserable frozen roads that melted and then turned to mud from the tank treads and how they had to use boards or a tree limb to get the tanks back on the slimy roads. He didn't mention that none of them had the luxury of a bath, a shave, or going to the bathroom inside a building for months and as a result, they all stank to high heaven. *We're damn lucky to have a cup of hot coffee once a week. I'm damn glad me and my crew get to ride inside a tank. Those poor foot soldier's uniforms get sop and wet from the snow and/or rain, then, when the temperature dips, their great coats and uniforms freeze to their bodies. It's a hell of a mess. We all attempt to huddle around the occasional camp fire but it doesn't quite get the job done. Then there are the poor saps in the cramped fox holes. They spend days and nights on top of a frigid bed of snow and mud. Most of the guys are getting so they can catch a few winks of sleep when and where they can.*

Arnold mentioned he missed his mother's good cooking, avoiding mentioning that in the field, they subsisted on C-rations and cold tins of Spam. "The tanks give us pretty good protection from the snow and rain and we're lucky that way." What he really wanted to say was-- *we're freezing our butts off inside these tin cans because there's no heat. Sometimes when we are parked, we take turns lying underneath the tank's transmission where at least, it's warm.*

He wrote:

I'll miss going to church on Christmas Eve. I will be thinking about you all sitting there singing Christmas hymns. I expect you won't be singing any in German this year what with the ban on anything that's German. (He couldn't tell them that they were waiting in ambush at the edge of the Ardennes Forest in ten-below weather; it's snowing again. We are instructed to remain soundless so the Germans don't know we're here. Reports have come in that there are three German battalions moving this way with Tiger and Panzer tanks in the lead. It's driving us nuts, sitting here, waiting and waiting for the immense fire power and battle that is crawling right at us. We heard they are calling this the Battle of the Bulge. We're on the far northern edge and the scuttlebutt is that Hitler thinks we are the weak spot in the Siegfried Line back into France.*)*

Say a prayer for us when you're in Church on Christmas. (We're gonna need every prayer you can send up cause we're in for one hell of a battle. We're all as nervous as a call girl in church on Sunday and can't even have a smoke—it's the shits!)

The last couple of weeks, Raisa had been holding her own, spending a great deal of time tending their granddaughter. The toddler was a hand full and occupied her grandmother's every waking moment. It was the first of December and Raisa and Beth began to make plans for Christmas dinner. They decided that Jimmy, Beth and their little girl would drive to Lovell and attend Christmas Eve services, spend the night and then have Christmas dinner the next day. Raisa actually put up the tree and a few decorations. She kept busy in the kitchen baking her favorite

Christmas recipes. Keeping busy was a blessing and a solution to her problems and Raisa knew it. The task was just getting her head into it. She sent three boxes of Arnie's favorite Christmas cookies and cakes over to Europe, hoping the home cooked food would help.

As she was preparing their traditional Christmas Eve dinner of chicken and noodles swimming in browned butter sauce, Raisa thought again about what Pastor Siebert had said to her last week. *"Raisa, I know you are a woman of strong faith. You are just going to have to let your faith get you through this difficult time. It's as simple as this; Faith deals with the anxieties and worries one at a time. You are worrying about every possible scenario that might occur with Arnold. Think about this, when you wake up tomorrow, tell yourself that you are going to deal with only the immediate, only the present concerns. Let go of tomorrow's worries. Wait until tomorrow to face them. By spacing your anxieties or worries out over the days and weeks, you will be minimizing what each day hands you. I know you believe in prayer and I am sure you have been beating a prayer path up to God every night. If your worries persist after prayer, then have 'faith' that God will deal with them. Let go—let God handle it for you, Raisa."*

With that thought, she felt the tension leave her body and she smiled to herself as she kneaded the bread dough. *Even in his sermons last Sunday, Pastor Siebert spoke of the strength of our faith. There was one particular Bible verse that touched me; "Do not worry about tomorrow, for tomorrow will worry about its own things. Sufficient for the day, is its own trouble." Matthew 6:34 KJV*

CHISTMAS EVE, 1944
"The lowest ebb is the turn of the tide." Henry Wadsworth Longfellow

Before they went to church, they went outside and posed for a family photo to send to Arnie. Raisa was warm and cozy in the fur coat that Jake had bought her a few years back—she loved that coat and wore it every chance she got. They were all in church, Arnold's grandparents, aunts and uncles, his folks, his sister and her husband and little girl.

1944 - Jake & Raisa Kessel, Beth and Jimmy with

Pastor Siebert gave a beautiful sermon about Christmas and the hope the birth of Christ gives to all. Raisa looked down at the bulletin and recognized the next hymn by its number— "Silent Night." Her breath caught in her throat as it tightened spontaneously. *"Oh mercy, how am I going to make it through this beautiful hymn when I know our son is fighting for his life in a brutal war? I don't know if he is in the middle of a battle right now or even if he's still alive. The night probably isn't 'silent' where he is."* The congregation usually sang the song in German, but with the war, they weren't allowed to do anything 'German'. Raisa looked up at the huge gold and white cross that hung in the center of the altar and just under her breath she sang the first verse in the only way that comforted her:

        Stille Nacht, heilige Nacht
        Alles schaft; einsam wacht
        Nur das traute hock heilige Paar
        Holder Knabe im lockigem Haar,
        Schlaf in himmlischer Ruh!
        Schalf in himmlischer Ruh!

The congregation continued to sing, softly and sweetly, the words of the favorite German hymn. The emotion and spirituality filled the far corners of the simple, small, wood-clad church. The candle light in the windows flickered with the movement of air and the scent of evergreen pierced the nostrils of all who breathed.

Suddenly, Beth put her face in her hands and her shoulders shook with her silent sobs. With her own tears running down her cheeks, Raisa put her arm across her daughter's shoulders and pulled her close and whispered. "Shhh now, Beth, please don't cry. It's okay, honey, God is watching over Arnie, shhhh now."

After church they went back to their home on Shoshone Avenue. Beth was still visibly upset. "I'm so sorry I cried like that in church. It's just that when we sang "Silent Night," all at once I got the most frightening chill and feeling that Arnold was in danger."

Jake got up and went to the kitchen, returning minutes later with glasses of Mogen David red wine for all of them. "Here, I think we need to toast Christmas Eve and celebrate the birth of our Lord Jesus. God will protect Arnold, we have to have faith and hold onto it." Jake lifted his glass. "Merry Christmas to all and to all, a good night. Now I think it's time for one little girl to be in bed so Santa Claus can come."

The months went by and Raisa continued to be absorbed with terrible thoughts of their son, fighting in Belgium. She was still having a difficult time getting her mind off the war, probably because the war news was plastered everywhere and simply impossible to forget. Jake and Raisa knew they were fairly ignorant of what was really going on with the war in both Europe and the Pacific. All they knew is that butter had disappeared from their table and something that resembled yellow lard called 'margarine' appeared in its place. That wasn't the first or last food substitution or extinction they would experience.

One evening after dinner in late March, Raisa was poring over the garden catalog that had come in the mail earlier in the day, while Jake sat in his chair reading the *Chronicle* before heading off to work the midnight shift at Marathon. Raisa turned the pages and began to jot down things in her notebook. "Jake, I am thinking of planting a bigger garden this year, you know, a 'Victory Garden'. I don't exactly understand how it is going to help the war effort only in that we will be supplying our own food and not taking it from the stores. I guess it gives the government more food to feed the soldiers with." She looked up from the catalog and, irritated by Jake's lack of attention, snapped, "Jake—Jake, are you listening to me? For Pete's sake—I might as well be talking to the wall."

Jake put the newspaper down and calmly lifted his head, "Well, Raisa, for your information, I was busy myself, reading an account of a big battle in France that our boy may have been a part of. I frankly, didn't hear a word you said." Jake stood and stretched. "Sometimes, I wonder if our government and the papers purposely deprive us of the real truth of what is happening over there. Maybe in this case, ignorance of the full-fledged war is a blessing for us; God knows our imaginations give us enough sleepless nights. I guess I better get into my work clothes and get on out to the job."

~~~~~

One day, shortly after Easter, Raisa was having a good day. She was absorbed with spring cleaning when she heard the doorbell ring. Instantly, she froze—*what if it's the government men in the black car? I feel sick every time I see a black car drive down the street.* Raisa shook her head to clear it from the nagging thoughts. She tidied her hair as she laid her dusting cloth on the table and went to answer the front door. There stood Beth, holding Karlie by one hand. In the other hand she held a towel-covered basket.

Raisa smiled ear to ear, "Well what a nice surprise, come in, come on in. I didn't know you were coming over today. What is the occasion?"

After giving her grandmother a hug, three-year old Karlie took her by the hand and led her to the sofa. "Sit down Grandma." She pointed to the basket and, clapping her hands in glee, she announced, "There's a present in the basket for you and I picked it out all by myself." She skipped across the room to retrieve the basket from her mother's lap and with great effort, carried it over and sat it on the floor in front of her grandmother.

"Hurry, Grandma look inside the basket, look inside! It's a kitty, just for you." Karlie took one look at her mother and realized she had spilled the beans, but Beth just laughed.

Raisa noticed the towel move before she pulled it back. There, snuggled down in the basket laid a golden brown and white kitten, wistfully looking up at her with the bluest-green eyes she had ever seen. Raisa reached out and slid her hand under the kitten's round tummy and pulling him from the basket, she held him up. "Oh mercy me, just look at you."

Holding the soft kitten against her check, Raisa asked, "Where did the kitten come from, sweetheart?"

The little girl said enthusiastically, "My momma kitty, Fluffy, had loooots of baby kitties. Momma said I couldn't keep them all-- maybe one. I have to give them away and I picked the best one for you Grandma Raisa, so you will be happy! Daddy said that it's a boy kitty. He was the prettiest one."

Raisa held the fluffy apricot-colored kitten to her face as unexpected tears rolled down her cheeks. "He's just beautiful sweetheart, I love the surprise." She held the squirming kitten up and looked at him again. "What should we name him? Hmm, let's see. What about Harry? I think I will name him, Harry. Do you like that name?"

Karlie giggled, "Why do you like the name, Harry? That's a funny name for a kitty."

Raisa smiled and stroked the kitten, "Because, he is---very hairy!"

From that day on, the kitten filled a void in Raisa's life and helped her through the bouts of depression. Harry gave her unconditional love. Her days were filled with caring for him and he took her mind away from the constant worry about her son. One afternoon she looked down at the kitten sitting in her lap. *Getting Harry has been a turning point for me. I can feel the difference. I still feel fear and concern for Arnie, but for some reason, now I am able to handle it better. I know that when I get the blues, Harry climbs onto my lap and licks my face until I stop.*"

Raisa reached down and scooped Harry up in her arms. She walked over to the old rocking chair Jake gave her on their first wedding anniversary, sat down and began to rock. Harry curled up in a tight ball in her lap and began to purr. He didn't even stop when she began to sing her favorite hymn: "*Mein Glau – be blickt* *auf dich, Lamm, das ge-op – fert sich, im Glo-rien-schein. Herr, ho-re mein Ge-bet, das um Ver-ge-bung fleht; eh noch ein Tag ver-geht, mach mich ganz dein."(* My faith looks up to Thee, Thou Lamb of Calvary, Savior divine; Now hear me while I pray, take all my guilt away. O let me from this day, be wholly thine.)

Raisa sang the hymn through twice more before her own head nodded with sleep. That was the sight that greeted Jake when he came home from work an hour later—Raisa and Harry sleeping in the rocking chair. He smiled and silently thanked God for helping her.

When Beth telephoned the next week, she asked her mother, "So, how is Harry working out for you? Is caring for him too much for you, Mother?"

Raisa laughed, "Oh Beth, Harry was probably the best present you could have given me. It's like having my own personal body guard, therapist, and child with me twenty-four hours a day. He doesn't leave me alone for a minute."

"Beth, I want to thank you again-- for thinking of giving me this kitten to fill my days, something to take my mind off Arnold. When I wake up in the mornings, instead of lying in bed, thinking about the bad things, I have to get up and take care of Harry."

~~~~~

A few days later, Raisa came home from the Women's League meeting at church with a smile on her face. That evening at supper she was full of news as she and Jake ate the meatloaf and fluffy mashed potatoes. "Today, I was appointed head of the district meeting that we are hosting next summer here in Lovell. Sadie Ritter volunteered to help me." Raisa smiled as she sipped her glass of water. "I worked with her during our remodel; she was a salesgirl at the hardware shop at the time. We've had lunch and run into each other a few times over the last few months. She even went to the movies with me a couple of time, then she found herself a boyfriend and I haven't seen much of her; he's been keeping her pretty busy. She's just the sweetest, most innocent young girl I think I've ever met. The sad thing is Jake, she's all alone in the world, both her folks are dead and she doesn't have any other family. She sort of adopted me as her mother or sister, whichever! I feel pretty protective of her as well I don't know why I wouldn't, she is adorable!"

Raisa wasn't sure Jake had heard a word she was saying but went on chattering anyway. "We have lots in common. She's in love with a soldier who was here in Lovell for just a month or so and now has left to ship out. I guess before she met him he was in boot camp and came back here to visit a sister or some relative. He asked her to marry him when he gets back; he asked her to wait for him and all that. You never know about those kinds of guys, he probably has a girl in every town. But I didn't tell Sadie that. I didn't want to throw cold water on her dreams cause she's head-over-heels for the guy."

Raisa pushed back from the table and stood, looking out the window. "Something about this whole romance bothers me. Like I said, she's all alone with no parents or anything and she's so in love with this guy. She told me she doesn't know what she'll do if anything happens and he doesn't come back. So see, I have someone else and something to look after, too. God has mysterious ways of helping us out of dark places, doesn't he?"

For the next two months, Raisa and Sadie Ritter worked side by side, making all the arrangements for the big district ladies aid meeting in Lovell that next summer. On Monday, after working all morning on their meeting plans they went out to lunch. Naturally protective of the young girl, Raisa noticed that Sadie wasn't eating her lunch. "Honey, is something wrong, you look a little peaked? Are you coming down with something?"

Sadie looked up from her half-eaten sandwich and burst into tears. "Oh, Raisa, how, could I be so stupid? I got myself into an awful mess, just awful and I don't know what to do."

Raisa looked around the half-empty restaurant. Nobody was paying any attention to them. On pure instinct, Raisa suggested they leave. She helped Sadie on with her coat and ushered her out the door after paying for their lunch. Raisa opened the car door and stuffed Sadie inside as she hurried around to the other side and slid in. Raisa reached out and covered the girl's shaking hand with her own. "Now, Sadie, what is going on with you? You can tell me honey, I'm your friend and I've been through lots of bad spots in my life. No matter what is wrong, I am here for you and I'll stay here for you."

Sadie looked blankly out the window, "I'm pregnant! Joey shipped out for Germany yesterday. He's been stationed at Fort Benning for the past month. I was so hoping he might get another leave before he left the United States and then we could get married. But now—he's gone and I'm here all alone and in a big mess."

Raisa slid over and put her arm around her young friend. "Oh, honey—I am so sorry. You are in a bit of a bind, aren't you? I'm pretty sure I've heard that there is a way you can get married long distance in a time of distress. I'll have to check into it and see what I can find out for you. That way nobody has to know it's for you. Do you want me to do that?"

Sadie wiped the tears from her eyes and blew her nose, "Oh, Raisa, I'm so ashamed. I'm not a bad girl. It's just that I don't have anyone else and I love him so much. He is my whole life and now this. I just don't know what to do. I simply can't bear it. I am so filled with shame."

Raisa asked Sadie to give her a couple of days so she could make some calls. "I'll pick you up on Thursday afternoon for our next meeting and hopefully by then I will have some good news for you. And Sadie, nobody else has to know about this except you and me. We'll get it worked out some way, honey. Pray, sweetheart, pray that God gives us some answers."

Raisa went home that day and she didn't say a word to Jake about Sadie. When he went out to work on some stuff in the garage, she made some calls but came up blank. *Oh dear, what am I going to tell that poor girl when I see her on Thursday. What is she going to do? We just have to think of something. There has to be a good answer out there.*

Raisa pulled up in front of Sadie's house promptly at 1:30 on Thursday. She parked by the curb and blew the horn. She noticed that Sadie's shades were down, but didn't think a thing of it because Sadie often didn't draw her shades up. Raisa blew the horn again and when Sadie didn't come out, she went to the door and knocked as she thought to herself, *Come on Sadie, we have things we have to get done today. You'd better be dressed and ready to go.*

After knocking the third time, Raisa tried the doorknob. The unlocked door pushed open and Raisa called out, "Sadie, are you here?" She went into the kitchen. No Sadie. Raisa saw the bathroom door was slightly open and as she passed it she peek in—no Sadie. She continued on her way down the hall to Sadie's bedroom and again, she called out as she stepped through the doorway. "Sadie, Sadie, it's me Ras--- oh dear God, NOOOOO! No, Sadie. No, you didn't!"

Raisa ran to the girl's cold body swinging from an extension cord. Even though she could tell it was too late, she tried to get her down. Raisa was about to call for help when she noticed a letter lying open on the table. Without thinking, she bent forward and read:

My dear Sweet Sadie:

I thought it best to write a letter instead of calling on the telephone. As you probably know I am shipping out to Germany tonight. Don't know what I'm going to find once I get over there, but I'll give it my best shot. You know me—always trying to do my best in a situation.

Sadie, I want you tell you how much you mean to me and what a swell gal you are. We had some great times when I was in Lovell and I won't ever forget you. I wish things had turned out differently for us, but one never knows how the hands of fate are going to swing. I know I asked you to wait for me until I got back from the war. But I ran into a bit of an unexpected problem when I got back here, to Fort Benning. When I was in basic training down here, I had been seeing this girl and we dated off and on for a month or so—had some swell times. But as it happens, one thing led to another and a situation developed that I had no idea of. You've got to understand that this all happened before I came to Lovell and met you.

When I got back here, Sandy told me she was pregnant and so we were married last week. I sure am

sorry kid, hope you understand. I'll never forget you and our good times.
Take care of yourself,
Joey

The letter fell from Raisa's hand onto the second-hand table. She put her face in her hands and wept. "Oh Sadie---you poor innocent girl. Why didn't you call me? I would have found some way to help you, protect you. We could have found another way to work this situation out. You didn't have to kill yourself and your baby too."

Still in shock, Raisa walked numbly to the phone. She picked up the receiver and hit the cradle until an operator answered.

CHAPTER TWELVE

Spring, 1945: Patton's Third Army convoy rolled at a steady clip toward a remaining bridge crossing the 'mother river' of Germany, the Rhine. Before crossing the Rhine, Patton's jeep paused and standing tall as a German pine, he gave the 'forward' jab with his right arm, pointing in the direction of Berlin.[9]

Sergeant Arnold Kessel's Sherman tank was third in line behind a troop truck in the convoy. Arnold stood in the open hatch, directing his crew along the rut-filled dirt road that wound through thick conifer and spruce forest and over gently rolling hills. They were now rolling unimpeded across once highly protected and impenetrable German soil, in high speed search-and-destroy mode. Arnold kept a keen eye out but so far they had met only small pockets of resistance.

The long line of tanks, trucks, and half-tracks as well as columns of marching foot soldiers moved at top speed. The guys called their pace 'Patton's minimum speed'—he was known for moving quickly, deceptively, and decisively. It wasn't any secret that the German high command feared and revered his fighting skill and unpredictable tactical command.

April 4, 1945 began like any other day as Patton and Gen. Courtney Hodges's battalions penetrated deeper into northern Germany. The 5th Armored Division, the 81st tank battalion, and the 89th infantry moved northeast, toward their intended target---Berlin.

Sergeant Arnold Kessel had no idea the impact this day would have on him as well as every man who witnessed what lay ahead, over the next hill. They smelled it, before they saw what it was. Many held their hands over their noses even though they were used to offensive smells, this was different and it took their very breath away. It desecrated and permeated the air, the trees, and the very minds of the men and all that was decent or humane.

Suddenly, the heavy forest road opened onto a man-made clearing. Captain Morris, who rode in the lead jeep, stood up and raised his arm to halt, then turned to stare at what lay in front of them. The entire convoy seemed to freeze. What their eyes saw stunned and horrified them beyond belief. All they could say was, "What the hell? Why would—how could, a human being do this to another human?" Skeletal forms of men and women—humans, reached weakly for help. They looked as if they hadn't had a bath or clean clothes for a year or more. Many of them had soiled themselves and could do nothing about it. Their faces were void of emotion—their eyes hollow orbs.

As tank commander, Arnold was standing in the hatch of his Sherman tank as they slowly moved in closer to the fenced compound. They passed the looming, unmanned guard towers, the ten foot fences topped with razor wire, and noticed the machine guns hanging limp. There were no German guards, just a crudely painted sign over the main gate which read, OHRODROF.[10]

Nothing could have prepared the combat-hardened troops for the horrific sights which filled their eyes. The 'walking dead' were one thing, but then the piles and stacks of rotting corpses were discovered, waiting for the ovens. No one there that day would have ever believed another human capable of the gross inhumanity seen at that moment. Now, they all knew why the Nazis had to be stopped—of what they were capable. Every man who saw and smelled the horror of that day never forgot it.

The men watched as battle-hardened General George Patton rode standing up in his jeep as it crawled through the open gates of the compound. The American troops stood to the side, their faces grim and ashen trying to digest the visions they had just encountered. They watched as Patton and his aides walked from one barracks to another, their jaws clenched and eyes narrowed-- trying in vain to take it all in, to contemplate it all. Arnold and his crew saw Patton's face when he walked out of the last building, the building where the ovens were kept. A ghastly pale Patton stop and put his hand up to brace himself as he leaned weakly against the outside of a building. Then, just as suddenly, he turned and shouted at an aide, "Get General Eisenhower on the phone. He's got to see this!"

The German civilians from nearby villages were caught in the middle of a terrible, escalating situation created by the Nazis and their supreme leader, Hitler. They had believed, at first, that Hitler would make Germany great again, as he promised. Instead, in the end he and his SS troops made the German people afraid and ashamed of their country and of their leaders, but it was too late. This camp was one of the first concentration camps liberated but it was not the last. The horror of what had happened only grew as allied troops discovered just how many camps there were like this one. As Allied Forces pressed deeper into Germany, they were astonished at the actual number of extermination camps. Each one was worse than the last.

On the other side of the world, the movie news reels and radio war news were filled with positive news as the Allied Forces pushed their way across Germany's borders, plowing through once immaculate villages and pristine farms. The Battle of the Bulge seemed to have been the turning point--when, at great cost, the Allied Forces drove the German army back toward their borders. Then, on April 27, the news flashed hot and furious: Italy's leader, Mussolini was killed, hanged in an Italian city square along with his henchmen. On the 30th of April, the teletypes buzzed with the jaw-dropping news that Adolf Hitler and his wife of several hours, Eva Braun, had committed suicide in their underground bunker in Berlin.

The entire free world was jubilant as an audible breath of relief and hope was shared. The end of the war was very near; the Allied forces could smell victory as scores of German soldiers simply dropped their guns and raised their hands in defeat. Raising their hands worked for some surrendering German soldiers and then again, for some it did not. Allied soldiers could not erase the horrific images of the blatant cruelty they had witnessed, time and time again in the Battle of the Bulge and Ardennes Forest. And once inside Germany, there were the unspeakable concentration camps. Someone had to pay for the atrocities; as in all wars, sometimes it is the surrendering soldier who stood with his arms in the air---he paid at that moment.

The final chapter of World War II in Europe came with the formal surrender of the German army in Italy, on May 1, 1945. On May 2, the enemy surrendered after the Battle of Berlin, followed by the surrender of all German forces on May 8, 1945.

Jake and Raisa were sitting at the kitchen table having their breakfast on a beautiful, balmy spring morning, the kind that makes you want to get out in the yard and dig in the dirt. Jake noticed Raisa was unusually quiet and seemed lost in her thoughts. "Raisa, what is eating at you this morning? I thought you'd be on top of the world with the news that our son is coming home. I'd think you would have a million things to do to get ready for his homecoming. But you seem sad and off somewhere else in your thoughts. What's going on? Talk to me, will you?"

Raisa looked up from her plate of eggs and bacon. "Ahhh, Jake, you're right, I'm sorry. Of course, our prayers are answered-- knowing that our son is coming home. But, we still have t-two brothers who are missing in the Pacific and we don't know if they are alive or dead. And we don't know when the w-war over there is going to end. It's the 'not knowing' that is so unbearable. I know it's hard for both of our parents to wait and wonder." Raisa took a sip of her coffee. "A-a-nd Jake, have you thought of your relatives who live in the Black Forest? What about them, we haven't heard anything from them in four years? I've read reports that many of the German civilians are starving and homeless."

Jake reached across the kitchen table and laid his hand on his wife's forearm. "I know honey; we have to hang on though. We'll hear one way or the other at some point about what's happened to our brothers and the cousins in Germany. I'm sure we aren't the only folks who are waiting and wondering about German relatives. Try and get the bad thoughts out of your mind, maybe go out and visit your folks today. That might help."

May 8th was declared V-E Day, the end of the World War in Europe. In every town, city, and state, the people of the United States celebrated with dancing and celebration in the streets, in homes, on table tops—even rooftops. The need to celebrate was as contagious as the flu.

Staff Sergeant Arnold Kessel came home to Lovell in midsummer, 1945 with his four bronze stars and numerous medals packed deep inside his duffle bag. His best girl, Noreen was there, waiting at the train station with his family, it was a picture he'd had in his mind's eye for two years. When Arnold climbed down the train stairs, the first one he hugged was his mother and next his dad. Then, he had eyes only for the shapely brunette who stood to the side. She looked up at him, eyes sparkling with tears as she threw one arm around his neck, winked and whispered, "Hi kid." She didn't have a chance to say any more as Arnold wrapped her in an embrace that had been a long time coming.

Raisa had noticed a Lovell couple standing toward the back of the platform, watching all the men get off the train and rush to their families. The woman's eyes were red and puffy and they held tightly to one another's hands as they stood and watched.

After Arnie gave everyone a big hug, he bent to pick up his army duffle bag and as he stood up he saw the couple standing near the station. "Just a minute, I have something to do. You all go on to the car—I'll be right there. Norrie, just wait in the car for me please, honey." Arnold walked toward the aging couple; their eyes met as Arnold pushed through the crowd.

"Mr. and Mrs. Randolph, I'm Arnold Kessel, I went to Lovell High with your son; we were assigned to the same battalion over in Europe." Tears filled Arnold's eyes as he struggled to compose himself. "I just want you to know that I thought a hell of a lot of Jack. He was a good guy and a hell of a soldier. I don't know, if—if it would help or not to know that he didn't suffer in the end. He probably didn't even know what hit him. If you'd seen what I did, then you would know that was a blessing, the way he died." Arnold wrapped his arms around Mrs. Randolph's shoulder and shook the hand of Jack's father. "If you need me for anything, to talk---anything, you just give me a call." Arnold nervously shifted his feet, not knowing what else to say. "Well, my folks are waiting and I better get going. Bye now!"

Back in the car, Arnold's face flushed as Norrie snuggled next to him and said. "That was really nice what you did back there Arnie. I know the Randolph's took it real hard about Jack getting killed." Arnold looked pensively out the window of his parent's car and said, "I just thought it was the least I could do, to try and give them some peace and let them know we haven't forgot."

Later that week there was a big parade down Main Street and a special memorial at the Lovell Cemetery for those heroes who didn't come home—for those men who gave the supreme sacrifice. Jake and Raisa still had no word on their brothers who were prisoners or missing in the war in the Pacific. They simply had no way to know what had happened.

It was hard to celebrate with their whole hearts but they did it anyway, for their son. Arnold tried to disguise his inner turmoil, but every once in a while, he had a particular haunted look that sucked the life from his sky blue eyes, especially when he didn't think anyone was watching. He couldn't seem to rid himself of the constant flashbacks of the war. The horror he had seen day after day would not leave him in peace—day or night. He wasn't aware that his mother heard the sound of his strained laughter and noticed the frown lines between his eyes that weren't there before the war. He wasn't aware that his folks had heard him cry out in the night, from the persistent and lingering nightmares. He was home now and he planned on getting on with the rest of his life, but he was starting to discover that it was easier said than done. *Everyone says to forget the war and get on with my life. But how in the hell am I going to just 'forget' what I heard, what I saw, and--what I did? Will it ever go away and leave me in peace? Do other men actually forget what happened after going through a war?*

Jake decided to bide his time in having a heart-to-heart talk with his son. *Think I'll wait until he's had a couple weeks to get settled in; maybe I can help or just listen to him I don't know exactly, but I gotta try to reach out to my boy.* Arnie was living at home until he could get his bearings, find a job, and get his life back.

It was a bright, sparkling spring day. Jake was at the breakfast table just finishing his pancakes when Arnie stumbled into the kitchen with an obvious hangover. Jake took one look at him and decided there and then, this was the day. "Hey son, have a short but eventful night, did you?"

With bloodshot eyes, Arnie peered at his father over his cup of steaming coffee. "Yeah, I guess you could say that, what I remember of it. I took Norrie to see that new flick, "A Tree Grows in Brooklyn". Was a pretty good movie, at least it wasn't about the war. I just can't take those kinds of movies any more. I seen enough of war and killing to last me a life time, if ya know what I mean." Arnie buttered a piece of charred toast and sat down across the table from his father.

Jake watched him for a bit and then said, "Son, I know war is terrible, I think we had this conversation before you left, but you have to try and let it go, make new plans for what you want to do now that you're out of the army."

Arnie's vile mood was matched by the vile hangover he was experiencing and that statement was all it took to set him off. He shoved his chair back, rose from the table and threw his half-eaten toast into the sink, then turned to face his father. "Forget it? 'Put the war and killing behind me, get on with my life.' That's the advice I get from everyone, especially those who haven't been in a war and I'm sick of hearing it!" Arnie punched his left fist into his right palm and ran his fingers back though his hair in obvious frustration. "Dad, for Pete's sake, have you *ever* looked a man in the eyes and shot him? Have you ever watched someone's face as the bullet tore threw him and blood gurgled out of his mouth as he died, all because of you pulling a trigger? Have you seen your best friend shot to pieces in front of your eyes or tried to shove his guts back into a body that was in shreds? How many of your friends have you held in your arms as they died, because they begged you not to leave them? Yet, we had to keep going forward, not stop to help, because the Krauts were shooting at us! Have you ever seen or smelled men on fire, running and screaming? Have you ever seen a field of perfect fallen snow, all white and pure one minute, and after an hour of fighting, looked at it again and it was covered with red, glistening blood, with limbs, with bodies and the endless screams of those poor SOB's who weren't dead yet?"

Arnie took a step toward his father, beads of perspiration dotting his forehead, his eyes wide and wild, with tears streaming down his cheeks. "Well, Dad—I have, I've seen it all and there is no damn way I will ever forget it. Do you wonder why I sit with my back against a wall facing the doorways? Do you wonder why I get jumpy during a thunder storm or when a kid runs yelling through the house? Do you wonder why I can't sleep some nights-- why I drink? It's because I can't get the sounds, the sights, and the smells out of my head, Dad. I can't make it stop—it comes back, all of it in a split second and I never know when!

"When the memories come slamming down on me, I feel like I'm back there in that thick, dark Belgium forest. I see the walking skeletons in those God-awful, stinking concentration camps in Germany. I remember the endless days and nights, when I huddled inside my tank, wondering if the next Panzer shell was going to incinerate me and my buddies. I'm scared to death that I will remember it all, until the day I die! Yeah, I'd 'love' to just forget it all and get on with my life—but I don't know how to do that and I think most guys who saw and did what I did, can't either."

Arnie turned to leave the room but then stopped and, with his back to his father, added, "And, I'm not out of the Army. I'm staying in the National Guard here in Lovell. At least I'll have some pay coming in while I look for a job. No harm in that, is there?"

PART THREE

1945

AFTER THE WAR

CHAPTER THIRTEEN

After a restless, humid night of tossing and turning, Jake and Raisa rose from their bed with the sun. The dew was heavy on the rose garden as the sun peaked over the Big Horns. They had decided the night before to rise early and get started on the job of hoeing their garden in the cool of the morning. Having spent a good portion of their lives under the heat of the sun in the sugar beet fields, they were both at a point where neither of them liked working in the hot sun. They grabbed a quick breakfast and swigged down a cup of coffee before heading down the back steps and across the wet grass to where the garden waited. With both of them working in the cool morning air, the task was finished in no time.

Two hours later, as they walked back toward the house, Jake casually mentioned, "Say, sugar, if you don't need me to do anything else, I was thinking of throwing my fishing gear in the back of the car and heading up to the Big Horns. Hoot and I've been wantin' to try that new creek we discovered above the switchbacks."

Raisa smiled, pushing the damp hair back off her face, "Oh sure, so that's how you finagle a fishing trip—help me in the garden first and then you know I can't say 'NO'!" Raisa squeezed Jake's muscular forearm. "Really, honey, you go ahead, I've been thinking about going out to the farm to spend some time with Mom and Dad anyways. Dad hasn't been feeling all that good lately. Maybe I'll call my sister and the two of us can drive out later this morning. Would you like a glass of ice tea before you leave? You can drink it while I am packing your lunch."

They went into the house. Jake washed off in the bathroom and changed to his fishing clothes while Raisa opened the refrigerator and took out the pitcher of ice tea. Then she reached into the small freezer area and pulled out a divided metal ice cube tray. She sat it on the counter and grabbed the handle, pulling with all her might as the ice cubes cracked and broke free inside the tray. Raisa shook the tray and pulled out four cubes of ice, and then she put the tray back in the freezer. *I still can't get used to this luxury of having ice cubes in my drink and this little tray invention is wonderful. All these new inventions like a toaster and an ice cube tray make living so much easier.* She poured the ice tea into two glasses and took one into Jake as he finished changing clothes.

Raisa watched as Jake took a deep drink of the refreshing cold tea. "Can you put the rest of that into my thermos? I don't want to drink it all right now, but know I will want more later? Thanks honey, guess I'm about ready to take off then."

Raisa finished packing Jake's sack lunch and handed it to him as he headed for the back door. He gave her a quick peck on the cheek as he grabbed his fishing pole and bait box then trotted down the back steps and out the door. Raisa called after him, "Have a good day and bring back some fish for supper."

Just then the phone rang. Wiping her hands on her apron, Raisa hurried to where the small telephone table sat against the dining room wall. "Hel-lo," she said, but the cheerful smile suddenly disappeared from her face. "Yes, yes I'm sorry, what did you say?" Her hand tightened on the receiver as the blood left her face. Raisa's face contorted into an anguished reply, "Oh, oh, NO. A-a-are you sure?" She listened to the voice at the other end of the receiver for a moment then said, "Yes, yes, I'll be right there. Thank you." Raisa tossed the receiver at the phone and ran for the front door. Jake was just backing their Mercury into the street as she threw open the front screen door and flew off the porch.

"JAKE, JAKE STOP! Oh, dear merciful—God. JAKE, STOP!" Hearing Raisa scream, then seeing her frantically run across the front lawn, Jake slammed on the brakes and whipped the car back into the driveway. He jumped out of the car door, not bothering to close it as he headed across the grass, straight for his wife. He didn't know what had happened but he knew it wasn't anything good.

Jake took hold of her shoulders and shook her gently as she sobbed, "Oh Jake, J-ake—the hospital just called. It's my dad, Jake. They said---they said my father is dead. He's DEAD, Jake, my Dad is DEAD!" She went down onto her knees on the front lawn covering her face with her hands, as great gulping sobs racked her body.

Jake put his hands under Raisa's armpits and pulled her up. "Come on honey, we'll go to the hospital right now. Did they say what happened to your Dad?"

Raisa tried desperately to get control of her emotions. "Yes, something about a m-m-massive heart attack out at the farm. Their neighbor brought him and Mama in to town, but it was too late. Oh, Jake, I can't believe this—not my Dad."

It was a record-breaking sizzling summer day when the family of David Steiner gathered to honor him and his memory. They were all there at his gravesite except for his first-born son, Jack, who was still missing somewhere in the Pacific. There had been no word from the military authorities and the family was beginning to lose hope, especially since hearing that Jake's brother, Johnny Kessel, had died at the very end of the war, after surviving the Bataan Death march and internment by the Japanese. They had learned that the Japanese slave ship he was on had been bombed by American fighter planes—not knowing its cargo was American POWS headed for slavery in the Japanese mines.

As Jake had feared, the death of her father sent Raisa into another deep depression over the next few weeks. She submitted to a program of medication and therapy sessions with her doctor and a psychologist. After a month or two, she began to act more like herself.

~~~~~~

One late summer evening, Raisa and Jake were sitting out on their front porch in the cool shade. The pungent aroma of the fresh cut lawn hung in the humid air as Jake enjoyed a smoke and Raisa mended a blue sock. Still concerned about his wife, Jake had been watching her out of the corner of his eye. Finally, he said, "How did you do today, honey? You look better—got some color in your cheeks again."

Raisa smiled weakly as she responded, "Yeah, Jake, I'm feeling better. I still find it hard to believe that my Dad is gone, and for it to happen so quickly. I wasn't totally prepared for it, none of us were. I knew he wasn't well, but didn't think the end would come so fast. I guess we never do, do we?" Raisa reached down in her dress pocket and pulled out a white, embroidered hanky. She blew her nose as persistent tears slid over her prominent cheekbones, the cheekbones she had inherited from her father. "He was everything to me, Jake. You know how close we were. I remember how I held on to his hand all those days we was on the boat coming from the old country. He was my rock; he was always there for me. I could always count on my Dad, and now he's gone."

She shook her head and looked into the distance. "It's just so hard to accept and, of course, I'm worried about Mama. Did I tell you that my brothers want to move her off the farm? They found a perfect little house just four blocks south of us. I suppose it's the best thing for her. She'll be in her own home but close enough to us if she needs help. If only we'd hear something about Jack, one way or the other. I pray to God he's alive somewhere. I don't think Mama could take it if he was dead too!"

Jake gazed out into the fading light, and after a few moments, he said, "I don't want to make a mountain out of a mole hill, but I think I might call in for a physical. I've been more tired than usual lately, and don't have much of an appetite, but am thinking it's just the heat and that shift work. It seems I just don't get a good rest when I'm on midnights and I'm no young buck anymore."

Alarm raced through Raisa as she reached out for her husband's arm, "I noticed that you've not been eating like usual—I just thought maybe it was the heat as well. Perhaps it's a good idea to call Dr. Welsey and get an appointment. We can't be too careful; you know it's best to catch things before they get worse."

It was November, 1945--the fall crops were all in and most folks were making plans for their holiday family gatherings. It was a Thursday morning, just a week before Thanksgiving when the shrill ring of the telephone startled Raisa as she was polishing silver. Jake had worked the midnight shift at Marathon Oil and was now sleeping in the other bedroom. Raisa wiped her hands on her apron as she hurried to pick up the phone before it rang again.

"Hello?" She listened to the voice on the other end. She blinked twice as tears filled her eyes and her mouth opened to speak but no sound came out. She stepped around the wall into the kitchen so as not to wake Jake. Then she said, "WHAT? Is this really YOU? Where are you? What happened" Where have you been? Are you here, in Lovell?" The voice on the other end of the phone said something and Raisa said, "Sure—of course, I have the car—I'll be right down."

Not giving any thought to the sleep Jake needed, Raisa threw open his bedroom door and walked quickly to the bed. She shook his shoulder to wake him. "Jake, oh my word, Jake, wake up. The phone—he called, he's at the train station---it's my brother, Jack. Jake, he's alive; he's home!"

Immediately, Jake jumped from the bed and threw on a shirt, a pair of pants and his brown loafers as they headed for the back door. On the way to the train station, Jake asked, "Did Jack say anything about where he's been or how long he's been in the states? Does he know about your dad, Raisa, did you tell him your dad is gone?"

Raisa looked out the window. "I don't know, Jake; he didn't say where he's been or anything. He said he would tell us all at the same time, that it's a long story. I don't know how long he's been back either. You know Jack—he likes surprises and loves an audience so I am sure we will all find out as soon as we can get everyone together. And—no Jake, I didn't have time to tell him about Dad. I don't think he knows because he said he wanted to go see the folks, first thing. How is he going to take the news, Jake? He always looked up to Dad. That is going to be hard for him, I know."

As Jake and Raisa pulled up in front of the brick train station, they spotted Jack sitting on a weathered bench out front. He was noticeably thinner and his hair was collar length. Raisa was beside herself with joy. "There, over there-- he is sitting on that bench. Anyway, I think that's my brother, he looks so different doesn't he?"

Raisa was out the car door before Jake had shifted into park. She ran to the man on the bench as he stood with arms open.

Jack embraced his oldest sister and the two of them just stood holding each other for several moments before Raisa broke the hug and pushed back against Jack's chest. "You are too darn skinny, Jack. But you are alive and that's all that matters."

Jake grabbed Jack's hand and then he too embraced his brother-in-law. Jake slapped him on the back. "It's a miracle, that's what it is, a damn miracle that you are home. You are going to tell us all how you survived, what the heck happened over there, but first we need to get you in the car. Where is your luggage?"

"Luggage?" said Jack, amused. "I don't have a suitcase or nothing, just this here shaving kit. I lost any luggage I might have had years ago, when the Japs picked me up and decided I was their prisoner! All I have is a change of clothes, compliments of Uncle Sam. Now, I just need to see my folks, so let's go!"

Jake and Raisa exchanged glances. There was no need for words at this point. Neither of them knew how to tell Jack that his father had died. The three of them climbed into Jake's car. Raisa took the back seat, letting Jack sit up front with Jake. Jack immediately began telling about being captured by the Japanese on Wake Island. Jake and Raisa let him talk; it just seemed easier that way. Anyway, when Jack was talking, nobody could ever get a word in edgewise.

But as Jake turned the corner on the street where Sofie's new house was, a bewildered expression crossed Jack's face. "What are you doing? Where the hell are you taking me? I said I wanted to see the folks, didn't I?"

Jake pulled the car to the curb in front of Sofie's house. Raisa put her hand on her brother's shoulder and said, "Jack, things are different with the folks, some things have happened that Mama needs to tell you. This is where she lives now, not out on the farm."

Not waiting for his sister's words to register, Jack jerked the car door open and bounded up the front steps. He knocked once and not waiting for someone to open the front door, Jack turned the door knob, pushed it open and strode purposefully into the house.

Once Jack was inside the small house, he looked right, then left, and locked eyes with his mother who was standing in the kitchen door, wiping her hands on her checked apron. Sofie waddled as fast as she could across the room, all the time crying, "Johann, my Johann, my son."

Jack folded his mother in his arms and they just stood that way for the longest time—it was something they had both dreamed of. Finally, Sofie pushed back and reached up to touch her oldest son's face. "Oh, Johann, you are so thin, and so brown! We all want to hear where you have been and how it was for you over there. Maybe we should sit down now, I need to sit down because my legs are shaking so." They moved in the direction of the couch as Jack said, "Okay, but wait a minute, Ma. Where is Dad? I haven't seen my Pop yet."

Sofie stopped walking and turned around slowly to face her son. "Oh Johann, you don't know, do you? It' a terrible thing but you should hear it from me. Your papa is not with us anymore; he has passed to his heavenly reward. It was just a few months ago and there was no way to get in touch with you, so you would know."

Jack couldn't have looked more stunned. His eyes were wide and his mouth opened, but no sound came from him as tears began to roll from his eyes again. Jack brought his hands to his face and cried like he had not cried in a very long time. Sofie pulled him to the sofa and pushed him down. Together they sat, waiting for Jack to get control of his emotions.

~~~~~

Jake and Raisa waited in the car. Then, they took their time walking up to the house, wanting to give Jack time to see his mother alone and to hear the news from her about his father. As Jake was climbing the front steps, he felt a sharp, shooting pain in the small of his back. Instinctively, his hand reached toward the pain.

Raisa noticed that Jake had hesitated behind her and, without looking at him, she said, "Jake come on, I think it's okay to go inside now." She turned to see why he wasn't coming and noticed he was pale and seemed to be wincing. "Jake is something wrong? What is it? Is it that same pain you mentioned last week?

FLESH ON THE BONE

Have you made that appointment with Doctor Wesley for a physical yet?"

Jake shook his head. "Naw, it's nothing, honey. Probably pulled a muscle or just getting old. Come on let's go inside."

Jake and Raisa entered and walked into the living room, where they found Jack and his mother sitting on the sofa. Jack's eyes were red and his jaw was clenched as he struggled to get control. He held his mother's hand in his as more tears spilled from his eyes. "Ahhh, Ma, Ma—I only missed seeing him by four months."

Sofie dabbed at her own eyes as she tried to console her oldest son. "Oh Jack, he tried so hard to wait. He never believed you were dead, he always said that you would find a way to stay alive. His heart was just too sick, he couldn't do it any longer; he didn't suffer, Jack. His death came silently and quickly; we have that to be thankful for."

Jack took his mother's hand in his and said, "When we were in the thick of things over there, there was no way for me to let you know I was still alive. I didn't even know the war was over for weeks after peace was declared because I was hidden way the hell back in the jungle on that God-forsaken island." Jack sat up, wiped his face and blew his nose into his handkerchief. "I want to tell you all about what happened. It was a day-to-day existence, depending on if the Japs found me or not. I'll tell you one thing, I owe my life to the Japanese family who hid me under a porch and made sure I had food. I'm going to bring their oldest son to the United States and put him through high school. That was my promise to them, if I made it out of the war alive; by the grace of God; I am going to do it! It was because of God that I'm alive, he gave me the opportunity to survive the war; I know that sure as I'm sitting here!" [11]

Raisa went into the kitchen to make them some coffee. In a short time, she carried a tray with the coffee pot and four cups out into the living room. "Here, I think maybe we all need to have a cup of coffee."

Sofie looked up and said, "Why don't you bring some of that fresh *Yagada Kugel Kuchen* that's sitting under the cake cover. That would go good with this coffee."

After they drank the coffee and ate the dessert, they talked a bit more until it was time to go home. Jake and Raisa left Jack there at Sofie's house. She had an extra room and for now, it was the best place for him to be.

Needless to say, their traditional Thanksgiving dinner was one to remember for both the Kessel and Steiner families: so much to be thankful for---so much. Jack and his mother, Sofie were at Jake and Raisa's table along with Arnold, his girl, Noreen, Jimmy, Beth and their little girl, Karlie. Their hearts were so full of thanksgiving, but the day wasn't over, there was still more. With his arm around his girl, Arnold and Noreen announced their engagement and plans to marry the next August. Then, Jimmy and Beth announced they were going to have another baby in the spring.

That night, as Jake and Raisa were getting ready for bed, they stood still, in each other's arms for a moment, so happy and thankful for their blessings. Their son was home safe from the war. Jack, too, was home safe, and they were going to be grandparents again. Everything seemed perfect.

After the holidays, things settled down and got back to normal. Jake went to work, played a hand or two of cards at the pool hall once a week, and was busy with his duties as president of the church council. Raisa tended to her housework, cooking, yard, and ladies church group. She still tried to catch the best movies that came to town—it was the one thing she did entirely for herself.

The middle of the next week, Raisa and Lizzie went to a movie called "The Bells of St. Mary's', with William Gargan and Henry Travers. It was pretty late when she got home and she didn't wake Jake, knowing he needed his sleep. Raisa undressed and slipped into her own bed without telling him about the movie.

FLESH ON THE BONE

Around midnight, Jake got up from his warm bed to go to the bathroom. He finished doing his business and before flushing, just happened to glance in the toilet bowl. The dim illumination of a street light came in through the window, but it was enough for Jake to tell that what was in the toilet bowl was dark. He quietly closed the bathroom door and flipped on the light. His face paled as he looked down—it was blood. As he walked back to the bedroom, that all-too familiar pain shot across his lower left back again, so severe that it took his breath away and stopped him in his tracks. He waited until it subsided, then crawled into bed—wishing and praying for it to just go away.

Unnerved by the blood and the pain, Jake had a hard time going back to sleep. He laid there worrying and wondering what was happening inside his body. Because he couldn't think of anything else to do, he said a prayer, *Dear Lord, I know I got something wrong inside; I know it as well as I know my name. Please help the doctors find out what's wrong and please help them to fix me up. I got a lot of livin' yet—guess you know best. Thanks Lord for everything. Amen*

Two days later, after getting the physical he'd been putting off, Jake sat in the doctor's office, waiting patiently for the results of the tests. Later that afternoon, after parking the car in the garage, Jake climbed the back steps and walked into the kitchen. Raisa stood at the kitchen sink preparing supper; she turned when she heard her husband walk into the kitchen. Alarm skittered up her spine when she looked at his face. "Jake---what is it, what did Dr. Welsey say is wrong? Did they find something?"

Jake slumped down in a kitchen chair. "You'd better sit down Raisa; this is serious."

Two weeks after Jake had the physical, he and Raisa drove to Billings where a kidney specialist removed Jake's failing left kidney in a six-hour surgery. They had to cut Jake from his belly button around to his back to get at the damaged and diseased organ. The doctors questioned Jake about any injuries to his back he might have suffered as a child, but he couldn't think of anything. Later that night as he settled down in his hospital bed, he thought about when as a boy, the numerous times his father beat him with his belt---across his back. *I wonder if that did something to my kidney—if that's how it was injured. Oh well, that's water under the bridge now. I've got good doctors and I can live just fine with one kidney or so they tell me. God was sure with me on this one!*

Jake took two months off work to recuperate. Actually, after the first couple weeks, he told everyone, "By gosh, I feel better than I have felt in a long time. I guess losing a sick kidney does that for a person." Jake saw how Raisa was running herself ragged, fussing over him. "Raisa, stop with all the fuss. I am fine, I just need to rest up—heal up, and I'll be ready to go. Now, you go find something that needs doing and leave me be."

1946: Beth, Jimmy and their three-year-old daughter drove over to Lovell to visit on the first Sunday of April. About to have their second child, Beth felt the stress of the final weeks of her pregnancy. Concerned, Raisa asked her daughter, "When does Dr. Welsey think this baby is due and will it come early? You look a lot bigger with this one than you did with the first."

Beth pushed the pillows on the sofa around, trying to find a comfortable position. "I know Mom, this is a bigger baby and I am feeling miserable. Maybe it's a boy—I know Jimmy is hoping it is. I'm just glad that I'll have it before the heat of the summer. Having Karlie in August during all that heat wasn't easy. With this one, I'll have all summer to get my figure back and for the baby to grow a little before winter. Dr. Welsey thinks I'm due around the first part of May."

Beth repositioned the sofa pillows for the third time. "I am glad Mrs. Wamhoff is still out there at the farm to help me, but after this second baby comes, she is thinking of finding a house of her own in Greybull. She promised she would stay a few months to help me out and then she will probably move into town. She doesn't have anything to keep her out on the farm—she has retired from being the community telephone operator and mail clerk. Besides, she said she is looking forward to living in town, closer to her daughter."

On April 24, Beth and Karlie came to stay in Lovell, waiting for the birth of her second child. Beth was having a hard time getting around. Raisa kept her three-year-old granddaughter busy helping take care of her mama and going for walks with her. "It's important, Beth, to walk as far as you can—it loosens up the muscles and ligaments. I know you are worried about having this baby, honey, but this one won't be as bad as the first one. That first baby is usually the hardest. At least you've been through it once so you know what to expect."

May 6th was a cool spring day in Lovell. Beth and her daughter were taking a walk around the block. Feisty blades of green grass pushed their way through brown mats of dead grass. Beth looked up at the tree branches that were as pregnant as she was with their own swelling buds. She breathed deeply as a soft breeze wafted from the south, bringing spring with it. White flower petals fluttered down from a nearby tree looking like snow drifting to the ground.

Raisa was busy washing clothes when suddenly she heard Karlie open the front door and run through the house, "Grandma, Grandma—Mama needs you, she just wet all over the sidewalk and she's crying!"

Beth and Jimmy's second daughter, Sharlie was born on May 7th, tipping the scales at eight pounds, three ounces. This labor and birth were definitely shorter, but the extra pound made a noticeable difference in the degree of difficulty. After being released from

Arnold & Noreen Kessel, Karlie & Lanning

the hospital, Beth came back to her parent's house to spend a week or two recuperating. Jimmy was busy in the fields—spring planting and calving. Beth knew her mother-in-law was there to help but she wanted her own mother to be there for her and besides she had Karlie to look after too.

It was proving to be a busy summer between the new baby and all the plans for Arnie and Noreen's wedding on August 1. They were going to be married in the yellow clapboard, Lutheran Church on Shoshone Avenue. Karlie was all excited because Noreen asked if she could be their flower girl. Beth remade one of her old pink prom dresses for her daughter. "Oh Mama—I love this bea-u-tiful dress—it's so fluffy, just like the dresses the ladies wear in the movies that I go see with Grandma."

After the wedding and a short honeymoon, Arnie and Noreen planned to move to Minneapolis where she enrolled in nursing school. Jake and Raisa invited the newlyweds over for dinner the night before they left for Minneapolis. After dinner, Arnie and his dad were sitting out on the front porch having a smoke. One thing led to another and Arnie told his dad, "I'm glad that I stayed in the National Guard; that extra money sure helps out until I get something steady. The captain told me I don't have to report for monthly drills while I'm in Minnesota. But to tell you the truth, I just don't know what I want to do Dad. I can't seem to settle down and sort things out. I even thought about going on to college but I'm not the student type and hell, let's face it, I'd didn't get that good of grades in high school. I guess I'm kinda like you, I like to work with my hands, not read it out of some book."

Jake looked across the porch at his son. "I know, Arnie, it's not easy sometimes figuring out what you want to do. I only had me a sixth grade education and I finally did alright for myself. I suppose you don't remember all the years I bounced from one job to another. Maybe when you get back I can check if there's something at Marathon for you. You'll have some time to think about it when you're gone. Don't worry son, things have a way of working themselves out."

It was going on three weeks that Raisa had continuous pains in her stomach, especially after she'd eaten. After putting up with it for a couple of more weeks, she called to make an appointment with Dr. Welsey but she couldn't get in until that next Friday.

That evening after a light meal, she and Jake were sitting out on the front porch, like they enjoyed doing after a hot summer day. Raisa sat up straight in her chair, "Jake how would you like a dish of peach ice cream? Highland Grocery had it on special today and I couldn't resist getting some when I was in there."

In no time, Raisa was carrying two bowls of ripe peach ice cream out to the porch. She and Jake sat back in their green metal spring chairs, enjoying the creamy, refreshing ice cream. When they had finished, Raisa stood up to collect Jake's dish and take them in to the kitchen sink. The minute she stood up, a searing pain tore around her right side, just below her ribs. She dropped her dish to the porch floor and went down onto her knees. She cried out, "Awwww, oh my word, oh Jake, something is realllly wrong---awhhhh!"

Jake stood up so fast that his dish went to the porch floor as well. He didn't break stride as he dropped to the porch floor beside Raisa. He tried slipping his hands under her armpits and pulling her up, but she was dead weight. "Can you stand up Raisa?"

She looked up at him, her face contorted with pain and fear, "Oh Jake—NOOOO—I can't move it hurts terrible, call the ambulance, hurry—awhhh."

The ambulance and Dr. Welsey pulled up at the emergency entrance to Lovell Hospital at the same time. The emergency room staff had Raisa out of the ambulance and onto an examining table in a matter of minutes. They made Jake wait out in the hall where he could hear Raisa crying and near screaming at times. He paced the floor, a million thoughts going through his head. *What in the world is wrong with her? I know she's been having some stomach problems. What a year we've had; first me with my kidney surgery and now it looks like something serious is wrong with Raisa. Be with her Lord—watch over my wife.*

It seemed like forever before Dr. Welsey came out of the emergency room. He put his arm around Jake's shoulder as they stood in the hall. "Jake, it looks like Raisa is going to need surgery—she passed a pretty good sized gallstone and from looking at her gallbladder, that isn't the only one rolling around in there. We are getting her ready for surgery right now. She said she's been having stomach troubles and some pain on that side, I know she called in for an appointment later in the week. It was probably that rich ice cream tonight that set that stone to moving. You can wait here or go on home and the nurses can call you when she's out of surgery. It might take a while; it's a nasty surgery. We will have to open her up from the front to the back on that right side to get at the gallbladder."

Dr. Welsey patted Jake on the back. "It's a good thing you are all healed up from your kidney surgery cause she is gonna need some nursing when she gets out of the hospital. Don't worry, she's in good hands. We'll get her fixed up like new!"

Jake waited out in the waiting room for four hours while the doctors operated on his wife. He tried to sleep but couldn't get comfortable, and smoked close to two packs of Camel cigarettes trying to pass the time. He was dozing in the chair when a nurse tapped him on the shoulder. "Mr. Kessel, you can come with me now and see your wife, she's out of surgery. She did really well and came through it all just fine. She's pretty sleepy and in some pain, but I know she wants to see you, she's been asking for you."

Jake spent a few minutes with Raisa. She was still groggy from the anesthesia and they were pumping her full of pain medication so she wasn't real talkative. Jake held her hand and gently kissed her cheek, "I'll be back first thing in the morning, honey. You relax now and let those pain meds help you sleep. It's all over and you did good—just got to concentrate on healing up now! I love you, sweetheart!"

It took Raisa a good two months of taking it easy to get back to her old self. Beth brought her daughters over to visit a couple of times and Raisa's sisters and women from the church carried in food, so there wasn't a shortage of something to eat. One evening as she was getting ready for bed and applying her ritual nightly layer of cold cream onto her face, she paused and looked in the mirror. I hope Jake and I are about done with these operations. What with those years of worrying about the war and our missing brothers and son fighting, I am about worn out. Things have been pretty good, what else could go wrong?

CHAPTER FOURTEEN

Early Fall, 1946: At the crack of dawn, Jake crawled out of his warm bed and stepped into his fishing clothes. He got his gear together and retrieved the lunch bag from the refrigerator that Raisa had packed for him the night before. Then, giving Raisa a quick kiss on her rosy cheek, he tiptoed down the back stairs and being as quiet as he could, he pushed open the back door. Once outside, he stowed his gear in the pickup, climbed in and backed out of driveway. Jake had a smile on his face as he headed east to the Big Horns.

I remember the first time I ever went fishing. It was with my Grandpa Christian back in Austria. I must have been just a little tyke, but I remember catching that first fish and I never did get the love of it out of my system. Opa told me that fishing taught you, patience. Now that I'm older, I see the wisdom in that. Fishing not only teaches patience, but endurance to stand in the middle of that rushing mountain stream and wait for the big one to take your bait. You know he's there—you know where to throw the line, then you just gotta have patience and wait him out. Sooner or later, he's gonna come after what you've got on the end of that line. He smiled to himself at the next thought. *In fact, that is exactly how I hooked Raisa into marrying me!*

It was a glorious Indian summer early morning and the snow melt in the mountains had dwindled significantly so the creeks were running slow and lazy, just the way he liked them. Jake stood in the middle of Nesbitt Creek with his new rubber waders. *Standing here in the middle of God's glory and peace is my opportunity to 'visit the still and restful waters'. The beauty, the quiet restores my soul. I've heard it said that silence can teach us more in a minute than all that blame noise we hear day in and day out. When I leave here today, I will be ready to face all of the pressures of life; I will be renewed. In the meantime, I aim to catch my limit!*

So it was. With a flick of his wrist, Jake expertly whipped his fly rod through the air several times until he zoned in on the spot he had eyed. Watching him throw that fly rod was like watching a ballet; it was a beautiful thing.

There was a deep, shaded pool lying to the north edge of the creek. Mountain ash branches skimmed the surface of the creek and the secluded pool was surrounded by huge granite rocks on three sides—the perfect target. Not getting a nibble, Jake reeled his line in real slow like, and then began circling the fly rod back and forth in an S-shape, high in the crisp mountain air until enough line had played out. He let it sail through the air and drop, smack dab in the middle of the target. A big grin covered his tanned, weathered face as the hook and buzzer fly landed in the shade of the pool, causing a slight ripple across the surface. Jake was just beginning to tease the line a little, reeling it in a little at a time and then letting it go slack when he felt the fish strike! Jake's muscles tensed as he pulled back on the pole, just enough to secure the hook in the fish's mouth, then he relaxed it some. *Yes sir, I think I got me a good one this time. Come to Daddy!*

Jake couldn't help but smile as he practiced the task of pulling, then reeling the line in a bit at a time, until the squirming trophy rainbow trout swam at his knees. Jake reached down and pulled the net from his waist; in one swift and educated swoop, he scooped the big fish up. He stopped for a moment and gazed at the squirming fish; *the scales on that fish are just beautiful—like a rainbow. I can sure see why someone named them rainbow trout—'cause you can see a whole rainbow of colors in them scales, especially when the sun hits just right.* Jake put the fish in his canvas creel and got set to cast the line again.

Yes-siree, I know them fish like that sort of cool, calm, shady water. Let's see if I can get me another. Here boys, look what I've got for you—go get it! After several hours and a full creel, he waded ashore. *I will never get tired of fly fishing—and I won't until the day I die. There's something about the seclusion of standing in a creek of pure, sparkling mountain water and throwing the fly in just the right place, to hook that big one. If me and my friends decide to come up fishing, they know to stay the* hell away from me. I don't fish with people around me. I'll go way upstream to get away because it's not just the fishing that I'm here for; it goes way deeper than that.

Jake looked at his full creel. *The wife and I aren't even that fond of eating these rainbows, but I can always find someone to give them to. Maybe I'll stop by the folks' farm on the way back to Lovell and see if they want a few of these beauties.*

~~~~~

It was just past noon when Jake turned his car into the lane leading to his parents' farm. He rolled up to the back door, stepped on the brake and cut the engine. Not seeing anyone in the barnyard or garden, he headed for the back porch. Jake was about to reach for the door handle when he heard loud voices coming from the kitchen. He paused for a minute, wondering if he should go on in or leave. *Damn it, they are going at it again. When are they going to get too old or too tired to fight all the damn time? That's what I remember about my parents, growing up—them fighting all the time.*

Jake rapped twice on the wood screen door then opened the door and walked into the kitchen, with the damp canvas creel of fish over his shoulder. His father sat at the kitchen table, finishing his noon dinner and his mother stood, back to him, at the kitchen sink. Obviously, they were in the middle of a major argument. Jake stopped, momentarily stunned by the venomous quarrel. His parents seemed oblivious to his presence. Finally he couldn't take it any longer. "Ma, Dad—what is going on here? Why are you arguing like this? It seems every time I'm around anymore, you two are always fighting. At your age, you are supposed to be getting along better. What in the heck is the matter now?"

Karl looked up at his oldest son with eyes of icy blue steel. "What business is it of yours if your mother and I have a quarrel now and then? You grew up in this house. You know we don't always see things the same way and we probably never will. What you got in that bag there? You've been up in those mountains wasting a good day fishing again?"

Jake walked to the kitchen sink and gave his mother a hug, handing her the canvas bag of fresh trout. "Yeah, that's right--I've been on the mountain fishing and thought you might like to have a couple nice big fish for your supper tonight. Take out what you want." Jake licked his lips as he smelled what remained of their noontime dinner. "You got any leftovers from lunch? I haven't eaten yet and your bratwurst and sauerkraut always were a favorite of mine."

Katja smiled as she motioned to the table, "Sit down, Jakob; for you I always have extra food. Here, I get you a plate and you help yourself."

Karl pushed back his chair, slapped Jake on the back and said, "What is this fancy thing calling our dinner—lunch? You are getting the ways of them town peoples. We still call it dinner at noon and supper at night and that's the way it should be. *JA!* Thanks for the fish. I got to get back to the field. I've only got half that field plowed and want to finish it up before the sun sets today. I don't waste my time sitting on a rock fishing like you do. Stay and visit with your mother; perhaps you put her in a better mood, *JA?*"

Jake wolfed down a quick lunch. After finishing, he looked up at his mother as she sat stone-faced and silent across the kitchen table, staring into her cup of coffee. She wasn't herself and Jake knew it. Finally, he reached across the table and took her hand. "Ma, look at me. What's going on with you and Dad lately? It seems like every time I am here you two are fighting like cats and dogs. What's the problem? Do you want to talk about it?"

Katja raised her head, her eyes narrowed and her jaw clenched tighter. Jake felt like she was staring right through him. "Ma, come on; you can talk to me. We've always been close; you helped me survive my childhood with that man. We have a special bond."

Katja yanked her hand from Jake's gentle grasp. With the same expression on her face, she shoved her chair back from the table and stomped over to the kitchen sink. With her back to her oldest son, she said, "What is wrong with your father and me is not, your concern. You would not understand; you have not lost a son in the war; you never had to leave your parents and have them die with never seeing them again. I am filled with sorrow and regret, Jakob. Your father never understood and he never will, so you forget it. I will not burden you with our problems; you can do nothing to fix what is wrong. That's all I have to say. You better go home to Raisa now; thank you for the fish, Jacob, I'll fix them for our supper."

Jake knew better than to try and change his mother's mind so he walked across the spotless kitchen linoleum to where she stood with her back still turned. Jake wrapped his arms around her and bent around to kiss her downy cheek. "Just remember, Ma, I love you and if you need me, all you have to do is pick up the phone." He walked out the back screen door, letting it slam behind him as he crossed the yard to his car. Jake glanced up at the kitchen window before he drove out of the farmyard, his mother still stood in front of the kitchen sink; she was not looking out the window, her face was buried in her hands.

~~~~~

That evening, Jake confided in Raisa what he had encountered at his parents' farm that day. "I don't know what's going to happen with the folks and their constant fighting. I've talked to my sister Louise the other day when she was out in her yard. We're all concerned about the situation."

Jake's sister Louise and her husband Bill lived right across the street and the four of them enjoyed picnics as well as a hand of canasta once in a while. Raisa got along fine with Jake's family. Most of them lived in or near Lovell just as hers did.

Two nights later, around ten o'clock, Jake and Raisa were getting ready for bed when they heard loud knocking at the front door. Jake went to answer it and found his father standing there. He was obviously very upset, "You've got to come back to the farm with me. It's your mother, she hit me, scratched my arm and I can't get her to stop crying. She is like—a crazy woman!" As Jake tried to get his father settled down, he asked Raisa to call Bill and Louise and ask them to ride along out to the farm. He knew something bad had happened between his folks. Jake drove his dad's car while Raisa hitched a ride with Bill and Louise.

What Jake, Raisa, Bill and Louise discovered at their parent's home was beyond their imagination. Karl and Katja must have had the fight to end all fights. Jake said, "Raisa and Louise, take Ma in the bedroom and get a couple of those sedatives pills down her that the doctor prescribed. We are going to have to make some hard decisions here, this can't go on!"

The decision was made for Katja to live with Bill and Louise and for Karl to move in with Jake and Raisa. Raisa didn't like it one darn bit, but there was little room for her opinion. They packed Karl and Katja up that very night and took them away to begin a long term of living separately in the homes of their grown children. The children purposely kept Karl and Katja apart, even though they lived across the street from each other. Katja became agitated whenever Karl's name was mentioned or he came near her.

Diagnosed with progressive heart failure and what the doctors called 'natural aging', Katja was in and out of the hospital that next year until one day, she didn't come home. Her family buried her in the fall of 1948. Jake and Raisa continued to take care of Karl for the next two years. Every day was a challenge, especially for Raisa. The man she was taking care of wasn't even her own father. She did what was asked of her because she was a Christian and it was what was expected.

January, 1950: It was a Sunday evening. Karl had gone to bed early as Jake and Raisa sat listening to the radio. Jake was smoking his pipe while Raisa worked on a green crocheted afghan. Suddenly, the announcer interrupted one of their favorite programs, "Jack Benny and The Lucky Strike Hour." "*Ladies and Gentlemen, the president of the United States, Harry S. Truman has just announced that North Korean troops have invaded South Korea. The United Nations has endorsed a 'police action' against the aggressors. The President has placed General Douglas McArthur as commander of the Pacific. Further details will follow as we are advised.*"

Raisa's face went ashen as her eyes filled with fear. "Jake, what does that mean? Isn't Arnold still in the National Guard here in Lovell? When are he and Noreen coming back from Minneapolis? She graduated the end of December, right?"

Jake crossed his legs and lit a cigarette. "Settle down, Raisa, all that means is that the North Koreans are acting up. I am sure the United Nations will take care of it in no time. As far as Arnie and his wife, they are supposed to leave Minneapolis around the first part of March. I'm pretty sure they'll be taking their time pulling that trailer."

Arnie and Noreen arrived in Lovell the end of March. They parked their house trailer at a local park, and spent the next few days getting caught up. Then Arnie seemed to disappear for two days—Jake couldn't seem to get ahold of him. Finally, Arnie called and told his father he wanted to stop by that evening. A couple hours later the doorbell rang and Jake opened the door to find his son standing there in his army fatigues.

Arnie walked in and sat down on the sofa. "Hey, Dad, you got anything stronger than Mogan David wine?" Jake went into the kitchen and poured two glasses of Jack Daniels over the rocks and carried the glasses back into the living room. "Where is Mom? Is she gone or something?"

Jake sat down and took a short pull of the whiskey. He had a bad feeling he was going to need it. "Yeah, she and Lizzie went to that new movie at the Hyart, *Singing in the Rain* with Gene Kelley and Debbie Reynolds. She'll be home about 9:30, why?"

Arnie leaned back against the sofa and tipped the glass of whiskey back against his lips. "That's just as well. I don't want her to hear what I have to say—right now, anyway. Well Dad, it's like this-- ever since we got back from Minneapolis, I've been at the National Guard yard every other day. They are really kicking up the drills because of that Korean mess. I'm starting to get a little unnerved by all the attention the news is giving to that, 'police action'. The top commanders of our 300th Armored Field Artillery Battalion know something that they aren't sharing."

Jake hadn't thought much more about the conversation he had with his son about North Korea. No news was good news as far as he was concerned. A couple of months later, it was after two in the morning when the phone rang. Thinking it had to do with work, Jake jumped up to answer it, letting Raisa sleep. He grabbed the receiver and moved into the kitchen so he wouldn't disturb her.

"Hello." Jake listened for a minute and a frown began to dig its way between his eyes. "Yeah, that's right." The voice on the other end of the phone said something else and Jake replied, "Just hold tight, I'll be right there."

Jake tiptoed back into their bedroom as Raisa sat up in bed. "Go on back to sleep, honey, something's come up and I gotta leave for a little bit. It shouldn't take long to take care of this." He kissed her on the cheek and headed for the back door. Once inside his 1949 Mercury, Jake hit the steering wheel with the heel of his hand. "Damn it to hell. Now what? That boy is out of control, no way for a married man to be acting at all. He better get a hold of himself and quit using the war as an excuse to get rip roaring drunk. I don't intend playing nurse maid to him at his age."

On the way home, Jake tried to hold a conversation with Arnie which was pretty much one way. "Son, what in the hell, can't you hold your liquor anymore? What is going on with you—is it still the war? Is all that still bothering you?"

Arnie tried to focus on something, anything to stop the car and the street from swaying from side to side. "Wel---l, Dad, I'll te-lllll ya w-w-what. Me a-and some of the--the boys from the 300th, deee-cii-ded to throw rr-ssselves a lit-ttttle parrrrt-ie to-night! That's right! Thaaat sure 'nough is righty, right!"

Jake turned and looked across the dimly lit interior of the car at his son. "Okay fine, you boys deserve a night out, but why go overboard? Does Noreen know where you are at this hour of the night? You better get ahold of yourself Arnie and find a job and start living your life like a married man!"

Arnold's face contorted into a semi-smile as he hit the dashboard with the palm of his hand, "Get a job? S-s-start living m-my life? Ya betcha Dad, ya betcha—thass the plan; juss-as-soon as me and the boys from the 300th, get back from that hellhole they call, Kor-reeea! T-th-ey told us to-night, we-re shippin out on August 19th. The whole damn bat-t-alion's got another war to fight on the other s-side of the wor-ld thusss time."

Jake slammed on the brakes and pulled the car to the side of the street. "What did you say? Your guard has been called up to go to Korea? Well, if that isn't the shits---that's unbelievable—just downright crazy! You've served this country long enough—you are married now and have other responsibilities."

Arnie wobbled on the seat, barely able to speak, but he had something else important to tell his father. "Ya, we-lll—that's wha' we get for signin back up with the Guard for that extra $200 a month. Ya Dad, I'm married and I gotta go back into a damn war and get my a-ass shot at s-s-some more. Annnnn-d, Dad," Arnie looked out the side window and hit the ceiling of the car with his fists as tears began to roll down his cheeks, "Thaaat ain't all, Dad—no sirree; ya know my wife—mieeee wifie, No-norrie? Well, my wiiife is, she is--N-Norrie is p-preg-nant!" With that, Arnie passed out and fell against the side window.

Jake sat motionless, staring at his son and trying his best to digest it all. He let his head drop against the steering wheel as his own tears rolled, unchecked, from his eyes. After a bit, Jake straightened up, wiped his eyes and started the car up. He pulled his son's body back against the seat then turned the car around in the street and drove slowly around town. He needed some time to think, to get this damn news straight in his head. He needed some time to figure out how he was going to tell Raisa that her son was leaving to fight in another war, and---that, he was more than likely going to miss the birth of his first child, while he was away. Jake angrily swiped at the tears that insisted on rolling down his ruddy cheeks as he pulled up to the house where Arnie and Noreen were living.

The whole town of Lovell turned out on August 19, 1950 to send off the 300th Armored Field Artillery Battalion—around seventy-five of the finest young men Lovell had to offer. The Lovell Chronicle ran a story and a picture of the battalion.

There weren't many happy faces standing on the streets that day. Their faces reflected the shock and injustice of what and why these boys from Lovell, in particular, had to fight in a 'police action'. [12] Staff Sergeant Arnold Kessel was driving one of the former, up-dated Sherman tanks that had been refitted with M-7, Priest 105mm howitzers mounted on the tank chassis. There was a string of eighteen tank-mounted howitzers that would be used as close support of the infantry over in the rolling, rocky hills of Korea. As Arnie told his dad, "It's a hell of a gun—fires 105mm cannon rounds faster than you can think."

As the troop train pulled out of Lovell, Jake and Raisa couldn't believe they were standing there for a second time in the last ten years, watching as their only son went back to war. It all seemed like a bad dream, a very bad dream. Chances were their son wouldn't be home to watch his first child be born in December. Before Arnie deployed, he had a chance to talk in private to his father, "Dad, I'm counting on you to take care of Norrie. I know she's got her Mom here, but since her father is dead and she doesn't have any brothers, you are the 'man' if she needs one. I know you and Mom will help her if I'm not back by the time our baby is born. I'm countin' on you Dad. Appreciate it, you know I do."

The morning after Arnie left for Korea, Jake and Raisa were having their breakfast in the kitchen. Raisa just picked at her waffle. She finally pushed back her chair, got up to throw the waffle into the slop pail. Jake had noticed she seemed a little down but decided not to stir the pot. He continued reading the Lovell Chronicle and puffing on the pipe he had recently substituted for cigarettes. Raisa poured herself another cup of coffee and stood motionless in front of the kitchen window, looking out into the lush backyard.

A train whistle blew, a familiar, faraway mournful wail, interrupting the peace of the early morning. Raisa put her head down as she said, "You remember, Jake, how I always said I loved hearing the whistle from the train?"

Without lifting his head which was buried in the newspaper, Jake responded, "Uh-huh, sure."

"When I was little, they reminded me of places I could go someday. Now, they remind me, they have taken my son away, again."

Jake still wasn't responding fully as he turned the page of the paper and took another sip of coffee.

Raisa turned and looked at her husband, "Damn it! Trying to talk to you, Jake Kessel, is about as satisfying as talking t-t-to the w-wall." She slammed her cup down on the Formica counter and stormed out of the room.

It was then that Jake came to the surface. *What the hell was that all about? What did I do now?*

Raisa knew from experience that she had to keep busy, had to keep her mind off the war news from Korea, and had to trust in the Lord that he would bring her son back safe and sound, just like he did in World War II. Her days were filled with taking care of her father-in-law which was a blessing and a burden. But every now and then, little doubts crept forward and she would have a bad day. *We were blessed and lucky the first time Arnie went to war, but will we be so fortunate a second time?*

~~~~~

The end of September, Jake got a call from his son-in-law in Emblem, "Hey, Dad—Ed and I was wondering if you could take a couple days off work, come over and help us combine the beans. With that rain last week, we got pushed back and they are ready to be threshed now. We need you to drive the truck alongside the threshing machine." Jake didn't need to be asked twice. He loved going over to Emblem and helping his son-in-law with the farming.

On the way to Emblem that next morning, his mind wasn't particularly on what he was doing, but on farming. *There's just something about being up on a tractor and doing something, anything with the land whether it's threshing, bringing in the harvest, or spring plowing. I guess it just got in my blood and it stayed put, even if I wasn't very good at it. I don't mind driving the truck alongside the harvester, but I almost wish it would rain and get all muddy out there. Then, I would get to drive that old beast of an iron tractor. That Minneapolis Moline would have no trouble pulling the harvester out of the mud. That iron lady can churn herself through anything!*

A split second later, a doe jumped from the barrow pit right in front of Jake's car. Shocked into reality, Jake grabbed the steering wheel and swerved hard to miss the deer as dirt and gravel flew from the edge of the highway. He braked hard as he drove down into the shallow barrow pit and then back onto the road. It had all happened in a split second. *I could have easily rolled this car if that barrow pit had been any deeper. Son-of-a-gun—where did that doe come from? That sure enough snapped me out of my day-dreaming. I better pay more attention here—getting close to Dry Creek and I know that's where the deer go to drink. Jimmy's expecting me to arrive in one piece to help them out.*

CHAPTER FIFTEEN

After Arnold left for the Korean war, Jake and Raisa were more than aware that his father, Karl's mental health was getting worse; some days were nearly unbearable. There were moments when Karl realized his Katja was gone from this earth; other days he barely knew his own name. The doctors diagnosed Karl with severe dementia and his care rested largely on Raisa's shoulders until her own health began to suffer. After a series of tests, the medical staff urged Karl's family to take him down to the State Mental Hospital in Evanston, Wyoming, because he needed to be in a lockdown facility. The sparsely-populated state had no other hospitals or dementia facilities to care for the mobile elderly. After a long family discussion, as the oldest son, Jake volunteered to drive his father down to Evanston and admit him to the hospital.

One evening before Jake and Karl were to leave for Evanston, Raisa and Jake were sitting out on the front porch as they so often did on warm summer evenings. Raisa glanced over at Jake, who was sitting in his green metal spring chair, staring off into space. "Jake, you look like you are a million miles away. What's on your mind, honey?"

Jake snapped out of his thoughts and turned slowly to face his wife. "I'm sorry Raisa, I just can't stop thinking about what that's going to be like--having to drive down to the mental hospital and leave my dad there. I never been in one of those places but I can imagine what it's like. It doesn't seem real or right, no way I look at it. I know it's the only thing to do with him. One thing I know for sure is that it's making you sick to take care of him—and I know the docs are right when they tell me it's in everyone's best interest. But I can't get the things I've heard about those there mental hospitals, out of my head." Jake slapped the arms of his chair with his hands. "I don't know how I am going to do what I have to do. All I know is that it's going to be a son-of-a-bitch."

Raisa stood and walked slowly to her husband's side. "You are going to get the strength you need from our Lord, Jake. We have to trust in him—he'll get us all through this and besides, your father doesn't realize where he is half the time. He probably won't even know he's not with family or not even in Lovell anymore once he's admitted to the hospital."

That morning in 1950, Raisa sent Jake off with a kiss and a prayer then she began to reclaim her home and go through the rest of Karl's belongings. She often thought about Jake during the next two days, praying--asking God to give him strength and comfort. Raisa cleaned her house from front to back, top to bottom. *I'm ready to recoup our life of peace and tranquility. I just could not deal with caring for Karl any longer. It feels so good to have everything back as it once was.* Then she paused and gazed out the window. *Except, that our son isn't here and Norrie is about to have their baby.*

Raisa was waiting for Jake when he pulled their Mercury into the driveway on Thursday. She walked down the back steps, pushed open the screen door and hurried to where Jake had parked the car. He was bent over the steering wheel, his head resting on it. Raisa didn't need anyone, to tell her what was the matter with her husband. She reached for the car door handle and opened the door. Raisa laid the palm of her right hand gently on Jake's back as her left hand reached for him. Not saying anything, she gently pulled her husband from the car and wrapped her arms tightly around him.

"Oh Jake, I told you not to go alone, not to take your father to that mental hospital by yourself. It was too much, too hard, but it was something you felt you had to do; it was the only thing that could have been done for him. It wasn't your fault, Jake, not at all!" Raisa and Jake held on to each other as she tried to comfort him. After a few moments, she took him by the hand and they walked up the sidewalk to the back door.

It didn't take Jake and Raisa long to get back into the swing of things. Raisa took care of the house and the yard, and went back to seeing a movie once a week at the luxurious new Hyart Theatre in Lovell. "Oh, Jake it's the biggest and most beautiful theatre in the state of Wyoming, I am betting. The seats are so plush and everything smells so new and good, not like old popcorn and cigarette smoke. They are even going to have concerts there. I got tickets for Beth, Karlie and me to see a ballet next month! Can you believe that, a ballet in Lovell, Wyoming?"

Even though she was due to deliver her first child in a couple of weeks, Jake and Raisa took Norrie with them to celebrate Thanksgiving at Emblem that year. It didn't turn out to be a very happy holiday—they all tried to be thankful, to be cheerful, but Arnold was missing from their midst and Norrie was downright miserable, mentally and physically.

The three of them left Emblem early and drove over icy roads, back to Lovell. When Jake pulled up in front of Norrie's apartment, he got out and opened her door. Taking her by the hand, he helped her climb the long stairway to her second floor apartment where she lived with her mother, Edith. Before he left, he warned her, "Now you be real careful climbing up and down those icy steps, that's all you'd need, to slip and fall!"

Jake hurried back to the car, his breath leaving vapor trails in the crisp night air and his boots crunching through the icy snow. "Brrrr, it's getting down right cold out there. Feels like we are in for another blizzard and that makes me real nervous with Norrie due in a couple of weeks."

Raisa reached across the dim light of the car and touched her husband's arm. "It'll all work out Jake. She knows we'll be there for her—anything she needs and of course, she has her mother to help her as well. I just wonder how Arnold is doing, we haven't heard from him in over a week. I can't help but think and worry about what he is going through in this war. Is it different than Germany? Is it as bad? From the news it looks like it's just as bad if not worse for our troops. One of the announcers mentioned that they are having the worst winter that they have had in years."

~~~~~

Jake had just gotten off midnights at Marathon and had walked through the door. He took off his aluminum hard hat and hung it and his jacket on the peg beside the back door and then headed for the kitchen. "Boy, that smells good—smells like waffles this morning. I need that and some good hot coffee and then I can hit the sack."

They were half way through breakfast when the phone rang. Raisa pushed back her chair and hurried to where the phone sat around the corner. "Hello." Jake turned and watched her face as she spoke. "Oh, that's a relief. It's going slow you say? Well, we are just finishing up with breakfast, Jake will probably try to get a couple hours rest and then we'll be over. Let us know if things pick up. Thanks for calling Edith."

Raisa looked at her husband, "Well, it looks like our third grandchild is on the way. You go ahead and get some sleep. Edith said she'd call when things were further along."

Jake headed for the bedroom, then turned and said, "Raisa, I just remembered—do you know what day this is? It's December seventh. Do you realize that December seventh is when the Japs bombed Pearl Harbor? How ironic is that—Arnold's baby being born on this day."

Raisa couldn't stand waiting at home and so with Jake sound asleep, she drove to the hospital to check on Norrie's progress. Raisa pushed through the front door of the Lovell hospital and up to the front desk. "Hello, I'm Raisa Kessel and my daughter-in-law is in maternity—having our grandchild. I want to go back and just say hi to her and give her a hug."

The nurse looked through her roster and found Noreen Kessel's name. Peering above her thick glasses, she stated, "Yes, Mrs. Kessel, I see her name here, but unfortunately only members of the immediate family are allowed back there. I'm sure you understand."

Raisa squared her shoulders as she said, "Noreen's husband, our son Arnold, is in Korea. He was sent there after serving in WWII. He asked us to be here for his wife when she gave birth to their first child. I am sure you can bend your rules just a little bit, or do I have to speak to Dr. Welsey?"

The nurses' eyes opened wide and her left eyebrow shot up. "Oh well, Mrs. Kessel, that does make a difference then doesn't it? Here, right this way, I'll take you back myself."

Raisa spent only a half hour with Norrie and her mother. Norrie had been in labor for about eight hours and things were getting rough. The doctor had given her a couple of hypos but they weren't doing much good. Being a nurse, she was well aware of what was going on. "I think I am getting close, Mom, you might want to go back home and get Dad—think you should both be here when this little one makes an appearance." Norrie's face wrinkled up as another hard contraction hit her. "Arrggghhhh----gotta breathe, breathe, and relax." Sweat beaded up on her forehead as Raisa took a damp cloth and blotted it away.

"You hold on honey, I'll go get Jake right now. We'll be here for you." Raisa gave Norrie a quick kiss and made a beeline for the car. When she walked into their house, Jake was awake and eating a bowl of cereal. He looked up as Raisa said, "Can you call someone to take your next shift at Marathon? Your grandchild is going to be making an appearance any time now. Come on, make a call then get your coat; we gotta get back there pronto!"

Jake and Raisa weren't in the hospital thirty minutes when the doctor took Norrie back to delivery. Her mother, Edith waited out in the front waiting room with Jake and Raisa. At exactly 11:35 p.m. on December 7, the doctor walked into the waiting room and announced, "You all have a healthy new grandson!"

Jake grabbed Raisa and swung her around. "Thank God! It's a boy, Raisa—we have a grandson! Arnold is going to be so happy. Well, son-of-gun, it's a boy, it's a boy and the Kessel name goes on!" As promised, Jake and Raisa went down to the telegraph office and sent a telegram to their son in Korea. "Congrats – *stop* – you have a son – *stop* – born 12/7 - -*stop* – all are well – *stop*.

Over the next several months, Jake and Raisa spent a lot of time with their new grandson, Terrill. A few months after his birth, Norrie decided to go back to work and she needed a babysitter. Raisa was quick to volunteer which made perfect sense. That way, Jake got to spend quality time with his grandson who, after a while, became very attached to his grandpa.

October 14, 1953: The war in Korea was over. Jake, Raisa, Norrie, and Karlie drove to the Billings, Montana airport to wait for Arnold's flight from San Francisco to arrive. There was a chill in the air as an early winter invaded the last days of fall. Norrie had left her son with her mother—she wanted to see her husband alone, if only for the night. Norrie wasn't at all sure this was a good place for eleven-year old Karlie to be, but Raisa had thought it would be a good experience for her to see her soldier, godfather get off the airplane. So, that's the way it was!

The four of them stood inside the terminal with other families, waiting impatiently for their military sons and husbands to arrive back home. Soon, they could see the lights of the plane as it circled the airfield before descending onto the runway. Jake, Raisa, Norrie and Karlie buttoned up their coats and braved the cool night, to stand against the chain-link fence, waiting for the plane to land, taxi, and come to a stop. The attendants rolled up a portable stairs to the plane and then the doors opened. They all had lumps as big as an apricot in their throats except for Karlie, who thought it was all very exciting.

"Why is everyone crying? Isn't this a happy night?" Karlie pointed to the top of the steps, "There, is that Uncle Arnold? He's so skinny and he looks so different, so tired."

Staff Sergeant Arnold Kessel was the third soldier out of the plane's door. He stood for a moment scanning the crowd, and then he spotted Norrie. He trotted down the flimsy steps and made a beeline for the gate when he saw her. There was no holding Norrie back as she busted through the crowd and security, into the arms of her husband. Raisa would have run out there too, but Jake held onto her arm. "No Raisa—those two have a lot of catching up to do. You just wait here with me and Karlie. He will get over here soon enough."

Karlie's eyes were open wide as she watched her uncle and aunt. "WOW-ZER—look at them kiss—that's pretty cool, isn't it, Grandma? They must have really missed each other, huh? Arnie and Norrie didn't let loose of each other except when he hugged his mother, father and picked Karlie up in a big bear hug. Jake put his arm around the thin shoulders of his son. "How are you feeling now son? Do you have your strength back after that bout of sickness? How did they treat you in that Japanese hospital?"[13] As expected, they all had a thousand questions, but now wasn't the time to ask them. They had tomorrow and the day after that too.

Arnie looked down at his wife and then at his parents. "I think I want to go back to Lovell tonight, to our apartment and to our son. So, let's get these bags in the car and head on down the road."

For the first couple of weeks after Arnold was back home, Jake and Raisa kept to themselves letting the young couple and their son get reacquainted. Raisa wasn't all that keen on the idea, "Darn it Jake, why do we have to stay away. We haven't seen our son for almost two years. I'd say we have some catching up to do, too?"

Jake just smiled and grabbed her around the waist, "Raisa, come on now. Those three need some time alone and Arnie needs time with Terrill. We both know that little guy is attached to me, like I was his father. I don't want to confuse him by showing up." Jake gave his wife a quick kiss and reached for his lunch pail. "I better take off for work. Now you behave yourself and stay away from those kids, okay?"

Raisa gave Jake a half-hearted smile and nodded in assent. "Okay, Jake, but how about I invite them for dinner on Sunday after church—would that be alright?"

Arnie, Norrie, and their son came by the house after services on Sunday. The minute they walked into the house, Terrill made a beeline for his grandfather and wanted nothing more to do with his father. Arnie forced Terrill to sit beside him at dinner and that didn't go well at all. Raisa tried to help the situation, "Here, let's put him between the two of you and see how that works."

Jake tried to make light of the situation even though you could cut the tension with a knife. "Have you found any work yet son? If you'd like, I would be happy to talk to Marathon. I know they are trying hard to find jobs for returning soldiers."

Arnie responded with a halfhearted shrug, "Sure, Dad that would be fine. I'd take a look at what they have. I'm sure as hell, oh sorry Mom—sure as heck not finding anything permanent around here. Norrie and I've been thinking about trying Billings.

She could get on at one of the big hospitals up there and I would probably find more job opportunities as well."

With that news, Raisa's eyebrows shot up and her eyes opened wide. "Billings? You would move clear up to Billings?"

Norrie replied, "It's not that far Mom, and besides, we think it would be good for us and Terrill. You know, to have a fresh start, new jobs, and perhaps another baby."

With his father's help, Arnie was offered a job at the Marathon refinery in Billings. He packed up his wife and son and made the move. It was a good job, with benefits and to top it off, Norrie found a nursing position with Deaconess Hospital the second week they were there. With both of them working, they qualified for a little two-bedroom, single garage house in west Billings. Norrie's sister ran a day-care and was more than happy to add Terrill to her group of kids. Everything was falling into place, or at least it seemed that way.

CHAPTER SIXTEEN

1954: The shrill ring of the telephone cut through the tranquility of the morning as Jake and Raisa were sitting at the kitchen table enjoying a leisurely breakfast. Raisa sat her coffee cup down, pushed back her chair and hurried across the waxed linoleum floor to answer the phone. "I wonder who is calling, at this hour of the morning. It always scares me when the phone rings when it shouldn't." She reached for the phone and put it to her ear. "Hello, yes he is, just a moment."

Raisa motioned for Jake to come to the phone. "It's for you, Jake. He didn't say who it was but he sounds very brusque."

Jake crossed the room, emptying the cold contents of his coffee cup in the sink as he went. "This is Jake." Jake listened to the voice on the other end. He looked down at the floor; then his eyes rose to meet Raisa's. "Yes, I understand. I think you need to send him back here. Yes, thanks for calling a-a-nd thanks for all you did for him, goodbye." Jake hung up the phone and when he raised his eyes again, there were tears. "It's my dad honey, he's died and they are shipping the body back here to Lovell for the funeral."

Raisa was beside Jake in an instant and wrapped her arms around him. "Oh, Jake, I'm sorry, but we knew it was only a matter of time. He's at peace now honey, he's in a place where he's happy with your mother and your brother. It's over."

Jake shook his head in agreement, knowing what she said was right, but his steel blue eyes were still glassy with tears. "I better get on over to the funeral home and make the arrangements. I don't think we need to call the rest of the family until we know when the funeral is going to be."

Thirty-five members of Karl's immediate family occupied the front pews of St. John's Lutheran church for the funeral of a respected member of the church and community. It was a large funeral—a beautiful tribute to a well-known and well-respected man. There weren't many tears because most of them had cried through the years Karl had spent alone at the state mental hospital. They had cried for the unseemly and unfair way his final days were spent. At least he didn't realize what had happened to him and like a child, was content to be taken care of. Now, his suffering was over and his family and friends were relieved.

After the funeral, Arnie and Norrie, as well as Beth and Jimmy, came back to the house with their parents. Raisa was fussing over Norrie, who was pale and still recovering from having given birth to their daughter, Arneen, only a few weeks prior. The women were sitting at the kitchen table having a second cup of coffee and the men were in the living room, talking about what men talk about. Raisa looked across the table at her daughter. "Speaking of being pale, are you feeling okay, honey? You are as thin as I have ever seen you."

Beth glanced up at her mother and forced a smile. "I'm fine Mom, it's just, you know--a woman thing. I'll be fine. I have an appointment with the doctor next week up in Cody. It's nothing out of the ordinary, don't worry yourself."

~~~~~

A month later, Raisa and Jake made the trip across the sage-covered hills to the south of Lovell, to visit their daughter and her family in Emblem. It was Raisa's birthday and they wanted to spend it with family. They went to church at the white, clapboard Lutheran church where Jake had been confirmed as a boy and where Beth and her family attended. After services, they drove back to the farm and Raisa helped Beth get their Sunday dinner on the table. It was unseasonably hot as Beth and her mother bustled around the kitchen. Suddenly and without warning, Beth leaned over the kitchen sink and gagged. Sweat beaded up on her forehead and she was deathly pale.

Raisa hurried to her daughter's side, putting her arm around Beth's waist. "Beth, are you all right, what's wrong, honey?" The answer to that question dawned on Raisa before she had another thought.

"Oh, Beth--do you think this was a good idea to get pregnant again. You have had so much trouble carrying a baby with your Rh-Negative blood and all. What are you thinking?"

Beth smiled weakly up at her mother as she splashed cool water on her face, "I know, Mom, but I want to give Jimmy a son and we thought we would try once more. The doctors in Cody are giving me this new drug called DES—it's supposed to stop my RH negative blood cells from attacking the baby's blood like before. They are telling me they are having good results with it."

Beth removed the wash cloth and sat up. "Really, Mom, I have felt pretty good, except I am getting a tummy already and I'm not even three months along."

~~~~~~

During the summer of 1954, a dreaded polio epidemic hit the area with a vengeance. County and state health officials closed the town swimming pools and canceled all public assembly as medical teams gave anxious long lines of bawling kids gamma globin shots at the local Elks Clubs. Then, people disappeared into their homes, pulled the shades and locked the doors. Everyone was scared, especially when several local kids came down with the dreaded disease; the worst cases were put into the confines of an iron lung which helped them to breath. Some cases were so deadly they didn't even make it to the hospital. Karlie cried when she learned that her playmate in Greybull, Dean had actually been one of the kids who died. Her cousin Susie was in the Cody hospital with a pretty severe case of polio in her legs. Fearing the worst, Karlie pestered her father until he drove her to Cody so she could wave to Susie through the hospital window. On the way back home she said, "Thank you Daddy. Now I know that Susie is still alive, but I'm gonna keep praying for her until she comes back home."

Throughout the long hot summer, Raisa and Jake made the trip across the hills to Emblem frequently to check on their daughter. Beth was just plain miserable. Her feet swelled so much the only shoes that fit were sandals. On their way home, after one of their last visits in early September, Raisa said, "Jake, I can't get over how big Beth is with this baby. I feel so sorry for the poor girl. It can't be easy to be 'so pregnant' in this dreadful late summer heat. Jimmy and Beth have had a heck of a summer, what with the polio epidemic and hoping Beth can carry this baby to term. I can see the strain on both their faces. At least she has those two girls to help her with the housework and light cooking."

As the summer came to an end, the polio epidemic disappeared as suddenly as it had appeared, but it left a lot of hurt and pain in its wake. Kids went back to school, people went back to church, social gatherings and life got back to normal. Raisa drove over to Emblem by herself when Jake was working days at Marathon Oil. She did what she could for her daughter who was big as a barn with her late pregnancy. "When is your due date, Beth? Does the doctor think the baby will come early? Since you are going to have to drive to Cody and not Lovell this time, are you going to stay up there instead of risk driving the thirty-five miles when you go into labor?"

Beth tried to be enthusiastic, but it took a lot of effort. "Ah Mom, the doctor thinks my due date is around the middle of October. I really can't go stay up in Cody by myself. I have two daughters to watch over and Jimmy is in the middle of threshing beans—he can't take the time off. I guess we are just going to have to take a chance and hope I don't deliver too quickly. I have never had that problem before. It always takes me a while to have a baby."

Raisa was watching Beth like a hawk and thought to herself, *she isn't telling me everything. I don't know what it is, but I can tell when my daughter isn't being totally truthful.* With great effort, Beth pulled herself to her feet and began to pace the floor. "Doctor Dominic wants me to walk as much as I can, to keep from getting blood clots. Sometimes, Mom, I feel like I am going to explode! Maybe it's my age. I am twelve years older than when I had my first baby." Beth seemed to force a laugh. "Maybe that's why I had the dream I had night before last. I dreamt that I was walking up the lane between the rows of cottonwood trees when all of a sudden my belly burst and all these babies came out and were flying around like fireflies! It was so funny!"

Early in the morning of September 21, 1954 the phone rang as Jake and Raisa were eating a late breakfast. Jake had worked the midnight shift at Marathon and had just gotten home; he was planning on going to bed and getting some shut-eye, but that was all about to change.

Raisa picked up the phone. "Hello." Jake watched her face as she listened to whoever was on the other end. "*What* did you say, its twins? Oh, Jimmy--thank God, I can't believe it." Raisa put her hand over the receiver and mouthed, "Beth had twin girls this morning." She listened a bit longer to her son-in-law. "So Beth and both babies are okay? It all went like clockwork? Oh, dear Lord—what a blessing." She listened while her son-in-law filled her in on the details. "Okay then Jimmy, I can come over tomorrow and stay for a couple of days with Karlie and Sherrie. When do you think Beth and the babies are going to come home?" Raisa nodded. "Is it okay for Jake and me to drive up to Cody today to see them? I can't wait any longer and I'm sure Jake can't either. It's been a long pregnancy and now to be blessed with two healthy baby girls—and Beth came through it all in fine shape. We all need to count our blessings!"

That afternoon, Jake and Raisa drove to Cody to see their daughter and new grand-daughters. Raisa fussed over Beth, "Oh, Honey, how was it and how are you doing, really?" Raisa walked to the edge of the bed and said, "You knew you were pregnant with twins, didn't you? Why didn't you tell us?"

Beth smiled weakly, "Mom and Dad, you know how many times I miscarried. We just didn't know how this was all going to turn out. One of the babies might not have made it or—we just didn't know and so we didn't share any details. I hope you understand and forgive us."

Beth gave her parents a big smile. "It's such a relief, I feel so much lighter and smaller. But, I have to tell you, when those babies decided to come, I could tell that it wasn't going to be a long labor—things progressed pretty quickly. Jimmy called the hospital right before we left the house to alert them that we were coming in. Doctor Dominic and Dr. Ridgeway had a full staff prepared and waiting for the double birth."

Beth took a sip of water and smiled. "Anyway, as soon as Myrna came to stay with the girls, Jimmy and I got in the car and he must have hit eighty a few times on that road to Cody. He was so nervous, so scared that he might have to deliver these babies. I have to admit the pains were getting pretty bad and close by the time he pulled up in front of the hospital. I think he even ran a couple of red lights going through town." Beth laughed, remembering how frantic Jimmy was to get her to the hospital.

"It was really amazing how everyone took over the minute we pulled up at the emergency door. They whisked me away in a wheelchair while Jimmy parked the car. I have to tell you, I was glad to be at the hospital and obviously so were the twins, because they were born about twenty minutes later and only ten minutes apart. They both weighed a little over six pounds each and are so pink and healthy. I guess it was worth it—that long, miserable pregnancy. Have you seen them yet?"

Raisa replied, "Yes, of course. They are beautiful and it's amazing how one reminds me of Karlie and the other of Sherri when they were babies. What a help your older girls are going to be with the two babies. You are blessed my dear, you are blessed."

Just one week later, Jake and Raisa were waiting at the farm house in Emblem when the newly enlarged family arrived home from the hospital. Karlie and Sherrie sat in the back seat, grinning ear-to-ear; each girl was holding a new baby sister. Jake and Raisa hauled in baskets of prepared food, most of which they put into the freezer for Beth to warm up later. Holding one of the babies, Raisa said, "Well, I know this is not what you all expected or were hoping for—but they are here and both so healthy."

On the way home that evening, Jake turned to Raisa and said, "Well honey, now we have six grandchildren, but the girls are outnumbering the boys. I hope Arnie and Norrie aren't done having kids—we need another boy."

It wasn't even two years later that Arnie and Norrie had another baby, but it wasn't a boy—it was another girl, Renee. They asked Karlie to be the baby's godmother.

~~~~~~

Jake and Raisa were sitting out on the front porch like they always did when the weather was nice. Jake was trying to cut back on the Camels again and so he lit up his pipe. "By gosh, Raisa, where has the time gone? Its 1959, our Karlie is going to be a senior in high school and will graduate in the spring. I hear she is going to go to college down in Laramie. How far we've all come— I doubt if either your folks or mine ever dreamed about their great-grandchildren going to college. They did a wonderful thing for us all, coming to this country."

Raisa looked over at her husband of almost forty years. "I know Jake, I think about all the hardships they went through and what we have now because of it. You and I didn't have such an easy time making our way during those first years either, did we? It's all a wonderful blessing; that it is." She stood up, stretched her arms and started for the door. "I'm going to get myself a nice dish of that peach ice cream, would you like a bowl?"

Jake smiled as he said, "Naw, you go ahead—but you better watch out, don't you go getting fat on me after all these years! I noticed you've been making a habit of that ice cream every night for a while now. Good thing you had that gallbladder taken out! I've gotta hit the hay, I have to get up early to go to work in the morning. I'll just sit out here with you for a while."

Back out on the front porch, Raisa held her bowl of ice cream like it was the last one on earth. Between spoonful's she said, "Say, Jake—I've been thinking that we should have our picture taken by Mr. Janssen for our fortieth anniversary—how about it?" A week later, Jake and Raisa climbed the steps to the town's photographer's studio to have their anniversary photograph taken.

Raisa and Jake Kessel on their 40th wedding anniversary

FLESH ON THE BONE

One day slid into the next, and year after year slipped by. In December of 1962, Karlie married her high school sweetheart and a year later they presented Jake and Raisa with their first great-grandson, Steven. As soon as possible, Jake and Raisa loaded up the car and headed down to Casper to see the new baby. As they were driving through the Wind River Canyon, south of Thermopolis, Wyoming, Jake commented, "You know, I think while we are in Casper, we might as well pay a visit to the Social Security office there and check on what I have to do for my retirement next year. Wow, I can't wait---fishing whenever I want to, puttering around out in the garage to my heart's content and home for lunch every day!" Teasing, he smiled and looked over at Raisa as he added the last part.

Raisa just rolled her eyes, thinking about having him underfoot every day. *What does he think he is going to do, go fishing every day? What about those days when he's just hanging around the house. That is definitely going to be a big adjustment for both of us.* Raisa gazed out the window, suddenly feeling depressed about what the future held for them.

Jake noticed her change of mood quickly and said, "Aw, come on honey, snap out of it! Don't go getting all blue on me now. We'll figure it out—maybe we'll hop in our Desoto and take a trip to Billings more often and see our kids up there and do a little shopping. We might even go out to dinner and catch a movie once in a while. It's not over for us, not by a long shot."

~~~~~

In 1965, Jake retired after twenty-three years at Marathon Oil Company. There was the traditional dinner, honoring him; they gave him a nice plaque and a watch for his dedication. Jake took to retirement like a duck to water—he grabbed onto it with both arms wide open, determined to make the most of the time he was given.

As promised, Jake and Raisa made numerous trips to Billings to see their son and his family over the next ten years, however it wasn't all for pleasure. As time went on, they found themselves making more trips up to Billings to see one specialist or another as their health took on a new face. So far, their aches and pains weren't anything the doctors couldn't fix.

Jake Kessel on the Minneapolis Moline tractor, in Emblem.

Jake was always eager to drive over to Emblem for a couple days when his son-in-law needed his help harvesting or tilling a field, getting it ready for the next crop. *I sure do enjoy driving those heavy sugar beet trucks. Just getting out into the field again and being a part of farming—just never got it out of my blood, no sir-ee, I sure didn't. I especially like driving that big old iron tractor he's got. That thing will grind its way through anything—it's a hell of a machine!*

Raisa enjoyed those days when Jake was gone as much as he did. She got more done around the house when he wasn't underfoot. *I notice I'm moving a lot slower these days—I just get tired out easier than I used to, but then again I have to realize that I'm gonna be seventy-four next March, so I guess I have an excuse. We aren't doing as much as we used to. We go to church, drive to Billings or over to Emblem to see our kids. We always enjoy visits from our grandchildren when they are near and those great-grandchildren are special. Lordy, how many do we have now, let's see, Karlie has four boys, Sherrie has three kids, Terrill has three, and Arneen has one. The other three aren't married yet. I remember last summer when Mike and Karlie came over for a visit with their four boys. They sure do have their hands full. They don't know it, but these are the best days of their life when their kids are little and all at home--all snug in the nest.*

**1973 - Jake holding baby Erick, Steven,
Raisa with Brett, and Todd.**

The days and years seemed to whiz past. Jake and Raisa kept busy with their yard and prize roses. They traveled some, but both admitted they like being home the best. Ten more years had passed and life was going by faster and faster. "Ya know, Jake—we're in a rut! But I am just content at the age of eighty-three to be in a rut—it feels comfortable here, don't you think so?"

Jake lowered his newspaper and smiled at his wife, "Yes, honey, I have to agree with you. I get pretty tired gallivanting all over the country. It's good just being here, living in this same house, with the same wife---doesn't get any better."

~~~~~

Jake had been over in Emblem for the last three days, helping Jimmy with the sugar beets. Raisa was expecting him home later that day, just in time for dinner. Raisa had roasted a fat chicken and put lots of potatoes, onions, carrots, and dill on it just the way he liked it. That evening as Jake and Raisa were sitting watching television, Jake couldn't help but notice that Raisa was working on her nightly bowl of ice cream. "Raisa, didn't Doc Welsey tell you to cut back on that stuff?"

Raisa looked up at Jake, "He sure did! I think it was about the same time he told you to quit smoking!" Raisa got up from the couch and carried her empty bowl into the kitchen and rinsed it out in the sink. Walking back into the living room, she bent over and kissed Jake on the cheek. "I think I'm going to call it a night, I feel sort of light headed. Would you like scrambled eggs and bacon for breakfast in the morning?"

Jake gave her a quick hug and said, "Sure, honey, that'd be fine—whatever you feel like cooking. I like it all, you know that." He watched as she turned and walked toward her bedroom. Jake turned the sound down on the TV and sat smoking his cigarette in the dim light. He heard Raisa opening drawers, sliding her dressing chair back, getting ready for bed. Then all was quiet, so he put his cigarette out and headed for his own bedroom.

Around four in the morning, Jake woke with a full bladder. It was still dark outside, so he turned on his bedside lamp, crawled out of bed and headed for the bathroom. He didn't bother to turn on the light in the hall. *I've made this trip often enough, that I know my way in the dark to the bathroom door.* As he walked quietly toward the bathroom, he tripped over something on the floor and grabbed onto the desk to keep from falling down. Shaken, Jake felt around for the wall switch and flipped it on. Shock and panic filled his face as he saw Raisa lying motionless on the floor of the hallway.

Jake dropped to his knees, hitting them hard on the cold wood floor. Pain shot up his thighs, but he didn't hesitate as he put his left hand gently under Raisa's head. Jake stroked her pale face as he tried to get her to respond. "Raisa, oh dear Lord Jesus please. Raisa, wake up. Open your eyes, honey—come on." Jake bent closer and felt a weak stream of air coming from her mouth. He closed his fingers over her wrist and felt for a pulse. It was barely there. Jake laid Raisa back down on the floor and grabbed the phone off the hall table. He lifted the ear piece and jammed the button for an operator.

A voice at the other end calmly asked, "Yes, is there an emergency? What can I do for you?"

Jake screamed franticly into the phone, "This is Jake Kessel, get an ambulance here, to my house quick—it's my wife! I'm not sure what happened! I found her on the floor and she's unresponsive, I can't wake her up. Oh uhh, and call Dr. Welsey to meet us at the hospital, tell him it's Raisa Kessel!"

Jake was shaking so bad he could hardly get back to Raisa, who still lay motionless on the floor. "Come on honey, come on, please, wake up. Why didn't you call out for me? Why didn't I hear you fall? Oh, dear Jesus, I will never forgive myself for not being there for you in the night, when you needed me." Jake bowed his head and quickly said a prayer, *Dear Lord, please hear me and take care of my girl. Let her be okay, please Lord, please— I can't go on without her. We've been through so much, please Lord.*

Jake hurried into the bedroom and pulled on some pants and a flannel shirt then grabbed a light jacket. He heard the ambulance pull up out in front and he was at the front door before the attendants climbed the front steps. "She's in there, on the floor. I was afraid to move her. I don't know what's wrong. I didn't hear her fall and I don't know how long she's been laying there."

CHAPTER SEVENTEEN

In the pre-dawn hours, Jake followed the ambulance in his car as it screamed south up the hill, to Lovell's new hospital. He was numb with fear. *What if she doesn't make it? I can't even imagine life without my Raisa. Please, dear Lord. Help my wife, don't take her yet. Please hear my prayer, Lord.*

Jake didn't know for sure what had happened to Raisa; he overheard the ambulance attendants mention that it was probably a stroke. Whatever it was, he knew it wasn't good and he winced as a shiver of fear wiggled up his spine.

He waited alone in the sterile but comfortable waiting room at the Lovell Hospital. *It's taking forever, what's taking them so long? Raisa, please be okay. I wish Beth and Arnie lived closer. This waiting would have been easier with them here. But I can't call them until I know what is happening to their mother.*

Jake went through so much coffee he had the jitters, and pacing the waiting room floor hadn't helped much either. *What I really need is a smoke and a stiff drink, but I don't think that idea would fly here in the hospital.* Finally, the double doors to the ER opened and Dr. Welsey walked into the waiting room. He motioned to a couch--for Jake to sit down beside him.

He shook his head, "Jake, I wish I had better news for you. The good news is that Raisa is alive and will more than likely pull through this stroke. It was a bad one, Jake. She's got significant paralysis on her left side and there is going to be some loss of speech I'm afraid. I'm not going to paint a rosy picture for you. She's going to have a long and difficult rehabilitation. I think we ought to transport her to Billings Deaconess Hospital where they have better facilities to help her through the physical therapy."

Doctor Welsey stood and extended his hand to Jake. "Raisa is stable for now. I suppose there are a few people you might want to call before the boys take her to Billings." The doctor headed back to the ER. "I'm going to watch her closely. We want to keep her in a semi-coma state, you know—to keep her quiet. It wouldn't be good for her to go getting all worked up and worried. I don't think she'll know any one today. On the other hand, she might come around enough for you to talk to her. If I know Raisa, she'll want to get her two cents in. You can go on back now Jake and see her if you want to." The doctor stood and patted Jake on the back. "I have to get on the phone and call Billings to make arrangements to admit her. I want to alert their docs so they are ready to take care of her when she gets there--probably early evening. Let me know, Jake, if there's anything else we can do for you. I want you to take care of yourself now too—Raisa's gonna need you—it's gonna be a long road back for her."

Jake walked across the waiting room and headed down the austere, sterile white hall that led to the emergency room. *I feel numb, like this is some sort of bad dream and I'm gonna wake up. Oh dear Lord, I wish it was a bad dream, I wish it was.*

Jake stuck his head inside the room where Raisa lay. Just the image of all those machines and tubes attached to her sucked the breath from his lungs. The attending nurse motioned for him to come on inside. Jake felt the blood drain from his face as he gazed down at the inert body of his wife of sixty-three years. Raisa lay motionless, her arms and hands lay on top of the bedclothes beside her body, needles and tubes were attached everywhere. Her eyes were closed and her breathing was steady and soft; she was so beautiful, like an angel. Jake bent down and took Raisa's limp, cool right hand in his. He stroked the thin flesh and spoke softly to her.

"Raisa, honey—open your eyes. It's me Jake. I'm right here beside you, I won't leave you. Aw, Raisa, I'm so sorry I didn't hear you fall in the night. If I had and had gotten you to the hospital sooner, everything might have been different. I blame myself for not hearing you honey, I blame myself." Tears rolled down Jake's ruddy leathered cheeks as his emotions got the best of him.

Jake continued to touch her face, to talk to her, hoping she might respond. "Raisa, the docs said they want to take you to Billings, to get top notch treatment. They said I could ride in the ambulance with you. I am not going to leave your side honey—no way. I'll be with you through whatever lies ahead, you can count on that. You are my life Raisa, we've been together too long to be apart now. I want you to rest. I'm gonna run home and pack a few things. I think I'll take Harry over to the neighbors while we're gone."

Jake started to put Raisa's hand back down on the bed when she opened her eyes, blinked and weakly squeezed his hand. Jake could tell she was trying desperately to speak. "Ja-Ja-Jake, w-w-what happen? Wh-where----? I scared J-Jake."

Jake bent over and kissed her soft cheek. "Honey, its okay now; take a deep breath—you are okay. You are in the Lovell Hospital. The docs have checked you over and think you had some sort of stroke. They are going to take you to Billings in an ambulance, to Deaconess Hospital where they have better equipment to help you get over this."

Jake kissed her again. "Raisa, it's going to be okay. I want you to try and stay calm, just rest sweetheart. I will be with you. I'll be back in a few hours. I'm going home to call the kids and pack a few clothes for us both. Just close your eyes now honey and rest. I love you, Raisa. I'll love you forever!"

Jake put her hand back down on the bed and turned quickly as he felt himself starting to lose it. He practically ran out of the ER and into the isolation of the sterile hospital hallway where he leaned his head against the wall and let the worry, the fear, and the guilt come spilling out. Suddenly, he felt a large hand on his shoulder. Jake turned and came face to face with Doctor Welsey.

"Come on now Jake, come on down here into my office for a minute until you get yourself together. I know it's a frightening situation and even us docs don't know how bad it is or isn't at this stage. We'll all know more when we get her up to Billings."

Ten minutes later, Jake shoved open the double doors of the hospital lobby and headed for his blue DeSoto. He grabbed the door handle and jerked it open, climbed in and slammed the door. Jake beat his hands against the steering wheel until they hurt. "No, no, no—what did she do to deserve this? Why, God? Why wasn't it me? And I wasn't there when she needed me the most—I was sleeping, all nice and cozy in my bed while she laid on that cold floor."

Jake wiped his face with the back of his work-hardened hand and turned the key in the ignition. He felt the engine turn over as he shoved it into gear and backed out into the street. On the way home, he made a mental list of everyone he had to call. He knew it wasn't going to be easy. He went to the cabinet in the kitchen where they kept a bottle of Black Label and poured himself a stiff drink. He sat down at the kitchen table and lit a cigarette. *I've got to settle down a bit before I call the kids, I don't want to start blubbering on the phone and scare them to death.*

Beth and her husband were in Lovell within the hour. "Dad, you go ahead in the ambulance with Mom, Jimmy can drive your car and I will follow him in ours up to Billings. That way you will have a car up there, too. Are Norrie and Arnie going to meet us at the hospital? It's a good thing we're going to Deaconess because that's where Norrie works. She can keep a special eye on Mom. Do the doctors know how long she will have to stay up there?" There were a thousand questions, but nobody had any solid answers at this point—it was pure speculation if Raisa would pull through or not and what kind of life she would have if she did.

Two days later, the family gathered in the head specialist's office to hear what the diagnosis was for Raisa's recovery. Doctor Wheaton sat behind his mahogany desk as he went over their findings. "I wish I had stronger reassurance to give you, but at this point Mrs. Kessel is suffering considerable paralysis on her left side and her speech is slightly affected. There doesn't seem to be any facial paralysis, only some limb problems. We want to keep her up here for a few weeks for some intense therapy and psychological counseling. We have learned that most patients need not only physical rehabilitation but also psychological in order to deal with their new bodies. We are quite sure we can get her moving to a point, but after that it's up to her. You are welcome to stay as long as you can, but it is not necessary and perhaps after a few days it will be best if you leave her with us. Sometimes family members inhibit the progress of the therapy with their empathy. I am sure you all have lives and duties that need attendance. We can keep you on a daily notification if that would be something that would make it easier for you. I understand one of our best nurses is her daughter-in-law. So she can check in on Raisa on a daily basis. That should cheer our patient up."

Beth spent an emotional hour with her mother before she and Jimmy left for the farm in Emblem. She hated to leave her but they were right in the middle of harvest and Jimmy had sixty acres of sugar beets to get out of the ground. Arnie promised to visit his mother every day or when he could. "I hate seeing her so humiliated and struggling to walk and move that arm. I think about the way we used to dance all night together---all the things we just took for granted have now been taken from us. Jake did attend some classes on how to care for Raisa once she went back home; they only depressed him and made him wonder how he was going to cope with it all. The doctors were hopeful Raisa would be able to do most things for herself, but at first, she would need help getting around and of course she's need constant encouragement.

Just before Christmas, Jake drove back to Billings to bring his wife home. Raisa was beaming when they wheeled her out of the hospital in her favorite fur coat, even though her left arm hung laid in her lap. She had color back in her rosy cheeks and her eyes twinkled with happiness as they helped her into the passenger seat. Jake went around to the other side, climbed in and turned the key in the ignition. They were off, on their way back to the safety and comfort of their home in Lovell.

Raisa didn't say much until they turned at Laurel and headed south, across the Yellowstone River and toward the Wyoming border. "Oh Jake, I am really going home. I can't wait to sleep in my own bed and walk around in my own house. How is Harry? Did he miss me? Have you been feeding him?"

Raisa gazed out the window at the winter wonderland. "Jake, thank you for spending so much time with me up in Billings. I know it wasn't all that easy for you either. I want you to know I am going to work really hard to get better or, as good as I can get. I'm scared Jake, I'm scared that this is the beginning of the end for me. There are so many things I can't do for myself and

I hate that! I hate how it takes so much effort to move my left hand and leg normally." Raisa looked out the window, as tears filled her eyes. "I don't want to be a burden on you, Jake. I want you to promise me that if you can't take care of me, you will take me to the nursing home at the Lovell Hospital."

Jake reached over and affectionately squeezed her forearm. "Aw, honey, come on now, we are in this for the long haul. Don't go getting down on yourself. We'll just take it a day at a time and do what we can. By the way, did I tell you that you look especially beautiful sitting over there?"

During the next six months Raisa struggled through her strengthening exercises and Jake struggled with his guilt—that her condition was his fault. Finally, Raisa had heard him blame himself once too often and she let him have it. "Jake, for Pete's sake, will you stop this. It was not your fault that I had a stroke. It was my fault for eating all that ice cream and gaining that weight—for not exercising like I should have. It was my fault, Jake. Sure you didn't hear me fall in the night, but if it had been you, I wouldn't have heard you either. So just stop it now, okay?"

That next week, Raisa discovered she had another mountain to climb—she was diagnosed as a diabetic. "I'm just like my mother Jake, she had diabetes too, but hers was much worse than mine. The doctors said I could control mine with diet and so I feel pretty lucky. And, while we are on the subject, you need to cut back on those Camels again. You are amazing, you stop smoking, then you start, then you stop, and pretty soon I see you smoking again. They are going to kill you someday, Jake, mark my words!"

Jake looked across the room at his wife, "I know, I know, Raisa. How long have you and everyone I know been pestering me about my smoking? I just can't seem to give them up completely or for long. I need that tobacco. I don't think it's going to hurt that I have a smoke now and then. For cryin' out, loud—I am eighty-four years old—something or another is going to kill me eventually. So, I elect to smoke once in a while on my way out of this life, so what?"

For the next two years, Raisa did her exercises and struggled to walk normally, but it was evident she was losing the battle. Raisa never did do well in the heat of the summer months and that July was a hot one. It was obvious that her physical health was deteriorating. One morning as she and Jake were having breakfast, Raisa suddenly sat her coffee cup heavily on the table and said, "Jake, I think I w-ant to go to the hospital. I don't feel right and I am having a-a-hard time breathing—I feel sort of light-headed too." She pushed back her chair and stood for only a minute before slumping to the floor. Jake caught her before she hit her head.

"Oh dear God, no, please God, not again!" He ran for the phone and call emergency. Jake hurried back to where Raisa lay on the kitchen floor. He grabbed the damp dishcloth from the sink and began to wipe her head and cheeks. She didn't respond.

Before he knew it the ambulance crew had her strapped on the gurney and were rolling her out to the ambulance. One of the guys turned to Jake and said, "It's probably best you drive your own car Mr. Kessel—it's pretty crowded inside the ambulance and we have some work to do."

Jake nodded in agreement and rushed back inside the house to call his two children and Raisa's sisters. He grabbed the car keys and ran down the back steps and out to the garage.

After Jake talked to the doctors at the Lovell Hospital, he called his family again. "They say she is going to have to stay in the hospital for a week or two, until they can get her stabilized. She had another small stroke but they think they got to her sooner with this one."

Religiously, Jake visited Raisa every day. He brought her flowers, a magazine, anything she wanted except candy or ice cream. Jake had a sinking feeling every time he walked back down the long hallway, back out to his car and left her there in that hospital, but he hung on to hope and faith.

After a couple of weeks, Doctor Welsey caught Jake in the hall one day and motioned for him to come into his office. "Jake, have a chair. We need to have a talk."

Raisa didn't come back home after a couple of weeks, instead she grew weaker and more despondent in spite of Jake's attentive visits and concern. Toward the end of July, she said to Jake, "I want to see our grandchildren, Jake. I don't think I have much time left and I want to see each of them before I go. That's what my dad did and that's what I want to do. Will you call them?"

Each of Raisa and Jake's seven grandchildren came to Lovell, came to the hospital to see their grandmother. Some of them acknowledged the reason they were called and embraced the time with her while others were in denial. Their grandmother had always been a strong and steady force in their lives and it was not easy to think of their world without her.

After church one Sunday, Beth told Jimmy that she was going to drive over to the Lovell hospital to spend some time with her mom. When Beth walked into her mother's room, she was startled to see Raisa lying on her side, curled up in a ball. Beth walked to the other side of the bed and gently touched her mother's shoulder. "Mom, are you in pain? Can I get you anything?"

Raisa opened her eyes and looked up at her only daughter. "Oh, Beth, I am so glad you came today. I'm having a bad day; will you help me sit up?"

After Beth got her mother upright in the bed, she adjusted the covers and sat on the edge of the bed. "What's the matter Mom? Come on, talk to me."

Raisa put her head down and wiped at her eyes with a tissue. "It's just that this is all so hard. I've not had an easy life and now, this! I am so depressed, I know I'm not getting better—it's so h-hard, Beth." Raisa blew her nose and laid her head back against the pillow and closed her eyes as more tears escaped. "I don't understand why God is making me suffer so. I have been a good Christian all my life, like my folks taught me. I don't know what I've done to deserve this suffering. I wish he would just take me and let this misery and humiliation be over with."

Beth moved closer to her mother, and wrapped her arms around Raisa's frail frame. "Aw. Mom, you know better than that. God is not punishing you—of course he knows you are a good Christian woman. I don't have the answers, Mom, but I know God loves you and He is waiting for the right time to take you. I guess I'm selfish in that I don't want that to happen, but we all have to go sometime. God loves you, Mom and He has some reason why He is waiting to take you. Just hang in there and try to bear it. I wish there was something I could do for you, but there just isn't."

Beth reached for the Holy Bible on the nightstand. "Would you like me to read to you from the Bible, Mom? That always seems to make you feel better." When Beth finished reading that afternoon, she asked, "Mom, would you like Pastor Schwieger to come by so you can talk to him about how you are feeling? It might make you feel better to hear what he has to say."

Beth called the good pastor that very evening and chatted with him about the torment her mother was going through with her faith. It was just after lunch the next day when Pastor Schwieger strolled into Raisa's room, unannounced. "Well, well, if it isn't Raisa Kessel. Do you mind if I visit for a few minutes? I'm out here on calls today and thought I would spend some time with you too, dear lady."

Raisa beamed at her pastor. "Oh, Pastor Schwieger, it's so good to see you. Of course, please sit for a spell and tell me what is going on at the church since I've been locked up in here."

After some small talk, the good pastor got down to the main reason for his visit. "Raisa, how are you doing, spiritually? I realize you are going through some difficult trials and of course you might have some questions. As your pastor, I am here to help you if I can. Now, let's talk—it's just you and me in this room. Raisa, I want you to relax and tell me what's on your mind."

A sudden melancholy mood fell over Raisa as she looked out the hospital window. To her horror, tears began to fall over her cheeks. She reached for the tissue box and dabbed at the tears. "Oh, pastor, I'm so sorry. It's just—this is just so hard. I know I am dying. I know it won't be long. I wish the Lord would take me tonight. I don't understand why I am suffering like this—I tried very hard to live my life as a good Christian. I have faith and believe in my Lord Jesus, but I don't understand why he is allowing me to endure this slow death. I feel like I am being punished for something and I don't know what it is."

FLESH ON THE BONE

Pastor Schwieger moved to the edge of her bed and sat on it, taking her wrinkled, frail hand in his. "Now, Raisa, Raisa—your Lord Jesus is not making or allowing you to suffer on purpose. He doesn't promise any of us a peaceful and non-suffering death if only we believe in him. That's not part of the deal. I know you are a woman of great faith, but as Christians we don't have faith and or trust in God just when it's convenient or when we need it. Faith is a daily thing. Faith is trusting in our Lord when good things and bad things are happening in our lives. We all come across things in our lives that we don't understand, that we question."

Pastor Schwieger paused. "Raisa, we all have our cross to bear one way or another—there are no guarantees. Just because we are Christians doesn't guarantee that death will come easy or without suffering. As the time of our death nears, as Christians, we lean on our faith and take courage in the promise of life-everlasting to sustain us. This promise of Christ is what helps us do what we have to do, to bear our earthly suffering during our lives and also as the end draws near."

The pastor leaned in. "Raisa, one of the hardest things we have to do as Christians is to wait on the Lord. We all get frustrated and irritated when we try to make things happen on our own. You know that your Lord Jesus is with you every step of the way and if it becomes necessary, he will carry you through your final days. Pray, Raisa, pray and have patience and faith that God will give you the strength. You are still here for a purpose you will someday understand. Perhaps the purpose is to show the others in your family how to act, how to have patience and faith. Our lives here on this earth, all have purpose—perhaps you are still here as a beacon of your Christian belief, to shine so that others may see the strength of your faith in your Lord."

In early August, the doctors told Jake, Beth and Arnie that they didn't expect Raisa to live much longer. Her organs were beginning to shut down and she was getting weaker. Beth decided to move, temporarily, over from Emblem and into her mother's bedroom, at the house on Shoshone Avenue. Beth went to the hospital every day to sit and read to her mother from the Bible.

One afternoon when Beth was spending time with her mother, Raisa commented, "In the final days my father spent on this earth, his Bible became even more of a comfort to him, just as it is to me. I especially like Psalms, the Psalms of David." Raisa gazed out the open window at the green leaves on the tree. "You know, David was my father's name. It was a perfect name for him; he was such a strong Christian. No matter what happened in his life he took it as the will of God—he accepted it." Beth nodded her head; she smiled as she opened the Bible to the Book of Psalms.

"Which psalm would you like me to read today, Mom?" She already knew the answer; she just wanted to engage her mother.

Raisa turned her head and opened her eyes, "Which psalm, why my favorite one of course, Psalm Twenty-three."

Beth began to read: *"The Lord is my shepherd; I shall not want. He maketh me to lie down in green pastures: he leadeth me beside the still waters. He restoreth my soul: he leadeth me in the paths of righteousness for his name's sake. Yea, though I walk through the valley of the shadow of death, I will fear no evil; for thou art with me; thy rod and thy staff they comfort me."* Beth looked up as she prepared to continue reading, but her mother's eyes were closed and she was breathing easier. Beth put the Bible on the night stand and walked out into the hall. She put her back against the wall and buried her face in her hands as quiet sobs wracked her own aging body.

Exactly a week later, around four in the morning, Beth was sleeping in her mother's bedroom at the house on Shoshone Avenue. Suddenly, she sat straight up in bed and called out in the darkness. "What? Who's there? Mama, did you call me?" Beth reached for the lamp beside the bed and pulled the cord. Light flooded the room as Beth tore back the covers. She grabbed her robe and ran out into the hall. She knocked frantically on her father's bedroom door. "Dad—Dad—wake up." She turned the door knob and opened the door, "Oh Dad—I just heard Mom call me. It was plain as day. We have to get to the hospital now, Dad. Get dressed while I throw on some clothes. We have to get to the hospital, Mom needs us Dad. I just know she is going!"

FLESH ON THE BONE

Jake and Beth ran down the back steps and out to the garage. They got into the car and Jake backed down the driveway and whipped the car around, out into the street. He shifted gears and they sped through the dark early morning, up the hill to the hospital. Jake pulled up to the front of the hospital and killed the engine. They burst through the hospital doors and down the hall toward Raisa's room. They saw several nurses and a doctor around Raisa's bed as they stood frozen in the doorway. The doctor looked up in alarm. It was apparent by the expression on his face what had just happened.

In her heart and mind, she knew the answer to her question, but Beth still felt compelled to ask. "I heard Mom call me—she called me, to come! Is she okay? Is she still alive?"

The doctor cast his eyes to the floor and walked toward Beth and Jake. "I'm sorry, but she passed away about five minutes ago. She died peacefully, in her sleep." Beth collapsed into her father's arms and they stood there together, weeping.

Just the day before, on August 8, 1986, Raisa prayed her last prayer and made ready her soul to meet her God as she took her last communion. Jake was in the hospital room with her, not realizing that it was their final day on earth together.

～～～

Jake had known this day was coming and he thought he had prepared himself for what lay ahead. After the funeral, family and friends gathered in the church's social rooms to talk about Raisa, her final days and their own problems. After the families all went home, Jake returned to his house. He sat in his chair, alone in the dark living room—alone with his thoughts.

Never in my life have I known such a vast emptiness. Life was always good, always hopeful with my beautiful Raisa by my side. What in the hell am I going to do without her? How in God's name am I going to get through the days without my Raisa? I always thought I would be the first one to go, not her, not her. Lately, I even had some crazy idea that after she was gone, I could do anything I wanted to do—I could go fishing whenever I wanted. Now, it's happened and I don't even want to go fishing.

Somehow he got through the next few days, keeping busy with final documents, thank you cards, and all those little things Raisa had always taken care of. *I feel like a duck out of water and am just glad Beth is taking care of most of the thank you cards.* He finished up with his supper dishes and, out of habit, wandered out to the front porch. Sitting by himself, Jake was at loose ends, down in the dumps. After smoking a cigarette, he stood and tossed it out into the street. He reached into his pocket and locked the front door. Jake walked around the house toward the garage and went in the side door. He climbed in his car and turned the key in the ignition. Suddenly, he remembered he had forgotten to raise the garage door. He sat there for a moment or two, his head buzzing with crazy thoughts.

Jake shook his head and ran his hands back through his hair. He reached down and pushed open the car door and walked back to open the garage door. He backed down the drive way and drove out to the Lovell cemetery. Jake parked near where they had buried Raisa and walked over to the grave. The dirt was mounded high over the grave, and still covered with the artificial grass, which itself was covered with wilting flowers. Jake looked at the gray granite headstone. He stared at Raisa's name and date of birth. They had already carved in her date of death—it was already done.

Jake dropped to his knees near the headstone and putting one hand on the rough edge of the cold stone, he shook with sobs. *It's my fault Raisa, my fault you died before you should have. I should have given you a better, an easier life. I should have done better by you and not played so many cards or been gone so much. I wish I had spent more time with you. I'm just a hell of a swell guy, aren't I? I disappoint my father and ended up checking him into a mental hospital to spend his last days. I didn't give you the life you deserved in the beginning, and in the end I wasn't there for you when you needed me most. Oh, Raisa, if only I had found you sooner on the hallway floor when you had your first stroke, maybe things would have—maybe we would have had more time. Now, I've lost you and it's all, my fault!*

CHAPTER EIGHTEEN

The Lowest ebb is the turn of the tide.   Henry Wadsworth Longfellow

It had been over a month since Raisa died. Jake was never much good in the kitchen and now he was entirely on his own. Of course, some of his female relatives tried to see that he had a good meal now and then, but that wasn't the problem. The problem was walking into that kitchen, Raisa's kitchen, and she wasn't there. It didn't even smell like it did when she was there and that was the worst part.

Jake opened the refrigerator and grabbed the mayonnaise, a loaf of bread, a tomato from the garden, some romaine lettuce, and a couple pieces of bacon. *I can probably make myself a bacon, lettuce, and tomato sandwich. How hard can that be? I watched Raisa make them often enough over the years. Now, where did I put that toaster?*

Jake toasted the bread and spread it with mayo. He threw a couple of pieces of bacon in the frying pan and turned on the heat. He remembered to cover the pan with a lid this time. Splattered grease is not easy to clean up, as he recently discovered. While the bacon was frying, Jake arranged the lettuce on the toast then turned the tomato on its side. He took a sharp knife from the drawer and zeroed in on the tomato. Feeling pretty apt, he successfully placed one slice of tomato on the sandwich and proceeded to slice another piece. Just for a second, he took his eyes off the tomato and glanced over at the frying bacon. The knife slipped through the tomato and his finger, with no effort.

"Gol damn it!" Jake dropped the knife as the blood began to ooze from a deep cut on his index finger. He ran for the bathroom and rummaged around in the medicine cabinet in search of Band-Aids. He no sooner got the finger bandaged up, when he smelled burning bacon!

Smoke was escaping from under the lid of the pan as the pieces of bacon turned a charred black and filled the room with an acrid smoke. Jake angrily grabbed the pan and set it off the stove, then opened the kitchen window. "Oh for, hell's sake, I can't even make a damn sandwich without it being a total disaster! I am completely useless and now the house smells like burned bacon. Hell, even the neighbors will know what I did."

Jake cleaned up the mess, poured himself a bowl of Wheaties and went into the front room. He turned the T.V. on and plopped down in his favorite chair. "It's just no good—I mess up everything I try to do. Oh, dear Lord, I miss her---I miss my Raisa. Nothing is the same, nothing." In spite of himself, tears began to roll over Jake's ruddy cheeks.

Jake had his good days and then he had some pretty bad ones too. He kept hoping things would get better. He hoped as time passed he would get used to being alone. He knew he was simply going through the motions. Jake tried to keep busy with all sorts of projects. He cleaned out the basement and then the garage. As he was walking back to the house, he glanced at their rose gardens. *I hate those damn roses—all they do is make me think of Raisa. She was the one who really wanted those things in our yard; she always loved the smell of roses.*

Jake walked back to the garage and grabbed a sharp spade. Clenching his jaw, he marched back out the garage door and headed for the first bed of roses. With a vengeance, Jake jabbed the shovel into the loamy soil right next to a luscious, Peace rosebush. He pushed down on the handle and the bush came out of the ground, roots and all. In two hours, Jake had dug up all forty of their rose bushes. He stood back and looked at the yard. *Hell, it looks like some ramped-up Rototiller came through the place----and, that woulda been me—fueled with grief.*

After Jake loaded the dying rose bushes in the back of his Scout, he turned and walked back towards the house. Glancing out of the corner of his eye, he felt a wave of guilt tighten his gut from having dug up all of Raisa's roses. *I'm sorry, honey, but they just reminded me of you and they are so much work. I just don't want any of those damn roses around without you here too.* Jake fought back the tears. *Tomorrow, I'll smooth out that ground and go get some grass seed. More lawn will be a lot easier for me to take care of all them roses.*

The next day, Jake made a couple of other drastic changes to his backyard, changes he wasn't certain his kids or friends would understand, but ones that would make his life easier and safer. Everything has it's time to live and flourish, and then................

~~~~~

The second Sunday in September, Beth and Jimmy drove over from Emblem to go to church with Jake. After church, they took him out to eat at the Rose Bowl Café and then they drove back to the house. "Dad, would you like me to fix a couple of dishes for you that I could put into the freezer? Maybe a tuna fish casserole and some macaroni and cheese would fix you up for a while? They would be there for you when you need them. You'd just have to warm them up."

If truth were told, Jake was still in a fog—still at loose ends. "Sure, honey—do whatever you want. Go ahead in the kitchen there and do what you women do. That's fine with me, I'm sure you know what I like. If you need something, I can run down to Winterholler's Corner Grocery and pick it up. Just let me know."

Beth headed for the kitchen to tidy it up a bit and start preparing the casseroles. Before Jake and his son-in-law settled in front of the television to watch a ball game, their quiet afternoon was shattered by a muffled shout from the kitchen. Both men jumped to their feet and ran for the kitchen.

Beth stood at the window, pointing to the backyard. "Dad, what in the world did you do to your beautiful yard? The roses are all gone and the, the willow trees -- Mom's willow trees --have been cut down? Mom loved those roses and the willow trees! Why in the world would you do that, Dad?"

With his head down, Jake walked across the kitchen to where his daughter stood. He stopped a foot or so away, put his weathered hand on her shoulder and said, "I had to take those roses out Beth, they are just too much work for me and they remind me—hell, it all reminds me of your, Mother. And, those there willow trees were getting trunk rot. I was afraid they would come down on the house. Trust me, honey—its better this way. At least your mother didn't have to see those trees come down. We can be thankful for that. I know how much she loved those blamed trees and the roses too."

~~~~~

That fall, Jake drove south over the sage-covered hills to Emblem once or twice a week, sometimes helping Jimmy with the harvest or Beth in her garden. He even spent the night when his son-in-law needed him to do something extra in the fields. Jake appreciated it that Beth always sent him home with a couple dishes of food because she knew he didn't cook much. Once a month he tried to drive up to Billings to see his son and family. But that was getting to be a pretty long drive; he was almost eighty-six.

Getting through the holidays that first year was rough. But Jake's kids made sure he was included in their family celebrations. After the first of the year, he tried real hard to get himself into some sort of a routine to fill his lonesome hours and days. On a sunny, Sunday morning in May, Jake sat in a pew at St. John's Lutheran church listening, or going through the motions of listening to the sermon Pastor Floyd Schwieger was giving. But his thoughts strayed. *I am sitting here like I do every Sunday, singing the songs, praying the prayers, and listening to the sermon, but it's like I'm not really here. I feel like a shell, like I'm invisible; it's like I'm on the outside looking in. I do remember hearing Pastor saying, "You may feel like giving up when you come up against a tough patch in your life. Just remember that the Holy Spirit gives you the peace you need and the power to face anything. Of course, we don't always understand everything that is going on in our lives, but we have to trust in God. He and he alone can put the pieces together even when we don't want to face tomorrow. Remember---don't expect tomorrow's answers to your problems to come, until tomorrow"*

Jake tried to listen, tried to let it all sink in. *Let's face it, I still feel lost without my Raisa. I guess that's what happens when you live with someone, love someone for so long. When they leave your life, nothing seems right any more. I gotta keep trying for the kids. I need something else to occupy my thoughts and my days. But shoot, it's not the days that are the problem here--it's the nights, alone in that house. Oh sure, I've got Raisa's cat, Harry. I lost count of how many cats named Harry she's had over the years. But even he doesn't act right now that she's gone. I think he actually misses her too.*

Over the past ten years, Pastor Floyd Schwieger and Jake had developed a mutual friendship. The pastor was a few years younger, but they had a lot in common and were on a first name basis, outside of the church. It was no secret that they both loved the outdoors and a good story. They had enjoyed years of spur-of-the-moment fishing trips, hikes in the mountains, and now, they had something else in common; they were both men living life alone. After the service, Pastor Schwieger pulled Jake aside. "Jake, do you have a minute? How about you and I go catch some lunch down at the Rose Bowl Cafe? I have something I want to talk to you about—something I think you are going to like."

Sitting in a booth at the café, Floyd took a sip of his ice tea, and then said, "How's that old orange Scout running?"

Jake looked up from the menu and smiled. "Probably better than that mistreated Dodge you drive, why?"

Floyd slouched down in the seat, smiled mischievously as he drummed his fingers on the table top. "Well, I have a little day-excursion planned for the two of us, now that the snow has melted in the back country. It's something I think we can really get our teeth into. And, we need to go in your Scout because there's some rough, off-road traveling involved. Interested?"

After giving their order to the sarcastic teenage waitress, Jake leaned over the table, "Okay, what is this big mystery? What do you have planned? You got your hooks into me now."

Floyd Schwieger laid a glossy 'coffee table' picture book on the table top and said, "Between now and Wednesday, I want you to take a look at this book. It's about the wild horses that roam that whole area around Pryor Mountain and the Yellowtail Dam, in the Bad Lands. [14]There's a good-sized herd out there Jake, and the government wants to thin them out, big time. I think those horses need us!"

Jake perked up and rubbed his chin. "You don't say? Wild horses, huh? How many are there and why does the government want to take them out? Why is the government sticking their nose into some open range horses? I sure as hell don't think they are hurtin' anyone except maybe the sheep herders who want all the grasslands to themselves. " Jake leaned back and pulled out his pack of Camels. He put a light to one as he draped his left arm across the back of the worn booth. "So, knowing you like I do, Floyd, just what is this plan of yours?"

Floyd flashed a gratified smile back. "Got ya, don't I?" he laughed. "Well, I've been thinking that the two of us need to go have a look-see and then plan our strategy of just how we are going to help those horses. Do you realize some of their history dates back to the conquistadors? There's a lot of history running around in those hills." Floyd waved Jake's cigarette smoke from his face and said, "You been hitting those 'cancer-sticks' pretty hard lately haven't you? You know, someday those things are going to kill you."

After lunch, Jake dropped Floyd off at his house, but before he drove off, he had one more little jab to deliver. "Hey, Floyd, I been a-thinkin'—if you changed the oil in that Dodge a little more often, it might run better. See ya, bright and early on Wednesday morning!" Jake slapped the steering wheel and laughed as he drove off.

That next Wednesday before daybreak, the two friends packed up the Scout and headed east out of Lovell. After a few miles, Jake asked, "So, do you have some idea of just where these horses are, out there in those hills? You realize that you're talking about hundreds of miles of range where they might be. Floyd looked casually out the window, smiled and said, "That's why I brought you along on this little jaunt; you always had a nose for where the animals were. How many times did we go hunting deer and you always knew where to find them by looking at the signs or whatever the heck you did?" Floyd laughed as Jake reached across the front seat and took a playful jab at him.

Jake thought for a few moments before saying, "Well, I was thinking of taking that road to the left up here, before we get to the reservoir, and head due north. There are some watering holes out in those hills that we might check first for fresh dung and hoof prints, is that a plan?"

Floyd thought about it for a moment, and then replied, "Sure, that sounds fine. Don't mean to change the subject, but look at that sunrise. See how it's just skimming the top of the Big Horns with a copper and pink halo and the rays of sun shooting clean up into the blue sky?"

Jake pulled over to the side of the road; both men got out of the truck and watched as the normally brown and barren landscape was transformed into a virtual painting of luminous colors—a flowing blush of pink, copper, mauve, gold.

Floyd turned to the west and pointed. "Look, Jake—how all that color is flooding down the sides of the Big Horns and washing across the basin. Just look at how it swims up the slopes of Heart Mountain, clear over there by Powell. That is truly a gift from our Heavenly Father." Climbing back into the truck, Floyd turned to his friend, "Jake have you ever thought that perhaps this Big Horn Basin is a gigantic ancient caldera—like they say Yellowstone Lake is? Maybe, when everything blew sky high and killed the dinosaurs; that might have happened. If this was a volcano and she blew, I can see why it would kill everything for hundreds of miles. This basin is probably a hundred miles in diameter from one end to the other, wouldn't you say?"

Jake turned to glance at his friend. "Now, that is some food for thought. I think you have too much time on your hands. You need to get out more—socialize!" Jake reached over and slapped Floyd on the back in jest. "Anyway, I think we are almost to that spot you mentioned that the horses prefer; do you want to pull over there or keep going a ways?"

Floyd looked out the window as the morning light bathed the red sandstone cliffs. "Sounds like a good place to start our search." He scanned the road ahead, looking for a good turn off. "So Jake, not to change the subject, but how are you getting along?

Are you making peace with being alone after being married for sixty-six years?"

Jake tensed but never took his eyes off the road. "Yeah well, Floyd, I don't think it's going to be easy to get used to it all. In the beginning I thought I would do fine, in fact I thought I would have all the time I wanted, to do the things I wanted, when I wanted, and I wouldn't have to ask Raisa first. I was thinking I would be fancy free. I sure never thought I would have this much trouble being fancy free or that having time to myself would be a problem, but it's pretty darn tough."

Jake rolled down his window and proceeded to light another cigarette. "Just like the other day, I was fixing or trying to fix myself something to eat, and turned to take my plate to the kitchen table to eat. I stopped dead in my tracks, just stood there and looked at that darn table. That table is where Raisa and I ate every meal, except when we had company. And, Floyd—she wasn't there. Even after all these months, I keep expecting to turn around and see her in the room, in the yard."

Floyd reached across the front seat and put his hand on Jake's arm as his friend continued, "Sometimes, I think I hear her in the kitchen or I'm sitting out on the front porch and I find myself waiting for her to walk out the screen door to join me. But, she doesn't come." He shook his head. "Then there are the nights. Sometimes in the evenings when I'm sitting in the front room all alone, watching that television, I purposely imagine her sitting over there on the couch with her crocheting, and I talk to her. Yeah, I actually talk out loud to her and I know she's not really there. It's better for me then."

Jake looked over at his pastor and friend. "I talk to her, like she was there, Floyd. I think it's because that's the only way I can get through the night—by imaging that she is still here with me."

Floyd smiled. "Jake, she is there with you, in spirit. Raisa was such a big part of your life for so long. It's not something that you can just get over or forget in a year or two. If it makes you feel better to talk to her, then do it. That doesn't hurt anyone, no one at all." Floyd slapped Jake on the shoulder. "It's just when she starts answering, that I'm gonna start getting worried."

FLESH ON THE BONE

Floyd pointed across the hills. "I've been watching some tracks, along the side of the road and I think the horses have been here, probably this morning. See, over there, is a pile of fresh dung. Perhaps over that next hill we'll see em'. Let's slow down a bit and see if we can maybe ease up on the herd."

Over the next couple of years, Jake and Floyd drew national attention to the growing herd of wild horses. The two friends had found a new mission in their lives as they put their heads together, sending out letter after letter to government officials and to the press to bring the plight and history of the wild horses to public attention. The press loved stuff like this and they were all over it. Jake and Floyd were thrilled when the story of 'their mustangs' reached the front page of national newspapers. When the wash was hung on the line---Jake and Floyd were instrumental in saving a substantial number of the horses that had literally been in the government's gun sights.

The two men made bi-weekly trips out to check on the herd's well-being and actually documented appropriate names for each of the twenty to thirty head of prime horse flesh. They were often thrilled at the birth of a foal and mourned the death of an old-timer. That old orange Scout held up pretty well, and Jake got a big kick out of taking his family members out to see the horses when they came to visit him.

One weekend, Karlie and her husband Mike came over to Lovell with their two youngest sons. Jake piled them all into the Scout, telling them he had a big treat in store for them. They headed east out of Lovell toward the Big Horn Mountains, and then veered to the north and the looming Pryor Mountains. They were flying over the better-than-normal dirt road when Jake yelled over the engine, "Hold on now, we are going down a hill."

The nose of the Scout shot skyward and then without warning dropped vertically—still on the road. They lost altitude at an alarming rate, evidenced by the screams of his passengers. Jake chuckled, "Well, I told you to hang on—that's a pretty steep drop off there isn't it? Kinda catches ya off guard, doesn't it?" He had a smile on his face for the next five minutes.

They drove on another couple of miles before Jake pulled off the road and killed the engine. "Okay, I think the herd will probably be over that next hill down by a grove of trees and a little creek that runs through there. They roam all over these hills, but they also have their favorite watering spots. Come on now, let's get out and walk as quietly as we can. I'll lead off and when I motion for you to move up, come on, real quiet-like. We're upwind, so I am pretty sure they won't smell us."

Jake was spot on with his prediction. A majestic gray stallion stood off to the side as the rest of the herd drank and grazed around the grassy banks of the slow-running creek. In irritation, the stallion pawed the crusty, rocky glacial deposits, left behind millions of year before. He was well aware of their presence and wasn't particularly comfortable with it. He reared up and whinnied; the sound of his unshod hoofs hitting the ground echoed through the solid rock canyons. Confidently, he began to trot down to where his herd grazed at the edge of the creek. With the skill of a thousand years, he circled his possessions, his mares and their foals; he drove them up and over the hill, away from the interlopers. Only the young, defiant stallions remained behind.

Jake looked down as his nine-year-old great-grandson pulled on his pants leg. "Grandpa Jake, do those wild horses ever get in a big fight and rear up and bite each other like I saw on television?"

Jake looked out over the arid landscape as he replied, "You're darn tootin' they do! They get in some real humdingers—bitin' and tryin to trample each other. You just look at the hide of some of those stallions and you can see the history of some of the fights they've been in!"

Suddenly, a high-pitched whinny split the air of the foothills as a fight broke out between two of the young stallions who had stayed behind. The young black and a beautiful roan obviously had a territorial disagreement and reared up in anger, snorting and pawing at each other. The roan let out a high-pitched squeal, swung around and took a nip out of the black's side. The black stallion shook it off; he whirled and kicked the roan in the head. Then, as suddenly as it had begun, the fight was settled and

FLESH ON THE BONE

over, as both horses disappeared over the hill in the direction of the lead stallion and the herd.

Karlie's two boys were in awe of the spirited battle the horses put on. "Do they do that all the time Grandpa Jake, huh? Do they fight each other? What happens if one really loses the fight? What then?"

Jake patted his great-grandson on the back. "Well, it's pretty much like nature takes its own course out here. If one of them horses gets beat up--cut up too bad, then they run off and often die alone, without the herd. There are mountain lions and even packs of coyotes that find them wounded horses and the old or sick ones and take them down. Sometimes they even get a colt or two. It's just the way nature is."

Pastor Floyd Schwieger and Jake Kessel were instrumental in helping build a museum for the wild horses of Pryor Mountain at the east end of Lovell. Through notifying government officials and the press they were able to bring needed national attention to the survival of the historic herd of the Pryor Mountain Wild Horses.

By late October, 1987, Jake had spent the better part of the week winterizing his yard. He raked a few leaves and burned them out back where the old outhouse used to sit. Jake looked around at the yard and its fading progression into winter dormancy. Suddenly, he felt a wave of weariness sweep over him and decided to call it a day. He hung up the rakes, then against its will--coiled the green garden hose up and put everything in order in the garage. Shutting the garage door, he leaned against the frame and took out his handkerchief to wipe the sweat from his head. *I am plumb tuckered out, think I'll head for the house. Maybe I'll cook me up a can of Campbell soup for my supper; I should be able to handle that.*

After eating a light supper and watching a little television, Jake pushed himself up out of his familiar recliner and turned out the light. *I don't know why I'm so tired tonight, I don't think I worked that hard today and my shoulders are killing me—feels like I've been stung or something. Guess I'll take a couple of Raisa's aspirin and get myself to bed.* Just after two o'clock in the morning, Jake woke from a restless sleep. The pain on one side of his back was so bad he couldn't sleep. Throwing the cover back, he climbed out of bed and went into the bathroom. *My right upper back hurts like hell—feels like pins and needle. This feels different, not like sore muscles from yard work; my skin actually hurts. I'm gonna slip my pajama top off and take a look at it in the mirror. Maybe I got a spider bite or something.*

The next morning, Jake was the first patient of the day at the Lovell hospital. Doctor Welsey took one look at Jake's upper back and knew immediately what was causing him so much pain and discomfort. "Jake, I hate to tell you this, but you got yourself a full-blown case of the shingles. Have you ever heard of this affliction? Well, I can tell you that you are in for a very uncomfortable few weeks. This stuff comes from the chicken pox virus and shingles is just as contagious, so I'd advise you to keep yourself at home. It's also made worse by stress, so try to keep yourself calm. Smoke a cigarette or two if you have to."

Jake looked at the doctor, someone he had known for most of his life. "Calm, you say? Hell, have you ever had this stuff? It hurts like a son of a bitch; can't you give me some creams or something to take this burning pain out of it, so I can at least sleep?"

Dr. Welsey looked down at his desk, then up at Jake. "I can give you some pills to knock you out so you can sleep Jake. Also ice packs—cold packs on it will help. Don't put heat on it—that'll make it worse. Take aspirin during the day—that's about all I can do for you, I'm sorry, my friend. This beast has just got to run its course."

Now Jake was physically miserable and alone. His kids couldn't visit and he didn't want to go anywhere in public and expose people to this stuff. He did take the Scout out once in a while when he got cabin fever so bad he wanted to tear the wallpaper off the walls. Jake gradually recovered, but by Christmas time, he still didn't feel much like traveling to Billings or Emblem to spend the holiday with his kids. He just didn't feel much like doing anything at all.

In eighty-eight years, this was the first Christmas Jake was going to spend alone and he knew it probably wasn't going to be a 'merry' one. For the holidays, Beth and Jimmy flew to California where three of their four daughters lived. Arnie and Norrie had asked him to come on up to Billings, but the weather forecast predicted a nasty storm and Jake didn't want to drive on the bad roads. So he went to church alone on Christmas Eve and then on Christmas Day, he sat all by himself in the house, ate a tasteless T.V. dinner and watched other people celebrate Christmas on television. He developed a pretty sound case of the blues—sitting alone in his home with his memories for company, alone on Christmas Day, a traditional family day.

For some reason or another, his persistent coughing was worse when it got cold outside and the past few days, it had been pretty bad. As all days do, this one finally came to a close. It was growing dark outside and Jake didn't bother to turn the front room lights on. He stood and walked to the big front window and looked out at the street. The neighbors had turned on their Christmas lights and he could see that it was beginning to snow. Big white flakes were drifting ever so slowly to the crusted snow that lay on the lawns and street. Jake just stood there, looking at the world go past—he felt like someone looking in the window at another life, at other people's lives. A devouring melancholy fell over Jake. He felt all his loneliness, his sadness, his missing Raisa—it all came on him at once. First one tear, then another and another, oozed from his blue eyes and rolled silently over his ruddy cheeks and dripped onto his plaid wool shirt. For a while, Jake just stood there, letting the tears come. Suddenly, he swiped them away and closed the blinds.

Jake sat back down in his old recliner, not bothering to turn on the lights. There was enough light coming through the window from the neighbor's Christmas lights. Jake looked at the walls that Raisa had painted and wallpapered. His eyes fell on the curtains at the windows, the green curtains that Raisa had made on her Singer sewing machine. She was still here, all around him. Maybe not physically, not so he could reach out and touch her, but her spirit her memory was still right here with him.

Jake rose from his recliner as another coughing spell stopped him. He struggled to cough the sticky phlegm up. Finally it passed and he made sure the front door was locked before turning back to the hallway. He stopped before he entered his own bedroom, turned and walked back, past the bathroom and into Raisa's bedroom. He hadn't changed anything in her room—it was all just the way she had left it three years ago. Jake slept in Raisa's bed that night, something he had never done before. Tonight he needed her--he needed---comfort. He slept like a baby.

The next morning while Jake was fixing himself a couple of fried eggs, he tried to forget how he had acted the night before. *It was just the damn holidays! I wasn't prepared for all the feelings that rose to the surface. That was darn silly of me and I better snap out of it. Things are what they are.* He started to carry the frying pan of eggs to the table when another coughing spasm hit him. He turned and sat the pan on the edge of the sink. He held onto the edge of the counter as he coughed and coughed. It hurt deep in his chest, same as it had for quite a while. Finally, he leaned over the sink and running the water, he spat into the sink. The spittle was bloody.

The next morning Jake called Doc Welsey to make an appointment for his yearly checkup. After the examination, Jake put his clothes on and walked out of the doctor's office. He didn't need to hear any more.

Son of a gun, maybe them people have been right all these years; these damn cigarettes are finally going to kill me. It's high time they did then, I'm gonna be eighty-nine come July sixth. I think maybe I'll treat myself to a birthday trip and fly to California and see five of our grandkids who live around San Diego. I've never been to California. I wonder if Terrill and his family might come down from Grass Valley to see me while I'm there. That would be a swell trip; I think I'll start checking on airline tickets. Ya know, I might even go on up to San Francisco where my niece and her husband live. I would love to see a professional baseball game while I'm out there. Maybe Cliff can get some tickets that would be swell!

Jake made the reservations the next day to fly out to California that coming July. It was set, he had his tickets and he would celebrate his eighty-ninth birthday with his grandkids. It was Saturday night and he wanted to go out to eat at maybe the Rose Bowl Café or the Wagon Wheel on the east end of Main Street. *First, I think I'll pay my widowed sister-in-law Maria a visit and see if she would like to come and grab a bite to eat with me.*

Jake drove up the hill on Shoshone Ave. to his sister-in-law's farm, where she still lived after her husband died. He walked up the narrow sidewalk to the front door and knocked. He knocked again and still no answer. Jake turned and was walking back to his car when the front door opened and Maria stood there. "Jake, is that you? What in the world are you doing clear out here?"

Jake turned and walked back toward the house. "Well, hello there, Maria. I was just lonely and wondered if you would like to come to dinner with me tonight, in Lovell. I get so tired of eating alone and thought maybe, just maybe, you do too."

A flush spread across Maria's face as she grasped the door frame. "Really – Jake? I certainly don't think that would be at all appropriate, me going out to eat with my sister's husband. What would Raisa think? You just go on back to Lovell and leave me alone now, ya hear?"

Jake started to say something but figured it was no use. Maria had always been a stubborn one and he got the message: she didn't want anything to do with him or his invitation to eat at the café. Jake just tipped his hat to her and said, "That's fine, Maria, just thought I would offer to take you to eat, that's all. And I am sure Raisa would not put any meaning to the gesture, as you obviously do. Have a nice evening, I won't bother you again. You can sit out here until hell freezes over if that's what you want."

Jake went down to the Rose Bowl cafe by himself to eat that night, licking his wounded ego. Over a chicken-fried steak and potatoes with white gravy, he started to mentally go through the list of eligible widows around the Lovell area. Not coming up with anything, he paid the bill and walked back to his car. As he was driving home, a light bulb went on in his head---Emmie Meyer. Her husband died a couple years back; she still lived on the family farm outside of Basin. Jake's face lit up as he began to think of Emmie. *By gum, she's a good German woman and I've tasted her cooking. Besides that, she's a pistol, and still pretty good looking too. I'm gonna call her up and see if she would like to go out to eat with me sometime.*

Emmie graciously invited Jake down to her farm to have dinner with her that next Sunday. "I'll tell you what, Jake, why don't you drive down after your church lets out? We can sit out on the patio and have a couple of beers and then I would like to cook you a good early supper. Does that sound okay with you? We can call it a day early, so you don't have to drive back to Lovell in the dark. See you whenever you get here."

Sunday after church, Jake headed south out of Lovell, down to Worland. It was just before two o'clock when he pulled into Emmie's farmyard. She came out of the door and waved for him to park and come on inside. Emmie was all smiles and offered him a cold beer as she ushered him out to the cool shade of her patio.

"So, Jake—how have you been getting along since Raisa passed away?" Jake took a long pull of the cold beer, wiped it from his upper lip and said, "Well Emmie, I guess about as well as you've been doing. Although for some reason I think you women do better with being alone than us men. I've been trying to keep busy, volunteer for things, I drive over to Emblem and up to Billings. There are times when there are those giant dark holes that pull me in. It takes a while to get myself back out on top. I hope you didn't think I was forward or anything Emmie, by calling you. I just would appreciate being able to take you to dinner once in a while, that's all—just for company. It feels good to get out of town now and then, if you know what I mean."

Emmie smoothed back her hair and wiped the dampness from her glass of beer. "I sure know what you are talking about, Jake, but I make myself find things to keep busy. I think it might be easier, like you said, for women to be alone. We always have chores and things we can do like cooking, baking, sewing, gardening, church work. But you men don't know how to cook or

FLESH ON THE BONE

frankly, to entertain yourselves for a long period of time and so I see where it is harder on you."

Emmie and Jake passed a couple of hours just chatting about her farm and their families. Looking at her large face wrist watch, Emmie rose from her chair, "Are you getting hungry, Jake? I just have a few last minute things to do to our meal and then we can eat and you can get back on the road before dark. I just fixed something simple; I hope you like sauerkraut, mashed potatoes, and I want you to taste some of our fresh German bratwurst—I think you are really going to like it. It's some that we made ourselves, me and the kids. You just make yourself comfortable and I'll call you when it's ready."

In twenty minutes, Emmie called from the kitchen for Jake to wash up. Jake pulled the chair out from the table and sat where Emmie indicated. She brought his plate already filled and sat it in front of him. She took her place across from him and said, "Okay then, you go ahead and say the blessing, then we can eat."

Jake enjoyed the traditional German meal so much. About half way through, he looked up at Emmie and said, "Emmie, thank you so much for spending time with me. I can't tell you how much I enjoyed the day and your company. The meal was just great, but it's the fact that someone else is sitting across the table from me that makes it all feel good."

Jake wiped his mouth with the napkin. "I never in my wildest dreams guessed how hard it was going to be to live alone, to eat alone, to simply go on alone. So, if you don't mind, I would like to do this again. You are good company and I feel halfway alive."

Emmie smiled half-heartedly and agreed that they should have dinner again sometime. She walked Jake to the door and just as she turned to say goodbye, Jake folded his arms around her and kissed her lightly on the cheek.

Emmie pushed Jake away roughly. "Jake Kessel---what do you think you are doing? That's taking this a little too far. I don't want you to go gettin' any crazy ideas in that head of yours. I think you better leave, now! I want no part of being with or taking care of another man. I had all that and I am content to be where and who I am. I think you should go."

Jake started to explain but then thought better of it. With his Sunday hat in his hand, he walked quickly out the front door and to his car. He turned before climbing behind the wheel. "Emmie, I am very sorry. I didn't intend for the day to turn out like this. Thank you for dinner; I'm sorry I just got carried away. I guess I just wanted to hug a friend and have a friend hug me back, that's all it was. I understand how you probably feel--I won't bother you again. Goodbye!"

Jake didn't look back as he drove to the highway and back towards Lovell. He and his badly damaged ego were about half way home before he could address what had happened with Emmie. *I just wanted to feel like a man again—I wanted to feel alive. I messed that up real good, didn't I? It's pretty clear; I'm not good for nothing now. Nobody wants me. Nobody has time to spend with me and I just have to accept that I'm not needed and learn to live with it. By damn—it's like I have no purpose left in this life—no reason for living. I look back at my life and I see light and laughter. I look ahead at my life and all I see is darkness and loneliness. I'm plain done with it, done. What's the use?*

CHAPTER NINETEEN

Who ne'er has suffered, he has lived but half. Who never failed, he never strove or sought. Who never wept is stranger to a laugh. And he who never doubted, never thought.
Author unknown

The sleek jet-prop airplane taxied across the runway and pulled into gate number fourteen at the San Diego International Airport. Inside the terminal, Karlie and Mike anxiously waited for her grandfather to come through the arrivals gate. "I am so excited that Grandpa Jake decided to fly out here. He must be feeling better to get on an airplane and travel all this way, I'm pretty sure it's his first time on an airplane. I was worried he wouldn't do well without, Grandma Raisa." Karlie put her hand on her husband's sleeve. "Look, there he is!"

During the ride north on interstate fifteen, Jake couldn't get enough of the blazing red bougainvillea that grew wild over the hills of San Diego. It crawled over fences and into people yards. "That's the prettiest flower I ever did see. Wish Mom could have seen them flowers, she would have loved 'em too."

Karlie and Mike lived in a stucco and tile patio home, high on a hill in a Del Cerro gated community. They didn't have much yard, but they had a heck of a view. Jake stood before the large bank of windows that faced the valley below. "I could stand here all day and just look at this view. You all can see probably twenty miles north. It's like living on the top of the world!"

Karlie showed her grandfather where he would be sleeping and left him to unpack and get settled in while she went upstairs and started their dinner. Karlie popped the baked potatoes into the oven and tossed a salad while Mike put the steaks on the grill. Suddenly, Karlie realized she didn't know where her grandfather was. She searched all over the house and couldn't find him. "Grandpa Jake, Grandpa Jake, where are you?"

She heard his voice coming from outside. Opening the front door, she looked down on the second level of exterior stairs that led up to their two story house. "There you are. I didn't know where you were. What are you doing sitting out here on those hard steps, you could sit up there on the nice soft patio chair, wouldn't that be better?"

Jake smiled up at her. "I'm fine right here honey. I just decided to come out here and look at this view while I have me a smoke. If I remember right, you're like your grandma—don't like people smoking in your house."

Karlie walked down a flight of steps and settled in beside her grandfather. She reached up and put her arm across his thin shoulders. "I thought you were going to quit smoking those cancer sticks, Grandpa."

Jake took another long, slow drag off his Camel. He blew the stream of smoke out into the evening air. "Well, Karlie, I'll tell you. I am eighty-nine years old now and I'm all alone. I guess something or another is going to get me sooner or later and these here nasty things have been my constant friend for a lot of years."

Karlie stroked her grandfather's back as she said, "Don't talk like that. You have lots of years ahead of you. You are a little skinny though, gotta start eating better I'd suppose." Karlie turned serious. "Grandpa Jake, how are you really doing without Grandma Raisa? I know she's been gone for almost three years now. Is it getting easier for you to be alone?"

Jake just looked straight ahead, not trusting himself to look into the eyes of his first grandchild. "Well, Karlie—I know it's only been three years, but it feels like a lifetime. A day, an hour doesn't go by that I don't miss your grandmother. I try to keep busy—me and Pastor Schwieger got those wild horses to take care of, but then there's the evenings alone in that house that we lived in for forty-seven years. This being alone without her is the hardest thing I've ever done, and I've done some hard things in my life." Jake felt his emotions welling up so he changed the subject. "What time is dinner? I can smell it and I'm feeling hungry."

The next day, Mike and Karlie informed Jake that they were taking him out that evening to eat at a special place. "You need to wear a suit and tie and be ready to leave around six thirty. We have a big surprise for you." That evening, Jake put on his navy tweed sports jacket, navy pants and a white shirt. He asked Karlie to choose a nice tie for him. When it was time to leave, Karlie called down the stairs, "We are ready to go Grandpa. Come on up here first, we will be leaving out the front door."

Jake thought that was a bit strange since the garage was just off the downstairs hallway, but he did as he was asked and climbed the stairs to the second floor. He thought to himself, *I haven't seen many houses like this, with the garage and some bedrooms on the bottom and the living and dining rooms, kitchen, and master bedroom on the upper floor. Suppose they did that to enjoy that beautiful view. But I still can't figure out why we are leaving out of the front door and down the steps to the street. Oh well, I better do what I'm told.*

Karlie straightened her grandfather's burgundy plaid tie and reached up to kiss his freshly shaven cheek. "Boy, you even put on aftershave—we are going to have a time of it keeping the women away from you tonight. You look so nice, Grandpa. Are you ready to go?"

Mike held the door while Karlie led the way out and down the Mexican stone-tiled steps. Jake held onto the wrought iron railing as he maneuvered down the stairway, keeping his head down and watching where he stepped. As he reached the bottom of the stairs, he lifted his head and was stunned by what he saw. "Holy cow, where did that come from?"

Karlie took his arm as she led him to the waiting, white stretch limo. "Have you ever ridden in a limousine before, Grandpa Jake?"

Jake was smiling ear to ear as he quickened his step toward the shiny car. "No siree, I have not—but it looks like I am going to get to ride in one tonight! Son of a gun, that's some snazzy-lookin' car. What make and year is it?"

Karlie climbed in first as Mike helped Jake slide into the car. Once settled in the back seat, Mike gave the driver the go ahead signal and they were off. Karlie dug around in her purse for her camera as Mike began to show Jake all of the bells and whistles inside of the car. Jake looked like a little kid at Christmas as he pushed the different buttons, getting a thrill out of each result.

Mike said, "Well now, I'll bet you might like a little something to wet your whistle. It's a ways to the restaurant and we don't want you getting thirsty." Jake's eyes opened wide as he replied, "Well now, that depends on what you have in that little cupboard."

Mike smiled as he searched through the contents of the liquor stock. "Well, Grandpa Jake, would you like a cold beer or something stronger?" Jake rested his arm casually across the back of the seat. "Why don't we split a beer? I'm saving myself for a glass of wine at the restaurant unless you are taking me to some burger joint!" Jake laughed and patted the back of the leather seat.

Jake reached for his half glass of beer and asked, "So, where are you two taking me to dinner tonight? I'm kinda spoiled you know, living in the big city of Lovell. I've been known to dine at the Rose Bowl at least twice a week."

Karlie clapped her hands in excitement. "Oh, Grandpa Jake, we are taking you to the island of Coronado and the famous hotel there that was built in 1888; it's the oldest and largest all-wood building in California. Many presidents have vacationed at the hotel including our President Reagan who ate in the Crown Dining Room. I've heard that Thomas Edison stayed here and even Babe Ruth. I think it was the first large commercial building, at least in California, to have electric lights." Karlie was excited about taking her grandfather to the famous landmark.

Karlie reached across the seat and touched her grandfather's knee. "And, you know what, Grandpa Jake? We have reservations to eat in the beautiful Crown Dining Room. I wouldn't imagine you have eaten in many dining rooms like this one, it's huge and elegant."

Jake just shook his head in wonder, "You say this Hotel Del is on an island? How do we get there? Does this limo tuck in its wheels and become a boat?"

Mike laughed as he took a sip of his beer. "Well no, not really, we will drive across on a huge bridge that connects San Diego to Coronado Island. It's really something, as you will see shortly. They had to construct it so big naval and other ships can sail underneath it. I've heard that when they were designing it, they were concerned that if we were ever invaded and that bridge was bombed, pieces of it might block the naval port and all the ships that dock on the other side. So, you know what they did? Each huge section of the bridge was designed with flotation devices that would enable the bombed bridge to float and make it easy for tug boats to push it out of the naval ships' way."

When they crossed the famous bridge, Jake was thrilled to look back at the night lights of downtown San Diego. "Now that's a sight to behold; we darn near have a bird's eye view from this bridge."

A few minutes later, the white limo pulled under the covered canopy of the famous hotel. The driver came around and opened the back doors so his passengers could disembark. Mike took hold of Jake's arm to steady him as he crawled out of the limo. The three of them walked into the hotel. Jake didn't say much, but Karlie noticed his eyes were wide with wonder.

Seated in the spectacular Crown Dining Room, Mike ordered a bottle of their best red Spanish wine and a stuffed mushroom appetizer. Jake sat straight on his burgundy velvet chair, just taking it all in—like a kid in front of the Christmas tree. Karlie reached across the table and put her hand over her grandfather's weathered hand. "Grandpa would you like some red wine or do you prefer white?"

Jake replied, "Why, I sure would like some of that there red wine, it looks pretty good. Not the cheap stuff, huh Mike?"

Mike reached around and patted Jake's shoulder, "Nope, Grandpa, only the best for you. It's not every day that you come out to visit us and we are having us a celebration." Mike poured the wine and then lifted his glass. "I would like to toast you, grandpa. Here's to a heck of a man—we're so glad you paid us a visit!"

Karlie grabbed her camera and snapped a picture of her grandfather lifting his wine glass with a pleased expression on his face.

They each ordered a steak dinner with all the trimmings. Jake only ate about half of his, which alarmed Karlie, "Grandpa, don't you like your steak or feel well?"

Jake rubbed his full stomach and said, "Aw no, that's not it—it's just that I'm not used to eating such a big meal and I want to save a little room for some of that *crème bro--lee* you were telling me about."

On the ride back to Del Cerro that night, Jake became nostalgic as he turned and looked out the window of the limo. "I sure wish your grandma could have been here with us tonight. We never did much traveling, pretty much home bodies. But, that woman did like the fancy things. We got used to a few of them when we lived out in Port Huron, Michigan in the 1930's. Wish I could have given her more nice things. She sure woulda liked eating in that fancy hotel and riding in this here limousine."

Karlie felt a shiver go down her spine as she reached over and took his hand, "Oh, Grandpa, I think she was here with us, in spirit. I feel her with me at different times and I know she is always near."

Karlie noticed her grandfather look away, then discretely pull out his handkerchief and blow his nose, so she quickly changed the subject. "So, Grandpa Jake, I understand that my sisters and their husbands are coming down tomorrow to pick you up and entertain you up in Carlsbad. They will take you back to the airport on Tuesday so you can fly to San Francisco, is that right? You are certainly making the rounds. I want you to promise to do this again next year, okay?"

Jake managed a weak smile as he replied, "Sure, honey, sure I'll try to get out here again." Jake pulled his handkerchief out again and coughed several times into it.

Karlie didn't like the sound of his cough. "Are you all right Grandpa Jake? Would you like some water?"

Jake tucked the handkerchief back into his coat pocket and said, "Naw, I'm all right, just my cigarette cough I guess."

The next day, Karlie and Mike kissed and hugged her grandfather as he climbed into his granddaughter's car. He waved out the window as they turned the corner. Karlie and Mike turned and walked up the stairway and into their house.

"I don't know what's wrong with me, Mike—but I have a funny feeling about his sudden visit out here and him wanting to see all of us."

Jake had been home from his trip to California for about two weeks when he noticed his persistent cough seemed to be getting worse, and he just didn't feel like himself. *I barely lift a finger and I'm out of breath. The last time I went to the Big Horns to fish, I could barely catch my breath and finally had to pack up and leave. Something is really wrong. My coughing spells are getting longer and more violent. I can't seem to stop coughing once I start—it's like there is something in my chest that is strangling me. The stuff I cough up is so sticky and sometimes it's got blood in it. I know I should see the doctor about it, but part of me doesn't want to or doesn't care.* Finally, after a particularly bad coughing spell, Jake called his doctor for a checkup.

Three days later Jake walked out of the doctor's office and climbed into his blue DeSoto. He just sat there for a few minutes, thinking—trying to make some sense of what the doctor had told him. *I knew my cough was worse and the blood in the mucus isn't a good sign, but I had no idea it was this serious. I guess it's a good thing I took that trip out to California, because Raisa, my darling--it looks like it won't be long before we are together again.*

Jake turned the key in the ignition and drove home without being fully conscious of what he was doing. He parked his car in the one-stall garage, climbed out, slamming the car door; he walked to the open area and reached up to pull the garage door down. *Well, son of a gun—just that little effort there has taken my breath away.*

On the walk to the house, he thought, *I need to get up to Billings next week and keep that appointment with the specialist. I've got to find out what options I have, if any. Maybe I'll wait until I talk to the docs in Billings before I tell my kids what's going on. But, it doesn't have to be right now. I am going to go in and fix myself a little supper and then I am going to sit out on my front porch and have me a smoke.*

CHAPTER TWENTY

Beth and her brother, Arnie waited outside of their father's hospital room while the doctors examined him. Uncontrolled tears rolled down Beth's face as Arnie nervously paced the hall. When the Billings specialist came out of Jake's hospital room, he motioned for them to follow him down the hall to his office. Walking into his office, he pointed to a couple of chairs in front of his desk; Beth and Arnie sat down, anxious to hear what the doctor had found.

"Well, I guess you've all been expecting something like this or worse, what with your father's life-long history of smoking cigarettes or pipes. It's just that when a person takes that much smoke into their lungs, over a long period of time it eventually clogs everything up in there and it's bad trouble. Your Dad has what we now call COPD or chronic obstructive pulmonary disease. In a nut shell, Jake's airways or tubes in his lungs are permanently obstructed, limiting how much air he is getting in and also out. Probably what saved your father from getting this condition sooner was the fact that he worked outdoors and was able to get good air into his lungs. However, give or take a couple of years, he's had this nasty habit of smoking for about sixty-five years and it's finally caught up with him."

The lung specialist shuffled some papers around on his desk while he searched for the words. "Your father's obstructed lung capacity is in the advanced stage. As I explained, he is having trouble getting sufficient oxygen in. Unfortunately, reduced oxygen forces the heart to work harder to pump the blood throughout his body. If the COPD doesn't get him, then he is going to have a heart attack. Because of the advanced stages of the disease and taking into consideration, his age, we don't think he has long. I need to warn you--the end is not going to be easy or pretty. We or the hospital where he ends up, will keep him as comfortable as possible."

Arnie moved to the edge of his chair. "How long does he have doc and how bad is the end going to be?"

The specialist folded his hands in a prayerful manner. "We can't be absolutely sure how long he has, but I want him to be admitted to the hospital in Lovell where they can monitor his symptoms and keep him comfortable. If your family doctor thinks he needs daily supervision and health care, then perhaps he should be admitted to the nursing home that's in conjunction with the Lovell hospital. I am signing his release papers right now and you can take him back home today. I assume that is where he wants to be?"

Arnie looked over at Beth, who seemed to be in a hypnotic state, watching the droplets of rain wiggle down the windowpane. As if to end their consultation with the specialist, a clap of thunder rolled across the city and echoed off the sandstone rim rocks to the north of the city. Startled, Beth snapped back to attention. "You said that I can take him back to Lovell today? I know he's going to like that part, but he is not going to like going into the hospital there. He can be pretty darn stubborn at times."

Dr. Riley smiled as he looked at the release forms. "I have discovered that trait firsthand. However, I think he is frightened enough that he will be cooperative. Jake knows he is in trouble and I don't think he wants to play the tough guy now and go it alone. He wants all the help he can get." The doctor handed over the forms which Beth put into her purse; she and Arnie shook hands with the specialist and thanked him as they prepared to leave his office.

On the ride back to Lovell, Jake was unusually quiet. Beth gave him the time and space to come to terms with the medical evaluation. "So, Dad, do you want to go home first? Do you have anything you have to do at home? Or, do you want to check into the Lovell hospital?

Jake didn't answer for a few moments. Looking out the window of the car, he said, "I might as well go directly to the hospital when we get into town. I have all I need in that duffle bag. There's nothing at the house that needs to be done, but if you don't mind—after you drop me off at the hospital, you might stop by the house to see that it's all locked up, you know—things like that."

Keeping her eyes on the road as her emotions surged to the boiling point; Beth managed to say, "Sure, Dad, that's not a problem. I will stay with you at the hospital as long as you want me to, but I should get home and fix Jimmy some supper. He's been on the threshing machine all day and I know he'll be hungry."

Beth slowed the car as they rolled through Bridger, Montana. Jake continued to look out the passenger side window at the changing foliage and at the leaves that had already fallen to the ground. *If I were a betting man, I'd say this is my last fall. I really don't want to go through another Christmas alone. I am so tired of being alone, without my Raisa. I'm sure as hell not lookin' forward to the kind of death I am obviously going to have to deal with, but in the end—it will all be good because I'll be with Raisa and my parents. The long, long struggle to live, to make it, will be over and I can rest. Bet I can even smoke all the cigarettes I want, in heaven."* His eyes went as they always did to rest on the cool blue cast of the Big Horn Mountains that rose majestically from the floor of the ancient Big Horn Basin. *I guess I won't be gettin' back up to my favorite creek anymore either. It's over for me, all over, I'm on that 'slippery slope'.*

Beth was feeling drowsy as the sun set and the long, curving stretch of asphalt wound out ahead, down into the valley and over the hills. To help stay awake and also to get her father's mind off of what she was imagined he was dwelling on, she said. "Dad, tell me about your life, what you learned, what things impressed you the most. You were born in 1900. Things have changed dramatically in the eighty-nine years you have lived, haven't they?"

Jake turned slightly as he too watched the black highway unfold ahead of the beam of headlights. "Well, I'll tell you, Beth, your mom and me, both being born in 1900, went from riding in a horse and buggy to automobiles. We saw the first cars—those 'tin-lizzies'—weren't much compared to what we have now. Them early cars were pretty basic, but to us they were darn incredible, yes siree. We were living high on the hog to be able to ride in a motor car. Your Mom and me both lived to see this country of ours put a man on the moon, riding in a rocket. Boy, we never ever even dreamed of something like that in our lifetime."

Jake took out his handkerchief and blew his nose. "I think the worst time was living through that Great Depression. Them were tough times, especially when we were still back in Port Huron. I was scared I wasn't going to get my family out of that big city before things got ugly. It was hard to describe how tough it was to make ends meet in them days. Mom, bless her heart, did all sorts of altering of our clothes, and putting together a decent meal and with hardly nothing to start with. I remember for us and our parents, when we got electricity—that was the beginning of a lot of changes that made life so much easier. Changes like having them indoor toilets, running water in the house, and no more kerosene lamps, but nice clean electric lights in every room. You know another invention that really was swell? Them darn pants zippers."

Jake smiled as he recalled having to button his trouser fly up like all the other men. "I heard somewhere that it was invented before we were born, but because of this and that, the public didn't get to see the invention until around 1930. Then with the Depression, a zipper wasn't used to close men's 'flies' until 1937. After that, it was pretty common for men's pants to have a zipper closing instead of those darn buttons." Jake laughed as he recalled some funny experiences in the early years, like trying to unbutton his pants in a hurry or fumbling with bitter cold fingers while standing in an outhouse.

"Course, sulfa was a miracle drug that saved so many lives in the wars and just general health care. It wasn't until after WWII that penicillin was discovered and that made another big difference. They also came up with better ways to treat diabetes, the disease that took your grandmother's life in the end.

"Another big thrill for your Mom and me was the year we got us a little Philco radio—I think it was in the late thirties. They were out on the market years before we bought us one, but course we couldn't afford one. Them little boxes were pretty nice, for us anyway—to be able to listen to music and ball games. That's when Mom got hooked on her soap operas—shows like Stella Dallas, As the World Turns, and at night I liked to listen to Mr. District Attorney. I was trying to remember when we got us a television. It was after we remodeled the house, after you and Jimmy got yours and that was in 1954, so I'd have to say we got our television in 1956-57. Mom quit going to so many movies then, when we had the television right here in our house."

Jake reached over and patted Beth on the forearm. "Yeah, I have no regrets. Your mom and me was blessed. We always found a way to put food on the table and a roof over our heads, although sometimes it wasn't much! Then God blessed us with you and Arnold. It was pretty darn hard on us when he had to go and fight in the war. As you might remember, Mom about had a nervous breakdown over that. Then, he had to go to Korea and fight in that war too. I was scared for her during those days; she got such terrible migraine headaches and all. But we made it through with God's help and now I face the end of my life and I am ready. Don't feel bad for me, honey. I've been blessed with a good Christian wife, two great kids, seven grandchildren, and sixteen great-grandchildren.

Jake put his head down in thought and then dropped a bombshell. "And Beth, just so you know, I've already made my own funeral arrangements. I went down to the mortuary and picked out my casket, gave them the instructions and paid for the whole thing right there and then. Pastor Schwieger has the paper with all the songs and Bible verses that I'd like at my funeral. It's all taken care of so you and Arnie don't have to worry about anything."

Beth's face was a roadmap of her inner feelings and fears. "What? You went down there by yourself and actually walked in and picked out your own casket? I've never heard of anything like that. What did you say to the funeral director?"

Jake laughed as he recalled the day and conversation. "I just walked into the place and told him that I needed to make some arrangements. He started showing me this casket and that, telling me I might like this for my 'beloved' and that for my 'beloved'. Finally, I turned to him and said, 'Listen Frank, I'm the' beloved' and I want the least expensive casket you've got. Don't try and pawn any of your expensive ones off, because I don't need it where I'm going.' Jake wiped his eyes with his handkerchief. "That was one of the funniest situations I ever been in. I could have knocked old Frank over with a feather, he was so shocked. He told me that was a first for him."

Jake changed the subject and kept talking about his life and all the interesting things he'd experienced. Just when Beth would think he was about out of stories, he'd think of another one and away he would go. Beth just let him talk; she knew it was good for him and she enjoyed it too.

Before they knew it, she was turning the car into the parking lot of Lovell Hospital. Beth pulled up in front and parked the car. She walked around to the passenger door, grabbed his duffle bag then helped her dad out of the car. Together they walked into the hospital. Putting her arm around his shoulders, she asked one more time, "Dad, are you sure you don't want to go back to the house first, yourself?"

Jake just kept on walking. "Nope, I don't want to go back there to that empty house, ain't nothing there for me. I need to get down to business here in the hospital, maybe they can help me breathe just a little better, or help me die a little faster."

~~~~~

The Lovell doctors kept Jake in the hospital part of the facility for about a week, doing some of their own tests and evaluating Jake's condition. They concurred that he would be better off in the nursing home area since he had no one at home to care for him and he wasn't going to get better. At this point, Jake didn't protest; he realized it was all a series of steps he had to endure here at the end of his life. He had lots of visitors, too many, in fact. Of course he enjoyed his family's visits, but most of all he liked to see Pastor Schwieger walk through the door of his room. They had some great talks, some about the wild horses, their fishing trips, and some about what was going to happen next. *Floyd is a great comfort to me. I enjoy hearing him read from the Bible and when he gives me communion every week.*

Jake hung on until close to the middle of October 1989. Suddenly, for no reason the doctors could come up with, his condition took a nosedive. They couldn't know that even though he was a fighter, at that point he willingly allowed the disease to take over. He was tired and he wanted it to be over. He wanted the eternal rest that his pastor talked about. And he wanted to be with Raisa again.

Jake was on constant oxygen, and they began a series of pain killers and relaxers as he struggled to breath. Beth brought his portable fan from home and sat it up beside his bed. Jake seemed to breathe easier with the moving air and he liked the sound of the fan as well. Beth and Arnie spent what time they could with their father. If and when the fan was inadvertently turned off, he became frantic. "Turn that damn fan back on and leave it on—I can't breathe if that ain't blowing the air."

Beth had been over to Lovell several times that week, seeing her dad and checking on his house. She sat by his bed for hours on end, reading from the Bible. Even though he seemed unresponsive, she knew he was aware she was there and reading the word. Late Thursday afternoon she kissed Jake's leathery, dry cheek as she tucked the bedcovers around him. He didn't open his eyes as she told him she'd be back on Saturday. All the way home, she had nagging feelings about her father. Flashback after flashback of her younger days growing up and of the fun they had in Port Huron, Michigan. She couldn't stop thinking about him, about her parents and their life together.

The sun was setting to the west as Beth drove down the lane between the rows of enormous seventy-five-year old Western cotton wood trees. She pulled into the garage, shifted, and turned the key in the ignition. *Aww, home again. I have to figure out something to fix for dinner, maybe just warm up that left over pork roast and potatoes we had yesterday.*

Beth was halfway up the sidewalk when Jimmy came out of the backdoor, coat in hand. "Beth, we got to go back to Lovell. It's your dad, the hospital called and said he has taken a turn for the worse and they don't expect he'll make it through the night. I grabbed some fruit and cookies for you to eat on the way. Come on, I'll drive—I know you are probably tired out."

Exhausted, Beth tried to sleep on the way back to Lovell. Finally, she sat up in the seat, "Oh Jimmy, I don't know if I can be there when my father dies. What is it going to be like? I don't want to see him suffer, I don't want to see it and then never be able to forget it."

Jimmy reached across the seat and put his large, work-worn hand over hers. "We do what we have to do, Beth. Your father needs you and I will be right there beside you."

They pulled into the dimly lit parking lot of the hospital as Jimmy found a parking place close to the emergency ward. He cut the engine and turned in the seat to face his wife. "It's time, Beth. I know you don't want to do this, but let's pray it'll be over quickly. It's the right thing. God and the doctors are right there with him too."

Jimmy pushed the buzzer and the door of the nursing home opened. They hurried down the corridor to Jake's room. As they walked into the room, Beth covered her mouth with her hand--- Jake wasn't in his bed. A nurse was stripping the same bed that, hours before held patient, Jacob Kessel.

"Jimmy is he, is he—dead? Where is my dad?" Frantically she inquired of the nurse. "My father, Jacob Kessel—did he, did he die? Where is he?"

The nurse shook her head. "He was in a bad way and so they took him back to intensive care over in the hospital. They have better facilities to help him at this stage. Check with the night nurse over in the hospital."

Jimmy and Beth literally ran down the corridor and into the hospital wing. The night nurse directed them down the long hall to the room where trauma nurses and doctors were working on the patient. Beth tore loose from her husband and ran into the room. The doctor took hold of her arm, restraining her. "We brought your father down here where we have more equipment to help him breathe. He is having a great deal of trouble and we think it is a matter of hours if not minutes. He is resting now, so you may go to him. He probably won't know who you are. We administered some pretty heavy meds.

Beth walked to the edge of the bed where her father laid. He had dark puffy circles under his eyes and his once ruddy complexion was pasty and pale. Jake's face was contorted as he continued to struggle to breathe—each breath labored. She took his hand and spoke softly to him, hoping he could hear her as she tried to—reach him. Beth turned to the night nurse. "Where is the portable fan that was in his room? We need that fan! It helps him to breathe easier." A night nurse hurried out of the room and soon returned with the fan. Jake seemed to settle down after they plugged in the fan and it began to osculate and whirr as it stirred the air in the room.

  Beth stood at the end of her father's hospital bed. He had tubes and monitors stuck everywhere—helping him to hold onto life. Beth put her head down as the tears started to roll down her cheeks, again. "I know Dad doesn't want all of these machines helping him to breathe and to live. He's such a fighter—he never was one to give up easily. But, if it's his time, why can't they let him go, or help him go?"

  Jimmy and Beth had been at the hospital for the last three hours. It was after midnight when Jimmy lay down on a visitor's couch in the waiting room. He had worked in the fields all day and was exhausted. Beth remained beside the bed of her father. She reached for the Bible and began to read to him, remembering that when people are in a coma they do sometimes hear what is going on around them. She read for a while until her eyes began to sting, then she stood next to the bed watching her father's chest rise and fall in an unsteady rhythm. Beth's eyes focused on her father's hand as she lifted it from the bed and held it in her own. It felt so cool and leathery, yet there was an alarming unresponsive frailty. She thought about all the things those hands had done in his eighty-nine years. Beth brought her father's hand up to her cheek as her tears rolled over it. "I love you so much Daddy. You were always my hero, even if you were pretty ornery sometimes. I know you want to go, to be with Mom. Its okay, Daddy, just let go; don't fight it. I'm right here Daddy, I'm right here"

  Reluctantly, Beth laid her father's hand back onto the bed. She moved her chair closer and leaned forward, laying her head on the edge of the mattress. Her eyes spontaneously closed for what seemed like only a minute. Suddenly, she felt the bed move violently. She raised her head and saw her father's body struggle and then jerk. His eyes were closed and a grimace of pain or fear was etched on his face—his mouth opened, struggling to breathe. Beth's eyes were wide with fear; she realized her dad was having what looked like a convulsion. She grabbed the bedside buzzer and pressed it over and over. Instantly, a group of night doctors and nurses flooded the room, pulling her back so they could administer to the patient. Beth heard her father wheeze, heard him gurgle, and then it was all quiet. The room held no sound as the machines and monitors were unplugged, even the oscillating fan. The doctor put his arm around Beth's shoulders as she stood at the foot of her father's bed. "I'm sorry, he's gone. He's at peace now—it's all over."

With a torrent of tears streaming down her freckled cheeks, Beth picked up his hand again and reached out to touch her father's face—relaxed and so peaceful, so cool. She whispered, "Goodbye, Daddy, Godspeed. I love you, Dad." She laid his limp, leathery hand back on top of the bedcovers and fled the room. Out in the dimly lit hospital corridor, she turned her face to the cold, sterile wall. Leaning into it, an overwhelming torrent of grief-driven tears tore from her small body. Silently, her shoulders heaved with choking sobs. She was alone, both her parents were gone. Suddenly, Beth was aware of two large hands on her shoulder, turning her around and pulling her to him. Jimmy wrapped her in his arms as she sobbed. He held her tightly, held her to him until she was empty of it all. "I'm here sweetheart, I'm here. It's over now—the worst, the dying part is over and he's with your mother. No more suffering."

Five days later, the large Kessel family gathered at the Lovell funeral home for a private viewing. The next day, Pastor Floyd Schwieger conducted a heartfelt sermon at the funeral service for one of his flock—for a man he knew personally. For him, this funeral was especially difficult because he also was grieving for his dear, long-time friend, Jacob Kessel. At the end of the day, Jake was laid to rest in the Lovell Cemetery next to his beloved Raisa, for eternity. It was now complete, their story was lived and told—it was over, the immigrants were no more.

Endnotes

(1) Wills Sainte Claire Automobiles were manufactured in Marysville, Michigan from 1921 to 1927. Jake worked for this company while they lived in Michigan. Childe Harold Wills first worked for Henry Ford, specializing in metallurgy. He was a perfectionist and focused on building the highest quality automobile, which eventually was the downfall of the company, another victim of the advancing Great Depression. Wills was instrumental in the development of vanadium steel and other alloys in the industry. The oval logo for Ford cars was also a product of Wills St. Claire's imagination.

(2) The first roads in this country were little more than rut-filled trails. Soon cities and larger towns began to improve their roads, paving with cobblestone or brick. Once out of a city, if you were lucky, most roads were covered with crushed stone, rock, or even seashells. Road construction methods were taken from techniques perfected by the Romans, who were the first civilized people to install curbstones and elevated sidewalks. Their gravel streets were constructed in an arc form—higher in the center to provide drainage.

(3) Beth and Shirley continued to be best friends and wrote letters back and forth for the next fifty years, until Shirley died in 1998. They saw each other only once more, when they were both married and had children; Shirley and her family drove through Wyoming on vacation and they stopped at the farm in Emblem.

(4) The first federal attempt to build a network of roads throughout the United States began in 1916 with the Federal Aid Road Act. WWI put a temporary stop to the establishment of a road system. In 1925, the Federal Aid Highway Act was passed to construct a system of interstate highways crisscrossing the United States. This act provided funds to state highway agencies as well as uniform 'shield' signs displaying the number of the road and the name of the state. The act was administered by individual states for the construction and maintenance of all interstate highways which ran

through their state. All east-west route numbers ended in zero while north-south routes ended in five. During the Great Depression, the Bureau of Public Roads created road projects which employed thousands of jobless men.

(5) "Hoovervilles" were makeshift transient camps mainly for those travelers who were down on their luck, had no other place to live or were just plain out of money. They were named in jest after the former Pres. Herbert Hoover, whose economic policies failed miserably. The camps were notoriously dangerous and dirty.

(6) The Terraplane automobile was built by the Hudson Motor Car Company between 1932 and 1938 in Detroit, Michigan. The name was derived from the public interest in aviation at the time. It was redesigned from an earlier version called the Essex Terraplane. This new, fully enclosed version was released during the Great Depression; it was inexpensive yet powerful. Marketing of the car was clever and effective, using this slogan: *"On the sea that's aquaplaning, in the air that's aeroplaning, but on the land, in the traffic, on the hills, hot diggity dog, THAT'S TERRAPLANING"*.

(7) In June of 1942, over two thousand workers began construction on the Heart Mountain Relocation Camp in the Big Horn Basin between Cody and Powell, Wyoming. It was purposely positioned near the Shoshone River for water supply and railroad tracks for transportation of inmates. This camp had one of the harshest living environments for Japanese internees, who came mainly from the temperate coastal California region. In sixty days, more than 10,000 Japanese Americans arrived at the camp. They lived in 468 quickly-built tar-papered, barrack-style buildings which were divided into single rooms and apartments for families. A family of nine might live in a two-room barrack. A single light bulb dangled from a cord in the middle of each room. They slept on single army-issued cots, covered with a thin mattress and an even thinner blanket; they took their main meals in the communal mess hall. There were separate outhouses for men and women as well as shower buildings—privacy was a non-existent luxury.

Military guards were positioned in the nine guard towers. The compound was surrounded with barbed-wire fencing and high-beam searchlights. The camp was self-contained with a post office,

FLESH ON THE BONE

hospital, schools, and fire department. The inventive internees ran a cabinet shop, garment factory, and silk screen shop. Many were farmers by trade and in the spring of 1943, they cleared the sagebrush, dug canals, and prepared fields for vegetables and fruits. They raised their own hogs, chickens, and cattle. They dug a swimming pool which turned into an ice skating pond in the harsh Wyoming winters. Some inmates were granted work releases in order to work off-site.

In the winter of 1944, internees were released from their harsh experience and most returned back to the West Coast to begin again from nothing. All of their businesses and homes had been sold by the U.S. government. The building of the camp was instrumental in stimulating the Wyoming economy still struggling after the Great Depression.

NOTE: Over 900 men and women from the Heart Mountain camp enlisted in the military during the war; twenty were killed in action. Enlisted Japanese men from the camp were with the '442 Unit,' the most decorated non-white unit in the history of the Army.

(8) President Franklin Roosevelt was re-elected and King Edward VIII abdicated the English throne in order to marry an American divorcee. The big movie of the year was "Gone with the Wind". The country and the world continued to be bogged down in the economic depression in spite of Pres. Roosevelt's 'New Deal'.

(9) The Allied Forces later learned that when the Germans received word General George Patton had crossed the Rhine River, they hastily abandoned the concentration camps, fleeing to the east. But before they left Ohrdrof Concentration Camp, the guards force-marched all who were able to walk to the nearby 'mother' camp, Buchenwald, where they were systematically gassed. Only those inmates who were near death and unable to walk were left behind, along with the unbelievable stacks of emaciated and rotting bodies of the dead.

(10) OHRODROF, Concentration Camp. This was one of the first Nazi concentration camps liberated by U.S. Army, in April, 1945. Prior to its discovery, it held over 11,700 prisoners. The 4th Armored Division and 89th Infantry Divisions were the first to

actually witness a Nazi concentration camp, near the German village of Gothe. Ohrodrof was a sister camp of the notorious Buchenwald camp. Generals Dwight Eisenhower, Omar Bradley, and George Patton were brought in to see for themselves the rooms and sheds filled with emaciated and dead bodies of prisoners. It was so terrible that Eisenhower cabled Gen. George C. Marshall and recommended that he and other members from Washington fly to Germany to see the camps firsthand.

NOTE: Even after 50 years, my Uncle Arnold was so overcome with memories of seeing the concentration camps that he could not continue speaking about the war. He had tried in vain to describe to my sister and me the hideous sight of human skeletons that could barely speak or walk. He mentioned that he believed he could still smell the indescribable odor from the camp that caused many of his fellow soldiers to vomit on the spot; it was the worst smell he ever experienced.

(11) Jack's promise: his real first name was Henry. Steiner was not his last name. The story about his capture and hiding under the protection of a Japanese family during the rest of the war in the Pacific is true. Once the war was over and he returned home, he contacted the family and subsequently brought their teenage son to Greybull, Wyoming to attend high school.

(12) Lovell National Guard: The entire Lovell, Wyoming National Guard was deployed to take part in the Korean Police Action on August 19, 1950. The 300th Armored Field Artillery Battalion of seventy-five men was sent overseas. Many of them had fought in World War II and had remained in the National Guard to supplement their income while re-establishing themselves in the workforce.

(13) Korean War Illness: Arnold contacted some sort of local virus or infection and had to be airlifted to Japan to be treated. This incident was the nearest he came to death while serving in both wars.

(14) Schwieger: Pastor Floyd Schwieger served St. John Lutheran Church in Lovell, Wyoming for many years. He and Jake were great friends and they did indeed work together to establish a museum for the wild horses of Prior Mountain. It was a cause near

and dear to both men. He passed away around 2004 from pulmonary lung distress, or COPD.

ACKNOWLEDGEMENTS

There is a saying, "It takes a village to write a book." This was definitely true in my case. There are so many people who were instrumental in helping me write this book. Initially, my grandparents were the key players, because this is their story; I know about it because they took time to tell us about their life experiences. As with the first two books, I thank my support system of talented and generous readers who took time to read the initial manuscript. A huge shout-out of appreciation goes to my confidant and mother, Beata Wamhoff; long-time friend and retired English/Reading teacher, Janie Lewis; retired, avid reading enthusiast, Julia Graham; former book critic for the *Coloradan* newspaper, Nancy Hansford; retired business owner and graduate of UC Davis and CSU, Betty Brown; Seattle University scholar and journalist, Morgan Schutte; and proof editor for the Greybull Standard, Kathy Ewen, who also receives kudos and credit for teaching me the proper use of the semi-colon. I appreciate your continued support as well as your unbelievable wisdom and finesse in guiding me through the forest and valleys of my words.

To my husband Mike – "You saved my bacon by reading the final proof for me!"

Finally, to my immediate family: my husband Mike, our four sons, Mark, Todd, Brett, and Erick and their wives and of course our grandchildren, I send my deepest appreciation. I never tire of your unending optimism and enthusiastic encouragement. It is for you that I have made the effort to research and write these novels about our family. I simply have to give kudos to our little Shih-Tzu, Sofie Su, who sits patiently or naps while I write, knowing there will be a walk later.

A special thanks to photographers Lewis Hine and Dorothea Lange and the exceptional gifs they left us all. Their work touched me deeply. I felt a kindred spirit in using their profound photographs to relate my own story of the hard times and the lives most immigrant people endured. They persevered through hardship and were forced to send their children out to work so they could make it in America. This was the only way for the majority of the immigrants to get ahead, to succeed. They all worked, worked long hours, long days, long years---saving every penny they could, so perhaps they could afford to rent a farm the next year or buy one the year after that. There were celebrations and times when they let down their hair and enjoyed a dance or a family gathering, but the next morning, it was back to the fields. Eventually, many were able to buy a place of their own, but even then, they never stopped working hard and long. They were grateful for the opportunity and the freedom they found in this country.

    I count my blessings and continue to be in awe of the direction my writing has taken. Having no formal education in this particular art, I strongly believe the thoughts, the stories, the words that appear on the page are guided by my Lord. I feel his presence every day and in every way, from the ability I suddenly discovered to tell a story, to the opportunities which have arisen which take my work to another level. This is all beyond me; I am a willing and excited participant. Finally--to my readers and my fans: I am eternally grateful for your support and encouragement. It means the world to me when I hear from one of you and I cherish the simple fact you are able to join me in the journey of these stories!

ABOUT THE AUTHOR

It is no exaggeration to say that my experiences or lack thereof, while growing up on a remote Wyoming farm, proved to be a daily inspiration for my imagination. Even as a little girl, I used my imagination to transform a forty-year-old horse-drawn threshing machine into an awesome pirate ship. I cherished the hours alone when I simply lay on my back in the long green grass of the pasture and gazed up at the accumulation of white billowing clouds. The game was to discover what shapes I could pull out of them as I daydreamed. I derived hours if not months and years of pleasure in creating other lives, diverse personalities, interesting characters, and outrageous plots complete with dialogue to fill my playtime.

I have always been an avid reader; reading took me to other places, I met other people, and I dreamed other dreams. I don't remember a time when I didn't love to draw—to create and imagine. I have always surmised that my situation, growing up on the farm, was actually an exercise in honing my imagination, preparing me for what I would do much later in my life. I was simply being me, letting my imagination run wild, enjoying my youth and the winds of summer.

After marrying at a young age and bearing four sons before the age of thirty, my early adult years were full and blessed. Yet, there remained a simmering desire to create – to become an interior designer. Through perseverance and hard work, this dream was eventually realized. I returned to college and graduated in 1987 with a degree in design/marketing, after which I practiced as an A.S.I.D interior designer for twenty-five years. Only when I retired and sat down to record my family history did I recognize that I also loved the task of historical research, the task of seeking the why and how of what had happened in the lives of the characters in my stories. I was always a writer, but soon discovered that an author was also inside me.

I will never forget turning over my first manuscript and reluctantly allowing a qualified friend to read my raw work. After reading my manuscript, she gave me an enthusiastic 'thumbs up'! Wow, I will never forget her response; it was the catalyst that propelled me to the next level.

Writing for me doesn't feel like a job, but a labor of love—the adventure and pleasure of creating. The research of historical fiction takes on the persona of a treasure hunt for me; the more I discover, the more I want to know. There is a saying, *"Becoming a writer means being creative enough to find time and the place in your life for writing."*

There are many reasons why I write about my grandparents' lives. I am the oldest great-granddaughter, and granddaughter on my mother's side. As a child, I was privy to the endless stories about 'the Old Country,' and I loved listening to them. I feel it is my responsibility of make sure these stories don't die—that they are remembered on paper as they are in my heart.

Of course, stories are interpreted differently by those who are involved. The core of my writing revolves around the stories as I remember them and the facts I have discovered in my historical research. I spent a great deal of my childhood with my grandparents; they influenced and helped shape who I am today. They enriched my life and planted the seeds of curiosity and pride in the history of our family.

Blending and applying the historical research to my family history is an enchanting passage between fact and fantasy. Writing allows me to explore, to enjoy the journey, and to use my imagination when an abyss in the story appears. The people I write about were fearless and strong in their faith. They were a relentless and extremely humble working class of men and women. They did their best to live the life they were dealt and to change what they could change. Above all, they never wavered in their gratitude for the freedom and the opportunity they enjoyed in this country.

By bringing these historical family stories to life, if I accomplish anything, I hope it is to inspire my readers to begin to uncover their own family history. There are lessons to be learned, discoveries to be made, and pride to be unleashed.

THE TICKET was my first novel, followed by SEED OF THE VOLGA. This third novel FLESH ON THE BONE is the final book in the trilogy---or is it? The fourth novel, THE TANK COMMANDER, will be a finale to the first three family books, in which Arnie Kessel joins the Army just in time to be assigned to Gen. George Patton's 81st Tank Battalion. He served under General Courtney Hodges, 1st Army, and 5th Armored Division, and was in Combat Command 'B'. I have some solid ideas of how I will begin this book, which promises to be emotionally difficult to write because of the number of brutal battle experiences and situations which Arnold fought in. Does he make it home?

I have current plans and bulging files waiting for the fifth and sixth novels—perhaps a seventh. I love what I do; writing gives me purpose and it inspires me to get out of my warm bed in the morning. It is my profound hope that I have continued success in channeling these adventures, these real life stories straight to you, the reader. I have been blessed to have met so many wonderful people during my many book tours and book signings. Thank you for your continued support and interest.

From the author of

   THE TICKET

      SEED OF THE VOLGA

      FLESH ON THE BONE

Coming soon,

THE TANK COMMANDER

"In war, there are no unwounded soldiers."

José Naroskey

CPSIA information can be obtained at www.ICGtesting.com
Printed in the USA
LVOW07s0201010814

396972LV00003B/7/P

9 780990 409502